DESPERATE: Joe Crane, a dedicated geologist willing to sacrifice his marriage and his life to find SEA GOLD...

DEVIOUS: Andrea Nolan, a sharp and seductive woman determined to be the first to claim the SEA GOLD...

DEADLY: Mr. Miel, a white-collar criminal ready to risk all their lives to get his hands on SEA GOLD...

SEA GOLD
by the bestselling author of *Firespill*
Ian Slater

Bantam Books by Ian Slater

FIRESPILL
SEA GOLD

SEA GOLD
IAN SLATER

SEA GOLD
A Bantam Book | May 1979

ISBN 0-553-12254-1

Bantam Books are published by Bantam Books, Inc. Its trade-
mark, consisting of the words "Bantam Books" and the por-
trayal of a bantam, is Registered in U.S. Patent and Trademark
Office and in other countries. Marca Registrada. Bantam
Books, Inc., 666 Fifth Avenue, New York, New York 10019.

PRINTED IN THE UNITED STATES OF AMERICA

For MARIAN

ACKNOWLEDGMENTS

I would like to thank the following for their help in the preparation of this book: At the University of British Columbia, Drs. R. L. Chase and J. W. Murray of the Department of Geology, and especially Robert Macdonald, an old oceanographic shipmate of mine.

I am also grateful to Lt. Commander Gary Davis, Canadian Armed Forces (Reserve), and Mr. John Sutcliffe for their advice on things nautical.

Thanks must also go to Mr. Rae Morris and Mrs. Helen Gatz for tea and understanding.

Most of all I am indebted, once again, to my wife, Marian, whose typing and grammatical skills have augmented her invaluable support to me in my work.

The oceans are not merely the repository of wealth and promise; they are, as well, the last completely untamed frontier of our planet. As such, their potential—for achievement or for strife—is vast.

> Henry Kissinger,
> On the Law of the Sea,
> New York, April 8, 1976

All over the world they are jockeying for position. In secret they are readying their ships for the assault on our last frontier—the oceans. Radar replaces telescope, chequebook replaces press gang but their motive is still greed and the means no less violent because they are modern. Who are these people you ask? They are tomorrow's pirates.

Jonkomo Watahai
World High Seas Commission,
Paris 1978.

1

"I know it's down there." Joe Crane's voice was barely audible above the howling of the forward starboard winch. "It's got to be there."

He walked quickly back to the ship's lab and opened the trunk marked "Dr. Joseph Crane, Maritime Institute (Geology), University of British Columbia," pulling out a parka as protection against the unusually cold summer wind. Despite his forty-six years the marine geologist was moving his six-foot frame with the agility of a much younger man. But it was the agility of tension—not fitness; Joe's middle-aged paunch showed even beneath the parka. His intense brown eyes darted from the recorder's jagged profile of the ocean's bottom out toward the black sea and back. He looked across at Frank Hall, his technical assistant, twelve years younger and working with the unhurried assurance of long experience. "I know it's there, Frank."

Though he was five feet ten, Frank had to strain his neck as he looked up at the cable jerking the davit. The arc light caught the rugged, sunburned cheeks beneath a shock of light brown hair, and the imperturbable blue eyes. "I hope you're right," he said.

"I'm right."

It was their last chance this voyage, and if they didn't find it Joe Crane knew it could be his last chance ever to be acclaimed as the discoverer of the world's last great treasure. Soon the bottom sampler would be aboard and they would know.

Frank watched the cable racing up from the sea, spitting and crackling as it ran over the block, down to the winch drum. Without taking his eyes off the meter wheel

that was frantically spinning backwards, showing the rate
of the sampler's ascent from the ocean canyon over six
thousand feet below, Frank switched on the deck-bridge
intercom. "Twelve minutes to surface."

Crane focussed on the white apron of light that, cast
from the deck, was now sliding up and over the quick succession of swells like a sodden sheet, holding the cable in
view one minute, losing it the next. Suddenly the winch
stopped and the shadow of an arm moved across the
lighted deck like a spear as the winchman changed down
gears for the final hundred-meter pull. The winch dropped
from a whine to a steady groan and the five-eighths-inch
cable that moments ago had been a long, thin blur now
rose so slowly that Joe Crane could see its individual
strands.

The cable's angle to the ship was wide and, like a fishing
line being slowly pulled away by its quarry, it was dragged
out of the dancing disc of light into the blackness. Every
thirty seconds or so the cable would reappear in the light,
only to slide out of view again as the ship dipped into
another trough.

"It's got to be there," said Crane, pushing the parka hood
off and running anxious fingers through his thinning gray
hair. "It's got to be there. Before the others beat us to it."

The wire came back in sight, then disappeared again.

"What others?" Frank inquired, without taking his
eyes off the meter wheel. "Some other university?"

"Whoever else wants to be first," said Crane. "Whoever
else wants to make a billion."

"Or two," added Frank.

"Exactly."

"Ten minutes to surface!" called Frank. Now his eyes
moved from the meter wheel to the sea.

2

"It's a little . . ." Andrea Nolan stopped talking as a stranger passed them on the quay bridge, hurrying across the gray span toward the polished green of the trees fronting the Burkliplatz.

Her companion, a tall, lean, angular man in his early sixties, looking as if he might be a Zurich banker, finished the sentence for her: "A little unorthodox?"

"Yes."

Klaus kept looking straight ahead, toward the edge of the lake. The cold asceticism of his eyes was perfectly matched by his uncompromising tone. "Perhaps, Miss Nolan, but the alternative is highly unprofitable. The oceans are the new Africa." He brushed a piece of fluff from the sleeve of his steel-gray suit as if it were a gross impertinence. "If we can maintain and secure a relatively inexpensive supply of metals and other minerals—the raw materials for the manufacturing companies we plan to acquire—we can expand into becoming one of the ten richest corporations in the world. Richer than half the *countries* in the world. Nickel for one. The United States uses nickel for the manufacture of everything from can openers and sinks to automobiles and missiles, but has to import ninety-eight percent of all the nickel it uses. *Ninety-eight percent*. And that is only one of the minerals at stake." He deftly flicked the remainder of his cigar in front of him onto the pavement, crushing it under his heel without the slightest change in pace. "I am a conservative man, Miss Nolan. I do not exaggerate. The riches in the oceans are enormous. Nothing like them has ever been seen on land. Next to them, the 'great' gold rushes—your Yukon, the Californian and the Kalgoorlie—will pale into insignificance."

3

Andrea Nolan was an attractive woman—she looked
closer to twenty-five than to her thirty-five—with a firm,
petite figure and pale blue eyes that seemed flecked by
gold whenever the turn of soft auburn hair changed the
light on her cheeks. Klaus' North American directors had
sent her over, claiming she was one of the best acquisition
managers in the mining business. And Klaus was hungry
for acquisition. But he was growing impatient with her.

Andrea knew that thanks to Klaus' nerve in expanding
into high-risk investment areas, his S.R.P. empire (Swiss-
Rhine Petrochemicals) was now the fourth most powerful
industrial complex in Europe, after Royal Dutch Shell,
British Petroleum, Unilever and Phillips, with employable
assets of 11.3 billion dollars. He'd just displaced Phillips
and was now marshalling his forces for a bid at first place
via the North American market. Andrea also knew that his
recent takeover of CANORE (Canadian Ore), the company
she worked for, would be only the first step, a beachhead
for an all-out assault on North America, and it wouldn't
end in Canada. Next he'd try to get a stronghold on mineral supplies to the United States.

There'd be many more deals like this one, and each
one would put her deeper into the murky waters of con-
glomerate intrigue. But she'd finally made it in a tough,
competitive male-run industry. To bail out now would
mean more than losing a job—it would be a grating personal defeat. She looked out at a pedal boat idly making
its way into the floating dock across the Limmat.

The dock owner was standing impatiently by the water's
edge glancing pointedly at his watch, but the young couple
in the boat didn't even notice. The woman was a blonde in
her early twenties and the man perhaps a little younger.
His arms were draped lazily about the girl's shoulder and
were covered by a cascade of long blonde hair each time
she laughed. The laughter came drifting across the water
and for a moment Andrea envied the girl. Spoilt-little-rich-
girl, she thought, American by the looks of her, over in
Europe on holiday—probably Daddy's graduation gift.
Andrea Nolan reflected how she'd never had time for that
kind of thing. She'd never been rich and she'd never even
known who her Daddy was. But she'd survived—and for a
moment that turned her envy for the blonde girl into
contempt. The only people worth anything, as far as Andrea Nolan was concerned, were those who had had to

work and fight for what they got. And she'd worked and
fought, out of the dark terrors of a battered childhood in
Vancouver's east end—waitress, typist, secretary, night
school, and then more recently up the ladder at CANORE,
showing them that she could equal any man when it came
to acquiring new claims to exploit. There hadn't been time
for pedal boats, or for anything like what was called a
"permanent relationship." Her relationships had all been
temporary and she'd ended them all because they threatened to hold her back from gaining a foothold in a suc-
cessful career. She glanced at the blonde again. Now they
were kissing. Andrea quickly looked back at Klaus. The
moment Vancouver had told her that Klaus wanted to
see her, she knew that this would be her big chance. She'd
come too far to give it up now.

Klaus flipped open the menu, and the lanterns hidden
among the decorative shrubbery suddenly came alive,
throwing a golden glow over the olive slate of the Limmat.
Andrea had the distinct impression that the lamps had
been lit solely on Klaus' cue. He ordered beer and *Rüe-
blichueche*, the local carrot cake.

Andrea didn't want beer but she didn't speak Schwyzer-
tüütsche and she was in no mood to dicker over food.
"The same," she said, making a note that she'd better
learn Swiss-German as soon as possible. Another language automatically gave you more power and authority.
She watched Klaus closely. He wore authority like a model
wears a coat, except that he wasn't just wearing it—he
owned it. He lit up another slim Dutch cigar, then took a
small, white box from his pocket and offered it to Andrea.
"While we wait for the cake. Chocolates, from Sprungli's. They calm the stomach."

"No, thank you." She smiled, then realized he was in
earnest.

"I firmly believe it," he went on, still holding out the
package. "You should take one. I am never without
them. They are much better than all those pills I hear you
take in America."

She took a soft cream. "I don't take pills."

"Then you are not worried—about my plan for
CANORE?"

"No."

"Good. It is the only way. We must secure Canadian
rights to whatever deposits are discovered. CANORE must

be the first to announce the discovery, with the sample
in hand, plus exact latitude and longitude. Before, with
only a three-mile fishing limit and a twelve-mile mining
limit, it was Captain Blood, right?"

"I beg your pardon?"

"Captain Blood—a pirate was he not?"

"Oh, yes."

"Yes. Well, until a little while ago it has been—how do
you say it?—grab as grab can?"

"It still is," said Andrea.

Klaus smiled. "Yes. But now that the world has finally
awakened to the fact that we are running out of raw
materials, your government—no different from the rest, I
must admit—has extended its territorial claim beyond the
continental shelf to two hundred miles—for Canadian companies only. Now, Swiss-Rhine Petrochemicals needs,
how shall I put it?, a Canadian advantage."

"Government protection from competition," said Andrea.

Klaus smiled appreciatively at her. "Just so. It's as simple as that."

"So now you have CANORE, a Canadian company," said
Andrea. "All you need do is equip CANORE with research
ships of its own to work the two-hundred-mile limit. It
would be expensive but . . ."

Klaus waved her suggestion impatiently aside with his
cigar. "You miss the point, Miss Nolan. It is not a question
of the money. Certainly it would be expensive to buy and
equip our own research ship, very expensive. Thirty million dollars, perhaps. But for SRP it would not be hard.
The real difficulties lie in hiding it from our competitors.
If Mr. Howard Hughes could not protect the identity of
the *Glomar Challenger* even with the help of the CIA, it is
unlikely that we would be able to camouflage a ship of
our own." Klaus surveyed the lake, its dark waters dotted
here and there with the bobbing lights of boats. "No,
let the Canadian government do it for us. After all, they
have built the research ships. Let them finance the university men to do the looking. Let them take the risk," he said,
smiling. "That is what they are for, is it not, so they can
serve the tax paying public? Correct?"

"But they may not find anything," ventured Andrea.

"They may not," agreed Klaus. "All the more reason for
not financing the ship on our own. You agree?"

"Yes," Andrea conceded.

Klaus inhaled deeply. "But if they do find it, we must be the first to know. We must be out there with them."

"We will be."

The financier paused, blowing a long stream of smoke over Andrea's head. "I hope so. It is solely to make that point, Miss Nolan, that I have asked you to fly all the way to Zurich. Telephones, telexes and the like are not to be trusted."

Klaus stubbed out the cigar and pushed the empty plate aside. "It is not only SRP who are seeking new mineral deposits, Miss Nolan. I need hardly tell you that. No, the race is on. The vast unknown regions are on the verge of exploitation. It is a decisive moment in history. Believe me."

He took out a fresh cigar, licked it, and stabbed it toward her. "And you will need information. Who knows where it will come from? Some laboratory, an angry graduate student perhaps, some assistant getting even with a greedy professor, a fishing boat even, with something caught in the net? Keep your ear to the ground, Miss Nolan." He looked out at the night. "We are at the new frontier—the last frontier." He turned back to Andrea. "We have to beat Inco, Noranda and the other companies who control the remaining Canadian land deposits. They will fight like the terror."

"Devil."

"Yes, exactly, devil. They will fight like the devil to get hold of it. Not to sell, but to stockpile, to protect their land deposits. They want to—" he hesitated, searching for the words, "they want to corner the market like the gold people in Johannesburg. And so you must watch." He waved the unlit cigar. "Vigilance, Miss Nolan, vigilance. This mining exhibition in Vancouver. It opens shortly?"

"In a few days."

"Good. You may pick up something there. What is the name of that company in Vancouver with its foot in the door?"

"That subsidizes research at the Maritime Institute?"

"Yes."

"Vancouver Oceanics."

"Try to find out where they get their information. How they decide what research to support."

"All right."

"And remember, it is just as important to learn where *not* to search. Knowing that a hundred-square-mile area has been pored over could save us valuable time."

Andrea was impressed. No wonder Klaus had already made so much money.

"I'll remember," she said.

"They tell us that in English Columbia—"

"British Columbia."

"Exactly. They tell me you are one of the best acquisition managers there." He drained his beer. "You may have to go beyond cocktail parties to get the information." He gave the cigar a final lick and flipped open the Dunhill lighter. "I expect you to do that."

Andrea nodded.

"Of course, if you have certain difficulties you must realize that it is SRP policy never to become involved in illegal activities. I hope you understand."

"I understand."

The cigar was fading and Klaus relit it, the tongue of flame giving his face the same yellow glow as a lantern nearby. "Naturally," he said, "there will be bonuses—if you succeed."

❧ ❧ ❧

Back on the ship the cable angle was almost zero, running straight down the side of the ship, and the water was erupting in giant bubbles. Ten more seconds and the shark-shaped mouth of the big pipe dredge broke surface. Another ten seconds and it was at eye level, bumping the rail.

"Watch it," called Frank, and just as the ship rolled he grabbed the meshed bottom with his bare hands.

"Be careful, Frank. It'll tear your arms off."

Bracing his legs against the roll, Frank held the ten-foot-high dredge hard against the ship's side until the swell had passed and they could lift it higher over the rail and quickly lower it before the next roll. As it was lowered to the deck like some great glistening prehistoric animal, the seawater poured out in torrents. When it was all gone Frank and Joe Crane knelt down to peer inside. It was empty!

3

Frank's small cabin cruiser, moored at the Burrard Dock Club, was ten years old and badly in need of repairs, all twenty feet of it, but he should never have hinted, even jokingly, that he could do with a raise, at least not to Joe Crane. Not after the empty dredge. His boss had merely grunted that he'd be lucky to get any more money for research, let alone pay people raises. Frank was about to explain that he'd only been kidding but he was too tired. He'd spent all afternoon, from the moment the ship docked at Ballantine pier, supervising the unloading of the oceanographic gear from the ship to the truck and then from the truck to the storage shed at the Maritime Institute, checking that the multifarious grabs, dredges, reversing thermometer bottles, current meters, underwater flash camera unit and piston corers were all intact. It was one of those days when Frank wished that instead of finishing his education with a B.Sc. in science he'd gone ahead and gotten his doctorate like Crane—then *he'd* be the boss.

After the unloading he looked forward to relaxing over a drink with the Cranes—at least with Mary Crane. It wasn't that he didn't like Joe Crane, but they'd seen one another every day at sea. On the other hand, he'd only seen Mary Crane occasionally at a rare party, or whenever she picked Joe up from the Institute. But he'd seen enough of her to know that if he were Joe Crane there wouldn't have been any time for drinks with the technician and chitchat. As soon as the ship had docked it would be straight home—the drinks could wait!

While Joe Crane was holding forth again on possible improvements to sampling gear, drawing a rough outline on the small deck table with his finger, Frank glanced up at Mary. She was looking right at him, her deep blue eyes contrasting with the long, golden-blonde hair. It was hot

and unusually humid for Vancouver, and he could see her
nipples clearly pressing against the white cotton dress. Even
her smile excited him.

"All I need," said Joe Crane, waving his Scotch, "all
I need is a little more time." He fiddled for a moment
with the keys to their Volvo, then lifted the Scotch and
drained it.

"That's your fourth, Joe," said Mary, more with concern
than irritation.

"It's my fifth," said Joe smiling, holding up his hand to
Frank for a refill. Mary turned away and watched Frank
pour the new drink. Even beneath his loose-fitting sports
shirt she could see the outline of muscles firmed by years
of deck work on various research ships. "Joe tells me
you want to sail around the world?"

Frank grinned, plopping in the ice. "Not in this tub, I
don't."

"In what then?"

"He wants to be another Joshua Slocum," cut in Joe.
"A thirty-five-foot sloop."

"That's the general idea," answered Frank, handing his
boss the fresh Scotch. Crane held the glass up. "Cunning,"
he said, peering at the short measure of whiskey. "Very
cunning, Frank."

"Frank's only trying to help, Joe."

"Help?" Crane laughed. "If he wants to help me, he can
go in and punch Thompson out."

Mary's hand went to her forehead in a gesture of
exasperation. "Joe, can't we leave off—"

"Thompson's a bastard. Don't you agree, Frank?"

Frank studied a beer label. He'd never seen Joe Crane
act like this—he'd never seen him drink like this.

"Isn't Thompson a bastard, Frank?"

"He's not my favorite dean."

"You said it."

Mary was looking out over the forest of masts piercing
the orange sunset beyond Georgia Strait. She could hear
the tinkling of a piano and the raucous voices of a party
warming up in the clubhouse. She reached over, gently
pushing a tuft of graying hair from Joe's forehead. "Don't
worry about Thompson, Joe. He probably just wants to
see you on some . . ." She shrugged in an effort to think of
the right words, and as she did so her bust was pulled in
tighter by the dress. "He probably wants to see you on

some petty detail," she said. "Everyone worries when their boss wants to see them out of the blue. Don't they, Frank?"

"I shiver all night."

Mary laughed, turning back to her husband. "It's when you don't worry, Joe, when you least expect it that you get—"

"Fired!" said Crane. "Oh, I know he's out to get us, all right." He lifted his glass, shaking the ice cubes from side to side. "And he has all the reasons he needs. We were hired to find manganese and we haven't found it. It's as simple as that. That's all he needs."

Frank could see that the clinking of the ice cubes was grating on Mary's nerves but she said nothing. If Frank couldn't remember Joe Crane drinking this much, Mary Crane's forced patience indicated it was nothing new to her. If he drank at sea, thought Frank, he surely kept it quiet.

"The trouble is," Joe went on, "these people in administrative jobs have no idea what you're up against. Right, Frank?"

"Right!"

"Don't humor me, Frank. I—"

Mary spoke quickly. "But Dean Thompson's a geologist too, even if he is an administrator. He should know how difficult it is, if anyone does. Besides—"

"He's a land geologist," Crane snapped. "He has no idea of what it's like at sea. He's head of the Maritime Institute merely because, of his seniority—that's all." Joe Crane looked at Mary, then at Frank, who quickly took his eyes off Mary.

"You know," continued Crane, "I think Thompson thinks it's just a big lake out there. I really do. People hear of the *Glomar Challenger* finding that Russian sub in '76 and they think you can find fifty million dollars' worth of manganese nodules—or any other minerals for that matter, in the same way. They've no idea. That was a four-hundred-foot sub, for Christ's sake, and the CIA knew exactly where to look. I'm supposed to cover an area the size of Alaska and find nodules the size of pancakes."

"Lower your voice, Joe."

"Listen," he went on just as loudly. "Some of those trenches are deeper than the Rockies are high. They make the Grand Canyon look like a pothole, and there I am putting down a chain dredge the size of a bathtub on a wire no thicker than your thumb. And they give me the gears because I don't come up with the mother lode. You know that over four fifths of the ocean is deep sea—over ten thousand feet?"

Frank agreed with Joe Crane. People ashore didn't understand the odds. To them five years of searching and no results merely meant failure. But Frank didn't want to talk shop, not with Mary Crane sitting three feet away. Even in the sticky heat she seemed remarkably collected, not cold or standoffish, but alluringly cool. She knew she was beautiful but didn't flaunt it. She crossed her legs and the evening breeze lifted the corners of the split hem revealing a firm, tanned thigh. It didn't matter to Frank that at thirty-seven she was three years older than he. It only made her seem more attractive—more challenging.

Joe gulped at the watery remains of his Scotch and ice and pushed the glass aside, knocking it over. Mary righted it. He pushed back the tuft of gray hair as if trying to hide it. "You know what I should have done? It would have been better for Frank—he could be sure of keeping his job, of getting enough to sail off into the sunset someday."

"What?" she asked idly, moving her hand over a frosted glass. The gesture, the languid movement of her finger, struck Frank as extraordinarily sexy.

"I should have started earlier," said Crane. "I should have started before 1980. I'd have tenure by now, which is as good as being in a union, and they couldn't sack me. Not without a hell of a lot of trouble, anyway. Thompson couldn't touch me." He glanced about at the red and white party lights. "The son of a bitch is after our blood. He wants to see me before I leave for the oceanographic conference in Fredericton. You see what he's up to, don't you? I won't have a chance to do anything, on the other side of the Goddamn country."

"Oh, Joe," sighed Mary. "I told you. You won't be fired. I know you had a bad cruise. So has Frank—but stop feeling so sorry for yourself."

"Sorry!" shouted Crane, rising from the chair. "I'm not sorry. I'm Goddamn mad! That's what I am. I'm mad as hell that idiots who can cut off my research and Frank's job don't know the first Goddamn thing about it. That

they can ruin our chance to be the first to . . ." Suddenly
Crane stopped and sat down, near exhaustion, his brow
beaded in perspiration, his face pale. "Maybe you're right."
He spoke slowly. "Maybe I'm just blubbering in my booze
. . . Silly bastard." He laughed, shook his head and got up,
steadying himself on a starboard grip.

"I'd better clear my brain." He tossed Frank the keys
to the Volvo. "Take Mary home, will you, Frank? She's
right—I'm messing up the party. Acting like an idiot."

Mary said nothing as Frank picked up the keys and
followed his boss off the boat.

"Where're you off to?" said Frank.

Crane kept walking. "I'll grab a cab. Bring the car
back here. I'll pick it up later. I'm going to check
out those depth profiles we did. Do something useful. Maybe there's something we missed."

"Maybe we did, but can't it wait till tomorrow? Look,
everyone sounds off about their troubles now and then.
It's therapeutic. You don't have to go."

"Thanks, Frank, but Thompson's still after us, and I
need all the evidence I can get to squeeze another trip
from him—if that's possible."

"I think you're wasting your time," said Frank.

"Fleming discovered penicillin in a dish he forgot to
clean, Frank. You never know. All we need is one more
trip. Sometimes you get this feeling, you know? It's based
on the work you've done, on the facts. But it's more than
that, it's, well, it's a feeling so strong that you know—you
just *know* you're almost there. It's the feeling you get when
you toss a piece of paper at a wastebasket, and you
just know the second it leaves your hand that it's going
in."

Frank didn't object further. He could see that the more
enthused Joe Crane was about his only passion, geology—
to be the first to make the big find—the quicker he'd lay
off the booze. It would have been easier to understand,
Frank thought, if Crane was driven solely by the desire
for money. Anyone could understand that; Frank wouldn't
mind more money himself. Indeed he saw his experience
at sea as a springboard to someday forming his own sea-
mining company. But for Crane a five-year search had
hardened into an obsession for recognition above all else.
Walking back to the clubhouse, Frank wondered what

denial during childhood could have been so great as to push Joe Crane so relentlessly toward his goal—so relentlessly that on the night of his returning home after weeks at sea he could walk away and entrust his wife to another man.

Nearing the motor launch Frank saw Mary's profile against the crimson-streaked sky. She was looking out toward the straits, her golden hair blowing gently behind her in the fragrant evening breeze, her fine, high cheekbones silhouetted sharply in the fading twilight. When he came aboard she kept gazing out to sea. "Where's he going?" she asked casually.

"To check some echo soundings."

"I've never seen Joe drink so much as he has lately."

"He only had five," said Frank loyally.

"I mean guzzling them like that—in fifteen minutes."

"He's under a lot of pressure. Thompson . . ."

She turned to him. "Let's not talk about Thompson, please. That's all I hear about."

"All right. Another drink?"

"Just soda."

When he gave her the glass her fingers touched his, remaining there for several seconds.

"He asked me to take you home."

"I heard. There's no rush." There was silence. She fixed him in her stare. "Is there?"

He put the car keys on the table. Darkness had now fallen but Frank could still make out the elegant line of Mary's dress. A gust of wind turned the hem and set the hailliards in the dockyard slapping frantically against the silver masts, so that every boat in the yard suddenly seemed alive. They didn't speak for the next few minutes. She tossed back her head with abandon, brushing the sheen of hair away from her eyes.

"Would you like another drink?" he asked again.

She laughed. It was an easy, sensuous laugh, uninhibited and fresh-sounding, as if she hadn't laughed in a long time. She held up the soda he'd just poured her.

"I forgot," he said happily. "It's the night air. Affects the brain."

She inhaled deeply. "It's marvelous," she said. "This is the most beautiful city in the world."

"With you—"

"Go on."

"With you here I believe it," he said. He could hear the hailliards flapping even louder than before. Suddenly he reached for the keys. "Let me take you home." Before she could say anything he hurried on. "Because if I don't, Mary, things are going to get right out of hand. And I'd love it."

"Let them, Frank," she said, rising and pressing hard into him. "Let them get out of hand."

"Mr. Hall? You there, Mr. Hall?" The voice was almost on top of them. It was the old caretaker.

"Shit!" muttered Frank. "Yes," he called out, trying not to sound as angry as he felt. "What is it?"

"Telephone, Mr. Hall."

It was Joe Crane. Where were the profiles for the last three sample stations? He couldn't find them in the jumble of boxes and sampling gear.

"By the piston corer," Frank snapped. "Got a blue sash on it."

"Okay, thanks. Listen, Frank, thanks for looking after Mary. Really appreciate it."

∽ ∽ ∽

When Frank returned to the boat the old man was still there, busily trying to strike up an acquaintance with Mary. She was trying to be polite, but there was a strain in her voice. The mood, invaded five minutes ago by the old man, was now completely gone. Driving her home Frank kept hearing Joe Crane thanking him for looking after her. A haze of guilt hung over the car like stale smoke.

"I suppose you think I'm some kind of tart," she said.

"Hardly," he said gruffly.

"You don't know what it's like. Joe's been—well, he's been acting strangely at home lately. At sea I guess he's too busy with his work. Sometimes I'm worried that . . . I'm worried that he's cracking up."

"Oh, anyone can act a little strange if they're under that kind of pressure and disappointment. If he didn't care about other people, like keeping me hired, it wouldn't be so hard on him. He's a good guy."

"I know," she said. "But how many men would have asked you to take me home if they still cared? *Really* cared, I mean?"

Frank didn't want to hear any more. "Look, Mary, you don't have to justify anything to me. I—"

"He's more interested in continental drift than he is in going to bed."

They sat in silence at a red light at Georgia and Burrard. They hit every red light there was.

At the door she fumbled a long time for her keys. Her hands were shaking. She was no longer the composed woman aboard his boat. "Would you have . . . ?" she began.

"Yes," he said.

"But it would bother you?"

"Right now? Yes."

"Good night," she said coldly.

"Good night."

Back in the car Frank punched the steering wheel. "Crowley," he said, recalling the old caretaker's interruption, "I could ring your Goddamn neck."

◇ ◇ ◇

Joe Crane got home around one fifteen a.m. He'd found nothing on the echo profiles that would indicate mineral deposits. Mary was still awake in bed, watching the late movie. He took her hand. "I'm sorry about tonight."

"It's all right."

"No, it isn't. Guess I'm just tired."

"Joe?"

"Yes?"

She switched off the TV, intently watching the dot disappear. "Would you like me to come out with you? On a cruise? If you get another chance, I mean? I've never been. It might be good for both of us if we spent more time together."

Joe Crane couldn't speak for a few seconds. "Hon— you don't know what that means to me. You know I've always wanted to share my work with you. I've always—"

"I'll go then," she said sleepily.

Joe kissed her cheek. "I love you," he said.

"I know."

"I love you," he said.

"Love you, too."

"I'll make it all up to you, Hon."

"I know."

It was just after two when Joe heard his wife softly groaning in her sleep. Stretching out his hand to comfort her, he stroked her hair and kissed her gently on the shoulder.

"Frank . . ." she murmured.

Joe's hand froze.

4

"Get down here fast, Ron."

"What's up?" asked Moody.

"Not on the phone. Get the first flight you can. How long will it take from Toronto?"

"Seven to ten hours."

"All right. I'll book you at the usual place. Meet you for breakfast."

"Got it."

∾   ∾   ∾

At seven a.m. Joe Crane, unable to sleep, was standing by the window looking over the gray harbor that came with the sunrise.

Fourteen hundred miles to the south, fifteen miles north of San Diego, Ron Moody was too excited to sleep. Besides, the quick plane trip from Toronto had left him suffering from dehydration, or what most people call jet lag. Aged forty-seven, looking fifty-seven and weighing thirty pounds more than was good for his bad heart, Moody trudged along the beach at La Jolla. It was the most strenuous exercise he'd had for three months. He watched a white fringe of surf push up on black rocks and saw the vast expanse of the Pacific turn quickly from darkness to a cobalt blue. He turned back toward the motel. It would soon be time for breakfast and his meeting with his partner Burke. Burke, an American, worked the west coast out of La Jolla, while Moody, a Canadian, worked the east coast out of Toronto.

At the motel restaurant he glanced at the previous day's headline in the *Los Angeles Times*. There was more trouble between Zaire and Shaba Province, formerly Katanga. For Moody that meant only one thing—copper would be scarce, since the rich Shaba mines would no doubt be closed once again by the dispute. That was the trouble with underdeveloped countries, he thought. Too busy fighting amongst themselves to develop. Still, he shouldn't worry. The big mining companies who couldn't invest in politically unstable countries would have to look elsewhere for their source of supply, whether it be copper or manganese. Which was where Moody and Bruiser Burke, or "Scouts Unlimited," came in. Burke's real name was Larry, but Moody had always known him as Bruiser. The nickname was an unimaginative tribute to Burke's methods of defending himself against those oil-company and mining employees who didn't like people pitching tents in the woods near company claims, and watching the workers through field glasses, or taking notes on drilling rates, or sampling mud holes and photographing drill record books and selling the results to other big companies.

Burke didn't waste any time. He didn't even order coffee. Moody flipped open a note pad. Burke closed it. Now Moody was really excited.

"It's that hot, huh?"

"It's that hot."

They were the only customers in the coffee shop but even so Burke did a quick check. "You know this big oceanographic conference?"

"Yeah," nodded Moody. "In Fredericton. Starts day after tomorrow. Don't worry, I was going to check it out. All the oceanographers send their papers in ahead of time —gives everyone a chance to bone up for the discussion groups."

"Right," said Burke. "Except there's one paper we don't want anyone to see."

"What is it—copper?"

"Everything. There's a guy here at La Jolla by the name of Shae at the Scripps Institute." Moody's ears pricked up. Scripps was the Mecca of oceanography.

"What's he on to?"

"He's been sampling off Santiago on the Chilean coast. He's found rust-red mud. Goddamn stuff is . . . You're the college graduate in geology. What do they call it? You know, when the sea bottom's a mineral porridge?"

"Son of a bitch," exclaimed Moody. "You mean sea gold—metalliferous muds?"

"Whatever. Anyway there's not much of it where he's been sampling, but the point is that this guy Shae—a young Ph.D.—has written a paper showing that there's exactly the same kind of seabed formation, only much larger, a hundred and seventy miles off the west coast of Vancouver Island."

"Son of a bitch. You get a copy?"

Burke's lips, those of an ex-boxer, visibly tightened. "I tried, but it seems our friend Shae isn't interested in flogging the exact position to vulgar industry. Wants to make a big name for himself in academia. Wants to make a big splash at the Fredericton conference. Lots of media coverage. Save the whales type. Not interested in selling it to the highest bidder."

Moody nodded knowingly. In his mind he quickly formed a picture of the young scientist. Late twenties or early thirties, beard, sandals, open-necked shirt, ecology T-shirt maybe, happy with his Ph.D. salary at Scripps, not interested in working in industry but hell-bent for glory in *Scientific American*. Genius geologist from the sunbelt.

"Goddamn idiot," said Moody. "All brains and no street sense. All he has to do is lift the phone. He could sell that info for a bundle."

Moody knew that there might not be massive deposits of sea gold in the area Shae had speculated on, after all, but the possibility alone was worth a bundle to the big mining companies. But if Burke had found out about the paper, if not the location of the area, how many other scouts knew of the paper's existence—even if they hadn't seen it. "Who else has got wind of it?" Moody asked anxiously.

Burke helped himself to one of Moody's cigarettes. "That's the problem. I don't know. I found out from one of Scripps' lab assistants I keep on retainer."

"Will he blab?"

"What do I know? He says no, but we aren't the only scouts in America, right?"

"Shit. We've got to act fast."

"Which is why I rang you soon as I heard."

"You got a plan?"

"I'm going to meet this lab kid at noon. I'll try giving him a bonus to do a little snooping around in Shae's office."

"Christ! You haven't done that already?" asked Moody incredulously.

"You move too fast," said Burke defensively, "and you scare 'em. They piss themselves and then you get nothing, period. Anyway, if he comes through, we could have the paper by tomorrow before the conference. You could fly up to Vancouver tonight. If we get it, we'd better not fart around. We have to work your connections on your side of the line. Sell it to a Canadian company. We don't know exactly where the area is yet. Could be anywhere in a hundred-and-seventy-mile radius from Vancouver, but wherever it is, it's in Canadian waters—Canadian economic zone."

"They mightn't buy it for themselves," said Moody.

"Why?" asked Burke, obviously puzzled.

"You're used to selling to big U.S. conglomerates. If it was in their territorial waters, a U.S. company would send their own ship out. Canadian companies haven't got that kind of backup yet. They share the cost of research with government outfits, universities and the like."

Now Burke was even more puzzled. "So how do the companies get an edge, if they share research costs with the government?"

Moody grinned. "I guess not all university scientists are idiots like Shae."

Burke nodded sagely. "Thank God for that."

"Maybe . . ." said Moody, looking pensive, "maybe we should sell it to *two* parties?"

"You got a lot of life insurance?" asked Burke.

"Just thinking."

"Yeah, well don't get too greedy. Play it safe. A ten-grand split between us isn't a bad catch."

"If we catch it."

Burke lit another cigarette—now he had two on the go. "I told you I'm seeing this kid at noon."

"Want me to come along?"

"No. A new body'd scare him off, sure as hell."

"So if we don't get it from him?"

"I've booked you on two return flights. One to Vancouver if I get it, one to Fredericton if I don't. Shae *has* to send advance copies of his paper to Fredericton. Conference rules, right?"

"He hasn't sent them yet," said Moody. "I have a geology graduate who checks the incoming stuff for me."

"Which means," said Burke, "that Shae is running true to form. Fucking prima donna. He sent them at the last minute. Not enough time for the delegates to read the paper before his big presentation, but technically the copies will arrive just in time to have him satisfy conference rules. He won't do anything to sour his big act. So if I can't get a copy this afternoon, then our last chance is at Fredericton. Chances are, no one'll read anything that comes in that late. Before the conference starts, everyone will be suffering from jet lag."

"Including me," quipped Moody. "I'm going to need a week's fishing after this. When will you let me know?"

"If I get it today?"

"Yeah."

"No phones. Meet me at the Townhouse Lodge at four—on Ash Street. It's only two miles from the airport. My room is two oh four. Smith."

"Original," joked Moody, adding more seriously, "I hope this kid hasn't blabbed."

"You and me both."

∽ ∽ ∽

When Burke didn't show at four, Moody went down and got another six-pack. He liked American beer; you could quench your thirst without getting too slow, and slow he couldn't afford—not today. If they didn't get a copy of Shae's paper here to take to Vancouver, he would have to hightail it to Fredericton and try to pick it up there before the oceanography conference officially opened—and before young Shae blabbed it for full effect in front of his colleagues and the press. It wasn't just the information, Moody reflected, so much as the timing that was all-important at the moment. Even an hour's delay in getting such information could mean the difference between huge profits or losses for mining companies.

∽ ∽ ∽

"Mr. Moody?"

"Yes . . ."

The police officer was very polite. Mr. Burke's car had

gone off Interstate 5 "around four twenty-seven p.m."
They couldn't find a next-of-kin in the wallet but there was
a card listing Mr. Moody at Townhouse Lodge.

It took Moody only a second in the sweet-smelling
morgue to identify Larry Burke. He looked like he was
asleep. Yes, the city would take care of the burial.
The state trooper on the scene had reported that when
he opened the door of the wrecked caraway-yellow Ca-
maro, it had stunk like a distillery, adding in his report that
an empty fifth of Jack Daniels was wedged underneath the
brake pedal. It was an open and shut case—that is until
the county coroner found that Larry, or rather Lawrence
Burke of no fixed address, had a .00 blood-alcohol
count.

It took Moody only ten minutes to get from Townhouse
Lodge to the airport. He boarded a plane for Toronto,
connecting with Fredericton, New Brunswick, twenty minutes later. As he clicked on the seat belt he said a silent
prayer of thanks that he hadn't gone with Burke. Then he
thought—a little guiltily—about the ten thousand dollars
that would now be all his. *If* he got a copy of the paper
first.

As Moody watched the sun setting over California, turning the sea blood-red, the floodlights at Vancouver's
Pacific National Exhibition, over a thousand miles to the
north, revealed the grotesque metallic monsters which
were the stars of the annual "Mining Exhibition."

∽ ∽ ∽

"Hi, Frank!" Andrea Nolan could see he hadn't heard
her, which was not surprising, given the noise of men and
machines. He was watching a huge strip-mining ripper
work over a two-foot-thick concrete slab. She tapped him
on the shoulder. "Hi."

"Oh, hello, Andrea. Didn't know COR was branching out
into coal."

"You're a bit out of your depth too, aren't you?"

"That's an awful pun. Someone tries that on me every
month at the Institute."

"Well, I don't get to see you every month. Unfortunately."

Frank laughed. He didn't know Andrea Nolan that well,
only through odd trade shows like this one. But he knew
her well enough to know when she was putting on her

honey blue-eyed smile. The eyes weren't as fetching as Mary Crane's, nor as warm, but they were always bright and calculating. He'd heard the stories. She'd work you over nicely: the Fado for dinner; she'd offer to pay half the tab—*insist* on paying half the tab. She'd pick the wines—to show how far she'd come, and if you weren't careful, by the time Spanish coffee rolled around you'd be telling her more about where you were going to sample on your next cruise than your boss knew.

"Want coffee?" she offered happily.

"Spanish?" he said pointedly.

She looked at him quizzically. "What—here?"

"Just kidding." He pointed at the nearby Hydro Dynamics stall. *"They're* giving coffee away free."

She waited till he was halfway through a doughnut before she really started on him. "I hear you're having trouble."

"News to me."

"Oh, come on, sweetie. It's all around town. Word is Joe Crane is washed up, that he's just this short of being canned." "This short" was a one-inch gap between her long, immaculately kept nails. One grab, thought Frank, and they'd de-ball you.

"So?" he said, trying to sound nonchalant.

Andrea's eyes were fixed on his. She patted her lips softly with the napkin.

"So, CANORE is on the lookout for a good oceanographic technician. We're branching out."

Frank saw one of Andrea's rivals. It was Nielsen, the acquisition manager from Vancouver Oceanics, the company which had subsidized much of the Maritime Institute research, and the company which might pull the plug on Crane after their last cruise. Frank couldn't stand the man, but he couldn't resist the chance to toy with Andrea.

"How're you doing?" he called out and waved. Nielsen nodded, somewhat nonplussed. Andrea coolly pretended that Vancouver Oceanics never existed.

"We're looking for new areas to mine," she said. *"At sea.* We need good people."

"Which comes first, the area or the people?"

"Well, we'd have to know we were onto something before we could hire—naturally."

"Naturally."

She broke off a little of her doughnut and playfully popped it into his mouth. He noticed that her blue eyes were flecked with gold.

"What we're really looking for," she continued, "is someone who knows where *not* to look. We could spend an awful lot of time and money going over old ground." She laughed. "I mean old sea."

Frank tossed away the Styrofoam cup. "No thanks—but thanks for the coffee."

As he moved away she tucked a COR business card into his pocket, her eyes still fixed on his in friendly invitation. "Don't thank me. Coffee's free."

"Nothing's *free*," he called back. "See you around."

The salesman from Western Hydro Dynamics took one look at Andrea standing alone and moved in. "See our new model?" he asked proudly, pointing up at the red and orange two-man submersible. Andrea took in the salesman, the crowd and the sub, all in one glance. "Yes," she said. "I've seen it."

"What do you think?" he inquired confidently.

Andrea handed him the cold coffee. "It's shit."

5

Fredericton, New Brunswick

At first it went so smoothly that Moody could hardly believe it.

When he walked into the University of New Brunswick's Residence Administrative Building, the clock read three minutes past nine a.m. He excused himself through a sea of suitcases and tired faces. He nodded to the security guard, who was watching a soccer game. "Who's winning?"

"New York. Brinowski just scored. Three-one."

"He's a killer, that guy. Talk about head work, I tell ya."

The guard lit a cigarette. "You can say that again."

Moody had never heard of Brinowski, but the conversation served his purpose. "Say, Chief, can you tell me where the conference papers are?"

"Tilley Hall," said the guard, without taking his eyes off the soccer game. "Head straight up the path back of here to the Student Union Building and take a right, top of the hill. You'll probably miss it."

Moody grinned. "Gotcha. Keep your eye on that Brinowski, eh?"

The guard saluted, still watching the set.

Like most of the buildings on campus, Tilley Hall was red brick colonial, but it was bigger than the others and all but deserted. Before he went in, Moody patted his left vest pocket, making sure his equipment was still there. It was an anxiety pat, to reassure himself that everything would go all right. Besides, he told himself, there wasn't any real law against what he was going to do in the next half hour. Well, there might be a law . . . So it might be a bit grubby. It certainly wasn't glamorous. But hell, he had to make a buck, didn't he? Same as any other scout. Same as anybody.

In the foyer there were blue cardboard arrows on stands pointing to the various conference rooms. He took the left hallway, turned left again at the men's toilet and saw the room marked "PAPERS" and, underneath, a sign reading "Only one per person—$1.00 each."

Moody smiled at the coed with the Learned Societies information button and let her return to her knitting. The knitting pleased him—she wouldn't be watching him closely. He noted the girl's name from her tag and began to leaf through the papers on the first desk, recognizing most of them from the graduate student's report of a few weeks earlier. As unobtrusively as possible he reshuffled the papers, transferring ten or so of each and mixing them into the other piles. This way it would take them hours to find out exactly what was missing. When he saw Shae's paper he could feel his heart quicken. He took care not to mix Shae's with the other papers. He looked at the title page: *"Juan de Fuca Ridge: The Possibility of Metalliferous Muds."* Moody began to read, his eyes racing across the pages.

Shae's article went into the geology of the ore-forming process in some detail. Moody passed the early sections by, anxious for the concluding remarks. The Chilean find, said Shae, though rich in deposits that included zinc, copper, nickel, iron, lead, silver, gold, and manganese, had been small, a few acres, and was not commercially viable —particularly in view of the volatile nature of the Chilean government. By extrapolation, however, he argued that the areas in and about the Juan de Fuca Ridge, off the coast of British Columbia, would be ideal for the formation of "massive" mineral-rich deposits, beside which the celebrated but politically inaccessible metalliferous Red Sea brines would pale into insignificance.

Moody looked around the room. The coed was still knitting. He forced himself to breathe slowly. Whenever he got too excited he was in danger of a heart attack. He popped a blue-white 10-mg. Bentylol capsule as an added precaution.

He read the passage again, dwelling for a moment on the word "massive." He thought it a beautiful word. His eyes darted back and forth over the article, quickly sifting out the key phrases quoted from the May '76 issue of *Geoscience Canada*: "Such potential reserves are impossible to estimate. In any case, there is little doubt that in the next few decades, oceanic crust will become a major source of raw materials . . . For this to be accomplished will require increasingly active international cooperation . . ."

"Yeah, yeah," mumbled Moody cynically, scanning the remaining background information. Of the Red Sea brines, Moody read that if the copper and zinc alone could be sucked up they would be worth over six billion—and that figure was based on 1974 prices.

Now, Moody knew, they would be worth eighteen billion. He considered it a typical academic's statement, completely devoid of political reality. Anybody trying to cash in on that Red Sea lot, he thought, would have Arab shrapnel up his ass before he dropped anchor— which made Shae's paper all the more valuable. He went back to Shae's estimate of mineral deposits in all the world's oceans, and the quote, "It's all there under the ocean and it belongs to nobody and everybody."

"Crap!" he murmured. "It belongs to whoever has the most muscle." He checked the latitude and longitude of the area off Vancouver Island that was the subject of Shae's hypothesis. In his excitement he'd forgotten to do this first, and silently castigated himself for it. It was the most important piece of information he would have to sell. He saw the map and memorized the latitudinal and longitudinal boundaries. He took a copy and paid the girl a dollar.

A minute later he returned, poking his head around the corner of the brightly lit room.

"Ah—are you Miss Michaels?"

The girl dropped a stitch. "Yes. Can I help you?"

"Not me," said Moody graciously, "but there's someone who wants to see you at the entrance. Got a pile of stuff. Special delivery. Looks heavy."

"More late papers," she sighed, putting down the half-finished mohair cardigan and walking resignedly off down the long corridor. Although Moody had made sure no one else was around, he knew the girl would be back in a few minutes. He worked fast, whipping out the two garbage bags from his pocket, putting one inside the other for extra strength. Taking two thumbtacks, he pinned one edge of the double bag to the table so that he could hold it open, with one hand. Then in one movement, using his free arm, he swept all the Shae papers into the garbage bag, tore the bag away from the thumb tacks, put a tie around it, moved the stacks of papers around so that the Shae papers wouldn't be missed immediately, lifted the bag over his shoulder and walked quietly from the room. He waited at the T junction near the washroom, his heart pounding. The girl wasn't in sight, but he could hear her footsteps clicking on the polished floor down near the main entrance. She was returning. He dashed across the T junction, looking like a truant trash collector, and turned left at the end of the corridor, heading down the ramp to the southern exit. A conference delegate opened the door for him from the outside and smiled.

"Ah, Santa Claus! Looks like you've got a body in there."

"Bottom samples from the University of New Brunswick," Moody puffed.

"Ah ha! A rare mixture of empties from the east coast."

Moody grinned politely and scuttled over the grassy lawns, making a shortcut between Tilley Hall and the administrative office, where he waited until he saw a luggage-laden delegate using a key in the entrance to the nearby Neill House residence. "Let me give you a hand," offered Moody, putting down his load. The man murmured his appreciation as Moody held the heavy swing door open. "They make these so elephants won't get in," said Moody.

The other man grunted, far too tired to wonder why Moody was lugging a trash bag. And that's what Moody had counted on: they would all be too tired until tomorrow when the conference started. And by then he'd be well and truly gone.

Once inside the dimly lit, barracks-like dormitory, Moody put one of the Shae papers in his pocket and dumped the rest in the lock-top anti-vandal garbage cans. This way, even if anyone had worked out what was missing and what wasn't, after his quick shuffling of the papers, it would be difficult to check what was inside the cans—if they ever thought to search—before the garbage pickup. A small thing, but together all the small things gave him more time—an edge over any possible competition. He lit a Player's, blew the smoke out hard, and looked at his Seiko. Not bad. From the time he'd decoyed the girl to the time he had dumped all the copies, it had only been twelve minutes. He went into the nearest toilet, but the cubicles only had lift-up wooden rims —no covers. He was going to use an internal phone booth but rejected it. Too risky. Some summer student would be sure to use it. He went downstairs and found a public phone booth. A scout was often under surveillance himself without knowing it, and it wasn't healthy to carry around the information you'd worked so hard to get—at least, not in such a bulky and visible form as a paper. He tore the last page, the bibliography, from the paper, printed "Out of Order" on it, pulled a thumbtack out of the nearby bulletin board and stuck the paper to the pock-marked door. Standing outside the cubicle with the door open, so that he could see if anyone was coming, he covered the glass half of the door with the garbage bag. Once inside, the weak bulb lit up the depressing chocolate-brown interior. He laid the paper on the floor, lifted out his Rollei A110, steadied the tiny four-element 23-mm Tessar lens camera against the telephone, and began photographing each page, pressing the orange inset button, pulling and pushing the film advance with an easy practised rhythm. As he turned over the last page, he

played it safe, altering the distance setting to four feet,
risking a little overexposure, and turned the pages backwards, photographing them again. Each time the flash went
off, the shaded cubicle looked as if it was exploding inside. He'd brought two extra rolls of the black and white
film, but the Rollei was his favorite tool and he didn't need
the additional cassette. After he finished, he ripped up
Shae's paper, put it in the garbage bag with the "Out of
Order" sign, dumped it all in the trash can, then pulled out
his tattered address book. He looked at his Vancouver list-
ings. There were two—Nielsen, the acquisitions manager
for Vancouver Oceanics, and CANORE acquisition manager
Andrea Nolan. The question was, who would it be? Whoever it was he figured he'd ask for his regular five-thou-
sand-dollar field price now and another five when they saw
the film, prints of which he would send by courier as
soon as he processed it in his Toronto darkroom.

The Howe Street suckers in Vancouver loved film. If
the *Globe and Mail* was on microfilm they'd think it was
hot and pay extra for it. Because he was so exuberant
it never occurred to Moody that his information, in
whatever form he wished to send it, might be considered
cheap at twice the price—and not just by his Vancouver
client.

6

As Joe Crane entered the cavernous foyer of the Maritime Institute, with its huge killer-whale skeleton resting
upon the aqua-blue carpet, he wondered if this would
be the last time—if he could somehow persuade Thompson to give him one last chance. It didn't help that, whenever he walked down the long corridor that led to the
Dean's office and saw the neat mineral samples and
the names of their discoverers lining the glass insets of the
walls, he felt intimidated. They were constant reminders
of what he was supposed to be doing. He recalled the

marine display he had seen at the Ala Moana shopping complex in Honolulu several years before. The big display board had confidently informed the passing masses that an estimated 140 billion metric tons of manganese nodules lay on the bottom of the Pacific. "Some scientists," the description had read, "think that the nodules are accumulating at the rate of 9.1 million tons per year." Sure, Crane had thought bitterly, and all you have to do is buy a big basket and pick them like strawberries.

Approaching the end of the corridor, Joe began to feel it closing in on him like an ever-constricting tunnel. He had the sudden urge to swear violently and smash the glass cases with his fist. He didn't know why. He'd had the same kind of feeling as a boy during communion—the fleeting impulse to jump up and yell an obscenity. Sometimes he'd been so afraid of doing it that he hadn't gone to church, and the more he stayed away from church the more afraid he became of doing it and so the less he went to church. He felt more and more like this lately. Not about church—he hadn't been in years, but about other things. He'd had the same closing-in feeling when he thought of Frank and Mary left alone, two nights before. What had gone on between them? His stomach tightened and the feeling that he wanted to smash something returned, now reinforced.

He counted the fluorescent tubes flicking past like white prison bars overhead. If there was an even number before he got to the Dean's office, he'd be all right: he would get another chance; he would keep his job; he'd find manganese. If there was an odd number it would mean trouble. When he reached the Dean's door he'd counted eleven.

Dean Thompson's office was spacious and carpeted with the same aqua-blue shag that surrounded the whale, a relic of earlier, inflation-free days. A large globe sat in front of the long, curved, mahogany desk. Thompson cultivated the loose, crumpled academic look—corduroys and pipe, with an oldish tweed jacket. But at the drop of a hat he'd don the three-piece pinstripe suit and call down to the Vancouver Club, where the menu was in French and had nothing to do with bilingualism. When he smiled, a gold flash revealed the extensive bridgework that had followed his running quarterback days at Jefferson-Davis

University forty years ago. At six feet he was no taller than Joe Crane, but he looked much taller as he waved Crane to the bucket seat set purposely, some said, four inches below his own. Thompson, halfway through a journal, looked down at Crane. The gray eyes were unsmiling, quick and intimidating. "Be with you in a minute."

Joe Crane nodded. He would have drummed on the armrests of the chair, but there were none. His foot began periodically jerking as he looked about the room. Behind him on the high cedar wall there was an old football photo. Thompson, the captain, was dead center. In the silence of the room the ticking of the antique mantel clock on the smooth desk filled Joe with a sudden despair. Forty-eight years old, and here he was sitting as nervous as a freshman. He wanted to tell Thompson to go to hell, and walk out. He shot an angry glance at the relentlessly ticking clock. It was already ten thirty, and he had to catch the plane to Fredericton at noon. By then of course he would have missed the beginning of the oceanographic conference. Goddamn the arrogant bastard, he thought, delaying him like this.

Thompson closed the journal, dropped it into the "out" tray, and looked quizzically at Crane's jerking foot. Crane stilled his foot and waited. Thompson began studiously stuffing his pipe.

"Joe," he began, and Crane felt his stomach turn. First names were used to soften the kick. "I could ask you around to dinner at the Faculty Club and do it all very diplomatically, but that would waste your time and mine. So I'll give it to you straight." Crane's face drained of color. Minutes seemed to pass as Thompson struck a long match, holding it over the bowl of the bent-stemmed Petersen, and sucked heavily. Hope you choke, thought Crane, as the thick, blue-gray clouds of smoke enveloped Thompson's head, then rose and rolled in waves off the silver-speckled ceiling. Thompson shook out the match with an elaborate flourish and let it drop into a crystal ashtray that was an old squash trophy. "The word is . . ." Thompson pushed the ashtray away from him. "Or I should say the word at the Permanent Appointments Committee meeting yesterday *was* that . . ." A small, orange light lit up on his oak-panelled switchboard and Thompson picked up the phone. "Yes? Yes, I know, old chap." Crane liked the "old chap" bit. Pretentious bastard. If he tried that on him, he'd tell him where to shove it. No, he wouldn't.

"Yes, I know you said you were ill," said Thompson, "but if I allowed every student who said he was ill the day of exams to rewrite, then where would we be? Why didn't you get a doctor's certificate? Hmm—yes, but surely you could have rung a doctor. Well, perhaps you couldn't get out of bed, but . . . No, no, I mean wasn't there a friend or someone who could . . . ?" Thompson spun the globe lightly, listening. The oceans became a blue blur. "The answer's still no, I'm afraid." There was a long silence. Crane imagined what was going on at the other end—one exam, one course, one degree, one career. Who knew?

"No, it's not possible. Good-bye." Thompson gently replaced the phone in its cradle. "Sorry about that," he said, but Joe could tell he wasn't. He had the distinct feeling that the interruption had suited Thompson's purpose very well.

"The word was, Joe, that in view of the fact that you haven't come up with anything in those dredges of yours . . ." The pipe went out. Thompson struck another match. Crane's mouth tasted like cardboard. His lips were parted, his tongue pressed hard on his bottom teeth.

"Well," he said, "I've tried . . ."

Thompson edged the tobacco pouch forward on the spotless blotter. "Oh, I know you've tried. It's no reflection on your persistence, believe me. Or your *theoretical* knowledge." Joe Crane winced. That one really hurt. "But you know how the outside is." Thompson's hands came up to form a wide Y. "If you don't bring home the bacon, industry cuts the research funds. Then where are we? These days we need their money to justify the projects in order to get the government grants."

Joe Crane was in a near panic. He could see his last chance going out the window. He leaned forward in his chair. "I know, I know. But it's not like mining on land where you can see exactly where you've been. At sea you never know exactly."

"But you must have extensive echo soundings, Joe? You've been looking for . . . what? Five, six years?"

"Five." Barely holding himself in check, Joe moved uneasily in his seat. "Yes, we do have records, but the navigation is just not pinpoint. Nobody seems to understand that. You could retrace your steps without even knowing it. Even the best . . . What I mean is, it's a process of elimination, and now I feel—"

"What about this satellite method? This Loran business? They say that's good to within half a mile or less."

"Sometimes, depending on the atmospherics. But everything is different at sea. I mean . . ." Joe Crane was perspiring.

Thompson glanced impatiently at his watch. "Yes, so you've said. Well, I'm sorry. The Committee's decision was that this is your last trip, then the money runs out. It's as simple as that."

Crane was stunned. "You mean . . . ?"

Thompson pulled out his notebook. "I received a call from Nielsen—acquisitions manager for Vancouver Oceanics—early this morning." He glanced up. "What I'm telling you, Crane, is in the strictest confidence. I want you to be quite clear on that."

Joe Crane managed to mumble his assent.

"They've come up with what I must say is a very generous offer. The most generous grant to date, I believe." His voice dropped. "Particularly in view of your record."

Joe Crane refused to take the bait—refused to do anything that might jeopardize his position as of that moment. He still felt that he was on a tightrope—exhilarated, but on a tightrope.

Thompson continued: "But obviously they're willing to overlook your record in the interests of speed. You are the only immediately available marine geologist who knows the general area. Speed, as they commonly say, is of the essence." He flicked open his notebook with his silver pencil as a pathologist might flick over a particularly repulsive specimen with his probe. "Apparently they have received information from a so-called 'mining scout'."

Crane could sense Thompson's disgust in the way he almost spat out the two words. "A spy?" ventured Crane, immediately ashamed at his attempt to curry favor in the wash of relief that was beginning to roll over him.

"Exactly," concurred Thompson. "This creature has somehow got advance notice of an area which Shae from Scripps—you've heard of him?"

"Yes," Crane lied. "Vaguely."

"Yes, well, it seems as if he's found a remarkable physical correlation between a small but metalliferously rich area off Chile and the area about Juan de Fuca Ridge. It's a little broad at the moment. All we have are the boundaries of the area—latitude and longitude." Thompson pushed a piece of paper bearing a set of coordinates across the desk. "I'll send the rest of the details out to you when Vancouver Oceanics receives them from this 'scout'."

Joe Crane had the urge to whoop madly, to run about the room. He'd heard enough to realize that this was infinitely more important than just finding manganese. Both men knew that in the quietest possible terms they were talking about the possibility of locating one of the richest mineralogical finds in history. A find that could change Crane's life—give him everything he'd ever wanted. That's why Thompson took his time about telling me, thought Crane. Just to make me sweat. Amid the fantastic images that danced in his brain he was aware of something he hadn't fully understood. "You said you'd send the information out to me. What about Fredericton —the Oceanographic Conference?"

Crane thought Thompson was about to choke. "Forget it. I've asked the *Petrel* to load tonight. They're on their way over from Esquimalt now. As you probably know, she's the most advanced research ship on the west coast. You haven't sailed on her, have you?"

"No."

"You've got five days. It's now Monday. I want you steaming out by Wednesday dinnertime—at the latest. And don't moan about only having five days. I know traveling time there and back will eat up nearly half of it, but we were damned lucky to squeeze that much time out of her. She was due for a refit. As it is, they're not happy about going out again so soon."

Thompson dragged another file across. "Needless to say, this is a rather sensitive business for all concerned. I want you to be circumspect about what you're looking for."

"You mean, tell everyone that I'm still looking for manganese?"

"Precisely. Your technician," added Thompson, his tone full of condescension, "the would-be Chichester—What's his name?"

"Frank Hall."

"Yes, well, he'll have to know, I suppose."

"It'd be useful," said Crane sarcastically.

"The fewer people who know, the better for all of us. Certainly no other company must know."

It sounded like a threat but Joe Crane said nothing.

"We *do* owe Vancouver Oceanics that much," pressed Thompson. "For past subsidies."

Joe Crane nodded curtly and got up. He hated agreeing with Thompson on anything, and it showed. As he opened the door he heard Thompson speak again. "One more thing."

"Yes?"

"Close the door. I don't care how much the University has got from Vancouver Oceanics. I told them, and I'm telling you. If I had my way I'd hold the ship until I could get someone from the east. Someone with more of a track record. You're lucky it's summer. It would take time to get a replacement. And we don't have time. What I'm saying is that—"

"You hate my guts but you've no alternative."

Thompson began knocking his pipe hard on the crystal ashtray. No junior member of staff, especially one without tenure, had ever spoken to him like that before. "That goes without saying. But what I mean, Crane, is that if you don't find those muds you won't set foot on a research ship again. And I'll be advertising a vacancy in Marine Geology." He smiled viciously. "I should also remind you that with only five days you won't have enough time to tow underwater vehicles, or use anything as slow as a submersible. You'll have to spot-sample from the surface."

Joe Crane nodded slowly. "Well, don't sell your Vancouver Oceanics shares just yet, will you?"

Thompson's face turned beet red and he looked down, opening his penknife. "The weather forecast is bad," he said. "At most you'll probably have two to three days in the area."

Joe Crane opened the door. Thompson was gouging deeply into the bowl of his pipe, the knife blade glinting in the morning sun. It must be hell, thought Crane, half wanting me to find it and half not. "When are you expecting the rest of the information from this scout?"

Thompson shrugged petulantly. "Whenever he can get it here."

Realizing now that Thompson would never give him another chance—that this time was unquestionably his last try; that after this his job would go to someone else—Joe Crane felt the old panic welling up in him again, threatening to explode. "And what if this scout, whoever he is, doesn't send all the details? These coordinates cover an area of over twenty-nine thousand square kilometers."

The knife's blade scraped into the black marrow of the pipe. "You've got five days."

～ ～ ～

On the other side of the country, Moody had been dreaming about what he would do with his money. He'd been dreaming so much that he awoke to find that he might have to pay an extra day's tariff at the Beaverbrook, having slept an hour past the noon checkout time. For all his sleep he still felt tired. He'd been joking with Burke about going fishing, but now he decided to do just that. He'd unwind in the peace of some place like St. Andrews-by-the-Sea. He didn't have any fishing gear, but after last night's work he could just go out and use his cards to buy whatever he needed. But first he'd have brunch.

It started badly. The waitress thought he said "grapefruit" instead of "grape juice," and he ordered a plain omelette, not Spanish. Though he was sitting facing the river with his back to the entrance of the dining room, he saw them the moment they walked in. They were reflected in the long window that looked out on the gray slate of river. It was the way they moved—as if they owned New Brunswick. He instinctively felt for the Rollei camera. There were two of them. One at least five ten, the other just over six feet; two-piece suits, striped ties on pastel shirts. The taller, neater one wearing Pierre Cardin sunglasses looked English—ex-army or navy. The shorter one looked like an ex-pug—heavyweight division. Moody thought of giving the camera to the waitress with an address and a five-dollar bill for postage, but she couldn't even get the juice straight. Besides, they were sitting just behind him, halfway between the long window and the bamboo gazebo, close enough to hear everything.

He watched in the window as they sat down and started

chatting pleasantly with the waitress. Then Moody began to laugh at himself. You're getting old, Moody, he told himself, relaxing, tearing open another packet of Sweet-'n'Low and dumping it into his coffee. What makes you think they're looking for you? So one of them might look like a boxer—so what? Could be two oceanographers looking for friends to eat with. After all, oceanographers, like everyone else, come in all shapes and sizes.

When he finished brunch, Moody walked out of the hotel and turned right down Queen's Street and headed toward the shopping center, passing through Officers' Square Park with its bronze statue of Beaverbrook. It was only when he stopped to tie a shoelace by the circular pool that he saw them again. The sunglasses were glinting in the sun and they were half a block behind him. He walked down to the York-Sunbery Historical Society's museum, paid his fifty cents and went quickly upstairs. He found himself in a dark World War One trench tunnel, complete with worn Hessian sandbags, gas masks, wax dummies of soldiers, periscope and narrow, winding duckboards. In the confined space he felt claustrophobic: he could hear his breathing and the echo of his footsteps. Then he heard the echo of other feet only yards behind him. It might still be coincidence, he thought, but that was wearing thin. He headed down the steps and out onto the crushed cream gravel, his heart thumping, back past the hotel to the Beaverbrook art gallery. Inside it was cool, and there were enough people to make it safe, at least for a while. Moody picked the first seat he saw, and found himself looking up at Dali's *Santiago El Grande*. He barely noticed the great white stallion rearing up, its rider's sword lifted high to heaven above the atomic blast, or the enormous sapphire sky that backed the explosion with an immense calm. The only thing Moody was conscious of was the small, crouching, refugee-like figure of Dali near the bottom of the painting. Moody identified strongly with the figure.

The two men stood at the back wall, looking at Dali's magnificent blue through their Polarized lenses. Christ, thought Moody, Jesus Christ help me! He couldn't stay in the gallery all day. Despite the air conditioning he was sweating, his heart banging in his chest. Christ! His hand was in his trouser pocket, nervously clutching the camera. It wasn't until he felt the two spare film cassettes that he

saw a possible way out. It would take him one, maybe
two minutes at the outside. That's all he needed. The problem was how to get out of their sight for even that
long. The bathroom was no good—they'd punch the door
down in five seconds. Still, it would buy him time while
he was working the plan out.

He got up slowly from the seat and stood back, ostensi-
bly for a better view of the Dali, adopting a thoughtful,
hand-under-the-chin pose. He moved to the far left toward
the window, then to the far right, then turned slowly to
face the winterscapes on the opposite wall. The two men,
temporarily blocking his view, separated on either side of
him and looked with him at the paintings. Walking up
past them to the information desk, Moody caught a
whiff of English Leather cologne.

"Could you tell me where the washrooms are?" Moody
said it loudly enough for them to hear.

"Down those stairs to your right."

"Thank you." He smiled and walked slowly down the
basement stairs, pausing to look at a recently acquired
Van Trier. The two men were about ten feet behind.
Then he made his dash—around the far corner of the room
out of sight and into the ladies' washroom. A woman
fussing with her hair in front of the mirror turned, startled.

"Sorry," he said. Then he was gone and running. A
few heads turned as he pushed past an incoming group
of oceanography delegates. By the time the two men
bashed open a door in the Gents and found an old man
having trouble with his zipper, Moody was sprinting the
two hundred yards to the Beaverbrook as fast as his hundred and eighty pounds would allow, frantically pushing
down the yellow button on the Rollei, pulling and slamming in the film advance, racing to use up the film.

They caught sight of him just as he reached the hotel's awning, nearly knocking a porter over on the steps.
That one of the two ancient elevators was empty was the
first piece of good luck Moody had had all morning. He
thanked God he hadn't left his key in the key drop. Once
inside he pushed the button, pulled out the camera,
flipped open the back, picked out the film cassette, and put it
on top of the false lattice ceiling. Then he took one of
the spare films, already half used, dropped it in his under-
shorts, and clipped the second unused film into the camera.

Again he began pushing the button and working the film advance, until half the film was exposed.

The elevator jerked to a sudden stop. As he half stumbled to his room and fumbled at the lock with his key, the first man was on him, breathing heavily, rivulets of sweat trickling from the edges of his sideburns after his run up the stairs. He grabbed Moody by the arm. There was a silent, intense struggle. Suddenly the door burst open and Moody, exhausted, fell against the wall. The second man, the taller of the two, patting his hair down, arrived a few seconds later having taken longer on the fire escape stairs. Both still had their sunglasses on. Moody noticed that the taller man had a small mole high on his right cheek. For a moment it was cherry red against the tan. "Mr. Moody," he said, extending his hand. Moody shook the hand limply. He smelled the English Leather again.

"I'm Jay," the man said. "And this is my associate— my aide-de-camp, as it were. Tony—Anthony if you like. Ah, may we come in?"

Still gasping for breath Moody mumbled, "What do you want?"

Jay smiled a little impatiently. "May we come in?"

Moody walked into the room, the two men following. Tony quickly stepped ahead of Moody so he could be in between. Jay went over by the window and looked out, all the time mopping his forehead. "Humidity's atrocious, don't you think?" He smiled. "Could I have a glass of water?" Moody indicated the bathroom.

"You see, Tony," continued Jay, "I told you. Didn't I tell you that Canadians were hospitable?" He took off his sunglasses, revealing deep brown eyes, soft-looking like a baby's. "Tony thought you didn't want to see us, Mr. Moody. He's an incurable pessimist, is our young Tony. Didn't I tell you, Tony? Didn't I say Mr. Moody would be a gentleman?"

"Yeah," said Tony, looking surly. "You told me." Tony patted Moody's jacket, felt the camera and dropped it on the bed. Jay emerged from the bathroom with a glass of water. "Tony!"

The other stopped. Jay indicated Moody. *"Manners,* Tony. Did you ask Mr. Moody?" Jay turned to Moody. "Do you mind, old man?"

"Take what you want," said Moody.

Tony carefully but quickly examined the camera, clicking his teeth all the while. Moody could see they were
false and obviously a bad fit. He noticed that, unlike
Tony, Jay still looked immaculate. The only sign that the
Englishman had just been running was a few tiny beads of
perspiration above the eyes. Tall and slim in his suit, he increasingly reminded Moody of an ex-British army officer.

"Let's sit down," said Jay. "It's too hot. I could do
with a drink. How about you, Mr. Moody?"

Moody nodded and reached for his jacket pocket.
Tony shot out a hand, gripping his fingers like a vise.

"It's only pills," said Moody weakly.

"Pills? Let's see." Jay took Moody's hand out slowly,
as if it was a cobra. When he saw the small brown bottle
of Bentylol capsules he relaxed visibly. "You shouldn't
be taking those things. Should he, Tony? Everybody's popping pills these days—uppers, downers, diet pills, fat pills.
It isn't healthy."

"I need them for my heart," said Moody.

"Oh," said Jay. "Then by all means, old man."

Moody quickly popped one. Tony picked up the remaining pills, took them into the bathroom and flushed
them away. Jay shook his head apologetically at Moody.
"Completely unpredictable." Tony then took the camera
off the bed, saw that the film was half used and tossed it
aside, shaking his head. "Jesus, Jesus. Will you look at
this?" he said. "The old Joe Tell shuffle. Now where's the
real film?"

"What—" began Moody.

Tony was starting to go through the dresser, clicking
his teeth in a tinny Morse code. Except for a Gideon
Bible and the Beaverbrook stationery, all the drawers
were empty. Jay motioned Moody to a chair and Tony
started on the suitcase, feeling each garment and tossing it
aside. Moody knew that if he had any chance at all he'd
have to play it cool. At the moment he was feeling far
from cool, but at least he was managing to keep his general plan in mind.

"Who are you guys?" he asked.

The back of Tony's fist came up and across, smashing Moody into the white Aborite TV table. The Toshiba
portable landed on the floor with a crunch. Tony kept
going through Moody's case. "No papers," he said, starting
on the pillows and bedspread.

"I detest this," apologized Jay, indicating Tony. "You see that? No respect for private property. And he's American!"

Tony drew out a small penknife, ready to slice open the suitcase.

"No, no, Tony. Do use the zipper—that's a good chap." Jay turned back to Moody. "I keep telling him, 'Tony, please use the zipper. Be civilized. What's someone going to do with a ruined suitcase?' But no. Not our Tony. Quickest way between two points is straight. Intelligence gathering by blitzkrieg, I call it. Now, I much prefer chatting. Intelligent men don't have to be bullies. You believe in sociobiology, Mr. Moody?"

One of Moody's teeth was loose and the blood was welling up, warm and metallic in his mouth. He was systematically watching Tony search his room. His heart was pounding and he was frightened that he would have an attack. "Socio- . . . No, I don't know what it is."

"Neither do I, completely." Jay laughed. "But I read a little about it. It's a theory about people acting as they do because of genes in the blood, or something like that. Not because of where they live. To tell you the truth, I think it's only the old innate-versus-learned squabble. Follow?"

"I—I think so."

"Right. Well I think Tony's got very bad genes. Very bad indeed. Difficult to control. Understand?"

Moody nodded. "Then why hire him?"

Jay spread his hands suppliantly. "Quite. But what can I say, Ron? It is Ron, isn't it?"

"Yes."

"What can I say? The scouting business isn't what it used to be. It's the same all over. Everyone's getting so violent. You need the protection. Used to be different, of course. After the war—in Rhodesia—all you had to do was . . . But that's another story. To the task at hand."

"I don't know what—"

"Now, do be sensible, old man. We know you've been in contact with your friend Burke. We know something is big in the air, and we know you're not here on vacation. We'd like some kind of copy of that paper. What's the name again, Tony?"

"Shae."

"Yes, some Shae paper. Our people want it."

"Who are your people?"

It was the bravest thing Moody had said in months, and the stupidest. Tony moved quickly toward him. Jay barely held up his hands in time. "Do go on looking, Tony." Jay smiled benevolently. "To tell you the truth, Mr. Moody, I don't know exactly who has hired us. We only deal with representatives—middlemen. They don't ask too many questions, as you know. Quite frankly they're not interested in the details of how we operate." He grinned almost sheepishly. "They'd disown young Tony here. But one thing I can tell you. They're impatient people, Ron. That's what they are. They want some of the sea gold business too. Now, we could have saved ourselves a lot of trouble if we could have flown up here earlier, before this scientific conference began, but you were one step ahead of us so now we're asking your cooperation. Right, Tony?"

"Right," said Tony absently, slitting open the lining of Moody's toilet bag.

Moody pulled out a wad of Kleenex. His bottom lip was numb, and he found it difficult to talk. "Maybe we can, you know, come to some arrangement," he mumbled through the tissues.

"Arrangement? You hear that, Tony? We're talking arrangements."

As Jay ambled over to the window and stood watching the river, Tony dragged Moody's case off the bed, kicked it, swung around, then walked over to Moody. He lifted him from under the TV table and threw him across the room, demolishing the reading lamp.

"Okay," Moody gasped. "All right, I'll get you the film."

"Now we're talking," said Tony, lighting up a cigarette, pointing it at Moody. "Let me guess. It's up your ass, right? That's all you had time for."

Moody gulped. He reached down into his underpants and drew out the film. Tony shook his head laughing and slapped Moody on the back. "You're a real pro. Isn't he, Mr. Jay? An honest-to-God pro. Always thinking." Suddenly he stopped laughing. "Now put it in a Kleenex, you dirty little bastard."

Moody did as he was told and handed the film to Jay who was standing beside him with his hand open. "Tony, get this processed," said Jay. "Pay whatever's necessary to have it done immediately. I'll wait with yon three-balls here until we see what's on it."

Without a word, Tony picked up the film and camera and walked out. Jay dialed Room Service, watching Moody cowering in the corner. "Let's have a drink, Ron." He was smiling again. "Beer or bourbon?"

"Beer," Moody mumbled. His hands began to tremble. He hadn't counted on them developing the decoy film. His plan wasn't so smart after all. It would only take Tony ten minutes to discover that the film in the camera was exposed, with nothing on it, and that the other hadn't even been shot. He would be back within three-quarters of an hour, and then they would really go to work on him.

Jay was on the phone. "Moody here, room two oh six. I'd like one bottle of beer." He cupped the phone. "Chips, Ron? Sandwich?"

Moody shook his head. "Make that four beers," continued Jay, "three club sandwiches and a bottle of Jack Daniels, please." When he put the phone down Jay pulled out a short bent stem pipe. "Your friend Burke—he liked Jack Daniels. You know that?"

Moody shook his head. He didn't like the past tense. It reminded him that he only had thirty-five minutes to get out.

"He did," said Jay, lighting the pipe and revealing a light tobacco stain at the base of his front teeth. "He loved that Jack Daniels. He really did."

7

Joe Crane walked quickly to the Faculty Club. Dean Thompson's secretary had rung with a message that Nielsen—acquisition manager for Vancouver Oceanics—wanted to see him. What the hell did Nielsen want, he wondered, anxious instead to collect the charts for the coming cruise. "Probably wants me to salaam for his passing on the scout's information."

As usual Nielsen's face was red and pudgy, matching his fake college tie. "Morning, Doctor," he said pleasantly, but the "Doctor" bit was forced, and so was the vigorous handshake. This wasn't the usual Nielsen.

"Morning."

"Beautiful day, isn't it?"

"Yes," said Crane. He'd hardly noticed. As Crane led the way to the lower lounge, solid and almost regal with its huge, deeply-padded leather chairs, he waved his hand toward the coffee urn and the silver tea tray with its nearby platter of pastries.

"Now you're talking," said Nielsen, beaming. "Those croissants are something else. We don't get this downtown."

"Benefit of the ivory tower," Crane said. Nielsen simply smiled, revealing that he was sensitive to what academics could say about themselves that outsiders couldn't. Filling his cup, Nielsen offered coffee but Joe Crane declined, pouring tea and squeezing the life out of a wedge of lemon.

"I heard you came back empty last trip?" said Nielsen.

"Yes."

Nielsen tore off a piece of Danish. "How old are you, Joe?" Nielsen had never before called Crane by his first name.

"I'm forty-eight, *Harvey*."

"How about that? We're the same age."

"Goodie." Joe Crane knew it was an impolitic reply, when he might be in continuing need of grant money from Vancouver Oceanics, but he'd never liked Nielsen and damned if he was going to crawl. To his surprise Nielsen ignored the remark.

"You haven't got tenure, have you, Joe?"

"No."

"Joe, I know you're anxious to get going, so I won't waste your time. You need a retirement plan." It was said with all the authority of an oracle. "Know what I mean?"

Joe Crane said nothing and Nielsen shifted uneasily. He wasn't used to dealing head on with bribery—it was usually done over cocktails and nuance. But with some academics—someone like Crane—you had to draw pictures. All right, he'd draw pictures. "A contingency plan."

Joe Crane was tense; the muscles at the base of his skull were drawn tighter than a drum. Then he saw it. "You'd be the insurer?"

Nielsen looked grave. "Times are tough, Joe, and they're going to get a damn sight tougher, but I think we can work something out in the way of a buffer against the future. Against hard times."

"Provided I keep you informed of what I find, or don't find. Who the hell are you working for, Harvey? Vancouver Oceanics, or yourself?"

Nielsen bridled at that one. "I'm working for Vancouver Oceanics, but I'm looking after number one. You think they give a shit what happens to you and me? We all need something for a rainy day. Some snot-nosed psychology graduate tells them I'm beyond my 'cost-benefit' peak and they'll shaft me. After what? After twenty years. And you, you're close to getting the shaft now from the University. You blow this trip and you're gone. So what have you got to lose? Here . . ."

Nielsen pushed the rolled-up *Province* toward him. "Read your stars. It could be a good day for you."

Crane looked at the paper; it was slightly fatter than it should be. He couldn't resist asking how much it was, how much to let Nielsen in on any big find he might make, so Nielsen could double-cross his employer by either starting up his own company or buying up stocks before word of the find got out. There were a dozen ways he could do it. Nielsen was chewing on the last of the pastries. "Ten thousand," he said, "as a sign of good faith. Another ninety thousand dollars' worth of Vancouver Oceanics stock that I bought on margin—*if* you find it."

Joe Crane gently pushed the *Province* back toward him. "Harvey," he smiled politely, "why don't you roll the newspaper up again? That way it'll be a lot easier."

"Why? What for?"

"So you can stick it up your ass."

Nielsen kept chewing until the Danish was finished. Then, reaching over with his napkin, he dunked it in Crane's tea, used it to wipe off his fingers, then tossed it to the end of the table.

"Listen," Crane began.

"No." Nielsen picked up the newspaper. "No, you listen to me, hotshot. So you don't figure you need insurance. So next time you won't get a chance to buy any. Not a

dime's worth. You don't come up with the goodies this
time and you're finished. You're gambling with your whole
career."

"I always have," said Crane.

"Yeah. Well, that's the biggest gamble there is, *Doctor.*"

"I know what I'm doing," said Crane, without conviction.

Nielsen rose, shaking his head. "No, you don't. I'm
telling you, Crane, I'll bust my ass to make sure you never
get another chance in your life. I know everybody in the
mining business. I've fixed more deals than you've had lays.
They won't even let you on a fucking creek dredge."
Turning, he left the club.

Joe Crane slowly finished his tea. That was the Nielsen
he knew.

∽   ∽   ∽

Sitting quietly in his car watching Crane emerge from
the Faculty Club, Nielsen had already thought of an alternative plan. He acted so quickly that even as Joe
Crane was walking along the main mall past the blinding
reflection of the tall mirrored skylights above the undergraduate library, he was dialing Crane's home number.

"Mrs. Crane?"

"Yes."

"Mrs. Crane, I'm a colleague of your husband's. You
don't know me and I haven't time to explain, but I'd
like to see you as soon as possible. The matter is urgent."

"Well I . . . How do I know . . . ?"

"It's about the trouble Joe's having with Dean Thompson. I don't believe he's thinking straight at the moment,
and I'm very concerned. I know it's presumptuous of
me—quite frankly I wouldn't blame you for hanging up on
me—but there isn't much time and I think he needs an
ace in the hole, as it were. With your help I think we can
save him a lot of problems."

"I'm not really sure—"

Nielsen cut in quickly. "I don't think Joe's talents and
efforts are really appreciated, that's all. I thought—only
if it's agreeable to you, mind—I thought we might be
able to help him get his due if he finds anything on this
last cruise."

"Last cruise?"

"Yes. I mean, why should the Institute bleed him dry? He should get something—you both should get something for your efforts."

"I don't think . . ." Mary Crane made a last attempt to halt the conversation, but once more Nielsen's voice rode over hers.

"All I'm asking is whether we could chat for a few minutes. Would that be possible? I know you wouldn't regret it."

"Well, I suppose you could come around . . ."

"Terrific. Now look, I'm not a mugger. If you don't like the look of me, don't lift the chain, and ring the police. Okay?"

Mary forced a polite laugh.

"I'll be around in half an hour. Now not a word to Joe. He'd kill me if he found out. You know how proud he is."

"All right—if it's to help Joe."

"It is."

∽ ∽ ∽

Nielsen had been extremely polite but to the point. And when she told him that if it might be Joe's last cruise, she'd be going with him, Nielsen beamed with pleasure. "Even better," he said, "even better." He wouldn't want to put this to Joe just at the moment, Joe was under enormous pressure. It would be better if Mary kept it to herself. Joe, just like anyone else, was apt to misinterpret things when under pressure. Of course he knew that Joe was an honest man. No question about that. But unfortunately the world wasn't black and white —it was gray. Right? He was merely calling attention to Joe's, well, unfortunate track record. He made it all seem so sensible, so coldly realistic and "prudent." Above all, "prudent." He was extraordinarily convincing. "Of course not," he said, "I have no intention of pressing you. Quite frankly I'd find that as offensive as you would, believe me. All I'm saying is that there are too many unknowns in our lives. We all need backup." He paused. "We can't rely on our employers. I work as hard for Vancouver Oceanics as Joe works for the Maritime Institute, but what long-term security do we have?" He held his arms out plaintively. "None! Absolutely none! If we do anything worthwhile it's not ours, it's theirs. And never mind *long-term* security or reward, what about the short term?"

If Nielsen had stopped talking for a second he might have seen that his carefully phrased appeals were completely unnecessary. Mary Crane was already convinced. Now that she'd had more time to think about it in the light of what Nielsen rightly called Joe's "unfortunate" track record, she saw all too clearly what she and Joe had to lose without "backup." The heavily mortgaged house overlooking the harbor, just to start with. And what would the University do if they did deign to give Joe one more chance and he found a rich manganese deposit? He couldn't profit from it personally. Oh yes, he'd be feted for a while. All the dull scientific journals would take his article, and he'd be ecstatic. That's what he craved, but what would *he* get out of it in cash? Nothing. It would all automatically become the property of the University and the subsidizing companies, just as Nielsen said. She didn't like Nielsen, but by God he had a point. Money wasn't everything, but at least it allowed you to be miserable in comfort.

"I have faith in Joe, Mrs. Crane," continued Nielsen. "I'll tell you what my backup is." He leaned forward and she could smell apple Danish. "My backup, Mrs. Crane, is two hundred thousand dollars' worth of Vancouver Oceanics stock that I've bought on margin."

Mary Crane wasn't exactly sure what buying on margin meant, but she knew what two hundred thousand dollars meant.

"Half is yours," said Nielsen, "if you agree we all need insurance." He gave her a small strip of white paper. The harmless-sounding message, to be sent from ship to shore, was addressed to a Mr. Y. Browner in Kerrisdale, Vancouver, asking him to contact a nonexistent Mrs. Lindert asking her to check that Crane's house security-alarm system had been activated while they were away. Nielsen explained that if Joe found anything, then the eight spaces left for a four-digit apartment number and the four-digit street address of Mrs. Lindert could be easily filled in with the four-digit latitudinal and four-digit longitudinal coordinates, indicating exactly where Joe had made his discovery. "It's really very simple," he said. "All you have to do is give it to the radio officer on the ship. The captain is the only other one who sees messages. He's

got to authorize it, but no one else will know. They're very
strict about that."

❦ ❦ ❦

The temperature had climbed into the high eighties
and the humidity was turning Fredericton into a steam-
bath. When Room Service arrived with the drinks and
sandwiches, Jay answered the door and signed, taking
care not to let the waiter see the shambles in the room.
It was fifteen minutes since Tony had gone. Soon,
Moody figured, he'd know that the films he had were
useless decoys. He didn't want to think what they'd do
to him when Tony returned. Even if they found the right
film, it was debatable whether they'd let him go. They'd
have guessed that he'd already passed on the information.
While it wouldn't interest them too much, provided they
were able to get it for their own client, they might not
want him going around creating any more competition.

The beer Moody had decided to accept after all was
ice-cold, and washed over a nerve. He winced with pain,
letting the blood-colored liquid dribble out of his mouth
into a wad of Kleenex. He decided to try the bourbon
instead—it might help ease the pain.

Jay pointed to the sandwich tray. "This is marvelous.
Sure you don't want some?"

Moody, barely two feet away from Jay, shook his head,
cringing. Intuitively, Moody knew that, for all their pro-
fessed urbanity, men like Jay liked to see people cringe.
He began to speak awkwardly through his split gum.
"Could you . . . give . . . ?"

"What's that, Ron?"

"Beer's too cold. Could I have some bourbon?"

"Of course, old man." Jay smiled expansively, sliding
the bottle a few inches along the edge of the dresser.
"Pour yourself a good glassful. Live it up."

Moody, his hands still shaking, reached groggily for
the bottle. He used both hands to pour the Jack Daniels
into the glass, his right hand holding the waist of the bottle and his left pushing gently down on the neck to steady
it. It was the left hand, held over instead of under the
bottle's neck, that should have tipped Jay off. But Moody's
cringing had served its purpose, and it didn't. The bottle
hit Jay above the left eye. There was no broken glass, no
cry, only a thud as his head fell back over the top of the

chair. His throat made a coughing sound as a wad of half-chewed bread and bacon caught in his throat. Moody crooked his finger, hesitated for a moment, then put it in the slack mouth and fished out the piece of sandwich. He would have gladly let him choke, but he didn't need a murder charge on top of everything else. He moved fast, grabbing a towel, his toilet bag, and a clean shirt, and headed for the door. He heard the rattle of keys and grabbed for the heavy glass ashtray. There was a faint knock. He lifted the ashtray, turned the doorknob, and stepped back. Just as he was about to bring his arm down he saw the hem of a white dress. A cleaning woman stood in the corridor. "I'm staying another day," he said, holding the towel over his bloodied face as if he had just finished shaving. "Don't want my room cleaned. Thanks all the same."

Moody waited until she passed down the hallway. He looked back at Jay. Jesus Christ! Half the Englishman's hair was hanging loosely over the chair back. Then Moody realized it was a toupee, and quickly pushed it back on the head, but it began sliding off again. Despite his rising panic, Moody tried to steady it. Then he came to his senses and left the room, went to the elevator and pressed the button. When the doors opened there was an old lady inside. She stared at him. She could see some of the blood. At the next floor she left quickly. Moody pressed the Basement button. As the Otis groaned he reached up and felt the latticework. His heart, which had been thumping ever since Tony had left, almost stopped. The film wasn't there. His hand groped frantically around the lattice frame. He felt something round, grabbed it and pulled it down. The film had slid six inches or so across the lattice. He pressed for the ground floor. "Mama mia!" he murmured, and put the film back in his pocket. As the door slid open he stood to the side, his finger hovering nervously over the Close button. Tony would be back any second.

Yes, Moody said, he realized the oceanographers had invaded the town, but his mother had just had a stroke and he must drive home immediately. He had to have a rental car. He slid a twenty-dollar bill across the hotel desk. "See what you can do." He tried to wink but the muscles pulled the loosened tooth, jolting the nerve.

"Yes, sir," said the girl, smiling graciously as the twenty disappeared.

The phone calls only took seven minutes, but it seemed forever. Moody kept his eyes on the entrance to the lobby, listening to the clock shifting noisily from minute to minute, and glancing from time to time at the elevator door beneath the faded picture of Queen Elizabeth.

"It'd be faster if you took a cab out to the Hertz office, sir. That's a few miles out on Vanier Highway. If you like, I can call a taxi."

By the time the cab came, Moody's heart was going wild. So far, so good, he thought. For a second or two he toyed with the idea of going directly to the airport. No. Too dangerous. If they traced him there, all they had to do was make one phone call and there'd be a reception awaiting him at the other end. A car was definitely the safest.

The cabbie looked to his left, then flipped down the meter flag and pulled out to Queen's Street. Moody slumped down in the backseat, out of clear view. A face wearing sunglasses was moving past the rose-dotted Memorial Gardens toward the Beaverbrook. It was Tony, and even with the curved Polaroids completely covering his eyes, it was easy to see he was not a happy man.

8

Frank had no sooner taken off his sweat-soaked shirt and thrown it to the floor of his boat than old Crowley was hollering: "Phone, Mr. Hall."

Frank walked toward the clubhouse cursing. All he wanted was to wash up and sleep. Crane had told him about the coming trip only three hours earlier, and for some reason he had been in a foul mood. Frank had been exhausting himself ever since, repairing and repacking all the gear they'd just recently unloaded a few days earlier from the other ship.

"Hello," he said grumpily into the mouthpiece. If Crane wanted something else checked, it could wait till tomorrow.

"Hello, Frank?" It was a soft, feminine voice.

"Yes? Mary?" he asked quickly, perking up, the sharpness gone from his voice.

"Who's Mary, pray? It's Andrea."

"Oh . . ."

"Disappointed?"

"No, I . . . No."

"Never mind, I'm liberated. Which brings me to the point. I'd like to take you out for dinner."

For the first time in months Frank didn't know what to say.

"Am I that depressing?" came the easy, seductive tone.

"No, ah . . . I was . . . I just got home."

"Lucky you. I'll pick you up at seven."

"Right. Sure." Frank was now over the confusion of thinking it was Mary—of hoping it was Mary. "What's the big occasion?"

"I'm lonely. Okay?" He didn't believe it for a second, but he could envision her gold-flecked eyes and he suspended his disbelief. "All right, seven."

∽ ∽ ∽

Frank hadn't eaten so well in a year, from the Caesar salad to the escargots and Tia Maria. Not once during dinner did she mention sea gold. All she could talk about was his boat, how she'd like to see it, how individualistic it was to just spit in suburbia's eye and live on the water.

It wasn't as glamorous as she might suppose, Frank told her. It was simply cheaper than a West End apartment. In many ways she reminded him of Mary—she had the same kind of sensuousness, the inviting gaze, the fullness of lips, but there it ended. Andrea was a barracuda. He kept wishing she could have been Mary. They danced closely and halfway through the first number he was hard as a rock, and she pulled him in closer. He didn't want to take her back to his boat and he was relieved when she suggested her place. He wouldn't think twice about going to bed with Andrea, but not on his boat, not two nights after seeing Mary there. He told himself it was silly, adolescent, but it still mattered to him. On the boat he would be thinking only of Mary.

The view of the harbor from Andrea's West End apartment was breathtaking, made even more beautiful by the cooling ocean breeze that pushed the wispy dress against her, and streamed her hair out behind. From a distance she could have been Mary.

The lovemaking was short, not so tender but enjoyable—Andrea pulling at him violently and him driving just as hard. It was five minutes or so before she spoke. "That was great. Can I see you again, Mr. Hall? Soon?"

You cunning bitch, thought Frank, looking down and stroking the long auburn hair. "Not for a while."

"You're going away?" The tone was pure innocence.

"Yes."

"Where?"

"To sea."

"Oh," she said, casually offering him a cigarette. "Where abouts?"

He refused the cigarette and laid back on the pillows. "I don't know," he said. "I really don't. Nobody tells me a thing."

She blew out a long stream of smoke. "You lying bastard," she said quietly.

"Really. I don't know."

She kissed him gently as he left. "Frank," she called softly.

"Yes?"

"You're very good—even if you are honest."

He looked back, grinning. "Don't you ever give up?"

She took another pull at her cigarette. Suddenly, under the sickly yellow hall light, she looked very tough and very cheap—not at all the soft woman he'd been having sex with. "Never," she said. "I never give up."

9

Moody was on the run. But Fredericton was too small to hide in. Besides, they'd know he was looking for a film-processing lab. While the woman at the Hertz office took his driver's licence and ID for the insurance forms, he rang ahead to St. John, sixty-eight miles away. Yes, there was a film-processing lab. Yes, they could process the Verichrome Pan 110, film if he got there by three p.m. If he could get there by four, could he pick up the negatives and a set of prints first thing in the morning?

"Yes, sure."

"Fair enough," said Moody. The numbness in his jaw was slowly giving way to a throbbing pain that ran up the whole left side of his face, as if a cord was pulling the back of his eyeball.

"Could I have your name, sir?" asked the voice on the phone. "I'll be leaving shortly, but I'll let the staff know we're expecting you. That way we can leave a space for you ahead of the regular orders."

"That's very kind of you," said Moody, giving them his name.

As he pulled out on Highway 7 alongside the St. John River, he was unaware that he'd just made his first big mistake.

The vistas of rolling green hills and wide reaches of placid blue tranquilized him, reawakening memories of the charter trip he'd taken to Scotland with his wife, Eileen, and their eight-year-old daughter, Susan. They had gone all the way up to Sutherland, across and down to Loch Ness. It made him wish he was with his wife and daughter now.

∽ ∽ ∽

Moody was an efficient scout, but he was used to tracking, not being tracked. It was almost insultingly simple for Tony. Once he had seen Jay into the Emergency Ward of the Everett Chalmers Hospital, he returned to the Beaverbrook and went directly to the desk.

"Excuse me. Ah, a buddy of mine had to leave urgently. Mr. Moody. He told me he left a forwarding address?"

"No, nothing here, sir." It was the same girl who had taken Moody's twenty. She could have earned another twenty, she guessed, but she didn't like the look of Tony. He looked like what he was. But the doorman didn't care what he looked like. Yes, he remembered the gentleman—seemed kind of upset, you know. No, he didn't see where he was going but yes, it was definitely Hertz.

∽ ∽ ∽

"This is the Beaverbrook Hotel. A Mr. Moody has left airline tickets here and we're trying to locate him. Could you help us?"

It was the politest Tony had been in two years, and he had to try hard to remember what a hotel clerk sounded like. But he needn't have worried—the Rent-a-Car people were so busy that they'd answer almost anything just to get him off the line.

"Yes, Mr. Moody was here. Yes, a Plymouth Satellite . . . Well, no, I'm sorry, he won't be back. He's turning the car in at our office in St. John."

"Thank you," said Tony, made unusually civil by the knowledge that he was gaining ground. Then he started telephoning the camera shops in St. John. "Has a Mr. Moody inquired about fast developing for a thirteen-mm film? He's a friend of mine. He's forgotten his camera and I can't reach him. I don't know what hotel he's staying at. Could you help me? I'd like to leave a message for him if possible."

It was 2:41 p.m. by the time Tony located the right store. "St. John Close-Up Processing," said the voice. The clerk, obviously busy, wasn't very cooperative. "Yes—what? Moonie?"

"No. Moody."

"Moody, I dunno. Hang on . . . Yes, someone says he called. What's the message? What—none? Okay."

The only thing the pilot of Fox Charters would remember, if he was asked about the medium-built man with the sunglasses who hired him for the short flight

to St. John was that he paid cash. No credit cards—
no chance of a trace.

∽   ∽   ∽

By the time Moody was driving through Parndenec, eight
miles northwest of St. John, Tony had already landed.

∽   ∽   ∽

In Grand Bay Moody pulled up outside the Imperial
station. In the washroom he decided to phone Vancouver
again. After all he'd been through, he figured he was entitled to some kind of bonus. He'd had enough of living
on his nerves. So just this once he'd break the one-
customer rule and make a double sale, a big one, and get
out. It was three thirty in Fredericton. It would be elev-
en thirty Vancouver time. Good, he'd reach her before
lunch.

"Hi. Miss Nolan?"

"Yes?"

"Moody here."

"Yes?"

"I've got something for you."

"Yes?"

"It's a piece of property in your area. I've just met
the owner. It's very hot. Will go any minute. I can send
you the details—property taxes, etcetera—later, but I
thought you'd like to know the approximate size right
away. Your client wanted a wide lot, you told me?"

"What's the size? It's approximately forty-eight to forty-nine and a half feet wide and a hundred and twenty-
eight to one thirty long."

Andrea Nolan scribbled down the coordinates. Latitude, forty-eight to forty-nine degrees, longitude, one
twenty-eight to one thirty. "All right, I'll see whether he's
interested."

"Ah, I'll have to bill you additional expenses."

"We've always paid before, haven't we?"

"Yes, but, well, it's a hot property, you see. Beautiful
view. I just wanted to make sure. Hell," added Moody,
with strained nonchalance, "I know you'll pay me."

"Anything else?"

"No."

"Good-bye."

Moody put the phone down and smacked his fist against
the side of the booth. "Christ," he murmured. "Hard-
nosed bitch. She oughta be begging to be let in on this.
The shit I've had to take. Son of a bitch ..."

           ❦ ❦ ❦

Cursing Klaus' neurotic fear of telephones, Andrea Nolan
immediately booked the flight to Zurich and arranged for
a local charter to fly her to Interlaken, where he was vaca-
tioning. She then began making a series of phone calls,
most of them to unlisted numbers, including several private detectives. She didn't trust scouts and, among other
things, she wanted to find out whether CANORE's competition, Vancouver Oceanics, were privy to the same information. Is that why she'd heard that Frank Hall was
getting ready so soon for another trip, just after it had
been rumored that his boss was about to be canned? It
started to add up. Now she knew what she had tried to
prise from Frank. But if Vancouver Oceanics knew, she
would have to act quickly before she left for Switzerland.
They would have a head start. She pressed her inter-
office intercom. "David, what's the research ship this
Crane's going out on? Is it the *Petrel?*"

"Yep."

"Give me a list of everyone who'll be sailing on her,
will you?"

"I'll try."

"No, don't try. Get it. Now!"

"Crew members only, or scientific party as well?"

"Everyone, David."

"Roger."

In five minutes her assistant rang back. "I haven't got
the list yet, but I've found out the *Petrel* is leaving
the day after tomorrow."

"Shit!"

"I beg your pardon?"

Andrea leaned back in her big leather chair, exas-
perated. "By the time I get this all together—with your
help—I'll have to go to Zurich and back in twenty-
four hours."

"And first class, too. My heart bleeds, Miss Nolan. Besides," he said cheerfully, "it's only noon now. You've
got fifty-three hours."

"When do I sleep?"
"In first class."

∾ ∾ ∾

"Listen, buddy," said Moody angrily, "I rang you two
hours ago and you said that if I got my film here by four
it would be ready by ten tomorrow."

"I never told you that," said the clerk, motioning for
the manager.

"Well, someone did."

The clerk glanced down at a note on the counter blotter. "Oh, are you Moonie? Moody?"

"Moody." He smiled triumphantly. "How do you know
who I am if you never spoke to me?"

"My mistake," said the clerk apologetically, as the
manager bore down on him. "Your friend rang. Said
you'd forgotten your camera."

When the manager reached them, Moody was quickly
pocketing the film which he had been about to hand over,
asking, "Could I use your washroom? I'm very sorry, but
I really have . . ."

The manager forced an accommodating smile, notic-
ing that his customer had gone decidedly pale. "Of course,
sir. This way."

Moody climbed out of the lavatory window. Then,
standing in the alley at the back of the store, he realized
that he had to find a way to get his car, sitting out front of
the shop, without his "friend" seeing him.

He still hadn't made up his mind which way to go
when Tony, having pushed past the futilely protesting clerk,
reached the back door. Moody began running up the
alley, turning right toward the Plymouth. Tony was gaining fast, and Moody barely managed to push down the
lock button on the door before Tony wrenched at the
outside handle, rocking the whole car.

Moody was already into the traffic as Tony, swinging
his Ford LTD violently, pulled out a hundred yards behind. Not knowing where he was going, only that he
wanted to get away from Tony as fast as possible, Moody
headed south on Highway 1.

There were times on the curves when Moody thought
he'd lost him. But the Ford stuck to his tail like a magnet.
Once out on the wide, lonely highway that followed the
slightly undulating hills and long flats of rocky coast,

Moody's fear increased. There were few turnoffs, and Tony was constantly in sight. Moody's sole comfort, apart from having made his contacts with Nielsen of Vancouver Oceanics and Nolan at Canadian Oceanic Resources, was his conviction that Tony wouldn't try to run him off the road. The goon didn't want a body—he wanted a film.

As the black rocks flitted past beneath the blue sky, now being invaded by low gray clouds from the cold Atlantic, Moody felt the crushing pain begin to spread across his chest, the sudden hammering of his heart. He had to stop, but he couldn't. For a second, at Musquash, he was tempted to swing hard left and head for Chance Harbor, but he was afraid of getting off Highway 1, where at least a passing motorist might stop and help. When he flashed by a camper parked at the picnic site at Lepreau, five miles west of the Musquash turnoff, he nearly pulled over; but there was no car near the camper and it looked deserted. By New River Beach two miles down the highway, where the brown, silty water was being sucked over the rapids into Maces Bay by the great Fundy pull, his heart decided for him. He would have to stop. He'd had three attacks before, and he knew the symptoms. Gasping for breath against the pressure in his chest, he thought of the film. He'd have to take a chance. Let the bastards have it. He had to gamble that whoever had hired them to get the information might leave him alone if he gave them the film. He lifted his foot from the gas, and the Plymouth slowed.

Moody knew he was taking an outside chance. He'd already double-crossed them once, so there was no reason they should believe him now. But he couldn't fight. Not until he'd had some rest and got a new supply of pills. He could only hope that Tony would be in so much of a hurry to beat the competition that he'd turn back to get the film processed. It was a long shot, but it was the only shot he had.

Three hundred yards behind him, Tony saw the arm holding the white plastic bag reach slowly out of the Plymouth's window. There was no other traffic in sight. Moody's arm flapped up and down like the wing of a wounded bird, and Tony began pumping the brake pedal. He was almost on top of the Plymouth which by now, he figured, must be doing only twenty miles an hour. He watched as the car started to pull in toward the side of the

pinkish gravel road. Then the hand opened up like a spas-
tic claw, and the white plastic bag dropped onto the
gravel shoulder. Moody's car sped up and swung back
onto the road. Tony wrenched the LTD over to the
right, keeping his eye on the bag. He pulled up, got out,
and looked up the road at the Plymouth topping another
rise like a red bug crawling over a log. Then he turned
about and looked back toward St. John. It was a question
of either getting the film developed or catching Moody.
Or maybe he could make time for both?

～ ～ ～

Up ahead on the blurred strip that was Highway 1,
Moody could dimly make out the Clipper Shipp Motel at
Pocologan, facing out on Maces Bay where the ebb tide
rushed over exposed reefs and through the black, wooden
stakes that marked the channels. For five minutes after
the car rolled to a halt in the motel lot, Moody sat
still, pallid and soaked in perspiration, his right hand
clutching at his chest as if he were trying to contain his
heart before it tore clean through his body. Gradually the
pain subsided and his vision cleared, not completely, but
enough to allow him to stagger out of the car, dropping
his wallet as he did so. At the end of the chain of credit
cards, his wife's photo flapped slowly in the sea breeze.

After one look at him, neither of the elderly husband
and wife team who ran the motel asked him to register.
The husband took him straight to Room 14. Plucking fee-
bly at his sleeve, Moody managed to reveal his Medic-
Alert bracelet. The owners had only a short conference.
Then they asked the next guest, who had kindly picked
up Moody's wallet, to wait until they had rung a doctor
in St. George, eleven miles further down the highway.

The sky was now overcast. After the waiting guest
was finally registered and shown into Room 15, the
proprietress remarked to her husband how funny it was
that he had kept his sunglasses on, even in the darkening
corridor. She had hardly finished speaking when the guest
rang the switchboard and placed a call to Toronto.

～ ～ ～

The potential heart attack passed and all the doctor
could do was advise the usual—rest, no tension. He chided

Moody gently for being so foolish as not to carry his Bentylol with him. The pills, he said, might have prevented all this.

"If I were you," said the doctor, "I'd stay a few days by the bay. Watch the sunsets, relax. You don't smoke?"

"No," Moody lied.

"Good. Just take it easy. What company did you say you represent?"

"Colgate Palmolive."

"Well, I'm sure your health is more important than selling a few cartons of toothpaste."

"Yes. I guess you're right."

"Yes, I am."

∽ ∽ ∽

The white-gold moon rolled through the thin stratus clouds, lighting the water with great silver sheets that would appear for a few moments, then vanish. The only sound was the lapping of little waves on the rocky shore. Moody, in open shirt and trousers, stood by the window watching the bay, telling himself for the hundredth time that it was time to stop running and jumping and settle down. But settle down to what? He was fifty and the only trade he knew was the one he was in. He put out his cigarette and lit another, opening the window and feeling the fresh ocean breeze that had become warmer with nightfall. The proprietress awoke as she heard the window open, wondering whether she should check to see if he was all right.

There was a gentle tap on the door. He turned. Nice people, the owners of the Clipper Shipp Motel—caring people, he thought.

"You shouldn't be smoking. Didn't you hear what the doc said?"

Moody opened his mouth, but the Hi-Standard .22 at his right eye silenced him. Tony pushed him gently back into the room. "Just a couple of questions, asshole," he said quietly.

Moody sat down on the bed. "I—I gave you the film."

"Not so loud. Get up. We're going outside."

Moody's hand reached out. Tony grabbed it and jammed the pistol under Moody's chin, pressing on the mandibular nerve that had been injured earlier.

"What the hell are you doing?" said Tony in a harsh whisper.

"My sweater—I want to put my sweater on. It's chilly."

The gun pushed further into the soft white skin. "Slowly, asshole." Moody nodded, wincing as the barrel caught the nerve again.

As they walked beside the shiny black rocks, the two men looked like black cardboard cutouts passing across the dust-gold moon. The tide was still ebbing. The lumps of rock over which the water had cascaded and frothed now stood out as distant islands in the moonlight. When the two men were far enough from the motel, Tony sat down and motioned Moody to a nearby outcrop at the water's edge. "Now, asshole, let's have the lat and long."

Tony was sitting with the moon behind him, and Moody couldn't see his eyes very well, but he could hear the false teeth clicking and knew that he could die. He was trapped. He could even tell him the exact coordinates and it still wouldn't save him. His only chance of survival now lay in making out that the film was another blank. That way Tony would have to keep him alive—for a while at least. And with every hour his chances would increase.

A lone car hummed by on the highway three hundred yards higher up. So near, yet so far. Tony reached into his pocket with his free hand and tossed something at Moody. "Take a good look."

As he bent forward, Moody felt the pain starting again. He still couldn't make out Tony's face clearly, but it looked as if he was smiling. Moody turned the small two-by-four-inch photograph toward the moon. A steel band was closing on his chest, squeezing the breath out of him and making every intake of air an agony. The photo was a picture of his wife.

Tony waved the gun at Moody. "You listen to me, asshole. I don't want any stalling or any bullshit coordinates. I want them right and I want them now."

Moody knew he couldn't stall, but he tried. "You took this from my wallet," he gasped, holding up the photo.

"Yeah, sure. But I'm not bluffing, asshole. Her name's Eileen, right? And that wasn't on the photo."

Moody's breath was coming in shallow gasps. He started to speak, but doubled up in pain. "You . . ."

"I made a call," continued Tony, "to Toronto. We've

got connections up there too, Moody. By tomorrow I'll even know how big her tits are."

Moody tried to lunge forward.

"Sit down, asshole." The semi-automatic was pointing at Moody's nose. "You tell me now. If it's on the film you're safe in any case, but if it isn't, what you tell me now had better be right. If our client finds out he's shadowing the wrong research ship in the wrong place, we'll come back and make you a widower. Understand?"

Moody felt nauseous. "Its latitude is—"

"Wait a minute. Here, write it down."

Moody scribbled, "Lat 48° to 49°50', Long 128° to 130°" and pushed the pad back. Behind the crushing onrushes of pain, through force of habit Moody found himself evaluating the opposing forces which his information had set into motion. Vancouver Oceanics on one side, Andrea Nolan's Canadian Oceanic Resources on the other, and whoever this thug worked for on yet another. What a bloody triangle, he thought.

Tony glanced at the figures. "So okay," he said. The teeth stopped clicking. He pushed the safety off. "Mr. Jay didn't like what you did . . ."

Moody gasped, clutched at his throat, and fell back like a mechanical doll, his eyes bulging, his lips dark blue—almost black, and his hands frozen, clawing at his heart. Tony caught him by the collar. The torso was already in the water. Tony lowered the unfired gun gingerly, easing the hammer forward. He placed his left hand on Moody's shirt in the center of the chest. He couldn't feel a thing. He felt for the carotid pulse. Nothing. Standing up, he slipped the gun back into its holster and walked slowly back to the motel.

∽ ∽ ∽

Tony was up early. He made a call to a Mr. Miel in Honolulu, collect. He was very polite to the motel proprietors. No, thanks, he wouldn't bother with breakfast. Yes, he had enjoyed himself and he'd pay cash.

∽ ∽ ∽

They found Moody two hours later. Covered by an army of tiny, russet-colored hermit crabs, the eyeless face staring darkly at the sun. Pushed up against two of the tall, muddy channel markers, the corpse was dappled now and then by the shadows of the gulls that screeched high above. In the hot sun, it was already beginning to bloat.

10

The train journey to the hotel at Kleine Scheidegg from Grindelwald had been a picture-postcard ride, the great arc of ice-polished mountains towering above green, flower-sprinkled valleys below. But Andrea Nolan had had no time for scenery.

When she told Klaus about Moody's call he crushed out his cigar. "No holds barred," he said. "That is how we'll fight. The best copper and nickel reserves are in Central America, Africa and Indonesia. Very unstable. So whoever can regularly deliver it from elsewhere will have enormous economic power. You realize this? This is our chance."

He rubbed his fingers together to get rid of a trace of cigar ash. "Now," he said. "We need a good plan. How is it to be done?"

Andrea nearly refused to answer. She could tell Klaus the same as she had told her colleagues at CANORE in Vancouver—that the fewer who knew about it, the safer. The old "need to know" principle of classic espionage. But looking at Klaus, she thought better of it. "We have someone on the boat," she said.

Klaus nodded approvingly. "Excellent." There was the beginning of a faint smile on his lips.

"We won't even have to wait until the ship returns to port," said Andrea.

"Did you arrange all this? Personally, I mean?"

"Yes. But the contact doesn't know who we are. I used go-betweens."

"Excellent. These things are . . ." Klaus' right hand tilted from side to side, "how do you say, awkward."

"Unorthodox," said Andrea cockily, remembering their first conversation some months before.

"Exactly," said Klaus, smiling broadly. Andrea was feeling good. A pat on the back from Klaus counted for something in this business. He understood better than the Vancouver fat cats how difficult it was to do the groundwork, to infiltrate, to bribe, and still keep your anonymity. Her Vancouver bosses thought it was just a matter of stuffing a few grand into an envelope and pressing it into the hand of anyone who would be on the ship. But if you did it like that, you were almost certain to find yourself splattered all over Fotheringham's column in the *Sun* the same evening. No, it took caution, and Klaus had obviously recognized that to arrange it all in the short time before the *Petrel* sailed was no mean accomplishment. Like Andrea, he had not inherited his position. He had worked hard and long for it, in the risky shadows of the rich *foyers*.

"Won't you have another beer?" asked Andrea.

"Why not?" said Klaus engagingly. "Tell me, do you think this scientist—this Crane—will find it?"

Andrea frowned. "I don't know. I wish I could say yes, but no one knows for sure. Even if he does, it may not be there in sufficient quantity—if it's there at all."

"Let us hope it is," said Klaus, raising his fresh glass of beer. "If he does find it, we get a sample?"

"Of course."

Klaus put down his beer, wiping a fleck of foam from his mouth. "How?"

After Andrea had told him, Klaus took out a fresh cigar, lit it and blew a long stream of smoke into the clear alpine air. "Ingenious," he said. "Absolutely ingenious."

11

"I don't care," barked Crane. "I don't want any information leaks, so I'm not having any marine geology student along to help. And that's final! We'll just have to put in more overtime than usual."

"You mean *I'll* have to put in—"

"Just do as you're Goddamn told, Frank. Just do as you're Goddamn told."

It had been a short, fierce exchange at the Institute as they finished loading, and Frank couldn't make out why. It just wasn't like Joe Crane. Frank had recalled what Mary told him about Joe acting a little strange lately, and he said nothing more. He hopped aboard the truck leaving for the ship. Crane would follow later.

〜 〜 〜

At Centennial Pier, Frank watched two yellow-beaked mew gulls fight over a crust as viciously as two men might contest sunken treasure. "Share it!" he shouted, but the two birds continued the battle. He paused at the top of the gangplank, rolling up the khaki sleeves of his work shirt and running his eyes over the sleek cream lines of the two-hundred-and-thirty-six-foot *Petrel*. Up forward, twenty feet below the slanting glass-faced bridge, two orange winches were bolted to the battle-gray well deck. The heavy-duty winch, with its drum of five-eighths-inch cable, squatted on the forward port side. The lighter, five-thirty-seconds-inch hydrographic winch squatted on the starboard forward side, just beyond the thirty-foot-long "wet" lab, which was designed for the testing and marking of fresh sea-bottom samples immediately after they were hauled up by either of the winches. Frank hoped that this time they'd finally get some samples worth testing.

66

On the starboard afterdeck, standing up like a long, one-legged artillery piece, an orange Austin-Western retractable davit, a twin of the one on the starboard side of the foc'sle, could be seen protruding directly behind the "dry," or electronics, lab.

Frank lifted his worn kitbag with one arm and started down the forward gangway. The "No Visitors" sign swung wildly as the Vibram soles of his boots rang on the serrated aluminium. He slid the kitbag off his shoulders onto the well deck, and a familiar voice called out from the stern. Frank pushed the brown hair back from youthful blue eyes, squinting into the sun. Against the glare and the background of spidery black pylons and crouching warehouses, *Petrel*'s bosun looked like a medium-sized bear. Frank grinned and thrust out a well-tanned arm. "Hi, Charlie. Long time."

The bosun shook his hand, punching him playfully on the shoulder. "Hey, Frank, what d'you know?"

"Not much. How're things with you?"

"Too fat, too old."

Frank could see that Charlie had put on weight, all right. At five feet nine inches he was almost the same height as Frank, but he was at least thirty pounds heavier than when they'd last worked together.

"Not too sober, I hope?" said Frank.

"Never! Only way to survive in this game. What are we out for this time?"

By way of answering, Frank dragged a microscope case and chart from the top of his kitbag and walked into the dry lab. Joe Crane had conceded that he would have to tell Charlie what they were really looking for. As bosun Charlie would have to help rig gear for various grabs, corers, and other bottom samplers. He was too experienced not to guess that it was something other than manganese nodules they were after. Glancing around to see that they wouldn't be overheard, Frank told him. "But watch it," he said. "Someone on board could have a big mouth. We don't want it out and about before we leave harbor."

"Okay," said Charlie. "It won't get past me."

"Good."

Frank spread out the chart, on which a series of stations had been marked over the Juan de Fuca Ridge system. Then he quickly set up the microscope, motioned

Charlie over, and slipped in a slide bearing an imported sample of metalliferous mud.

"Doesn't exactly dazzle you, does it?" said the bosun. All he could see through the microscope was a dull, reddish-brown mass, flecked here and there with silver spots of reflected light.

Frank leaned over the lab sink and lifted one of the portholes, hooking it up onto the small chain. Immediately outside, a surly-looking deckhand who had been standing directly below the porthole moved slowly down the gray deck, unenthusiastically pushing and pulling a scrub broom, heavily tinted blue glasses hiding his deepset eyes. Frank turned back from the porthole and flicked off the microscope light. "Doesn't have to, for a billion."

Charlie let out a low whistle. "A billion! That much?"

"If Crane ever finds it. Could be ten square miles of it somewhere out there. Makes manganese nodules look sick."

Charlie picked up his jacket. "So it all depends on him?"

"Always has. That's the problem." Frank immediately regretted saying it—a moment of pique, after his words with Crane earlier. It was easy enough to be flippant, he knew, when you weren't carrying the load. So what if Joe Crane had been acting a bit strange, he thought.

It was probably due to the fact that now he'd been given one more chance, the full reality of what failure would mean was upon him. Frank had never seen him so agitated. So apprehensive. Trying to put it out of his mind, Frank began packing the microscope and slides away, reminding himself that even with the extra work, he looked forward to being on board the *Petrel*. She was the latest naval auxilliary research ship to come off the Farris slips, and she was the only one he and Crane hadn't worked. Reputedly she was the most up to date in the world, complete with bow thrusters to help her maintain exact station positions in rough weather, and an echo and seismic sounding system that its designers boasted could pick up a pimple of rock five thousand meters below.

Charlie opened the starboard rear door of the rear lab. Watching him as he stepped wearily over the sill onto the stern deck, Frank could see that no one had to remind Charlie that he was fifty and overweight. It was easier on the younger men. At least they still had hopes of moving from the deck to the ward room. He followed the bosun on deck. "You look beat, Charlie."

The bosun grunted and scratched the old tattooed heart on top of his left hand. Like most tattoos, it had turned from blue to deep purple over the years. "I'd feel better if I'd been home," he said.

"Bit short on the old shore leave?"

"Short? Haven't seen the wife for eight weeks. Load up, go out, come in, unload, load up, out. Like a bloody merry-go-round."

"But the overtime, Charles. Think of the overtime."

"To hell with the overtime. I want a good lay, that's what I want."

Frank slapped him on the back. "Well, we'll only be out five days. Not too long."

Charlie yawned and spat over the side. "Yeah. At least that's a change." He stared out over the harbor where the sun's image played dreamily on the water, turning its oily surface into a kaleidoscope of reds and greens. "You think he'll find it?"

"I don't know."

A gull dived and picked up a piece of cabbage, then let it fall back into the dirty water.

"What's his wife like? I hear she's hot stuff."

Shielding his eyes, Frank looked up at the conglomeration of oceanographic equipment on the quay, towering above them like a pile of scrap iron. The tide was low, and the ship seemed imprisoned in a jungle of scarred pilings like a petrified forest. For a split second Frank felt oppressed by it all. "Let's load the barrels for the corer first," he said quickly, pointing up at the dock. "We'll need them up for'ard."

Again Charlie spat into the oily water. "What's she like?" he repeated.

"I wouldn't know," said Frank, halfway up the steep gangway moving toward the corer barrels. The "No Visitors" sign swung wildly again.

"I don't mean what color pants does she wear," said Charlie. "I mean what's she look like?"

Frank kicked at one of the core barrels, separating it from the rest. "Nice," he said, without turning around.

"Big tits?"

Frank heaved one end of the barrel off the deck. "C'mon," he snapped. "Give me a hand."

12

The tide had risen and the ship was straining to be free.

Captain Tate, glancing impatiently at the Smith's chronometer, paced up and down on the bridge. "Did you give them another ring, Johns?"

The first officer looked up from the chart table. "Yes, sir. Dean Thompson said Dr. Crane had already left."

"Their gear?"

"Loading now, sir."

"So we're only waiting on His Lordship?"

"Yes, sir." The First Officer knew that "His Lordship" always meant the head of the scientific party. At thirty, Johns was relatively young for a First Mate, but he'd been aboard the *Petrel* long enough to know that Tate had little time for scientists with whom he was increasingly required to consult and to share his authority regarding the planning of cruises. Above all, he didn't like scientists who weren't punctual.

Tate stepped out onto the bridge's starboard wing and looked aft, the four worn gold rings on his sleeve catching the afternoon sun. The Austin-Western's motor whined and its long telescopic boom slid out, then stopped with a thud.

Charlie, standing over the control levers on the starboard side of the now disused helicopter deck behind the bridge, swung the boom toward Frank on the dock and began to lower the four-foot-square loading pallett. He heard a click below and looked down as a flash of light exploded from the dry lab onto the afterdeck. He peered in. Someone was taking pictures with what looked like a 35-mm camera.

"Hey!" shouted Charlie. "What the hell are you doing?" It was a dock laborer.

"Nothing. Just looking around."

"So I see. Did you look at the 'No Visitors' sign too?"

Frank watched from the dock as Charlie put his hand on the man's back, half pushing, half guiding him toward the gangplank, all the time grinning broadly. "Dangerous around here when we're swinging the boom about," Frank heard him say, indicating the Austin-Western above as they approached the gangplank.

The man looked up to where Charlie was pointing. Frank had to bite back a laugh as Charlie faked the trip, bumping hard into the man's shoulder, knocking the Leica out of his hands into the oil wash below. One splash, and it was gone.

"Shit!" said Charlie. "Son of a bitch, these decks are slippery."

The man's mouth was still wide open. It took him a full thirty seconds to find his voice. "Christ," he said, "that's—that was a Leica, you clumsy bastard. You'll have to pay for that."

"Pay for what?"

"That's a Leica! That's worth . . ."

Frank almost felt sorry for him.

"Piss off," said Charlie, then turned away as if the man didn't exist and shouted up at Frank on the dock. "How about the heavy stuff—got much of it?"

Frank didn't even bother checking the truck. He knew it by heart. "Three pipe dredges, two Petersen grabs, two Van Veens, a piston corer, the big grab, some boomerang corers—you haven't seen them before—and that silly bloody Japanese dredge."

"Oh, Christ," said Charlie, showing a row of tobacco-stained teeth. "I've never seen one of those Goddamn things work yet. Rides underwater like a surfboard."

"Well, this time we're going to put a couple of amateur photographers in as ballast."

Charlie's black teeth showed again. "Yeah. Listen, Frank, we'd better pull our fingers out—the old man'll be steaming by now. Send down the light stuff first."

∾ ∾ ∾

In the ship's galley, surrounded by the huge stainless-steel pouring pots, meat slicers, and giant dough mixers, which it was his job to keep scrubbed and spotless, George sat peeling potatoes. He was bored stiff. Strapped to his belt like a small holster, a mini cassette recorder crackled with raucous rock. He took a potato from the sack and examined it. Though there was no blemish, he threw it back and took another. "Hey, cook, you ever seen these nodules we're after?"

The cook grunted as he lifted a big pot onto the stove in preparation for the evening meal, which in accordance with tradition would begin at four thirty. "Sure I seen them. Not on this tub, though."

George, eager for any diversion from potatoes, looked up inquisitively. He was seventeen, squat and muscular, but his baby face and light brown eyes made him look fourteen. The cook hoisted another pot. George's voice was loud even above the sound of one of the giant mixers. "What do they look like?" he asked.

"The nodules?"

"Yeah."

"Cow shit."

"Cow shit!"

"Yeah, that's right." The cook's mind was on the stew in the pans. "Cow shit, but hard."

"Yeah? What color are they?"

The cook disappeared in a cloud of steam. "Same color as cow shit. Get moving with those potatoes."

~ ~ ~

On the bridge First Officer Johns shuffled uneasily. The Captain, his dark eyes flashing with impatience, was still stalking from port to starboard like a grizzly just awakened from hibernation, tugging at the neatly trimmed gray-black beard that failed to hide the angry line of his mouth. The intercom on the steering console buzzed. Johns pressed the bridge button. "Yes? Good." He turned to the Captain. "Chief says we're all revved up, sir."

Tate's voice was sharp with annoyance. "I know, but where's Crane? Ring them again."

Johns dialed the University via the ship-to-shore line. When he hung up he managed to keep his voice bright. "Should be here any minute, sir. Dr. Crane just had to stop off and pick up his wife."

"His *what?*"

The watchman started as the Captain's voice boomed

and bounced about the bulkhead. Johns turned his gaze downwards through the knee-high window that curved around the full length of the bridge. He fixed his eye on an imaginary point on the foc's'le. "His wife, sir."

"Good God! Soon as he's aboard I want to see him."

"Yes, sir."

∽ ∽ ∽

The now-cameraless photographer hopped onto his forklift truck, wove his way through the last trunks of gear and made a sharp left turn toward a B. C. Tel booth at the far end of Centennial Pier. He dialled the local Honolulu number for the Royal Lanai. He had barely dialed the last digit before the operator came on the line. "Can I help you, sir?"

"Yes. Mr. Jonas Miel—collect from Harry Larn." Larn glanced at his watch. It was seven after four. That would make it seven after one in Hawaii. After his rough handling on the ship, Larn thought, it was only fair that he should be getting Jonas Miel away from his liquid lunch. In fact, Miel, his leisure suit strewn about the bottom of the bed, was right by the phone. He'd been there ever since Tony had called from the Clipper Shipp Motel.

"Miel here. That you, Larn?"

"Yeah. I saw that boat you're interested in. It's the right one. The coordinates you gave me check out."

"You sure?"

"No. That's why I'm ringing you. I like phoning people."

Miel grabbed the massage girl's hand and pushed it into his groin. "I suppose you asked them where they were going?" he sneered.

Through the greasy blue glass of the telephone booth, Larn could see the *Petrel* rising and falling impatiently on the tide. "Don't worry. I made like a sightseer. Took some pictures." He didn't mention losing the camera.

"You *what?*"

"No sweat. They just thought I was curious. Lots of guys take shots of them oceanographic tubs."

"All right, never mind that. Just tell me how you know."

"I saw the chart on the dry-lab table. It's number three oh oh one."

"So?"

"So—that covers Juan de Fuca Ridge."

Miel pushed the unprotesting girl down on her knees. "So the chart's the same number. Same Goddamn chart every fishboat in Vancouver uses."

"Yeah but they had a track drawn on it."

"Over the ridge area?" Larn could hear the excitement in Miel's voice.

"Yeah, bang on. A hundred and seventy miles south-west of Vancouver Island and west of Seattle."

"Okay. Okay, I'll send you a draft."

"How much?"

"A hundred."

"Okay. Hey—"

"Yeah?"

"You ever want me again, I'm available. I can keep it all confidential."

"Sure, sure. Like giving me the chart number over the phone. Why don't you hire a band?"

"Hey—"

"All right, all right. Just be sure you keep a lid on it."

"Don't sweat it, Mr. Miel. Mum's the word."

"It better be."

Larn hung up and jumped back on the fork truck. He drove toward one of the warehouses and was quickly swallowed up by its cavernous, tar-black interior.

〜 〜 〜

In his room at the Royal Lanai, Miel pulled the drape cord and sunlight flooded into the room. Fifteen floors up, he was unlikely to be seen by anyone but low-flying aircraft—not that he would have cared. He lay down on the bed, his legs hanging over the edge, and grabbed the girl's hair, pulling her down. "We're in the game, sweetheart," he said. "We're in the game. If we play it right we'll own half the Goddamn world."

The girl didn't answer.

"That's beautiful," he grunted. "Damn, that's beautiful."

The girl tried to say something but it only came out as a mumble. Miel roared with laughter and threw a pillow, knocking over the dresser lamp. "It's beautiful," he said. "Damn, it's beautiful."

〜 〜 〜

The bridge phone rang shrilly. Johns grabbed the receiver, listened for a moment, then held it out to Tate. The Captain, his tall, thick frame hunched over, strode from the starboard wing, looking as if he'd squash anything in his way. *"Petrel* bridge!"

"Main gate here, Captain. Dr. Crane's just passed through."

Tate grunted acknowledgment, hung up and turned abruptly to Johns. "I'll be in my cabin," he said, striding through the center rear door, past the radio room on his left and onto the upper deck, where he turned sharp right and disappeared behind a royal-blue curtain. It was his habit to make the chief scientist come and knock, especially if he was late. Some thought that Tate's sense of punctuality was out of place on a government-run research ship, but they hadn't known him in his younger days, when he had been captain of a south-sea trader out of Suva. The climate might have been conducive to relaxed living, but the copra trade wasn't. It had been a cutthroat business, where a late sailing could mean the loss of a fortune for the owners, and a job for the captain. Though Tate didn't know it, Joe Crane would have sympathized with him entirely.

∽ ∽ ∽

If any of the crew had been watching Joe Crane come aboard they would have seen his slight pot belly jumping up and down as he walked, and the pale, parchment-textured face marked by heavy dark pouches as if he hadn't slept for a week. But no one was watching him, not with Mary Crane descending the gangway at the same time. Her blue eyes looked even bluer than usual, reflecting the color of her indigo sweater as she looked down, cautiously stepping over the aluminium slats. Her long blonde hair caught the sun. Even in her baggy sweater she drew immediate attention from every deck hand in sight. An off-duty oiler leaning against the door of the ship's machine shop moaned softly. "Will you look at those nipples," he said. "They're like navy beans. She's not wearin' a bra." The oiler's buddy switched off an acetylene torch and lifted his protective visor. "I don't care," he said. "She's mine."

Frank watched Mary carefully wind her way through the unstowed gear on deck. As the Cranes approached

Charlie, he pushed the foc'sle door open and paused, suddenly worried that Charlie was going to come on to Mary like Don Juan. But Crane had no sooner introduced his wife to Charlie than the bosun bellowed, "Sam, watch the Goddamn cable. Use your palm on the lever. Tap it back, don't pull it like a Goddamn handbrake."

Crane stood awkwardly for a few seconds, feeling as if he should help in some way but not knowing how. Frank had seen it before, every time Crane stepped aboard a ship, in fact. The change it induced in him was as noticeable as the shift from daylight to dusk, and as much a part of the load he brought aboard as any of his equipment: it was the instinctive embarrassment of men who can work with their heads but not with their hands.

"Well," Crane said finally, "we'll see you later, Charlie."

"Yeah, Doc," said the bosun, still watching the cable.

Frank closed the foc'sle door.

Crane passed through the wet lab on the starboard side and motioned Mary to follow him. He walked quickly down the cream-colored passageway, stopping next at the "On Call" posting which listed the ship's forty-man complement. He showed Mary the Chief Scientist's lifeboat station, marked in red Dymo tape. She would board the same boat should anything go wrong.

A sailor walked past. "Thinking of going overboard already, Doc?" he asked.

Sliding down the polished rails from the upper deck, Frank cut in. "With our work schedule that might be a good idea." The seaman laughed, but Joe Crane's smile was strained.

Outside, the whine of the Austin-Western rose to a scream as it lifted a clutch of heavy bottom samplers and moved them across the deck. Removing the high, navy-issue toque he was wearing, Frank looked straight at Mary. She met his gaze and said, as nonchalantly as she could, "Hello, Frank."

"Mrs. Crane." He was surprised—almost shocked—to feel his heart race. "Good to see you again."

There was a silence, then Crane spoke. His voice was taut, as if under considerable restraint. "Mary, our cabin is at the top of the stairs on the right. You want to unpack?"

She paused as if to say something more to Frank, then

turned and made her way gingerly up the stairs. Frank
watched her as she climbed. Her legs were firm and lithe
all the way. For a second he glimpsed an edge of white
lace against the tan.

When she was out of sight, Crane snapped, "Why
did you mention our work schedule? I told you not to say
anything that might cause anyone to wonder why there's
only one scientist."

Frank was incredulous. "You think a deckhand will
worry about that? The only thing in his mind is the fewer
people we have, the harder he'll have to work. That's
what *I* think about. You might like twelve hours on and
twelve off, but I sure as hell don't."

"You're getting paid."

"I'm getting paid for a forty-hour week, not eighty-
four."

"Why don't you quit?"

"If we weren't in the middle of a bloody recession, I
just might."

"No, you wouldn't. You'd like to find that stuff as much
as . . ." Crane paused as a seaman passed them. "As much
as anyone else. And capitalize on it."

Frank flushed angrily. "What the hell do you mean
by that? You think I'd sell—"

"No, no." Joe Crane knew he'd overstepped his mark.
"I just mean you'd like to be in on it too."

"Look, *Doctor*," growled Frank, "I'm just the bloody
donkeyman. If you're so upset with me why don't you
fire me?"

Crane's eyes went to the wall posting again. "Because
you've spent more time bottom-sampling off this coast
than any other technician."

"Looks like we're stuck with each other then, doesn't
it? Like man and wife."

"That's enough!"

"What?"

"You leave Mary out of this."

Frank stood in something like a state of shock. "What
the hell are you talking about?"

Crane's finger jabbed the air. "Leave my wife out of
this. I know what you're getting at."

"Jesus Christ! All I said was man and—"

"I know what you said. It was the way you said it.

I've never commented before, but I've seen the way you look at her. Now knock it off. I don't care how much I need you, I . . . You watch your manners, that's all."

Frank stared at Crane as he walked away toward the pantry.

Charlie poked his head through the forward door. "We're all set here."

"The bastard's mad," said Frank.

"What?"

"I said the bastard's mad. He's cracking up. Paranoid."

Charlie grinned; surely Frank was joking. He jerked his thumb toward the bridge. "They're all paranoid." He put his hands out and made them shake. "You know. The-loneli-ness-of-command."

But he could see that Frank didn't think it was funny.

$\backsim \quad \backsim \quad \backsim$

After his bad start with Charlie and Frank, Crane hoped he would get on better with the Captain. As he walked past the Second Officer's cabin on the port side, he could hear the joyful strains of a Mozart violin concerto. Through the curtain he glimpsed a faded photo of a smiling wife and two small children. Joe had wanted kids, but Mary hadn't, so he'd given up the idea.

When he came to the Captain's door, he knocked sharply on the bulkhead.

"In." The voice behind the curtain was deep and loud. Crane had barely stepped into the spacious cabin overlooking the forward deck when Captain Tate charged. "You're thirty minutes late, Doctor."

Crane flushed. "Sorry about that, Captain, but we had a real scramble to get everything ready."

Tate waved a thick, hairy forearm toward the white-and-yellow contour 3001 chart that covered his table. "How far this time?"

Crane could see that to Tate it was simply another scientist, another cruise. The Captain's brusqueness, his failure to recognize him—they had met once before—annoyed Crane. "It'll be about a thousand miles all around," he said.

"About?"

"Well, yes. It depends on the grabs, you see. We've only got a couple of working days, I know, but we might be able to do it all. It's possible we could be finished earlier," Crane lied.

"You people never finish early."

"And you people can always squeeze a few more knots heading home than you do heading out."

Tate ignored the remark. "I hear you brought your wife?"

"Yes, well, this could be my last trip and I thought—"

"Yes, well. I know that as Chief Scientist you can bring who you want—up to six extra bodies. But I would have liked some advance notice. Have to inform the stewards, y'see."

"I'm sorry—"

"Not much privacy, you realize."

"She'll be all right."

"I've no doubt."

"What d'you mean? If you—"

"I meant nothing." Like Frank, Tate saw the sudden change in Crane, from near civility to outright aggression. "I just hope she understands there'll be no special facilities."

"She doesn't want any."

"Good. I hear you'll be doing some seismic work?"

"Yes."

"Normal incidence reflection, or refraction?"

"Refraction. We want to get good traces of the substructure—not just the surface layers."

"Explosives, then. Not towing that bloody Sparker?"

"We might use both, depending on the bottom."

"I'd rather the explosives as the noise source for the echo than that thing cracking every ten seconds. It's like a cannon through the ship."

"We'll use it on the run out. See where we're going. But I'll probably try to use the explosives later. They're much louder, of course."

"Yes," said Tate, "but they don't go on continuously."

"They're more dangerous," said Crane, trying to create some leeway for later decisions.

"Yes," said the Captain. There was the trace of a grin. "But they're much more fun. Keeps the crew interested."

"We've loaded a thousand pounds," snapped Crane, "but by God I'll use what I please. No matter who's against me!"

Tate started to roll up the chart. "Give me the course as soon as you can."

"Can't do everything at once," said Crane, turning to leave.

The Captain stared after him, eyebrows raised. "Oh, Doctor?"

"Yes?"

"I hope you find your nodules."

Crane muttered something, slapped the curtain aside and withdrew.

After Crane had left the Captain called for the First Officer.

When Johns walked in, Tate was looking pensively out of the porthole.

"Sir?"

"Do you know what paranoia is, Johns?"

"Sir?"

"Paranoia." The Captain had his eyes fixed on the deck. "The feeling that someone's out to get you. Persecution mania. Often caused by fear of failure. And pressure."

"Yes. I think so, sir." Johns sounded puzzled.

"I think we're carrying a load of it this trip."

Johns grinned. "A mild case, I hope?"

"I'm not so sure," said the Captain, looking down at the chart. "I want you to keep an eye on the good doctor."

∽ ∽ ∽

13

As the *Petrel* pulled slowly away from the wharf, heading into the wind, the assorted smells of the docks mingled with the salty smell of the sea to envelop her.

On the foredeck the mess boy, still in his stained, spotted whites and apron, the cassette recorder blaring at his side, was watching Olly, an old seaman, pull in the forward line. Other crew members were lashing down the sampling gear. The wharves and warehouses quickly re-

ceded astern, the ship's engines throbbing like a great beast
awakening below decks while the brown-white wake boiled
up to the surface. The sharp cream bow sliced through the
water toward the main channel and a growing fog bank
that lay over the Strait of Georgia. The yellow nylon rope
slid from the old seaman's hand like a snake, forming an
almost perfect coil.

A few minutes later, Olly was sitting on one of the starboard bolins puffing his pipe. He was staring at one of the
outgoing fleet of fishing boats that flanked them in the
Narrows like sharks closing in for the kill. The big gray
trawler was astern and to starboard of them, midway
through the channel. Olly ran an admiring eye over the
sixty-foot, tuna-rigged craft. He recognized her as one of
the Frostad freezer boats. Her equipment was so highly
automated that it would take only three or four men to
work her fish gear. Despite her twenty-foot beam and her
deep tuna-boat's hull, Olly knew that the "Jimmy," her
G.M. 671 ninety-horsepower engine, could give her fifteen
knots—five more than the smaller and lighter salmon trawlers that looked like rowboats next to her. George looked
over and, to please Olly, said, "Nice-looking boat." Actually, he didn't know a good boat from a bad one.

Olly blew slowly into his pipe and a stream of smoke disappeared into the mist. By the dry lab door, Frank was
watching the trawler too. On her stern, watching the men
on the *Petrel* through binoculars, stood a man in blue coveralls.

"He must be short-sighted," quipped George.

Olly struck a long wooden match. The orange flame
burnt fiercely in the gray fog as he pressed it to his pipe.
The man on the trawler moved his glasses up toward the
Petrel's bridge and out beyond the Point Grey peninsula
to the Strait of Georgia. Then he disappeared back inside
the cabin.

❧ ❧ ❧

On the trawler the skipper, a short, squat man of forty,
moved awkwardly in the faded blue coveralls. His breathing
made a hard, labored sound, as if he was continually fighting for air. He put down the binoculars and took over the
controls from the American, Doyle, who had hired the
boat. Then, unconsciously, he began winding his self-
winding Timex.

"Well?" said Doyle, pulling out a pack of Gitanes from his thin green windbreaker. "Does the equipment jibe with that info we got from Honolulu? Is it deep-sea sampling stuff?"

The Captain turned down the radio static coming in from Vancouver Control. "Think so. The big grab isn't for collecting pebbles, that's for sure, but they could use it anywhere, even in shallow water. It's the length of wire that counts. They've got a hell of a big drum on that winch. Looks like half-inch or bigger, and there's about three thousand fathoms. I'd say it was deep-sea."

"Juan de Fuca Ridge?"

"That's an awful lot of guessing."

"Okay, so we just trail them like Honolulu said to do."

The Captain ran the wheel through his fingers, scowling. "I'd rather go out and wait for them. Wouldn't look so suspicious."

"I'd rather you did what you were told."

"It's my boat," said the skipper, looking up at the American. Doyle was as old as he was but the years didn't show.

Doyle tore the foil from the Gitanes. "It's my money, Captain. The half I've already paid you is more than you'd earn in six months on this tub. It'll pay off your boat. You want to give it back?"

The skipper grunted bitterly. "The mortgage company's already got it."

Doyle blew the pungent smoke and casually tossed the match out the port window. "You should've started small."

"I've been starting small all my life."

"Cigarette?"

"No, thanks."

Doyle patted the skipper's back. "Don't sweat it. You'll get the other half when the job's done. Anyway, too late to back out now. The people I represent in Honolulu don't like unfinished work—if you know what I mean . . ."

The skipper suddenly looked frightened. "You threatening me?"

"I'm telling you facts."

"You never told me that before."

"I'm telling you now."

There was a sudden silence. Then the skipper, knowing he was trapped, grumbled, "I still think we should go ahead and wait for them. Looks suspicious, following them."

"And what happens if they don't show up? No, just tail 'em. If they find what they're looking for, we take a sample off them to stake our claim with Energy, Mines and Resources. That way everything's clear with COMDEV."

"What's that?"

The American smiled. "You Canucks really should learn more about your country. It's the Commission on Ocean Mining and Development. Used to be, you could just stake a claim by sending in the coordinates, lat and long. But now you have to have evidence of the find in your hand, and you have to pay the government ten thousand dollars per square kilometer for the right to mine—*and* you have to start mining within a month. Otherwise you lose the option and it goes up for auction. But that's not too much to pay if you have the sample in hand—then you've a good idea what you stand to make."

"Why all the restrictions?"

Doyle grinned knowingly again. "To stop speculators who haven't got the equipment to mine—guys who just want to stake out half the ocean and hang on to it for twenty years until someone finds something interesting."

"Didn't stop you guys, did it?"

Doyle shrugged good-naturedly, watching a group of Sabots tacking off Ambleside. "We've got the mining equipment but we're not going to pay ten thousand clams a square kilometer on hearsay. A hundred square kilometers means a million-buck deposit. That's some overhead."

The Captain nodded toward the *Petrel*. "How are you going to get the sample if they find it?"

"That's my problem."

The Canadian nodded in the direction of the cabin below. "Is that why you brought Laurel and Hardy?"

"Well, things could get a little rough."

"It's a race, then," said the skipper grimly. "Whoever gets the goods into Vancouver first gets the mining rights."

"You're bright."

"What good will it do Honolulu? Juan de Fuca's in Canadian waters. It's a hundred and seventy miles out—within Canada's two-hundred-mile limit."

"It is now."

"Meaning what?"

"Ever heard of territorial lobbying, Captain?"

"No."

"It's called moving boundaries over martinis. You know —you give me some of your territory and I give you some of mine. The politicians are very good at it in Washington. You guys are learning up here in Ottawa, but you're behind the times."

"Why's Honolulu interested, then? Why not Washington?"

"Washington is, but Honolulu's closer. Anyway, ever since they found manganese nodules off there, it's been the biggest ocean-mining center off the west coast. If something's found, those boys have the tubs to get it up."

Half a mile away, the *Petrel* was barely distinguishable in the fog bank. "What if we lose them in that soup?" asked the skipper. "Weather's going all to hell. They're predicting force seven further out."

"What's that?"

"Over thirty miles an hour. That's not much on land, but out there it means waves up to nineteen feet high."

"What about your radar?"

"Won't be able to tell them from the fishing fleet for the next few hours."

"So?"

"If we lose 'em I think we'd better go straight to the coordinates."

"Hm. I suppose you're right."

"You know I'm right."

"Okay. If the fog keeps up and we lose 'em, we'll go out and wait for them. But only if the fog keeps up."

"It will."

The Captain turned up the radio for the weather bulletin, but all he could hear was a rush of static. "I don't think they'll find the bloody stuff anyway," he said.

The American turned to look at him, squinting in the golden glare of diffuse sunlight. "I think they will," he said.

14

As the giant sand-sweeping truck ground along the beach in front of the Honolulu Hyatt, Miel sat in the terrace bar sipping his Mai Tai and watching the bright-eyed traffic stream in the purple twilight down Kalakaua Avenue. His companion, a short, dark man who was attacking his Teriyaki steak as if it might try to escape, spoke with a full mouth. "So we lobby for the new Pacific line, eh?" Juice from the steak ran down his chin.

Miel sounded tired but satisfied. "We sure as hell do, Freddie. Personally I think it's a cakewalk. If I didn't I wouldn't be trailing that Canuck boat."

"The *Petrel?*"

"Yeah. Anyhow, I think it's a cakewalk. What does the Seattle office say?"

Freddie wiped his mouth with the giant-sized napkin. "The problem is, it's still very uncertain. There's internal waters, continental shelf, continental slope, territorial waters, contiguous areas, high seas, and . . ." He paused, mopping his chin again.

"You know, Freddie, for a hotshot lawyer you're a real slob."

"Hey—"

"Hey nothing. No really, you embarrass me. Rippin' that steak apart like that. You got no class. And don't give me all that garbage about territorial-sea bullshit."

"It's very complicated," said Freddie, trying to fit his vocabulary to his pinstriped suit.

"Complicated, my ass. You think I know nothing about it? All you lawyers coming over here telling me how complicated it is. I could've saved you the trip. The Canadians want to fish off the east coast, so we lower the line— give them more of the Georges Bank to fish so they'll give us a higher line off the west coast, 'cause they think there's nothing there. So okay. If they don't think that's

enough, we give 'em a bit more of Dixon Entrance off the
Panhandle and maybe a bit more of the Beaufort Sea off
Alaska so they can drill for more oil. It's all trade-offs. Poli-
tics." He lit a slim cigarillo. "Trouble with you is, Freddie,
you spend all your time in fucking seminars and you
never look at a map."

Freddie pulled out a small booklet entitled *Third Law
of the Sea Conference*. "It's more difficult than you realize," he said, sounding more Harvard Law School by the
second. "The boundary disputes are very delicate. I've got
a report here . . ."

Miel grabbed it and flicked to page seventy-two. "Read
that, Freddie—aloud," he said, stabbing his finger at the
last paragraph.

Freddie took the blue monograph sullenly.

"Well?" said Miel, holding up his hand for another Mai
Tai. "I can't hear you."

Freddie glared at him and began reading. "'If the na-
tions of the world do not soon reach an accord on the
international seabed's legal regime, two equally undesir-
able consequences may occur . . .'"

A blonde walked by and Miel waved. She smiled. "Go
on, Freddie, I'm listening."

"'First, development will be retarded because potential investors will lack internationally guaranteed security
of title . . .'"

"The last sentence," said Miel, "where it says 'but still
within the realm of possibility . . .'" He picked up the
swizzle stick and stabbed the piece of pineapple.

"'Still within the realm of possibility,'" continued Freddie, "'the developments that do take place could suffer a
form of international anarchy very much akin to the
Wild West claim-jumping experiences.'"

"Now," said Miel, pointing his swizzle stick at the report,
"there's a scientist with some savvy. 'Wild West,' he says.
You got that, Freddie? That's what it's all about, babe.
Horse trading. Don't matter what you lawyers call it,
it's good old horse trading. So if they find something out
there, I want our ship to be the first back with a sample.
Then we pay our deposit and file our claim."

He smiled at Freddie. "With that behind me I can lobby
for anything else I want. You think I'm bullshitting? You
draw the U.S./Canada land border straight out to sea
and it cuts right through the Juan de Fuca area. That,

together with a sample in hand, is lobbying material, babe. Look at the maps, Freddie. It's all in the maps."

Freddie was looking glumly out at the darkening turquoise ocean, watching the late surf riders coming in near the Royal Hawaiian Hotel.

"So," said Miel, punching him playfully on the shoulder, "you still haven't told me what Seattle says."

"They agree with you. They say we can trade. We've got another congressman on the Boundary Commission now."

"Beautiful!" Miel's hairy arms stretched out to embrace the world, the new Mai Tai in his right fist. He took out the flower and put it behind Freddie's right ear. "That means you're waiting to be asked."

Freddie took the flower from his ear and threw it on the table.

"Hey, don't be sore, Freddie. You came three thousand miles so we can talk about what to tell those stupid congressmen to do. You think I invite you here without doing my homework? I can read too, you know. You don't have to go to Harvard Law to be able to read."

"You don't have to make cracks about my table manners."

"Who's making cracks? I'm just observing. You're a pig. With some things, I'm a pig." He slapped Freddie playfully again. "So we're all pigs—hey?"

Freddie grinned slightly.

"I'll get you another steak," said Miel.

"No thanks, I'm not hungry."

"Order another steak. That one's cold."

"Well, maybe . . ."

"How do you like it?"

"Rare."

"On the hoof?"

"Bloody as you can."

Miel smiled broadly. "You got it. Waiter?"

15

Joe Crane went on deck. Standing at the bow, away from
the heavy fumes of the dieseline, he found the wind cold
and refreshing. But everything else seemed to conspire
against any sense of well being. The sun had fought a
losing battle with the fog and now hung weakly on the
horizon like a faded moon.

Above the wall of fog the anvil tops of the giant cumulonimbus flattened at nineteen thousand feet and spread,
umbrella-like, over the altostratus below, further filtering
the sun's rays.

As he watched, the hazy ball disappeared altogether
and night came down, transforming the sea into a great,
brooding expanse of darkness. Crane had the uneasy feeling that beneath him some vast and unkind intelligence
was awakening.

As the ship began pitching higher, heading into the
fringe of the rough weather, he could hear the swishing of
the ballast diesel rolling from side to side in the flume
tanks. As the ship rolled one way, the diesel rushed to the
other side to compensate. Crane felt that this anti-roll
scheme was somehow unnatural, and wondered what would
happen if the diesel spilled out of the vents when the
ship encountered force-seven swells and winds. But the
designers at the Farris yard had said that such spillage was
impossible, and he decided to take their word for it. After
all, they were the experts. If he was to find the metalliferous muds, he would have to have the same kind of faith
in his own ability. The same kind of self-confidence he
saw and envied as he watched Frank working on deck—
the unconscious self-assurance that comes from just *knowing* you can do things. Through a small hole in the sky
he could see a clutch of stars blinking. He took it
as a sign, and felt a surge of optimism. Then, without
warning, the cumulonimbus closed off the hole and the

stars were gone, and he knew that this too was a sign. He could hear a chain on one of the grabs clanking and shifting to and fro against the bulkhead. It sounded like a tired prisoner shuffling through the darkness. Another sign.

He stood for a long time, watching the sea. His eyes had grown accustomed to the night now, and he could see much further. Though there was no discernible horizon, he had a sense of the immensity of the ocean, and it drove home to him the huge area he had to search. It seemed to dwarf his effort. With all the sophisticated equipment and the Loran navigational aids, the task before him suddenly seemed futile and his hopes a gross presumption. He remembered how often he'd failed before.

The *Petrel* rolled, rose high on a swell, yawed sharply to starboard, and dropped into a deep trough. A shudder went through her steel, and Crane gripped the railing. Even after the swell had passed, his grip remained. He thought of how easy it would be to just slip off a ship at night—just to let go—to slip into the dark oblivion below. And who would know?

〜 〜 〜

While the seamen off watch sat in the crew's mess smoking, playing draughts and poker, and watching Victoria's Channel 6 fading to a washed-out blue on the television, Mary Crane, high up in the Chief Scientist's cabin immediately below the bridge, was getting ready for bed. It was only seven-thirty, but she wanted all the rest she could get. She'd been told that once the stations began, the noise would make it impossible to sleep. The small bunk light only dimly illuminated the spacious twelve by fifteen cabin, and as she laid out a flimsy negligee she could see the reflection of one of the running lights in the glass of the porthole that overlooked the well deck and beyond. After a few seconds she could barely make out the dark figure of someone standing by the windlass. The only distinguishing feature was a high toque. She could hear the wind rising now, howling about the ship's superstructure. She turned off the bunk light and in the blackness unzipped her teal-blue skirt, stepping out of it quickly before the next roll could pitch her off balance. She reached into the closet for a coat hanger, steadying herself against the door while the ship lurched hard to port, buffeting its way through a cross wave that flung a wisp of spray against the porthole.

Now that the light was out she could see the man by the
windlass move toward the forward mast. In the next instant the ship rose high and shuddered, and she thought
how brave it was of the lone figure there not to be frightened by wind or sea or night. She stared at the dark form
for several minutes. Though it was warm enough in
the cabin, the sound of the cold air howling made her feel
chilly. She hugged herself for warmth, but all the time she
kept her eyes on the man. One of her hands, as if of its
own will, moved across her body and passed fleetingly
against her nipples. Then it passed back, and back again.
Suddenly, for the first time in months, she became fully
aware of her body. In a few more years she would be old.
She looked out again at the figure on the bow. After a few
moments she turned, sliding her hand along the cool, hard
rail of the cabin, past the bunk light, until she felt the
main switch. Her hand froze over it for several seconds.
Then she quickly flicked it on, and in the soft burst of
fluorescent light she slowly, and as casually as she could,
turned toward the starboard bulkhead so that she was
side on to the forward porthole. She unclipped her bra,
then, bending over slowly, pulled down her panties.

There was a sharp knock on the door. In panic she
grabbed the silk dressing gown, put it around her and
pulled the belt tight. The knock came again. She opened
the door, her face flushed with fright. It was one of the
seamen, beaming down at her, making no attempt to hide
the pleasure he took in watching the quick rise and fall of
her breasts. "Y-y-yes," she stammered, pushing back her
hair in a satiny cascade.

"Your main light, ma'am." The seaman's grin widened.

"My what? I don't . . ."

"Your main cabin light, ma'am. It's all right if you keep
the porthole covers shut, but the main light throws too
much glare, you see. The officer on watch gets it all reflected in the bridge glass. Can't see a thing. Sort of like
turning your light on in a car at night. Makes it harder to
drive. Mr. Johns sent me down the moment he saw it."

"I'm sorry."

"Here, I'll close the cover for you, then you can have
all the light you want." Before she could say anything, he
stepped forward, brushing up against her, and was halfway across the cabin, glancing approvingly at her under-

wear and looking back at her. "Sometimes these covers are a bit tight," he said, grunting as he secured the wing nuts. "There you are." He stopped at the door. "Anything else I can do for you?" He looked straight at her.

"No, thank you."

"Good night, then."

After the man had left she quickly turned off the light and opened the porthole cover. The figure was gone. She shut the cover again, then slid in between the crisp linen sheets. Switching on the bunk light she began to read, but the motion of the ship prevented her from concentrating. She began thinking again about the last time she and Joe had made love. It had been months ago, and it had been miserable.

The heat of the reading lamp caused its shade to give off a smell like burning paint. She turned it off. In the darkness she still thought of the abortive lovemaking. Afterwards they'd sat together watching a late movie, a love story from the thirties where all the women made apple pies and the husband was utterly amazed when his wife began to knit baby socks and coyly told him she'd paid a visit to the doctor, and, well, there was going to be an addition to the family. Joe had tried to apologize and, forcing herself, she'd told him it was all right. Then they had sat on the sofa, holding hands without much conviction, until she'd fallen asleep before the second feature. More nights had ended like that than she cared to remember.

The door opened and a figure stood silhouetted against the bright light of the passageway. She started. "Who's that?"

"It's only me," said Joe, softly clicking the door closed. He could hear her breathing fast in the darkness. "Sorry, didn't mean to frighten you."

"I didn't recognize you," she said. "That toque. I've never seen it before."

"Oh, it's standard issue on the research ships. Keeps my brains warm."

"Where were you?" she asked, trying to keep her voice level. She could feel the deep beat of the engines.

"Up at the bow," he said. "Why?"

She heard him begin to undress. "Joe . . ."

"Yes?"

"Come here." Silence. He'd stopped moving.

"You should get some rest," he said. "Once we start sampling—"

"Please."

As he came toward her the ship took a heavy roll and he almost crashed into the bunk. She grabbed him and pulled him down. "You were at the bow," she said. "All alone?"

"Yes, I—"

"Love me, Joe," she said. "Make love to me." She threw the sheets aside, arching her body toward him.

"Wait," he said. "I'm not undressed." But he knew she would take no excuses, and in a few seconds his seaboots clumped to the floor.

Five minutes later, she knew it wouldn't work. His caresses were forced, dutiful rather than passionate. Oh, he was trying—he was always trying—but nothing was happening. Finally she stroked his head. "It's all right," she said. "I should—"

"Goddamn it!" He rolled off her body and slammed his fist against the side of the bunk.

"You're worried," she said. "You're too worried about the cruise. I know."

"No!" he exploded, tearing off his shirt and flinging it against the toilet door. "No, you don't understand. If you did you wouldn't—"

"Wouldn't what?" she snapped, sitting up in bed and bumping her head against the bottom of the top bunk.

"You wouldn't—"

"Bother you?" she said. "Well, pardon me for living, Joe. Last time we fucked—"

He swung around at her. "Don't be cheap."

"Last time we fucked, Joe, was during the Centennial. You probably did it for Canada."

"That's not funny," he growled.

"It wasn't supposed to be." She began to cry.

"What's the matter?"

"Oh, nothing," she said. "Absolutely nothing."

"Then stop that Goddamn whining. I'm the one who's under pressure."

"You bastard," she said, between sobs.

The toilet door rattled and he kicked it violently. "Fucking door."

"Be quiet," she said, ripping a Kleenex from its box. "Someone will hear you."

"I don't care."

"Yes, you do. You care what everyone thinks of you. That's the trouble."

"Well, I'm glad someone cares in this family."

"*What* family?"

He walked into the toilet, slamming the door behind him.

"I'm sorry," she called. "Joe? I'm sorry. That was cruel. I . . . Joe?"

"Oh, God," she said, gripping the side of the bunk to keep her balance. "Oh, God." She rolled over on her side, facing the cold steel bulkhead.

A few minutes later his shadow passed across her, as he hoisted himself to the top bunk. "I'm sorry, Joe."

There was silence. The *Petrel* shuddered and yawed hard to port. "I'll kill him if he touches you," said Crane.

"Who? What are you talking about?"

"You know who I'm talking about."

"I don't—"

"I saw you," he said, his voice trembling. "I saw you. I know what you were trying to do—what you were thinking. You thought it was Frank out there, didn't you? You rotten—"

"I don't know what you're talking about," she said.

"If he touches you I swear I'll kill him. If he—"

A metallic *whack* hit the ship. Mary sat up. "What's that?"

"It's only the sparker," he snapped, almost contemptuously.

Whack!

Mary tried to shut out the noise by cradling her ears with a pillow, but it made little difference. The monotonously persistent echo induced in her the kind of nerve-racking anticipation that comes from sitting next to a chronic cougher on a long journey. But she knew that the real reason for her jangled nerves wasn't the noise of the sparker but the overwhelming loneliness that now swept over her like a tidal wave.

Out in the darkness the sparker kept firing. Every ten seconds, forty-five hundred volts jumped across a gap between two electrodes, producing a whitish-green flash twen-

ty feet in diameter twenty yards astern. Now and then a
fish would be illuminated for a second or two, blown to
the surface by the force of the explosion, its backbone
snapped like a twig.

～ ～ ～

Despite the incessant whacking of the sparker, Frank
dreamed on, unperturbed.

In the deep India-ink sea, he felt himself descending
without scuba tanks, without diving suit, without submersible. He was descending effortlessly toward the top of one
of the sea mounts, the dead volcanoes that rise from the
ocean floor in the Northeast Pacific and thrust to within a
few hundred feet of the surface. On the sea bottom he
saw the strange, cone-shaped encrustations of iron oxide
standing still and silent on the mud flats like the ancient ant
hills of the vast Australian desert, each one a fifty-foot
column of incredibly rich mineral deposits. Swimming with
him was a woman with long, flowing blonde hair that swept
gently back and forth like golden wind coral in the deep
currents. Suddenly his chest began to compress in a silent
scream of pain and he was thrown against one of the
mounds, causing a fragment of the iron oxide to crumble
and burst like dried blood, turning the sea into a vivid
red and orange cloud through which he could no longer
see the woman. He pushed up with all his strength, but his
body wouldn't move and he was caught, kicking furiously
in the effusion of escaping breath. But then the sea
calmed and the soft lips of the woman blew air into his
lungs and together, embracing, they rose until they broke
surface and floated, exhausted but peaceful, in long and
gentle swells.

16

At four in the morning it was a different world. The
Petrel was ploughing through the seas at latitude 48°59′

north and longitude 128°31' west, a hundred and fifty-five miles west of Cape Flattery, the northernmost tip of Washington State, and a hundred and fifty-two miles west of Carmanah Light on the southwest coast of Vancouver Island. The twenty-knot winds had increased to thirty knots, and waves that had been ten feet high had now risen to fifteen. It was unquestionably force seven on the Beaufort scale. Before, it had been plain bad weather. Now, it was a near gale.

To Frank, sharing the bosun's cabin on the starboard side below the waterline, it felt like force nine. The atmosphere was so black he felt as if he was in a sealed coffin. He was tossed to and fro, up and down, and periodically wrenched to the edge of his bunk, where all he could do was hold on precariously before being thrown back against the bulkhead as the ship compensated for the sudden yaw. Among the slidings and creakings of the cabin, further sleep—even rest—was impossible. He'd spent years at sea as an oceanographic technician, but the first twenty-four hours of a new trip, particularly one this rough, always upset him. Over the moaning of the wind he could hear the closet door squeaking, but he felt too sick to get up and fix it. Each time the *Petrel* rolled he could hear the irritating rattle of a toothbrush inside the wash-basin cabinet, and the smell of diesel was heavy in the cabin. They were still running against the wind, he guessed, and it was forcing the fumes from the funnel down the aft vents. The smell added to his general nausea and he longed for fresh air. But the ship, being of modern design, was fully air-conditioned, which meant that the only air below decks was the sucked-in belching of the diesels. He cursed the *Petrel*'s designers, and hoped that as the weather was so bad the voice from the bridge would never come. But come it did, at about three minutes after four.

Crackling like static, the First Mate's monotone invaded the blackness of the cabin. "On station in ten minutes. On station in ten minutes. Let's find some manganese, you lucky devils, you!"

A dim light came on and Charlie sat up on the edge of his bunk, groaning, holding onto its lip for support with one hand and reaching for his bosun's jacket with the other. Frank too sat up, trying hard not to swallow. His stomach did a slow barrel roll in unison with the ship, which then rose, hung for a second, and bucked violently before crashing into another wave. As he pulled on his boots, his mouth flooded with saliva that tasted like dieseline. "This isn't research," he mumbled. "This is insanity." He swung his legs over the top bunk and kicked Charlie in the head.

"Oh, Christ Almight—"

"Sorry."

Frank, his legs hanging limply, waited for the ship to reach the apogee of its next pitch. Then he jumped down, steadying himself on the small writing desk as they went into the next roll. Staggering like a drunk, he made his way to the toilet.

The fluorescent light flickered fitfully for a moment, then stayed steady. Frank stood whey-faced over the stainless steel basin, clinging to the two chromium rails, his knuckles white. He dimly heard Charlie asking him how he felt. "Fine," he whispered. Then the saliva dribbled over his bottom lip and his head dropped.

The voice came over the intercom again. "On station, on station." Frank stumbled out of the toilet, bumping into Charlie. Mustering all his concentration, he dragged on his cold wet gear, cursing a stuck zipper. The two of them rinsed their mouths, then shuffled their way through the door and along the alleyway like two robots, clumping heavily up the steps from the lower deck, hanging onto the rails. To enter the dry lab aft they had to step over a compartment bulkhead, and in Frank's condition it required an enormous effort. On the wet lab's blackboard Frank read: "Station #1, Depth 7–8,000 feet, p.v.c. Claw Grab to determine mud type—3001 chart indicates a possible 25° slope."

The ship corkscrewed violently, churning the bile in his stomach, and he went out on deck. As they tackled one of the smaller, hundred-and-fifty-pound grabs, spray enveloped the ship and a wave sluiced green across the decks and drained through the scuppers. Charlie steadied himself against another roll. "You were right," he bellowed, above the howl of the wind. "This is madness. Surely to Christ Crane won't make us work in this."

A crewman switched on the starboard afterdeck winch, and its high whine cut through the noise of the approaching gale. But the afterdeck floodlight was not yet on. The bridge hadn't realized that they were ready on the deck. "On station," the Mate bellowed. "On station."

Frank felt incapable of reaching the intercom only a few yards away. "Will someone tell him to shut his cake hole?" he said, then leaned over the side, retching. The wind felt good on his face, but it was so cold that it soon began to numb his forehead. He made his way back to the protection of the winch on the port side. Every now and then a whiff of diesel would send him lurching back toward the rail.

On the bridge, First Mate Johns began "jogging" the *Petrel*, maneuvering her so that he could keep her head into the wind, which would push the grab cable clear of the twin props as it was played out and trailed along the ship's side. The water churned white under her stern as she tried doggedly to maintain station.

Frank forced himself to attach the grab to the winch wire. Every few minutes the props would clear water as the ship pitched heavily. From long experience he avoided watching the blades—their spinning only adding to his problems of balance. Finally, the ship turned straight into the wind. The wire was clear of the props but the *Petrel*'s slow speed meant that more diesel fumes were being swept over the afterdeck. Frank finished attaching the cable and went to rest against the port-side winch, trying to catch a few gasps of unpolluted air.

"Ah, feeling a bit rough, chaps?" It was Johns, the First Mate.

The mumbled obscenities were lost to the wind.

"Okay," said Charlie, now fully awake and scratching the tattooed heart vigorously. "Let's go."

Frank, wrenching himself away from the winch, bent down and tightened the shackle and swivel that would allow the grab to move around freely without twisting the wire. A crewman released the big handbrake on the side of the winch, and the whine grew shriller. When the wire was taut, having taken up the weight, Frank turned stiffly into the wind and raised his thumb to the winchman, who tapped back the control level. The five-eighths-inch wire started moving through the block that swung from the davit, and the grab rose slowly from the dock.

Frank caught the collar of the grab with his boathook, trying to keep it from swinging. The winchman and Charlie

started to laugh. Each time the ship rolled heavily, the
weight of the grab pulled Frank across the deck like a
dog on a leash. The second time Frank went past, Charlie
reached out and looped a rope around his waist in case
the swinging grab dragged him over the side.

Once the grab was high enough off the deck to clear
the safety chain that replaced the normal rail, Frank,
holding the boathook precariously with his left hand, signaled with his right for the winchman to swing it over the
side. The bosun quickly cranked the davit outboard. Frank
pointed down with his thumb and disengaged the boathook from the collar. The winchman dropped the grab
into the sea, then let the winch have its head. As the cable
rasped out at ten meters a second, a small white arrow
on the davit meter spun madly while a slower needle
registered every hundred fathoms.

Frank was feeling a lot better now, breathing in cold,
salty air, watching the echo sounder.

"Will you core here?" asked the First Mate.

"Depends on what we get in the grab."

"How's it look?"

"Fifteen-degree slope now. It's all right, I suppose."
Frank glanced forward but all he could see was the dim
outline of the funnel, and the red-white-red lights swinging
wildly high above the upper deck, signalling that scientific
research was under way. "Is Crane up?"

"On the bridge."

"That figures. Safe and sound. Well, safe. Is he sick?"

"No. Very cheery."

"He would be."

∽　∽　∽

The small galley was warm as Frank and Charlie waited
out the grab's long descent, wedging themselves into a corner and letting the ship take care of their balance while
their legs rested. It was just as they were finishing their
coffee that the winchman stuck his head around the door.
"Frank, you'd better come aft."

"What's up?"

"The echo trace. It's very sharp. Looks like we've
drifted over a precipice. Could tangle the grab."

When they reached the dry lab Crane was there, bending over the echo sounder. Frank could see by his face that
something extraordinary had happened. When he saw the

trace he forgot the weather outside. The winchman had been right. The line on the trace had taken an extremely sharp dip. They had started on a 15° decline, but now they were over a 47° slope—a bad bet for a good grab bite. But what made it really striking were the sharp crags that stuck up from the side of the cliff. Between the crags there would be basins of considerable size—perhaps several square miles each—perhaps filled with mud.

A seaman just off watch was the first to speak. "What do you think is down there, Doc?" Frank noticed that it was Sam, the deckhand with the thick, blue-tinted glasses, who'd been outside the porthole when Frank had shown Charlie the metalliferous mud sample. Much to Frank's disgust, he was munching on a piece of cold custard pie. Crane didn't answer. Instead he turned to Frank. "I'll be on the bridge if you want me. Bring the small grab back in, and we'll come at it from another angle." He left the lab, heading forward.

Frank watched the trace for ten minutes, then turned to high magnification. He glanced up at the wall compass. It read 187°. On their first run it had registered 11.5°. That meant they were turning and coming at the formation from the opposite direction. He heard the Mate's voice come over the intercom: "How wide is it?"

Frank studied the trace, which now looked roughly like the silhouette of a nude woman. Before they had turned to approach the formation longitudinally, the ship had crossed the formation's stomach. It was this width that Frank was now trying to measure. "It just keeps going—could be miles. Looks like the edge of the Cascadia Plain. Could be fifty miles long, judging from the chart. It's not an isolated formation, if that's what you're thinking."

There was silence from the bridge, then Crane's voice came on. "We can't be sure." Further silence. "What do you think we should do?"

On the bridge, the First Mate raised his eyebrows at the Captain, who had just come in and was still buttoning up his gold-braided jacket. Frank's voice crackled on the intercom. "We've wasted enough time already. I estimate we've only forty-eight hours left before we reach force ten. Let's drop Big Bess and see if we can't bite in."

"You think it might be a manganese bed?" said Crane, hoping everyone would hear the deception.

"I'm not a prophet. Let's try to find out. That's what we're here for."

"I don't know . . . Why waste precious time rigging the big grab, Frank? Try the little one again."

An outlaw wave suddenly punched the *Petrel* amidships, putting her into a heavy roll and throwing Frank off balance. He steadied himself. "No, that little job will roll over on a slope, trip itself and just grab water. The big one will plough right into the bottom, whatever it's made of— slope or no slope."

"All right, go ahead. You're the boss."

Frank slipped the "talk" level, then spoke into the mute mouthpiece. "No, I'm not. You are, for Christ's sake!" He turned to Charlie. "And they pay him twenty thousand a year to tell me that."

"Relax, Frank, it might be manganese." Charlie winked.

Sam, still standing near the sounder, looked excited. He had got himself another piece of pie from somewhere. Even in the bright light of the lab it was difficult to see his eyes through the tinted lenses.

"Huh?" said Frank to Charlie. "I don't give a damn what it is. I—"

"Yes, you do. Come on. Let's unleash Big Bess."

Huddling into their wet gear, the two men walked out into the open beyond the lab's after bulkhead, heading toward the cold, windy foredeck.

Big Bess was huge. She stood six feet high, weighed a thousand pounds, and her steel jaws had a ten-foot bite.

Most grabs are designed to sit gently on the bottom and close their jaws. Bess was different. Her function was to plunge into the seabed and tear off her huge mouthful. To allow her this plunge, a twenty-foot length of slack cable was coiled and clamped together above her. Twenty feet above the sea bottom, the looped slack would be let loose to allow the grab to free-fall the length of the coil. The coil was held together by two hand-sized metal jaws at the end of a long horizontal metal arm, and the jaws were held closed by a two-hundred-pound lead trip-weight attached to a twenty-foot wire on the end of the arm. This meant that the trip weight hung twenty feet below Big Bess, and when it touched bottom the tension, which had previously kept the arm down and the jaws biting hard on the coil, was gone and the coil would unwind rapidly, allowing the grab to plummet into the bottom. On deck, when her jaws had been cranked open, a trip-prevention pin one inch thick and twelve inches long was inserted in her neck. The pin would prevent her from pretripping on the deck, or in any of the rigging, as she was lowered overboard. If she did pretrip before the waterline, she could punch a gaping hole in the ship's body, slice a man in half, or both.

The covers were off the Swann winch on the port side, and the First Mate was trying to maneuver for the same angle of approach as before, but he was having difficulty in finding the same line.

Finally the port winch screamed, lifting Big Bess and lowering her just below the sea's surface. Lashing himself to the deck, Frank leaned overboard to pull out the safety pin.

Though the grab was resting half submerged, there was still the risk of a wave pushing the submerged trip weight against the ship's side the moment the pin was out, causing a premature trip that would let the grab rip down the ship's side in free fall. The sudden thousand-pound jerk on the coiled cable could neatly decapitate anyone nearby.

Frank, perching precariously by the taut main cable, watched the big swells that were lifting the bow toward the gradually lightening sky. He waited until a particularly heavy swell swamped the grab, pushing her away from the ship's side, then reached down and pulled the pin. It came out clean. As he stepped back quickly from the chain, Charlie slapped him on the shoulder. Frank looked up at the spinning meter needle as the grab dropped out of sight. Beyond the meter, he could see Mary Crane watching him from the bridge.

The Captain went down to the dry lab on a rare visit, stared at the trace, grunted his surprise and walked back up to the bridge to wait it out. As dawn broke, a growing crowd of sailors below joined Sam around the after-lab depth sounder.

∽ ∽ ∽

Bess was so big that her shape was readily discernible on the moist Hardiger trace paper when the magnification was set at maximum. The shape which the returning blips gradually built up as she descended resembled that of a blurred bulldog clip. After twenty minutes Frank, on deck, saw the sudden jump of the five-eighths-inch cable as the grab tripped.

By now the ship was drifting off position at two knots, but as the grab had reached bottom the bridge wasn't unduly concerned.

"She won't budge," shouted the winchman.

Frank looked up. The wire from the winch stretched out from the starboard side at a thirty-degree angle. They'd drifted well off position. The only trace on the sounder now was a flat bottom. The winchman was forced to let out more cable, yielding to the drift. The bridge was loath to back up, for fear of the heavy swells suddenly pushing the props into the cable, but reluctantly rang down for "dead slow astern." Someone called out, "We'll never get her out!"

Frank kept his eye on the tensionometer as Charlie took over the winch controls and began to play Big Bess in much the same way as a fisherman plays a snag, winding in, letting out, going sideways and sometimes risking a short jerk forward. Each time the winch howled, the needle on the tensionometer would shoot up past the three-thousand-pound pull mark. He nodded approvingly as Charlie quickly let out a few fathoms, as each big swell took the ship higher, threatening to increase the tension on the already dangerously taut line. Suddenly the cable sang like a plucked piano wire. Frank grabbed the nearest body and pulled it down to the deck, the winch screaming above his head as Charlie fed out line as fast as he could.

"What's the matter?" It was only then that Frank realized that the body he'd been holding was Mary Crane's. Slowly he let her go.

"Whenever you hear that zing, vacate the premises," he said.

"You mean the cable is breaking?"

"No, but it's got an awful hernia by now, and if it zings again it could snap. Sometimes it breaks underwater and goes slack like a wet rope, but it can just as easily go near the waterline and whip back over the deck. Could cut you in half."

"She's free," called Charlie. The Swann began groaning as it started to haul up.

It was seven o'clock now, and the sun was flooding the

gray horizon with a pale wash that revealed endless ranks
of whitecaps. The tensionometer held steady at around a
thousand pounds.

"Think it's mud, Frank?" said a seaman.

"Don't think so."

"Manganese?"

Frank didn't answer.

"You think it's manganese, Frank?"

Frank shrugged. He wondered how long the deception
would hold.

When Joe Crane came onto the forward deck, he looked
like a different man. He walked out of the dry lab and
stood there, hands behind his back, without moving his
feet. His body, compensating for the rolls, leaned in the
opposite direction to the swells. At no time did it even
look as if he might slip, though often his body leaned at an
angle of nearly forty degrees to the deck. He had the
attitude of impending victory, as if he were admiral on a
ship of the line and the whole fleet awaited his order, and
his alone, to fire.

Frank wasn't as optimistic. Maybe they should have
used the small grab, then moved on. If they were going
to try other stations, they couldn't afford much more time
here. The improvement in the weather was only a lull;
the forecast for the next twenty-four hours looked bad.

The whine of the winch rose as the grab came nearer
the surface from three thousand meters below. To Frank
the whitecaps looked like the tents of a surrounding army
that had advanced in the night to within striking distance
of their enemy's camp. He glanced at his watch again.
It was seven twenty. At seventy meters per minute, the
grab would be up in eleven minutes.

17

It was Mary Crane who first saw the lone mast less
than a mile to the west. She had been standing on the

forward deck, listening to the splitting sound of the wire as it rolled tightly onto the winch drum, and she moved to the protection of the foc'sle's overhang to avoid the ice-cold droplets that splattered down as the wire passed overhead from the block on the starboard side. She was watching the meter needle moving counterclockwise, recording the decreasing length of wire as the grab was brought up more slowly now to avoid flushing out its contents. But after a few seconds, the rocking of the stationary ship upset her sense of balance and made her feel queasy.

Frank noticed the greenish tinge in her cheeks. "Sit down and watch the horizon," he said. "You need to fix your eye on something distant."

As she made her way toward the bollard a swell pushed her against one of the square, mesh-covered air vents, sending her dangerously close to the gap below the safety chain. Joe Crane, who'd been standing by the port winch, moved toward her, but Frank had already caught her arm. Instinctively she grabbed at him. Putting his other arm around her waist, he lowered her gently onto the bollard. "You okay?" Recovering from her fright, she didn't answer immediately. Frank touched her arm softly. "Mary, are you all right?"

She looked up. It was the first time on the ship that he'd used her name. "Yes," she said, smiling, still holding the sleeve of his wet gear. "Thank you. I . . . ." There was a moment of silence. Frank patted her arm and turned back toward the winch.

"Frank!" Joe Crane's voice was strained almost beyond control.

"Yes?"

"Inside the dry lab."

"What?"

"I want to see you. Inside the dry lab."

High in the tractor chair behind the winch, Charlie threw his cigarette overboard and shook his head as Frank, moving stiffly in the heavy wet gear, followed Crane toward the lab.

Once inside, the two men faced each other.

"I warned you," said Crane.

Frank pulled out a paper towel and wiped the itchy, drying salt from his face. "About what?"

"About messing around. Playing Sir Galahad."

Frank stared at him. "I'm not playing anything. Mary looked ill—"

Crane clenched his fist. "It's not that. It's how you do it. You know what I mean."

Frank crumpled the towel into a tight ball. "What the hell are you talking about?"

Crane's mouth tightened and he moved forward. Frank gripped the towel tightly, his hands clenched.

"Doctor?" It was Charlie's voice from the deck.

Crane hesitated. Then he let his arm fall and walked out toward the winch.

∽ ∽ ∽

Charlie gave him the Zeiss binoculars. "Over there. One o'clock. Your wife just saw the mast."

Crane snatched the binoculars. "Can't see anything," he said, handing them back to Charlie and scowling at him. "I know what you're up to." He stalked off toward the starboard side. The wind blew back his parka hood, whipping his hair into a mat that lay forlornly over his face. The look of impending victory was gone.

Charlie passed the glasses to Frank. Then he stopped the winch, wound out a few feet to straighten a kink, reset the wire guide and started the rewind. "There's a deep-sea trawler out there."

Frank searched the slices of horizon between swells. It was some time before he saw the blur of the mast dipping between the distant whitecaps. He wiped the glasses free of spray and altered the focus. Now he could see the tall trolling poles as well, standing upright, one on either side of the mast. "Yeah. Tuna, I guess."

Charlie checked to make sure that the nearest seaman was still yards away, under the meter block. Then he bent down out of view by the side of the winch, fiddling with the wire-guide control. No one but Frank could see him. "Tuna, my ass."

"What d'you mean?"

A wave smashed amidships and water gushed over the deck. "I mean he's following us," said Charlie.

Lifting the binoculars, Frank steadied his arm against a stanchion and looked at the trawler bobbing up and down in the bottle-green swells half a mile away. As the *Petrel* topped a wave, Frank felt a chill. A figure on the trawler was looking at him. On the next wave the figure was gone. Frank swept his gaze toward the stern of the trawler, but all he could see was Mary Crane's head. He moved the glasses back and waited for the next wave to lift him higher, but the swells had temporarily fallen off. Finally he got a glimpse of the trawler again. There was a Canadian flag fluttering at the stern. He looked at his watch. The grab would be up in five minutes. He scrambled up the ladder to the helicopter deck. Much higher now, he could see more of the trawler each time the *Petrel* rose. It took him three minutes of hard concentration, but eventually he could make out the name on the bow.

"Two minutes to go," came a seaman's voice from below.

Clambering heavily back down the ladder, Frank took off the binoculars, grabbed a long boathook and stood ready by the rail.

"You get the name?" asked Charlie. The winch ground into low gear for the slow heave to the deck.

"Yeah," said Frank. "*Sea Wasp.*"

"That's right."

"You recognize her?"

"Don't you?"

"No."

"It was one of the fleet that passed us going out of Vancouver."

"Wait a minute. The guy that Olly saw watching us through the binoculars in the Narrows? That big gray job?"

"The same."

"Ten fathoms to go," came the cry.

Frank thought hard. "But it could be a coincidence . . ."

"Yeah," said Charlie, rubbing the tattoo. "Sure it could. And I'm Aristotle Onassis." He looked around guardedly. "How many people know what you're really after?"

Frank wiped the seawater off the slippery aluminum boathook. "Don't know."

"Well, someone told Crane, didn't they?"

"Yeah. Of course."

"Who else did *they* tell?"

Frank looked up at Charlie in the high chair. "Or who else found out?"

"You got it," said Charlie. "You got it."

"Five fathoms," called the seaman.

It was then that the squall struck, without warning. The wind howled down on them at fifty knots, whipping the tops from the waves, and forcing the wire, despite the weight of the huge grab, to stream out another ten degrees. Charlie thumped both feet down on the footbrake and heaved the handbrake back for good measure. "Everyone inside," he yelled. The *Petrel*'s engines began pounding to bring her head to wind.

18

The squall missed the *Sea Wasp*, rolling and pitching in the growing light just over a mile to the east. In the trawler's wheelhouse the Canadian Captain was moving his Gerber variable rule across chart 3001, plotting their position. Doyle watched the *Petrel* through his glasses. With the squall enveloping her, all he could make out was the sharp bow that lifted and plunged in the huge gray swells that had rolled unimpeded more than ten thousand miles from Antarctica. Doyle tried to visualize the vast distances of the Pacific, but his musings were interrupted by the sound of noisy vomiting below.

Wheezing for breath, the Captain leaned over the table, drawing a line from their present position to Vancouver Island. Without lowering the glasses Doyle said, "Where are we?"

The Captain placed the transparent bottom-contour map over the navigational chart and followed the course he'd drawn. "We're in the southern part of the Cascadia Plain. It's northeast of what's called the Middle Ridge. There are three ridges, East, West, and one in between— the Middle Ridge. They're all in the northeastern corner of the Juan de Fuca Ridge system."

"Never mind the lecture, Professor. How far are we from the coast?"

"What coast?" said the Captain, looking at the U.S. Olympic Peninsula and the adjacent stretch of Vancouver Island on the Canadian side.

"The China coast," said Doyle derisively.

The trawler rolled and a cup tipped over, spilling coffee on the overlay. The Captain slammed the cup into a wooden holder above the chart table and mopped the spill.

Doyle altered the focus of the glasses. "How far off Vancouver Island, dummy?"

"About two hundred and forty-nine kilometers from the Carmanah Light."

"What's that in miles, for Christ's sake?"

"A hundred and fifty." The Captain was winding the self-winding Timex again. "We're still well within Canadian waters."

"I know," said Doyle irritably, still staring through the glasses. The sound of vomiting came again from below. The Captain grinned. "Better get Laurel and Hardy topside before they stink us out."

Doyle scanned the horizon once more. "Listen, my friend, let me give you some advice. I can take a joke." He used his sleeve to wipe the lens, which had fogged up in the warmth of the wheelhouse. "But those two can't. They get very annoyed with people. Get what I mean?"

"They're gorillas."

"That's right. They look pretty pathetic right now, but once they get their sea legs it'll be a different story, believe me. Honolulu didn't ask the Seattle office to send them along for a holiday. So cool the sarcasm, okay? They're on our side."

"What side's that?"

"There you go again."

"Okay, okay, I get the picture." The Captain cuffed the wheel, bringing the trawler back into the wind. Doyle opened the door to the galley below. "Hey, Jay, Tony. Come up topside. You'll feel better away from that gas stink."

On deck the two men clung morosely to the gunwale. Jay retched and Tony moved further upwind, taking out his false teeth and letting the salt air go to work on the nauseous torpor that had kept him prisoner below, all the way out. He looked out at the windswept sea ·and felt much better—until he saw the distant matchsticks of the *Petrel*'s masts. Their swaying made him feel sick again. At that moment he didn't care who was on the research ship or what it was doing. All he knew was that it was the cause of his being out there, and he hated it as he had never hated anything before. He wished he could sink it and kill everyone on board. He hoped he'd get better quickly and that things would turn nasty, so he could do what he knew best. He felt the burning in his throat again and threw up over the side.

"See the ship?" asked Doyle cheerfully, pulling out a Gitane and pointing in the direction of the *Petrel*. "Here, use the binoculars."

Jay was too sick to bother, knowing instinctively that to take his eyes off the horizon would mean more throwing up. "No," he dribbled, trying to get as far as possible from the smell of Doyle's cigarette. "I see it already." He let his arm flop in the direction of the port side. "I see it."

"No," said Doyle, "it's over there, off the starboard beam."

As they took yet another gut-wrenching roll, Jay's arm pointed spastically to the port side again. Doyle stared for half a minute. "Jesus Christ," he said and stepped quickly inside the wheelhouse. "Have you got your radar on?"

"What for?" asked the Captain. "You can see the *Petrel* from here. Why waste power?"

"I don't care, turn it on," said Doyle.

"Why waste power? We can—"

"Turn it on, damn it!"

The Decca 101 began humming, and shortly the arm began its hypnotic sweep. Doyle saw a large dot within the three-mile range—the *Petrel*—and then, at five miles, another, smaller dot. "Surprise," he said sarcastically. "Who's that?"

"I dunno. Could be another trawler from the Vancouver fleet."

"They all headed north?"

"Well, I dunno. Could be Japanese or the U.S."

"In Canadian waters?"

"Could be." The Captain shrugged.

"Yeah? Well, we'd better find out. And fast. Let's go."

As the ninety-horsepower "Jimmy" engine jumped from quarter to half speed, spurting blue-white fumes from the stack, Tony began to feel better. At least they were moving. With every knot they gained, the wind blasted harder on his face, reviving him. He put his teeth back in. He was certain that soon he'd be feeling his old self again.

19

When Frank saw the green gush of bubbles breaking the surface, he felt his throat tighten in anticipation. He held up his hand and the winch stopped. Charlie changed to a lower gear and gently eased out the throttle, holding the lever upright with his left hand and gently slapping the tattooed heart with his right. Bess began rising again. Her outline resembled a giant blue stingray with the cable for a tail. Beneath this shape the water was whalebone white, the effervescent salt bubbles streaming downwards as well as upwards. Frank was mesmerized by the rising shape, but the grab was no more than six inches out of the water before he remembered to shout, "Surface!"

Charlie switched down to the lowest gear. The seamen crowded to the rail.

The Captain, relieving the First Mate on the bridge, ran his fingers through his tousled mane of hair and picked up the intercom mike. "Stand clear! Stand clear!" he shouted, but no one took any notice. Charlie trod on the brake. The grab was halfway out of the water now but its contents were invisible in the sloshing of the heavy swells. "Stand back!" bellowed Charlie. "I can't see the grab. Go to the port side. Go on, move!" The seamen retreated from the rail, grumbling.

Gradually the head of the grab appeared above the rail, like a huge metallic bug. The ship rolled away from the grab, then smashed into it on the return. The Captain's voice came over the intercom. "Up smartly, Bosun."

Charlie waited till the ship was fairly steady in a long, deep trough, then lifted the grab high above the deck in one pull. No one expected what they saw next.

Stuck in the jaws of the grab, water pouring off it in streams, was the biggest and loneliest geoduck clam that any of them had ever seen. A foot long and six inches wide, with a three foot siphon dangling from it like a brown snake, it looked as if it would weigh in at between twenty and twenty-five pounds. A heavy swell came and the grab swung inboard, without any restraint from sea or wind. No one had moved. They all stood there, buffeted by the remnants of the night's foul weather, staring at the clam. When Big Bess swung over them they ducked their heads, but the clam struck the railing. The impact sliced off the exposed siphon and ripped out the innards. They fell into the sea. The only thing that remained in the jaws was a half-shattered shell. The grab was empty. Joe Crane bent down and morosely picked up a piece of the broken shell that was rolling about the deck like a skull. He looked at it for a moment, then put it in his pocket and went below.

Some of the seamen began to laugh. "All this way to catch a Goddamn clam."

"Can't even eat the Goddamn thing."

"Never mind eating it—they can't even catch the God-damn thing."

Frank walked off the deck, barely hearing the voices around him, leaving Charlie to lash down the grab. He could hear the engines pick up as the ship moved on. As he made his way through the wet lab, George appeared with a big smile on his face, his belt cassette blaring country and western music. "Clam chowder's better than nothing, eh, Frank?"

"Piss off."

Back in his cabin Frank took off his boots, throwing them viciously into the corner. Charlie began scratching his tattoo. He spoke quietly. "Ah, Frank, the old man wants to know where the next station'll be. He says we'll have to cut some out now. We spent too much time here."

"How the fuck should I know? Ask Crane."

"I can't find him." There was an awkward silence.

"He'll be up at the bow."

"In this weather?"

"That's where he broods." Frank swung his legs up onto the top bunk and closed his eyes. "Sorry, Charlie."

"Aw—it's okay."

"No, it isn't. Crane's obsessed with finding this bloody mud. Guess it rubs off. Sounds weird, huh?"

"No. It's a pain in the ass to keep searching without finding."

"You seem happy enough."

"Yeah," said Charlie, shrugging. "But I got Lola." He opened his locker and exposed a Playboy centerfold. "You like her?"

Frank nodded and forced a grin, but his eyelids were dropping with fatigue. He lay back on his bunk, and within five minutes he was asleep.

When Charlie reached the bow, Joe Crane was on his way back. The ship nosed into a wave and spray covered both of them. To Charlie's surprise Crane smiled. "How are you, Bosun?"

"Not too bad, thanks. The old man wants to know where to next."

Joe Crane nodded wearily and kept walking. When he entered the bridge, Tate pointed to the chart. "Where to now, Doctor?"

"Oh, just keep going."

The Captain's face creased, puzzled. "Just keep going?"

"Yes."

"Don't you want to miss a few stations? Otherwise we'll never complete the line before that gale hits us."

Joe Crane exhaled heavily, as if he couldn't care less. "Yes, all right."

The Captain turned to the wheelman. "Hard-a'-starboard. Steer zero seven eight."

"Hard-a'-starboard, zero seven eight, sir."

The ship was now running with the sea and barely rolled at all, despite the storm-whipped water. The huge, white-crested swells slipped under her and slid quickly by, as if benevolently granting her safe passage during the daylight hours.

Joe Crane went to his cabin to wash up for breakfast. He sat down for a moment on the bunk to rest his legs, his muscles aching from the effort of battling gravity. It wasn't until he was taking off his wet gear that he realized he couldn't remember where he'd put the pieces of clamshell he'd found. From habit, like any other ocean-ographer, he never wasted anything brought up in a sample, aware that those few broken fragments had been retrieved at a cost of thousands of dollars in ship time. Slowly he remembered that he had put the fragments in a drawer.

The lapse of memory frightened him. He had always had a secret fear that one day his brain might give out on him. But no, he told himself, this time it must have been the storm. No sleep had meant no appetite, and the long dog watch had worn him down even more. But still, as he sat exhausted on his bunk, all his failures crowded in on him, ganging up to sneer at his latest defeat. This was the last chance and it was going the way of all his other attempts. To make things worse, an old guilt surfaced—his terror of working the heavy equipment. The heavy gear made flesh and bone appear so fragile and insignificant. And always, over the years, it seemed as if the giant dredges and grabs were the instruments of fate's conspiracy to crush him. They could kill him in an instant, before he had accomplished anything worthwhile in the world.

In the past he'd managed to cover this fear by busying himself on the bridge and with paperwork in the lab. He'd even managed to establish a reputation for always being around no matter what shift it was, which meant he was taken for a worker by many of the ship's crew and even by other scientists. Only Frank knew how little manual work he really did on the ship. Of course, he could always say that as Chief Scientist it was his job to supervise, and that was true; but he knew that even as Chief Scientist he was supposed to be ready and able to lend a hand in any tight situations on deck.

His fear of deck work had eventually become terror, the night he and Frank had seen a man cut in half by the trip cable of a long corer off Florida. He'd gone to his cabin and vomited until there was nothing left but bile. He'd never told Mary of his fear, and now that made it even harder to bear. He'd let her believe that he'd always handled the heavy equipment, that he knew exactly what to do on deck as well as in the lab. Exactly as he had let her believe that Frank was just the helper.

He unlaced his boots slowly. Then, telling himself he should eat something despite his fatigue, he began, according to tradition, to dress up for breakfast. Staring blankly into his locker, he tried to concentrate long enough to choose a tie. It seemed an impossible decision. All he could see before him was the massive clam shell caught in the grab. And inside the grab—nothing. The emptiness kept growing until the blackness beckoned him like a vast, soft oblivion. All he had to do was leave the ship—let go. It would be the easiest thing in the world . . .

∽ ∽ ∽

On deck, Mary Crane stood by the stern's A-frame nursing a cup of coffee and watching the ocean, the wind sweeping back her hair and chafing her cheeks. A blackfooted albatross with a seven-foot wing span swept low, gliding effortlessly over the troughs and crests. Then, just as effortlessly, it rose in the convection currents created by the *Petrel*, passing over the ship with such confident grace that Mary envied its freedom. She knew the birds were at their best during stormy weather, that in calmer times they were clumsy and ineffectual in their attempts to get airborne. But for the moment they were free of impediment—free to act on instinct. If only she and Joe were free too, to start their journey all over again. Despite the coffee, which was the only thing she felt her stomach could take after the sleepless night, she began to feel drowsy. She lowered herself into the starboard corner of the afterdeck, away from the breakfast smells that had pursued her each time she'd sought the shelter of the dry lab.

She continued to watch the bird. Soon there were two of them, diving and swooping together in carefree harmony. Suddenly she was overwhelmed with nostalgia for the early days in Vancouver, when she and Joe had been so happy together.

She'd been half asleep for about ten minutes when she was awakened by the scratchy sound of the P.A. system. It was the Second Mate's voice. "Ten minutes to station. Ten minutes to station."

She got up to make sure Joe was awake. On the horizon she could see the dark gray dot of the trawler. She thought of Nielsen's message, then tried to put it out of her mind. She could think of that later—if they found anything.

∽ ∽ ∽

Mary saw Joe in the wardroom. As she entered, his back was toward her. The tall, dour Scottish Second Mate, seated at the table, rose immediately. She began to smile in acknowledgement, and barely caught herself in time when Crane turned about.

She was shocked at his appearance. It wasn't his color that alarmed her so much as his eyes. They were extraordinarily bloodshot, and they stared at her without apparent recognition. It was as if he was looking at a stranger.

The Captain shot a quick glance at Johns, then addressed Mary. "Sleep well?"

"What? Oh, yes. Quite well," she lied. "Thank you."

The Scotsman, oblivious to the tension in the room, uncharacteristically broke into good humor, the red splotches on his face increasing in numbers and complexity. "You slept over the whack of that sparker? Ach, you're the best sailor here."

The ship was no longer running with the sea, but taking its punishment head on. In the galley, the cook braced himself against a heavy roll and watched helplessly as the small platoon of eggs on the hot plate, as though in time to a slow ballet, slid first to port, then to starboard, yellow overflowing white until not one yolk remained intact. Looking through the serving hatch, he saw Mrs. Crane smiling at the Second Mate. Angrily he took a large spatula and in one swift moment swept the hot plate clean.

Joe Crane took it as an omen.

20

No one on the *Petrel* had yet seen the second trawler. It wasn't until they were nearing the second station, just over seventy kilometers from the first at latitude 48° 48′ north and longitude 128° 40′ west, that George, on deck to throw the breakfast slops over the stern, spotted her. She was nothing more than a blue smudge on the broken horizon.

Frank, still groggy from being awakened for the second

station, picked up the binoculars and turned them in the direction that George was pointing. All he could make out was a small Canadian flag trembling from a blunt stern.

"Trawler?" the mess boy asked.

"Yeah. I think so."

"Canuck?"

Charlie, resting against the stern winch, wiped a piece of grit from his eye, examined it for a second, then flicked it over the side. "Well, whoever they are they'd hardly be flying an Arab flag, would they, George?"

"Arab?" The mess boy was bewildered.

Frank rubbed the binocular lenses against his khaki sleeve and lifted them again. "Two-hundred-mile limit, George. They'd fly a maple leaf no matter who they were."

George looked down thoughtfully at the sea under the *Petrel*'s stern. Her wake was less turbulent now that she was slowing down for the station. "Must have a name, though? Home-port registration."

Frank could see the other gray trawler, the *Sea Wasp*, a few kilometers to the west, but the new ship lay beyond her, and there was no hope of making out its name. "Maybe it doesn't have one," he said.

Charlie was not looking at the trawlers but at the horizon, ringed with heavy, anvil-topped cumulonimbus. "Shit!"

"What?" said George, alarmed.

"We've got a gale coming."

"Jesus, not another one!" George was happy to be cussing along with two such veterans as Frank and Charlie. He looked at the long line of cloud as if expecting it somehow to announce its intentions.

Frank, still glued to the binoculars, turned eastwards. "George?"

"Yeah?"

"If Crane sees you throwing those slops over the side just before this next station he'll cut your knackers off."

"What? Why?" George couldn't work out how Frank could be watching him and looking through the binoculars at the same time.

"We're just off the northern end of the middle valley here. The good doctor's marked this down as a water sampling station. Any crap you fire overboard can sink and pollute the water that goes into the sample bottles."

"Aw, horseshit! It'll just sink."

Frank was still watching the trawlers, the muscles in his

brown arms moving under the skin as he altered the spacing between the lenses. "Only thing that'll sink to the bottom is that stew you guys make. Everything else'll be saturated. It'll only sink so far, then it'll break up and spread around."

"How come?"

The *Petrel* was slowing now, and Frank began his mental checklist. Charlie was up forward, letting a few feet of 5/32-inch wire down from the block so as to hook up the Niskan five-liter PVC water-sample bottle.

"On station—five minutes," the intercom blared.

"How come?" repeated George.

"What?"

"How come all the slops won't sink?"

"Oh, they might eventually," Frank conceded irritably. "But the density, the thickness of those ocean layers, varies a lot. Differences in salinity, salt content and all that. Some layers haven't intermixed since the time of Christ."

This was beyond George. Deep in thought he turned the cassette recorder down, put the bucket on the deck and made his way toward the passageway between the dry lab and the mess.

The *Petrel's* engines had died even further, and now they were moving carefully over the northern mouth of the twenty-mile north-south middle ridge, jockeying for the exact position Crane had indicated on the chart. It was the valley, lying between the east and west ridges of the Juan de Fuca Ridge system. On the basis of the details of the Shae paper, passed on to him by Dean Thompson, Joe Crane hoped to find evidence of temperature differentials in the middle valley—anomalies which would point to the kind of upwelling that was characteristic of the metal-rich brines. If there were temperature and salinity differences, he would take core and grab samples to assay the mineralogical content of the bottom of the valley's mouth, which spread out northwards into the vast Cascadian abyssal plain.

Frank walked to the forward deck as the winch started to scream. The thin wire ran out fast. A fathom above its weighted end was the orange pinger, and five feet above that, the yellow five-liter Niskan water sampler. As it sank through the surface layers of the middle valley, the pinger's echo was already being monitored by the dry lab's oscilloscope, the small emerald dot moving smoothly across the screen, hiccuping like a heartbeat in a sine wave.

The pulse from the pinger's waterproofed thirty-volt nickel-cadmium battery also made a thin, arching gray line as the styluses raced across beneath the seismic recorder paper, burning into it a permanent record of the water bottle's descent. Frank pushed the timer button on the recorder, checked his watch, and marked the time. Next, he pressed the lab intercom button and asked the Captain for the position. He wrote down: "Cruise—Juan de Fuca Ridge—middle valley/July 7—position latitude 48° 48' north, longitude 128° 40' 10" west, depth 2200. Pinger at 1800 meters." As he waited to see the pinger almost touch bottom, so he could be sure of getting the temperature and salinity sample as close as possible to the seabed, he became aware of someone standing behind him. He glanced over his shoulder, frowning, thinking it was Crane. It was Mary. She smiled at him.

"Good morning again," she said.

Looking at her, he forgot his anger with Joe Crane's paranoia. His eyes simply responded to the presence of a beautiful woman.

"How far to go?" she asked.

"A thousand meters."

"Why don't they use a metal sampling bottle? The plastic looks a little fragile."

"It's tough enough. Anyway, plastic's better. If you use metal bottles you can get metal contamination in the sample."

"You think we'll find anything?"

There was only one crewman in sight, and he was ten yards away on the afterdeck, checking the lashing on the twenty-foot sections of core barreling. "Might find hot springs," said Frank.

"How hot is hot?" They were talking easily now.

"Oh, it can vary quite a bit. Around here bottom temperature would be about two degrees Celsius—almost freezing. But it can go as high as sixteen degrees. It's not so much the temperature, though. It's the variation at any one place. Sometimes a difference of ten percent is all you need to indicate an anomaly. Then again, off the Galapagos Islands the variation is enormous, from freezing to sixty-three degrees Fahrenheit."

Mary nodded.

"You know how it works?" he asked.

"No—not really," she said, laughing. "I've no idea."

He motioned toward the laboratory bench. "I'll show you."

She eased herself slowly off the bulkhead, and Frank could see the fullness of her breasts even beneath the bulky wet gear. As he pressed the timer again, watching the mark appear magically on the paper, she leaned closer against the piled aluminum trunks. He could feel her hair, silky against his cheek. He pulled down a paper towel and drew the line of a valley between two peaks with a felt tip. "The line is the sea bottom, okay?"

"Okay."

He shaded slightly below the line. "This is the crust." He shaded in long strokes beneath that. "This is magma. Very hot stuff. Okay?"

"Hmmmm."

"Okay, so here we have volcanic activity in the earth's magma zone which bursts through the earth's crust due to separation of part of the ocean rift system—in this case the Pacific and Juan de Fuca plates. The lava coming up cools when it hits the cold water, and some of the minerals in the porridge settle out. The cold water comes down from above because it's dense and heavy. When it's heated, chemical changes take place and it becomes more acidic —a brine, if you like—because as it passes through porous rock channels, often hundreds of miles long, in the earth's crust, it absorbs minerals. The water gets hot and carries the minerals up to the sea bottom, where they separate out and fall on the sea floor, or in catchment areas on the newly formed ridges as metalliferous muds. If they aren't disturbed by mudslides, they get thicker and thicker over the years. A rich area ten miles by a half would be a big mine —worth billions."

The *Petrel* took a sharp roll, throwing Mary against the recorder. Frank caught her. "All right?"

"Never better." She brushed away a wisp of hair that had fallen across her lips.

"You didn't get it all," he said, carefully smoothing back a thin, blonde strand. He could hear the soft, insistent swishing of the styluses racing across the paper. "What was I saying . . . ?"

"Something about turbidites."

They both laughed, though Frank didn't remember saying anything about turbidites as such. "Yes. Well, some of the deposits are covered by mudslides—turbidites from the ridges. The deposits high on the ridges aren't as affected by this, so they should be the richest, or anyway the most accessible."

"What do we do if we find a temperature variation?"

"We run an analysis of the sea water that's been collected near the bottom, and look for abnormal readings of Radon two two two and Helium three, which would indicate very deep aquifers—rock channels leading into the magma. Den ve send down the cameras und see vot ve got on the bottom, and den ve core and dredge and grab and get as much sediment and rock as ve can. And den ve see how much of za copper, nickel, lead, manganese, iron and other goodies ve got, and if ve got a lot— den ve have a party."

She giggled. "Am I invited to this party? I thought you couldn't tell anyone." The ship went into a long, slow roll, and she was moving toward him, falling further and further.

She was almost on him when she grabbed the rail. He looked intently at her, and for the first time he noticed that from some angles her blue eyes appeared slate gray. "The Institute tells the government," he began. "COMDEV —the Commission on Mining and Development—like we're supposed to. After all, it's the taxpayers' money we're using."

"And the companies like V.O. that contribute?"

There was something in her tone that put Frank on alert. It seemed strange that for someone who supposedly didn't know beans about what they were after, she'd made specific reference to Vancouver Oceanics—especially as "V.O." Maybe she knew more than he—or anyone else—supposed. He recalled her mention of turbidites. "They'll get their chance to bid, like everybody else," he said coldly. "The government knows who contributed and who didn't. The highest bidder will get a tax break if he's contributed to research. They all know that."

"You're very honest," she said.

The pinger was almost on the bottom. Frank pressed the lab-winch intercom. "One hundred meters to go. Hold her steady for the messenger drop."

"You're very honest," she repeated.

He pressed the timer and glanced at the chart again, frowning. "I'm old-fashioned."

"I *know*," she said, putting her hand on his shoulder. "I like old-fashioned people."

"Do you?" He swiveled back to the lab-winch intercom. "Slow speed. Fifty to go."

"Slow speed—fifty," came the confirmation from Charlie up forward.

Mary Crane moved back a pace. "I mean it," she said.

"Stop winch!"

"Winch stopped."

He could hear the thump over the intercom. The long, slightly curving trace of the pinger line stopped on the paper, even though the styluses kept racing frantically across the record.

"I mean it," she repeated.

"That's nice," he said, looking at the trace and calculating how many minutes it would take to send down the eight-ounce metal messenger that would trip the water bottle closed, trapping the water sample and simultaneously reversing its three Yoshino Keike thermometers so that the mercury columns of two of them would be broken, allowing the temperature recorded at the bottom to remain the same on its upward journey. The third thermometer, having been set upside down to begin with, would record the surface layer on the way up. The reading could then be compared with that of the deeper layers. He heard the forward door of the lab shut behind him.

Mary Crane was gone. Angrily he punched the intercom button again. "Send messenger."

"Messenger in transit. Messenger E.T.A. twelve minutes."

Frank looked at the door. Jesus, he thought, maybe it was just his imagination—maybe she wasn't pumping him for information at all. I'm getting as bad as Crane, he told himself. She was probably just being nice. Hell, that's what he wanted, wasn't it? He'd been dreaming about her last night. But that was why he was vulnerable, and he knew that Mary was all too aware of it.

That was why he couldn't entirely rid himself of the suspicion.

∽ ∽ ∽

While the grenade-sized messenger slithered at two hundred meters per minute down the long arch of hydrographic wire into the constant night of the middle valley, Crane paced the bridge, pausing at the end of each lap to check the sounder. First, he would scowl through the clear-vision window at the darkening anvil tops of the cumulonimbus interlocking like a gigantic fortress about the horizon. Then he would turn and walk out onto the starboard wing, to check that the wire angle wasn't so flat as to slow down the messenger's rate of descent. Then he would return to the sounder and repeat the whole procedure in exactly the same way, lest any variation in routine might bring him bad luck. At one point the helmsman heard him muttering to himself and glanced over at the man on watch.

"We're drifting," the Captain said quietly. "You want us to maintain station with the bow thrusters?"

"Drop a buoy!" instructed Crane, savagely pushing a lock of gray-flecked hair from his eyes. "Water bottle'll be closed soon. Any time now."

"All right."

"Then we'll know," said Crane excitedly. "Got this feeling. We're going to win the fight."

The Captain saw the man on watch grinning.

"See anything, watchman?" he asked pointedly.

"No, sir." The grin disappeared.

Tate stepped back out of Crane's path as the Chief Scientist, robot-like, retraced his steps for the hundredth time that station. "Yes, by God," announced Crane. "We'll beat the bastards!"

The Captain recognized the symptoms easily enough. He'd seen them once before, between Wellington and Suva —a Fijiian mate distraught over some affair with a white woman. The same fixed look in the pupils, as if the rest of the eyes had departed from the body, leaving deep black holes behind.

"Beat who?" asked Tate quietly.

Crane motioned him to the chartroom. Once inside Joe Crane slid the door closed, looked out at the helmsman, then at Tate. "Can I trust you?"

"Of course, Doctor."

Crane swallowed hard. "I'm very worried, you see."

"Yes, well, you've been under a lot of pressure. Happens to all of us at times, you know."

"Exactly! You understand. That's why I trust you.

But . . ." Joe Crane lowered his voice. "They've sent spies."

"Who has?" asked Tate politely, easing the other's claw-like grip on his arm.

"Sorry," said Crane.

"No, that's all right. You've just been under a lot of pressure, that's all."

"Pressure, right. See, that's it. That's exactly it."

"Of course. Ah, who's sent out the spies?"

"I don't know. Trouble is—"

There was a crash as Crane suddenly punched the illuminated lower bar of the chart-room intercom. Tate jumped. He could see that Crane's forehead was now glistening with perspiration.

"Could anybody hear us?" inquired Crane nervously, looking suspiciously at the intercom. "I don't want anybody to hear us."

"No. That's just an operational light. Just shows that it's on. You have to push to speak."

"Point is, you see—"

The watchman tapped on the chart-room window. Joe Crane whirled.

"Coffee?" came the watchman's voice, muted by the glass.

Crane shook his head. Tate, guessing what the man was up to, said yes. The watchman walked away.

"If I know," continued Crane, leaning over the map, "if the Maritime Institute knows, who else knows? The more steps there are, the more leaks." Crane's eyes darted over the chart.

"But you've been after manganese for quite a while."

"I'm after more than that."

"Oh?" For the first time there was a note of resentment in Tate's voice. "I wasn't aware—"

"No offense. No offense. No need to know, you see. In Hawaii captains like you don't even know where they're going until they're well out of port. They have to open sealed envelopes at different latitudes and longitudes."

Tate's face went beet red, and it was only with difficulty that he kept his voice even. "We're not in Hawaii, Doctor. And I would have thought that the captain ought to have been informed before . . ."

Crane's bloodshot eyes flashed to the chronometer and

then to the barometer. "Jesus! We're running out of time."
He looked at the ring of clouds on the horizon. "That
storm's building. What's the forecast?"

The Scottish Mate, having been surreptitiously called by
the watchman, appeared with two mugs of coffee. Sticking out of his back pocket, hidden from Crane's view,
was a two-foot length of two-by-four.

"Let's ask the Mate," said the Captain. Crane slid the
door partway open.

The Scotsman passed a mug of coffee to Tate, returning a minute later with the weather report:

Crane's lips moved quickly, and his face paled.

MARINE FORECAST ISSUED IN VANCOUVER AT 8:00
A.M. JULY 7—SYNOPSIS. WEATHER SHIP (50 N 145
W) REPORTS LOW PRESSURE AREA IN THE EASTERN
PACIFIC IS NOW INTENSIFYING AND MOVING MORE
RAPIDLY. PRESSURES ARE DROPPING ALONG THE
COAST AND WINDS HAVE SHIFTED TO NORTHWESTERLY
AND INCREASED TO SPEEDS SOMEWHAT HIGHER THAN
AT FIRST ANTICIPATED. WINDS OF 40 TO 50 KNOTS
HAVE BEEN REPORTED IN SOME EXPOSED NORTHERN
WATERS ACCOMPANIED BY HEAVIER RAIN AND INCREAS-
ING GUSTINESS. GALE WARNINGS HAVE ACCORDINGLY
BEEN ISSUED FOR SOUTH COASTAL WATERS AND
SMALL CRAFT WARNINGS FOR JUAN DE FUCA, GEORGIA
AND JOHNSTONE STRAITS AS THE FRONTAL SYSTEM
PRECEDING THE LOW MOVES TOWARD OLYMPIC
PENINSULA AND VANCOUVER ISLAND.

"Jesus! Jesus!" said Crane, closing the door. "Winds
forty to fifty. Haven't got much time."

"Time for *what?*" asked Tate, as cautiously as his patience would allow. On shore it would have been relatively
easy. He could simply have called an M.D. and had him
pump 20-cc of Diazepam into Crane. But the *Petrel*
carried no medical doctor and he had to be damned careful. He knew that any act of forced restraint at sea was
ten times more serious in its implications than it ever would
be on shore. As Captain, his authority might be total in
such matters, but when he exercised it he did so alone.
There was no one to share the responsibility—or the fall-
out. Tate wasn't afraid to use such authority, but he knew

that once he took the first step he would most likely have to go all the way and literally tie Crane down. Then there was Crane's wife. In the old days he'd have hit Crane on the head with a cosh and that would have been the end of it. But nowadays it would be a lawsuit for sure. *That* would look good on the record, he thought. Basher Tate.

Crane thrust his finger at the chart. "Got to hurry. We have to hurry."

"What's the rush, Doctor?"

"I need to get it before the winds hit." Crane began to pace back and forth. "If I don't find it quickly, the storm will give the others a chance to catch up. The longer we take, the more time they've got to catch up."

"Who?" asked Tate. "Who'll catch up?"

"Them." Crane pointed through the glass, three points off the starboard bow. Tate saw the dark blobs bobbing up and down in the heavy swells beneath the darkening scud of cloud.

"The *Sea Wasp?*" he asked with surprise. "That's just a trawler out of Vancouver."

"What's it doing here?" snapped Crane.

"Fishing."

"In three thousand meters of water?"

"Well," said Tate, "maybe it's come to fish for tuna off the Heck sea mount. Lots of snapper there, and pomfret."

Crane stabbed at the chart. "We're ninety-four kilometers from the sea mount. And what would they be doing fishing in this weather?"

The Captain was beginning to feel uneasy. There was a disturbing thread of logic in Crane's paranoia. "Well, maybe they've locked on to a deep-sea school. Not to worry. What can they do anyway?" He smiled soothingly.

Crane was staring wildly. "Watch us. And wait. That's what they can do."

"So? As I understand it COMDEV has to have an actual sample of deposits from an area—whatever they are," the Captain said pointedly, "before anyone else can claim it. COMDEV can quickly match it up with the area that the finders claim it comes from. So anyone in competition with you can't just give a position and chuck any old bottom deposit across the counter, can they now?"

"No. But what if they got a sample from us?"

"Now how would they do that, Doctor?"

Crane sat down, exhausted. His face was sallow and drawn. He looked like an old man. "I don't know," he said. "I don't know . . ."

"I think you're worrying about nothing. Besides," Tate put his hand gently on Crane's shoulder, "we haven't found anything yet."

Crane's voice was now so low as to be almost inaudible. "No, but we might. Juan de Fuca Ridge is so similar to the other area." For a second it sounded like the old, cool, rational Joe Crane. Then his voice rose. "We'll just have to work through the storm if it comes, that's all."

"It would be far too dangerous," said Tate. "Winds forty to fifty knots. That's pushing force ten—waves as high as forty feet. Working on deck in that weather, well, it's never been done—not on my ship."

"We'll do it," said Crane.

Before Tate could object further, Crane had torn open the door and was running down the steps to the flight deck on his way to see what clue, if any, the water sample had brought up from the depths of the middle valley.

Tate came out of the chart room. The Scottish Mate looked up, angry new splotches of red on his face. "The bastard's gone mad. Absolutely raving bloody mad!"

Tate nodded slowly, deep in thought. "Next thing he'll be suspecting us. Where's his wife?"

"In her cabin. I thought it best not to bring her up. I—"

"Quite right. That's all we'd need. Her trying to calm him. Did you see him this morning at breakfast? I thought he'd strangle her when she smiled at us."

"Aye," said the Scotsman, "but what do we do?"

Tate could see the watchman and helmsman staring out at the whitecaps dead ahead, hanging on every word. He tugged at his beard and took the Mate to the privacy of the chartroom.

"You're a drinking man, Mr. Redfern?"

"The occasional snort, Captain."

"Right. Now, as officer in charge of medical supplies, you know which crew members take medication. Correct?"

"Yes, sir."

"The cook. He takes chloral hydrate?"

The dour Scotsman actually began to grin. "Yes, sir."

"It's not meant to be amusing. Crane's half off his bloody head. I don't find it amusing. I just want to calm him down and we've no doctor aboard, now have we?"

"No. Sorry, sir."

"All right. It'll be your birthday tonight."

"Ach, I see. Yes, sir. It's my birthday."

"And at dinner we'll have some wine from the officers' mess supply."

"Good idea, sir."

"Not a word to anyone."

"No, captain . . ."

21

While the Niskan bottle passed out of the valley into the translucent regions of the upper layers, the *Sea Wasp* was a mile away from the unknown trawler and closing in. Doyle was watching it through the binoculars. "Can't make out her markings yet. That's weird to begin with."

The Canadian Captain, keeping one calloused hand on the wheel, tried to get an Export A from the top pocket of his coveralls, but ended up pulling the whole packet to the floor.

"That's funny," said Doyle. "Now she looks like she's got a name. But it's still a blur. Could've sworn she had no ID markings before—other than the flag."

The Captain flicked his lighter on and inhaled deeply. "She'd have to have some ID marks in case of a Fisheries 'inside limit' check."

"Didn't know you had any planes," said Jay.

The Captain ignored him. Jay put out his hands for the binoculars, but Doyle handed them to the Captain. Jay, his mouth closed firmly over a stubby pipe and standing apart from the others by the port gunwale, watched impassively, both hands sunk comfortably into a war-time duffel jacket. Every now and then, as unobtrusively as he could, he checked that his toupee was still in place.

Tony, standing by the skiff on the starboard side, broke wind. The Captain turned to him. "Come home and meet Mother sometime."

Tony gave him a finger, but the Captain fixed the binoculars on the other trawler and didn't notice. "No, it's still too far away," he said. "In a calm sea you might be able to make it out, but not in this chuck. Maybe you're getting your balls in a knot over nothing," he said to Doyle. "Ever think he might be fishing? Just because *we're* watching this Crane guy doesn't mean they are."

"They're watching us," said Tony, pulling a fifth of bourbon from his oilskins and taking a swig.

"Oh?" said the Captain. "Spent a lot of time at sea, have you?"

"Listen, Columbus, you don't have to be a fucking mullet head to figure the odds against three buckets being out here at the same time."

"Well, he could still be fishing."

"But he's not, is he? He's doin' the same as us," said Tony.

"Of course he is," said Jay imperiously. "But perhaps we should look as if we're fishing."

Doyle walked over and took the bourbon from Tony. "Christ, it's cold for September."

"Fucking cold, period," said Tony. Doyle felt the Jack Daniels burn his gut. He offered the bottle to the Captain, who wiped the top on his sleeve. Tony looked at him angrily. "We haven't got leprosy, sweetheart."

Doyle kept watching the trawler. It was now less than a quarter of a mile away. He took up the glasses again. "You know, Captain, Jay might be right."

"What do you mean?"

Tony grabbed the bottle back, stuffed it in his pocket, and began marking time to keep his feet warm. Doyle lifted the stiff, cold safety strap of the binoculars from around his neck. "I mean his idea about fishing. We should be pulling in some lines or something. It would look better all round. Especially if one of those Fisheries planes comes in low and starts taking snapshots."

The Captain grunted. "No way. If we have to move fast all of a sudden, we'd be—"

"I'll be a son of a bitch!" bellowed Doyle. The other three men turned toward him as he braced himself against the roll and passed the glasses quickly to the Captain, who took one look.

"Those bastards—"

"You said it," cut in Doyle. "Tony was right."

The pale mole on Jay's cheek began turning red. "What is it?" he demanded, snatching the glasses from the Captain. "What the hell is going on?"

Doyle took hold of a stay, ducking a wave that smashed on the bow, drenching the wheelhouse in spray. "The name on the boat," he said. "It's *Sea Wasp!* The bastards! They've used our name so if there's any trouble we'll take the rap."

Tony ripped open another stick of gum. "If there's any rough stuff . . ." He patted his coat pocket. "We'll take care of them. Right, Mr. Jay?"

Jay sucked heavily on the pipe.

Doyle shook his head. "Not yet. We might be able to get what we want the way we planned. We get the tipoff when Crane finds it, pick up the stuff, head back to Vancouver and file a claim before anyone else."

"So," began Tony, "if you figured it was all going to be so easy, why didn't you and Grandma just come out by yourselves?"

Doyle shrugged nonchalantly, but it was unconvincing. "Honolulu said to bring you. Sea air. Thought it would do you good after all your hard work back east."

"Sea air, shit!" said Tony, who was hating the sea the more it rolled. "You think we're dummies, huh? Honolulu told you to bring us because there might be some knuckles needed. So now you and Grandma need 'em. So let's do it. Let's scare off the competition, go home and get off this pisspot."

Doyle shook his head again. "No, not yet. No point in starting anything."

Tony was chewing vigorously. "We started something the minute we left port, Doyle. Let's do it. Let's do it right now!"

Doyle changed the scale on the Decca to the half-mile radius. The other trawler was close now, riding high then disappearing between the swells that seemed to be getting bigger by the minute, as the wind grew. A gust pushed the needle on the Danforth-White gauge to forty knots. The gale was coming, and soon. "Okay," he said. "We check 'em out. Maybe we scare 'em a little. That'll buy us time. What's your plan—if you've got one?"

Still outside the wheelhouse, Jay pulled his right hand from his pocket and tossed a small, black object over to Tony. The Captain went white. "Jesus Christ, watch—"

But Tony had caught it and held it up in front of the wheelhouse window, laughing at the Captain. "Not to worry, Grandma. The pin's still in."

"Jesus Christ, Doyle! You've got to control those bastards."

Doyle lit a Gitane and inhaled deeply. "Who we going to call in for help? The Mounties?"

The Captain spun the wheel to avoid taking a wave beam on. "So what do we do now?"

Doyle turned away, jabbing his cigarette toward the other trawler. It was now three hundred yards dead ahead. "We circle them. Try to see who they really are."

"They're hardly going to advertise."

"No. But we give them a chance. We tell them to get lost."

"And if they don't?"

Doyle was staring out to sea, watching the blackening sky. "We give them a scare."

22

Disregarding the standing order to wear lifeline and hard hat as well as life jacket when working over the side, Joe Crane stepped out on the small, chain-protected platform that dropped down like a drawbridge from the starboard side of the *Petrel*'s forward deck, and caught hold of the heavy, water-filled Niskan bottle.

Captain Tate looked at the inclinometer—a bad thirty-eight degrees—then glanced through the bottom half of the bridge glass. "Bloody fool'll get washed overboard."

"Save us a lot of trouble," said the Scotsman. The helmsman laughed.

Tate frowned at the suggestion, then pushed the P.A. button. "Scientific party to wear lifelines and safety jackets." He didn't mention the hard hat—that rule was made by some Compensation Board official who'd never worked in force nine.

If Crane heard Tate through the banshee howling of the wind, he gave no indication, but Charlie moved to the rail and took hold of his jacket. Once the bottle was off, Crane made his way precariously to the white plywood bottle rack that was fixed to the bulkhead outside the wet lab, clipped the bottle in place and began marking down the temperatures. Frank opened the bottom valve and let it run for a second, ridding the sample of any contamination caused by the bottle's seal. He then ran the water off into ground-glass-topped flasks and put them into the sectioned box, ready for the titration test that would give them an oxygen reading and the salinometer test that would reveal the salt content of the bottom layer.

Joe Crane's voice was sharp, cracking with strain. "Salinity?"

Frank watched the needle swing over and made the correction from the temperature tables. "Thirty-two point six parts per thousand."

"Damn it!" said Crane.

"What've you got for bottom temperature?" asked Frank.

Crane didn't answer. He scribbled furiously in the log for a minute, smacked a hard hat from the counter and strode outside to the windward side where he stood alone, muttering to himself, as the ship pitched and tossed. Frank reached over and pulled the station log toward him. In the "temperature" column, Crane had scrawled "2° Celsius." Normal deep-sea temperature in these parts. So that was why he had flown off the handle. If it was normal for the whole northeastern part of Juan de Fuca Ridge, from Revere Channel in the northwest of the sector to the Cascadia Plain in the northeast, from Heck sea mount in the southwest and on past the Endeavour Trough to the valley in the southeast, they were finished. It would be all over. Beside the reading, Crane had angrily scribbled, "No abnormal temperature variation. No abnormal salinity. No evidence of geological anomaly."

Frank went out to the starboard side. He stood beside Joe Crane and started to speak, then stopped and went back inside. He stabbed the intercom. "Station Two completed. Proceed to Station Three. Repeat, proceed to Station Three—middle valley, latitude 48° 37′ north, longitude 128° 46′ west. Seventeen kilometers sou'southwest."

"How is he?" asked Charlie, peeling off his canvas work

gloves and stamping his feet for warmth. A seaman was turning the wheel on the lab door, shutting out the rising wind.

"Okay," said Frank. When the seaman had gone and they were alone, Frank took a cloth from the rag box and wiped the spray from his face. "He's going nuts. Bawling his eyes out like a kid."

"Huh. Time he gave it up."

Frank nodded. "I've never seen him this bad before." He tossed the rag into the oily waste bucket. "I don't know. One minute I hate his guts, next minute I feel sorry for him."

"He'll be lucky if he finishes the trip with his marbles."

Frank struggled out of his wet-gear top, loosened the trouser suspenders and stretched. "We'll be lucky if he doesn't make us work in this gale."

"Christ! We can't work in that."

"You tell him."

"Not me. I would have once, but not now."

"That's the trouble. No one can. He's likely to kill some poor bastard for even suggesting we ease up."

"He's likely to kill some bastard if someone *doesn't* suggest it," said Charlie. "You ever tried to handle Big Bess in seas like this?"

"No. She's a bitch when it's calm as a pond."

"Well, it's no pond now, and that's not the half of it." He indicated the wind gauge. "That's force nine already, my friend. Even if the old man wanted to outrun it, it would be touch and go. We're over a hundred and fifty miles from the coast."

Frank slid backward as the *Petrel* turned into the sea, taking a forty-one-degree roll. "Christ almighty! When does this tub capsize?"

"Sixty-seven degrees is maximum."

Frank looked at the bottom topography map. "Who's got the key to the explosives store?"

"Second Officer. Jesus, Crane wouldn't try seismic recording in this blow?" Even as he said it, he knew that Joe Crane would—that he was so desperate he'd try anything.

~ ~ ~

The Pacific was not living up to its name. The edges of the new gale had arrived, tearing at the waves, sending long streaks of white foam stretching down from crest to trough and up to oncoming crests. This gale howled like all the others, but like all others it was unique in form and structure.

Thanks to their size, the trawlers could ride the swells much more comfortably than the *Petrel*. Even so, Andrea Nolan was feeling far from comfortable. There'd been no chance to sleep on the way out from Vancouver, as the *Tench* ploughed into the heavy seas in pursuit of the *Petrel*. Klaus, she thought, would have admire her initiative in switching the name plates as soon as she'd seen the competition's. She knew that if she won out on this one, Klaus would be certain to push her to the top of the pile, which was exactly where she figured she belonged. That was why she'd stayed with it this far, and that was why she'd told herself she'd see it through—no matter what.

She pulled off the oilskin hat, enjoying the feeling of freedom as her auburn hair swung free of restraint. The Captain, a tall man with a neatly clipped Vandyke beard, watched her as she turned toward the stern, observing the crooked wake with the intensity of someone who is never bored. Even in the heavy, overcast light he noted how the pale blue eyes caught the light, revealing small, golden flecks above the ripe-peach cheeks. It was a flash of beauty, almost innocence, that surprised him, in view of what he'd learned about Andrea Nolan in the past eighteen hours.

A wave amidships knocked the *Tench* sharply to port, throwing Andrea against the Captain and he put his arm tightly around her waist, feeling her body give against his. But it was gravity pushing, not Andrea Nolan. She wrenched free from his grasp.

"I haven't time for that," she snapped. "Not now. If you have to grope, play with the wheel."

"I was just—"

"You were just groping. This is business, Captain. I want it kept that way."

"You're the boss."

"That's right." The innocence had fled. She looked steadily over the bow, at the great hills of water rolling toward them from the inky horizon, and at the other trawler bearing down on them. "They can send men to the moon, but they can't tell just what the weather will do," she said after a while.

"No, ma'am," said the Captain. His tone was apprehensive, but Andrea couldn't detect it above the roar of static filling the tiny cabin, the creaking of stowed gear, and the constant crying of the wind. In a lull she could hear Henry, the deckhand, below, restacking a cutlery drawer that had been flung from its cabinet. The approaching trawler was not much bigger than theirs. There were men standing in her bow.

"They're too close for such unpredictable seas," said the Captain. They were barely two hundred yards off, and closing. "What the fuck are they doing? Excuse me, ma'am," said the Captain, his frosty Vandyke darting up and down as he spoke.

Andrea Nolan had never seen Jay and Tony before, but there was something about the way they stood—too rigid for sailors, clinging to the gunwale for safety yet unafraid —that told her that this was the competition she'd expected, and perhaps more besides. She had no illusions as to what they were doing. They were playing the same game she was—spying on the *Petrel*. But something told her that these men bearing down on her and her two companions would make their own rules, if there were any rules. As Klaus had said, there were no holds barred.

With some difficulty she had gotten a radio message through to Vancouver Oceanics, who in turn passed it on to Klaus. It sounded innocent enough but, decoded, it informed him that Swiss-Rhine Petrochemical had opposition present in the trawler *Sea Wasp*. It took Klaus and his sources just seven hours to find out that he was up against Miel—or North American Oceanics.

Andrea glanced nervously at the Captain. "Don't let them get too close," she said, zipping up her down-lined parka against a sudden draft as they turned into the wind. But it wasn't the wind that made her shiver so much as the cold, gnawing feeling inside. Up till now she'd been so busy planning the operation that she hadn't really understood what "no holds barred" might mean. Now she was afraid she'd find out.

The Captain spun the wheel five points to port, putting his boat's nose up the incline of a massive thirty-foot wave that lifted them softly toward the leaden sky before dumping them hard into the yawn of an oncoming trough. "How am I supposed to keep my distance from a boat as powerful as that? In this weather?"

"Never mind the weather," said Andrea. "Do it." A sheet of spray blinded the wheelhouse windows. As it cleared, she could still see the two immovable oilskin-clad figures standing at the other boat's bow, falling and rising like wooden figureheads in the storm.

～ ～ ～

As the *Petrel* approached Station Three in the middle valley, she was smashing through waves forty feet high. The spidery lines of foam had become torrents that criss-crossed the gray sea like white lava. The wind made normal conversation all but impossible on deck, and the routine lowering of the Niskan bottle and pinger had become a brave man's task, as the research ship tilted through forty-five-degree rolls that tore well-lashed equipment loose, flinging hundred-pound coring weights tumbling across the well deck like cannonballs. Frank was used to big seas, but these waves were the worst he'd seen. It wasn't just their size that was so awesome but their power. With each wave the eighty-yard ship would slip from her seemingly invulnerable perch atop a mountain of water into deep, racing ravines walled by thousands of tons of water towering high above, tearing past in great gray-foaming cliffs. His hair plastered flat to his head, his face stinging from the constant onslaught of spray, Frank stood in the forward lab door contemplating the job ahead. He knew that once the ship stopped, she would turn head to wind and that would be a change for the better. But still it would be damned dangerous. Crane's voice crackled through the intercom. "Nearing station. Prepare to lower pinger and bottle."

Charlie stood by the sink in the lab, pretending to put on his gloves. He was waiting for Frank's decision. As they neared position, the rolling grew worse and several waves smashed beam on. Charlie lit a new cigarette from a stub and nervously started scratching his tattoo. He knew that with the two-way intercom open he could be heard on the bridge, but he said it anyway. "You're crazy if you go out there, Frank."

"I've got a lifeline."

"Maybe, but if you go out in that lot you've got no bloody brains."

"Station—one mile," bellowed Crane from the bridge.

"We've come this far," said Frank.

"Famous last words."

Frank pointed to the intercom box. Charlie shoved two
fingers up toward it. "Why isn't Crane down here?"

The bosun's words threw the bridge into tense silence.
Mary Crane pretended not to have heard. Tate kept his
eyes on the radar, while the helmsman watched the bearing above the clear-view window and the watchman looked
fixedly through the glasses at a solid sheet of spray. Crane
thumped the chart desk. "I'm Chief Scientist!" he shouted,
as if that automatically excused him from working on deck.

"Quite," said Captain Tate. "Two degrees starboard,
helm."

"Two degrees starboard, sir."

The Captain pulled the engine-room telegraph back to
"slow ahead," and the ship's props dropped to fifty rpm.
"Could we check that position again, Doctor?" He walked
toward the chartroom door, Crane following.

Inside, the Captain spoke calmly: "Might be just as well
to pass this one up, Doctor. We're in for quite a blow. We
can weather it all right—I think—but to work on deck is
pushing our luck." Tate was careful to give emphasis to
"our," to save Crane's pride from further bruising. Tate
tapped the position on the chart. "Now I checked the
Annual Mariners' Report last night, and over here . . ."
his finger slid a little to the northwest, ". . . there've been
reports of rips. Only reports, mind, but in this weather . . ."

Crane seemed to be looking through the map rather
than at it. Tate pressed his lie. "It is possible, isn't it, Doctor? After all . . ."

Crane nodded. His voice was almost a whisper. "It's
possible," he said.

"Yes, well, there we are. In this chuck," his arm indicated the massive seas all around them, "you couldn't
possibly see a rip surf. Whole sea is surf."

Crane nodded again, still looking through the map to
the brightly lit frosted glass beneath. Again his voice was
barely audible. "Also possible that the bottom contains
what I'm looking for. If I don't find it now, I'll never be
given another chance." He spoke very deliberately and
very slowly, and Tate could feel the tension building, ready
to explode. "The very presence of such adversity confirms
my belief, Captain. Adversity is the sign of impending discovery. Adversity is nature's way of doing away with the

timid." He slammed his fist down on the chart table. The glass splintered and sliced through the center of the chart. Mary Crane and the watchman ran for the chartroom, but both were thrown hard into the bulkhead as the *Petrel* leaned twenty-nine degrees in only three seconds.

"Don't you see?" yelled Crane. "The storm is sent to try us. It is a test. If I surrender now, if I bend, if I run for home like you all want me to—run like a frightened hare . . ."

The color rose in the Captain's face, but he checked himself and steadied his body against the next roll.

"If I run," continued Crane, "run like a coward, I'll never know. I just can't . . ." Mary entered the chartroom and took his arm. Crane shoved her away. "I'm all right. I'm all right." As suddenly as he'd exploded he was calm again. The ship shook violently under the ceaseless charging of the sea. "I'm quite all right," said Crane quietly. "Quite all right."

Tate was equally as calm—and determined. "Doctor, you're senior scientist and I'm senior officer, but it's my ship and if I say we don't sample, we don't sample. I've been as patient with you as I can . . ."

Crane smiled maliciously. "Run for port if you like, Captain! I won't say a word. No one'll ever know from me that you ran." With that Crane left.

Tate's face turned crimson and he stomped to the starboard side of the bridge. Mary Crane followed him. His head darted in the direction of the tinkling broken glass of the chart table, the pieces sliding about with each new roll. "Get that mess cleaned up," he called to the watchman.

"Yes, sir." The watchman made for the chartroom, hanging onto the radar set's grips for support.

"No!" shouted Tate. "Not you, you fool. You're on watch, man. Ring for your relief."

"Aye, aye, sir." As the watchman lifted the phone and rang crew's quarters, Mary Crane, holding onto the waist-high bar that hugged the curve of the bridge, began talking to the Captain. "He's—he's not himself. He's—"

Tate turned on her. "I should bloody well hope not, madam! By the living Jesus I've not had a man accuse me of cowardice in all my days."

"But he was only—"

"What he was doing, Madam, was impugning my reputation. He'd have it on my record—explicitly or not—that I, that I was afraid of—"

"But he's upset. He's—"

"He's mad, madam! That's what it is. By God, I wish I had a doctor aboard."

The wind almost drowned Mary's outburst. "He is *not* mad!"

"Near enough to make no difference," retorted Tate.

"Then why are you so worried about what he said? *Are* you afraid?" Mary shouted.

"Madam! Leave the bridge!"

"If he's mad, why are you so afraid?" A wave, riding on another, broke over the bow, smashing itself to pieces in a solid sheet of spray that shot up from the anchor and windlass guard and covered the bridge. Mary shouted her question again. "If he's mad, why are you so afraid? *Captain?*"

Tate turned to face her. His tone was cold as ice. "Because, madam, a rumor at sea is no different from a rumor ashore. It can ruin a man's career. The source of the rumor, sane or not, is never questioned. Is it?"

Before she could answer, Tate turned sharply, into the chartroom and closed the door. As she left the bridge Mary Crane began to cry, the sobs wrenching at her throat as her anger at having to defend her husband mixed with anger at herself for having impulsively humiliated Tate, whom she respected.

Tate carefully taped the split chart, gently ran the Gerber variable rule across it and drew his line. After checking their position, he stepped out and shifted the rev handle from 50 to 30. The frantic thumping of the great pistons immediately slowed. Tate bent toward the bridge-forward lab intercom. "On station. Stand by to lower gear."

In the wet lab Frank stamped his feet into the heavy-duty boots.

"You're a fool," said Charlie. "A damn fool."

"What—for doing my job?"

"For working for him."

"Come on, Bosun. On deck."

The depth was 2.3 kilometers. Frank watched a cliff of foam-dappled water slide by. No other man would make him work in this. It was insane. "I want twice as much wire as normal. Forty-six hundred meters."

One moment Charlie was bent over, trudging uphill toward the winch like an old man, the next he was fighting against slipping downhill into the winch, so violent was the ship's pitch. And the rate of shift from starboard to port was so fast that the flume tanks were rendered all but useless. On each big roll the overflow vents spewed gallons of diesel ballast out onto the deck, greasing it until it was as slippery as ice. Charlie used the long handbrake on the winch as a safety hold while he eased out enough slack to allow them to clip on the bottle, but not enough to let the wind whip it horizontal.

∽ ∽ ∽

"I've never been so humiliated in all my life!" she said. "What are you doing, Joe?"

Crane punched the timer button, then sharply demanded latitude and longitude from the bridge. Knowing they'd hear her on the open line, Mary stayed silent, barely controlling herself, clinging to the stanchion that passed up through the middle of the after lab like a giant spear. After Crane took his eye from the intercom, she pushed the button to "off." "They aren't scared," she said. "You are. It's you that's scared, but you—you shamed him. I know how upset you are, Joe. I understand it. But you shouldn't have—"

"*I'm* scared!" Crane screamed at her. "If it weren't for me this Goddamned ship would be high-tailing it for Vancouver—for Ucluelet—for the first Goddamn harbor on the west coast. *I'm* scared! Jesus Christ!"

Mary tried to speak, but no sound came. Her throat was dry and she hadn't stopped crying. She swallowed hard. "You know what I mean. You're afraid to be out there with them. On deck."

"On station!" came Tate's voice over the P.A. "Lower when ready."

The winch started up, its whine all but inaudible against the wind.

"I'm Chief Scientist. My responsibility's here in the lab. Frank's my technician. That's what I pay him for. I can't do everything."

"No one expects you to, Joe. But . . . Joe, you'll help yourself if you go out there and help—"

"And help *him!*" Crane swung away from the recorder. "Isn't that what you mean? That's all you're concerned about—and help your nice, stiff-cocked boyfriend, eh? That's what you mean, isn't it?" His arm swept the counter clean of marking pens, pencils and erasers. "You don't give a damn about me. About me, Tate, or anyone else, you pious little bitch. You just want that dirty bastard safe and fucking sound, don't you?" She backed toward the door as he advanced on her. "He could get washed overboard," he said, smiling.

The lab to lab intercom hummed. It was Frank's voice. "Ready to lower when you are."

Crane hit the "talk" button and screamed, "Then lower it!"

When he turned around Crane saw that only the mess boy was standing there. The cassette player was moaning a blues number. "Would you like some tea, Doctor? We've got the kettle on." Crane stared at him for a moment, as if suddenly realizing where he was. "Tea? Yes," he said quietly. "I'd love some."

He leaned against the sounder, watching the thin, gray trace of the descending water bottle. Beside him, the oscilloscope pulse hiccuped softly on the calm green background.

"Sugar and milk, Doctor?"

There was no answer.

∽ ∽ ∽

In their cabin Mary Crane was shaking. She locked the door, afraid to venture out until the station was over. There was a sharp knock. She could feel her heart thumping. "Who is it?"

"Steward, ma'am. Will you be wanting lunch?" Silence. "I could bring it to you if you're feeling a bit under the weather?"

"No. No, I'm not hungry. Thank you. I won't be down." But as soon as she was left alone with the raging of the storm, distraught at what had just passed between her and Joe, and hating herself for having hurt Tate when she knew he was right in wanting to turn back, she longed for company. Though she tried not to, she thought of Frank. She got up from the bunk and watched him through the forward porthole, wondering whether they would find anything in the middle valley—and wondering what she would do if they did. She turned slowly and looked at the

Cricci purse by the lower bunk. Inside it Nielsen's message—what he'd called her "back-up"—was safe. She looked out again. Frank was bending dangerously out from the wildly swooping platform. Clutching the wing nut on the porthole, she turned it tighter and tighter.

~ ~ ~

When she could see that the Niskan bottle was down, Mary Crane's finger hovered nervously above the cabin-lab intercom for a second, then she pressed down, hard.

Five minutes later she left the Chief Scientist's cabin and made her way carefully but quickly down to the lower deck.

Frank's cabin smelled of men. Away from the natural light, the air conditioning below didn't make up for the fresh-air ventilation of the cabin above. But she didn't mind. In fact, even in her despair over Joe—perhaps because of it—she found the smell peculiarly exciting.

Without thinking she instinctively put her arms out to Frank as he entered. Holding her, he could feel her body still trembling from her most recent fight with Joe.

"I had to see you," she said, her voice tremulous with fatigue and fear. "I—I had to talk to someone. Frank I—I wasn't trying to get information out of you before. I only wanted to . . ."

He lowered her gently to the bunk's edge, then took off his oilskin. "Where's Joe?"

"In the lab." She almost stammered. "He—he might go back to our cabin. That's why I came down. I—I was so afraid. I'm so afraid of what's happening to him, Frank. I . . ."

Frank took her hands in his, cupping them tightly. Gradually she relaxed, as if the storm outside had somehow been abated merely by Frank's presence.

"Now look," he comforted her. "I know there's no point in saying, 'Don't worry.' You've got something to worry about. But as long as he doesn't get violent, I think it's best to just hang on, not only you but all of us."

"I'm terrified," she said softly, "for Joe. I'm so afraid all this has pushed him too far—too far to come back."

"Is this what you meant? I mean is this what it's been like at home for you?"

She nodded and looked forlornly into the middle distance of the tiny cabin. "Oh, at first it was only little things, petty arguments, forgetting names of close friends, petty suspicions and then bigger suspicions. Always there were suspicions. And some of them even made sense. Thompson was out to get him, he said."

"Which he is," said Frank.

"That was only the beginning." She fell silent for a moment, and all they could hear was the raging of the storm. Finally, she turned pleadingly to him. "What do you think the Captain will do if . . . ?"

"If nothing," said Frank firmly, putting his arms about her, drawing her toward him. She felt warm like a child and he could have kissed her tenderly, passionately. But not now, not when she was pouring out her anguish. Not now, when she'd come to him for understanding, for the sharing of her troubles. If he kissed her, she would know it was more from pity than from love, and in the future she'd remember it. No. When he made love to her—if he was to make love to her—it would be uncamouflaged, uninhibited and unashamed. It would either be that way or not at all. It would be on equal terms or it wouldn't be.

～ ～ ～

The growing winds had finally driven Jay and Tony into the already cramped wheelhouse of the trawler, where they stood stomping their cold feet and lacing their coffee with Jim Beam.

"You always put turds in your coffee?" Tony asked the Captain.

"Fuck you," said the Captain.

Tony flipped the lapel of the fat man's coveralls. "Thought you had your master's ticket?"

The Captain glared at him. "I do."

"Then why can't you get any closer and ram that bastard, huh? We were right on his ass. It's cold out there, huh, Mr. Jay?"

"Freezing."

"I told him to hold off," said Doyle.

Tony sneered. "But we settled that, sweetheart. Didn't we? Thought we were going to get rid of the competition while we could still see 'em."

Doyle looked apprehensively at Jay but the Englishman gave no indication that he was even listening—let alone interested in taking sides. He merely puffed his pipe, his eyes fixed on the other trawler and his hands still stuffed deeply, squire-like, in his jacket. He was waiting.

"Plan's changed," said Doyle. "This weather's getting worse."

"No kidding," said Tony, holding out his hand for the bottle.

"Well, I've been thinking. Why not let the competition do the hard work for us?"

"So?" Tony sniffed loudly and went to spit out of the windward side.

"Other side," grunted the Captain disgustedly. "Jesus Christ!"

Tony shuffled past, spat, and looked back at Doyle. "So, Einstein, what's going on?"

"Well, look. The competition have had more time to get things squared away. If we'd gotten the information from the east quicker," he said, looking pointedly at Jay, "they wouldn't have had the edge. But we didn't and they did— so there's nothing we can do about it. But why not let them get it for us, then intercept? If things don't work out we can always fall back on the S.O.S. plan."

Tony said nothing, and tossed the empty bourbon bottle out to windward. They heard it crash on the deck.

"Brilliant," said the Captain.

"Shut your face, motherfucker."

Jay knocked out the sodden remains of tobacco against his shoe. "How do we know what they'll do?"

Doyle could see that at least he was making sense to someone. "It's an even bet that our friends in the other trawler have a contact on the *Petrel*."

Jay unconsciously rubbed his head where Moody had bashed him and grimaced in pain. "So they've got a plan too," he said. "Why not get rid of them? Then we've only one plan to worry about. Ours. Too many cooks spoil the broth. Correct?"

"Look, what I'm saying is if our friends over here . . ." Doyle jerked a thumb at the bobbing masthead of the other trawler half a mile off the port bow, "are frightened off, we could lose a free chance. Who wants to pass up a free-bee?"

Tony broke the seal on the second fifth. "What you think, Mr. Jay?"

The Englishman stuffed his pipe with studious detachment. "How d'you know their contact will signal? *If* they have a contact."

"Smoke signals," said the Captain. No one thought it was funny.

Doyle shrugged his shoulders, tapping out another Gitane. "Probably a lamp," he said. "They had time to work out something more detailed than we did. Their home base is Vancouver. Honolulu had to organize whatever it could in a shorter time. That's the guts of it."

Jay grunted. Doyle could tell that the Englishman didn't like the way he kept rubbing in the fact that they'd lost valuable time because they'd let Moody slip away at the Beaverbrook. Jay sucked heavily on the short stem, the glow turning his face even redder. "So how are they going to know any better than we are? How are they going to pick up the sample?"

"Ring Room Service," said Tony, laughing.

Doyle's face clouded over. "Haven't figured that out. Their contact on the *Petrel* won't want to show his hand too early."

The Captain held the wheel tightly as a wave slapped them hard aport, throwing Tony into the corner. "Well, I can tell you one thing—that research ship sure as hell knows neither of us are fishing in this weather."

"That's why we have to be careful," said Doyle. The Captain nodded, spinning the wheel back to starboard. "One thing you haven't thought about."

"What?"

"Maybe that other trawler, maybe they're waiting for our contact to make the move. Maybe they're waiting *us* out?"

Doyle exhaled heavily. "Could be. But I'm betting against it. It's more their territory. They've had more time."

"Maybe they haven't had more time," said Tony defensively, finally getting Doyle's point. "That's a mighty big bet you're making. If you're wrong, Miel'll break your legs. Or worse."

At the mention of Miel's name Doyle swung around angrily. Jay could see that it was really fear; he smiled.

"Shit!" said Doyle. "I don't know. Give me a drink. I'm not a Goddamn prophet."

"So?" said Jay. "What you want us to do, old man? Have a nervous breakdown?"

The trawler took another wave beam on and the bottle fell, smashing against the deck.

23

"Nothing," yelled Frank, trying to make himself heard over the noise of wind and sea. "Not a thing. Temperature normal. Salinity normal. No anomaly."

As Crane's voice came through from the dry lab, Frank steadied himself against the wet lab's hand bar, trying to find a grip amidst the web of lashing rope that held down the equipment.

Suddenly the *Petrel* fell to starboard, driving up a sheet of water two hundred feet long that fell back over the ship's superstructure and filled Frank's boots, leaving him standing in two feet of water. "Jesus Christ! Yes," he shouted back at Crane, "I double double-checked. We struck out. Nothing. Zero. Zip."

Crane started to speak but Frank cut in. "You can run the test yourself if you like." The intercom went silent.

Charlie came in from the deck, cupping his hands around his cigarette. "What's the story?"

Frank shrugged. Crane was talking again, but a sixty-knot gust flung the hatch of the side door away from its holding hook, slamming it into the bulkhead. Inside the lab it sounded like a gunshot. "Didn't hear you, Doctor," said Frank.

"Bring the bottles into the lab out of the weather."

"Roger. We headed home now?"

"Bring the bottles into the lab, Goddamn it!"

"Would Dr. Crane please come to the bridge? Would Dr. Crane . . ." Frank switched off the intercom. "There'll be shit to pay now, brother," he said to Charlie, who was lashing the door back, bending against the fresh onslaught of wind.

Charlie heard Frank but didn't answer. Instead he beckoned him over and pointed out to sea. "Those two are still out there."

Frank tried to speak, only to find his breath snatched away in the wind's slipstream. He turned in toward the shelter of the lab. "Ah, don't worry about them. Probably sticking close by for safety in the storm. I would."

"Would you?"

Frank looked at Charlie, wondering if it was a double-edged question. "Yeah," he said defensively. "I would."

〜 〜 〜

On the bridge Tate's left hand tugged at his beard as his right alternately tapped the rev lever and the engine room telegraph. Finally Crane, his eyes as wild as they had been earlier that morning, clumped up the last few stairs from the deck below. Tate glanced at the chronometer. It was eleven thirty.

"The center of this storm is only eighteen hours away," he said, pointing at the chart. "We're now a hundred and seventy miles west of Cape Flattery. At half speed, ten knots, which is the maximum we can safely do in these seas, our best time to make shelter in Neah Bay is seventeen hours." Tate shoved the latest forecast at Crane. "So, Doctor. Now that we've all proven how tough we are—and found *nothing*—we must go in before we're in force ten or worse. The weather boys are calling for force twelve plus, at the center of the storm. And in case you didn't know, that's called a hurricane."

But Crane wasn't listening. He was watching a brown albatross, momentarily suspended in mid-air above the ship, serenely riding the hot air stream of the funnel above the turmoil of the boiling sea below. Beyond the albatross he could see one of the trawlers dipping out of view one second and reappearing the next, suspended high on the crest of a wave like a toy. He could hear Tate talking, but something about the albatross commanded all his attention. He was transfixed by it. Finally the Captain's voice came through: "Doctor?"

"Uh, yes, what?"

"Are you finished on this station?"

"Yes."

"Good. Then we can head back."

"No! We go to Station Four." Crane handed him a

piece of paper. It read: "Lat 48° 35.8′ N, Long 129° 00′ W." The position was further west.

"Doctor, I've had just about all . . ."

The spell of the albatross was shattered and Crane's voice was shrill. "Get a hold of yourself, man. Take a hold. You're too old, eh? Is that it? No more lead in the pencil, eh?" His arm thrust out at the horizon. "What's that, then, eh? Two other ships. Are they running for home?" He turned to the helmsman and the other man on duty. "Well, Lookout? Are they running in?"

"Ah—no, sir," said the lookout nervously.

Crane swung toward Tate and pushed the "general address" button. He could now be heard all over the ship. "No, sir. You hear?" he yelled. "No, sir! *They* are not running away, Captain. They're not running."

Tate, now humiliated before his crew and aware at the same time that Crane had gone berserk, stood immobile for a moment. All he could think to do was to flick the "general address" button to "off." Before he could find words, Crane snapped, "How far away is this hurricane?"

Tate glared at him. "Eighteen hours."

Crane snatched up the weather report. "You said maximum speed ten knots. But the wind's behind us—that's a hundred and eighty miles in eighteen hours. We're only a hundred and seventy out. Got an hour to play with, even if your weather pals are right. Let's move on to the next station."

"Under no . . ." began Tate, but Crane had pushed the "general address" button again, holding his finger up at Tate like a scolding schoolmaster, as though to say, "Naughty, naughty!" With a wild-eyed stare he called, "Next station, last station. What do you say?" His voice echoed throughout the ship: "Next station, last station . . ."

Tate, his hands shaking with fury, shut off the address system again. "All right, Doctor." His voice was a hoarse whisper. "Done."

Crane smiled. "Great!" He glanced up at the chronometer. "Join me for lunch?"

The Captain's voice was almost inaudible. "Shortly, Doctor."

"Good." And with that, Crane turned, steadied himself on the radar console, and left the bridge.

Immediately he was gone Tate picked up the phone and called the Scottish Mate. When Redfern appeared, his usually florid face tired and haggard from the storm, Tate got right to the point. "Did you hear that—that exchange?"

"Yes, sir."

"Bloody bastard would make me out a coward because those stupid bloody fishermen don't know any better. They'll run for it soon enough. You'll see."

"Aye, sir, I'd bet on that."

"Yes, well . . . Damn it!" said Tate, almost losing his balance on a roll. "I won't be bludgeoned by that lunatic into risking this ship and its crew."

"No, sir."

Tate motioned the Mate into the chartroom. As the door shut, he slid the 3001 chart slowly toward him. "Is the wine to be served at lunch?"

"Yes, sir."

"You have the material?"

The Mate glanced out through the chartroom glass. The lookout was watching one of the trawlers through the binoculars, and the helmsman was busy trying to keep the *Petrel* headed into the wind until he received the next order. Redfern dug into his pocket, and produced three orange-red capsules the size of jelly beans. "One and a half grams."

The Captain grunted, smoothing his beard and toying with the chart, not looking directly at the capsules.

"Is that enough?"

"Aye."

"For how long?"

"Six hours. It's a bitter taste, so I'm using a Chianti. Could give him more, but it can affect his blood pressure."

Tate kept fidgeting with the chart, still not looking at the capsules. "No risk of—I mean . . ." He toyed with the variable rule.

"Ach, no, sir. He'll just have a terrific bloody hangover. That's all."

Tate lifted a pair of dividers and let them fall. "Christ, I hate this farting around." He looked up at the Scotsman. "But what else can I do? I can't thump him, can I? We'd have a bloody lawsuit on our hands. His wife can't control him. No telling what he'll do next."

"No, sir."

"Meanwhile he's undermining my authority. He'd happily make us the laughingstock of the west fleet." He picked up the dividers again. "As I said before, you only need one charge of cowardice against you in this business —official or unofficial—and that's that."

"I know, sir. I remember that chap on the *Merlyn* in '79. He—"

"Exactly!" Tate hesitated for a second. "Crane's just gone down to wash up before lunch." He paused again, then said awkwardly, "You used to go in for amateur theatricals, didn't you?"

"Aye, sir. The Clydeside Players, sir."

"Right," said Tate, drumming his fingers on the chart. "Well, give a good performance."

"Not to worry, sir." The Mate slid the door open.

"And Jock?"

"Sir?"

"Mum's the word."

"Of course, sir."

As the Mate left the bridge Tate's throat constricted with disgust. It was an unmanly thing to do. It was petty and cheap, because no matter how necessary such action was to safeguard the ship and crew, he knew that in part it was to protect his own pride from further assault by Crane's deranged brain. And in arranging this charade aboard his own ship, he realized, he'd lost some of the very authority he was seeking to preserve.

∽ ∽ ∽

George had been complaining all morning. Despite its air conditioning, the ship had been invaded by cold drafts of air through the open door of the lab during the last station, making it twice as cold as normal down in the six by eight by four-foot lockers where the wine for the wardroom was kept. What's more, heavy seas made it impossible to bring up more than two bottles at a time. But as he carried up the last two bottles to the wardroom, the Captain turned the *Petrel* to run with the sea during the meal. Soon, in the relative calm, it was possible for George to help set out cups and saucers on the starched linen tablecloth, dampened for extra friction in rough weather. Even so, he was still complaining. "The Mate must be crazy, celebrating a birthday in this weather."

The senior wardroom steward set out the celery sticks,

raw carrot slices, dill pickles and pickled yellow cauli-
flower that was traditional fare aboard the naval auxiliary
vessels. "Yours not to reason why, George. Yours—"

"To do or die—yeah, I know. Keep the lads' spirits up
by getting them all pissed. That way they won't know
there's a storm on—not bloody likely."

The senior steward wiped the neck of the HP sauce
bottle. "Second steward's down sick, so I want you to help
me pour, okay?"

George looked frightened. "Gee, I don't know anything
about what side you stand on and all that."

A voice came from behind them. "I'll pour, seeing it's
such a crazy idea to celebrate your own birthday." George
and the senior steward spun around. They hadn't seen the
Scottish Mate quietly sitting behind the latticed partition,
which separated the wardroom from the small lounge
area. Blushing, George began to apologize. "Ah, sorry,
sir, I—"

"Ach, it's all right, lad. You're probably right. It's
daft, I know, but variety is the spice of life, and all that."

"Yes, sir."

The senior steward spotted a fork with a piece of en-
crusted egg still on its prong. He scooped the fork up,
scowling. "I'll still need you to clean up when you're
through with the crew's mess, George. And turn down
that bloody tape."

"Okay," said George easily, glad to be rid of wine
steward duties.

The Scottish Mate took the bottle of Chianti. Tearing
off the plastic seal, he started in with the corkscrew.
"Where's the Doctor sit for lunch, steward?"

The steward pointed to a catsup-stained napkin on the
port side of the second of three tables. "He could do
with a bit of good cheer, Mate."

The Scotsman nodded noncommittally. "Aye. Could use
a wee drop myself. Think I'll have a dram before soup.
I'm not on till four."

He took his glass of wine back into the lounge, set it
between his knees and reached into his pocket for the
small vial, half-full with the contents of the broken capsules. The wardroom door began to open. He quickly put
the vial back into his pocket just as the second engineer
appeared. "Hello, hello. Boozing before lunch? Lost the
bloody Empire doing that, didn't you, eh?"

The Mate smiled. "True enough, true enough. How's Diesel Valley?"

The second engineer was pulling out his chair. The Mate could just see him through the lattice partition.

"I'm telling you, Scottie, there're a few whey-faces doon there, and tha's a fact."

By now the Mate had poured the contents of the vial into the goblet. He walked to the first table and casually rearranged the napkins so that he would be sitting opposite Crane, ready for the switch.

Ten minutes later, after most of the officers had arrived and the meal was in full progress, the Captain rang down from the bridge asking for the Second Mate.

"Yes, sir?"

Tate's voice was low. "When do you want me to call him to the phone?"

"The steward's just pouring the wine now, sir. I'll keep some for you," he said, so that everyone could hear.

The weather-beaten face of the first engineer looked up from the far table. "Tell him it's horse piss anyway." There was raucous laughter.

"I'll call him in five minutes," the Captain said.

"Roger, Captain."

When Crane was called to the phone a short time later, the Mate, to the astonishment of the second engineer and the radio officer, pulled the switch—his glass for Crane's. With schoolboy embarrassment he winked awkwardly at the two officers. The second engineer smiled. The radio officer didn't—birthday or not, he didn't think it was funny.

"Cheers," said the engineer.

Several others, including the Scottish Mate, raised their goblets. Crane never even heard them as he returned to the table. He was watching a low-gliding albatross slip past the porthole and out to sea, where it now swept with consummate grace over the valleys and ridges of the gray-white ocean. "How do you like the wine, Doctor?" asked the second engineer.

Crane looked up. "What?"

"The wine. What do you think of it?"

"Huh—never drink red wine. Too many histamines. Must stay alert." He looked out at the albatross again. "Must stay alert."

The radio man smiled smugly at the Second Mate. The

Mate scowled, gulping the remainder of his wine and excusing himself before anyone had a chance to begin any "For he's a jolly good fellow" nonsense. He went and told the Captain what had happened. Redfern was still irritated with the radio officer. "There's something I don't trust about . . ." he began, then checked himself. The last thing the old man needed was bad blood among his officers.

"You don't trust who?" asked Tate.

"Nothing, sir."

By the time they'd changed course after the meal, heading for the last station, the plates had begun to slide and one wineglass had already fallen over, splattering Chianti on the wardroom carpet and all over the senior steward's newly laundered jacket. "What a fucking mess," he yelled, racing to clean up before the ship completed the turn. "George! Get in here quickly."

When George arrived, his long, stained apron in stark contrast to the immaculate tablecloths of the wardroom, the steward directed him to the goblets. "Wine off first—hurry up."

The steward collected four goblets, put them in the empty sink between the wardroom and crew's mess, then reached for Crane's. It was still full. He drank it in one gulp, picked up the Second Mate's empty glass, and turned toward the pantry.

Twelve minutes later he began to weave badly toward the second table.

"Stop fartin' around," said George. "Give us . . ." George caught him just as the pile of plates slid from his hands and crashed in a heap by the cutlery sideboard.

∽ ∽ ∽

"Like a light!" said George, half-frightened, half-excited. "Out like a fucking light, Mate," he said, and hung up the receiver.

When the Captain heard about it, he was in his cabin telling the radioman and second engineer, with acute embarrassment, about the Mickey Finn. When the two officers left the cabin, sworn to silence, he rang Crane and asked him to come to the bridge. They were less than ten kilometers from what they had agreed would be the last station, but the Captain believed he knew how the Mickey Finn could still be used to advantage.

A few moments later Crane appeared, nursing an

oceanographic text. "Yes? What now?" he asked irritably.

"Doctor, we have a seriously ill man aboard. He just collapsed in the wardroom. Last station is canceled. We have to get him ashore as quickly as possible. Any objections?"

Crane was watching the albatross again. Two more had now joined the first, floating serenely above the ship in the stream of hot air.

"Any objections, Doctor?" repeated Tate, with obvious relish.

"No," said Crane softly, and walked off the bridge.

"Jumping Jesus!" said Tate. The helmsman began to splutter and the lookout's shoulders were shaking as he raised the binoculars to look at the trawlers.

As the *Petrel* turned, the trawlers turned too.

〜 〜 〜

Having heard over the P.A. system that they were heading in, Mary Crane was certain that whoever it was knocking softly on her door, it wasn't Joe. It was a discreet tapping, a polite request to be admitted. But when she opened the door, it was Joe she saw. No longer the frantic paranoid of an hour ago, he now looked utterly defeated. He lifted his feet laboriously over the doorsill, shuffled into the cabin and slid down exhausted into his Chief Scientist's chair. His eyes no longer seemed alive; they were dulled and bloodshot with fatigue. Mary couldn't begin to explain to herself what had gone wrong with her husband over the past year. She only knew the symptoms, the totally unpredictable rages fueled by the terrible repetitions of failure. She knew that she had every right to be angry, every right to feel humiliated, after his most recent behavior. But anger would have signaled some remaining vestige of care or desire, and all she could feel right now was the sad realization that they were becoming completely and unalterably estranged.

Watching him sitting quietly in the chair, she found it hard to imagine that a short time before they'd been screaming at each other. She gently closed the door, holding onto the bunk as the *Petrel* slid into a fast, deep trough. The porthole turned gray, then lightened. She could see a patch of whitish cloud as they rose high and slipped over the crest of the wave. She closed her eyes and she prayed, for the first time in years—prayed that something would happen to make it all right. But as she said the words in her mind she felt it was too late. Joe Crane stared straight at the bulkhead. In front of him on his lap, spread out like an apron, was the Oceanographic text. But it was only as Mary watched him more closely that she realized he wasn't really staring at the bulkhead but through the porthole, at an albatross gliding high over the well deck, riding weightlessly on the funnel's exhaust.

"I've found it," he said, as casually as a neighbor might say good morning.

On top of his words, Mary could hear the shrieking laughter of the wind tearing into the aerials and rigging, and shearing off the tempered steel of the ship. Suddenly, everything seemed hopeless. Now Joe was so overcome by depression, she thought, that a creeping delirium had quietly, quickly, engulfed him. He was now the victim of a massive delusion.

"I thought so at lunch," he said, still staring out of the porthole, "when I was watching the albatross again. I knew the birds were telling me something, but I wasn't sure what. Now I know. Now I'm sure. Finally, I've found it."

She felt the hot tears welling up, but she was too tired even to cry.

"Nielsen, you bastard!" Joe shouted. "You'll eat crow!" His eyes sparkled as if from electric shock. He walked to the porthole and thrust a finger at the two trawlers, yelling, "Those Goddamn hyenas. Christ!"

"Joe! Joe, what's the—?"

"Christ! They've got gadgets so small they can pin them to you and you'd think it was fly dirt. What do you think they're doing?" he yelled, even louder. "They're probably listening to every Goddamn thing we're saying." Then he fell silent, put his finger to his lips, and frantically began to search the cabin, riffling it like an enraged burglar.

Mary edged toward the door. Joe rammed home the bolt, pointing to the corner. Mary was trembling half from fright and half from the realization that, for all his derangement, his paranoia might not be entirely unfounded. The two trawlers *had* been following them everywhere, no matter the weather. And while his belief that the *Petrel* was actually bugged was fantastic, well . . . if the trawlers were shadowing, they must have some method of contact in mind. Against her will she remembered

magazine articles she'd read at her hairdresser's about
infra-red and laser equipment that could pick up conver-
sations merely by pointing a beam at the target and
bouncing them back to the listener. The beam was im-
pervious to rain and wind. It seemed logical, now, that the
trawlers would have a contact on board. Or contacts. But
what if the contacts weren't people, but invisible beams
of light?

Quickly, Crane scribbled some words on a piece of paper: "Don't tell anyone I've found it."

Mary wasn't looking at the message, but at Joe. His
face was so distorted, so consumed by his obsession, that
she doubted in that moment that he fully understood who
she was. This terrified her more than anything else. She
buried her face in her hands.

Had he found it?, she wondered. But then you either
found something or you didn't—there was no half-truth
in discovery. If he thought he had found it, did he have an
actual sample or merely a hunch? And if it was a hunch,
what did it have to do with the albatross? Or was his
new conviction nothing—and only a part of his madness?
Her brain reeled with unanswered questions. It was as
though she had been physically battered. Suddenly, she
felt as if she, too, were going insane.

Then, though she tried to stop herself, she thought of
Nielsen's visit the morning Joe had left for the University,
and the strip of paper with the message—the message that
was still in her purse. She remembered Nielsen's parting
advice: "Think about it. Think about the odds against
Joe. If you change your mind, send the message. I'll make
it worth your while." She tried again to push the memory
from her consciousness, but she couldn't. She was chilled
by the thought of what would happen to them if Joe
couldn't work again. She looked at her husband once
more. He might have been a stranger.

And what would happen to her? Someone should pay
for what had happened to Joe, she thought bitterly. Maybe Nielsen was right—you needed more than hope and
love. You needed insurance.

24

At latitude 48° 44′ north, longitude 128° 50′ 2″ west, they were 13.7 kilometers east of what was to have been the final station. When Crane made his way to the bridge, the ship was over the northern part of the western ridge that separated the west valley from the middle valley.

First Mate Johns' cherubic face was tufted here and there with patches of blond stubble as he checked the ship's position for the sixth time during his watch. Despite the leaden skies, and the forecast of hurricane-strength winds, he took comfort from a faint patch of blue that stood out gamely in the mass of metallic gray clouds.

Crane smiled at Johns and walked past the helmsman, who eased forward against the wheel to allow the Chief Scientist enough room to pass in his wet gear. He could hear Crane's rubber boots dragging against the grill of the steering platform. In the relative quiet of the bridge the sound reminded him of a carcass being dragged away after the kill.

Johns was surprised to see Crane looking so tranquil. Even so, with the Captain's permission, he'd slipped a homemade blackjack inside his navy duffel jacket, leaving the top toggles undone for easy access.

Tate, the strain apparent in the bags under his eyes, mumbled his customary "Good afternoon." Crane smiled again. Without a word, he walked into the chartroom, took up the Gerber rule and drew a line eastward from their present position. He intercepted the line with another running north-south, and pushed the rule off the map. "I want to do a station there," he said. "It's on our way back. Forty-four kilometers east of here. Same track as we came out on."

Before Tate had even begun to object Crane added, "I'll want a seismic run all the way back home—Big Bess and corer sampling at the station proper." Crane pointed to the barometer. "Barometer's rising. There's a lull."

Tate rubbed his eyes and spoke slowly. "Doctor, you know that's only temporary. There's a line of storm from here to Japan. There's a hurricane on the way. You know that."

"There's a lull *here*," said Crane. "All we need is a few hours."

"Doctor," said Tate quietly, trying not to set Crane off again, "just look at those waves. Do they look any smaller?"

"Yes, they do. Your steward—the chap you said was so ill, he looks better too. I called in to see him. No need to rush home after all."

Crane pulled out a piece of English toffee. He ripped open the silver paper and offered the candy to Tate.

"No, thanks."

Crane began to chew the toffee, grimacing as his teeth bit into a piece of foil. "You don't think I know the smell of chloral hydrate?"

Tate reddened. "Chloral what . . . ?"

"Chloral hydrate. We used to call them Mickey Finns. Oh, hell," he said, crumbling the foil into a tight ball and popping it into the wastebasket. "I don't want to have to make an official complaint, to call your fellow officers as witnesses against you. So childish, really. So unnecessary, and so undignified. 'Captain charged with assault.' These smart-ass lawyers nowadays. They'd get damages from a stone. And the bastards make it look so bad in the papers." Crane smiled. "But look—let's not be unreasonable." He held up four fingers. "Four hours on station. At the outside. Then home. *Fini!* Well?"

Tate could hear the ticking of the chronometer even over the wind outside. "You're very distraught, Doctor. One minute you're all right, then—you're distraught. God knows I have witnesses enough to that."

To Johns, who had expected a shouting match, the conversation inside the chartroom seemed strangely subdued. Crane was barely moving his lips.

"You're Goddamn right I'm distraught. But that's nothing to what you'll be after the newspapers and lawyers finish with you. Even if *you* don't care, what will the Navy think?"

"I might not give a fish's tit what the Navy thinks. Has that occurred to you?"

"Horseshit! It's your future." Crane tapped the new position with a finger. "And this is mine."

The Captain stepped forward, his fists clenched. "If I wasn't on this ship, in this uniform, I'd—"

"Four hours," repeated Crane. "That's all—the final station."

"You said that the last time."

"Final station." Crane smiled. "Scout's honor!"

"What's the bearing?" snarled Tate.

Crane turned to look at the chart just as the ship rolled and Tate's body came falling toward him. Crane saw him coming but had nowhere to go. The Captain crashed full into him, pinning him against the bulkhead. The First Mate reached inside his jacket. Tate stayed on top of Crane until the ship rolled back to starboard. Only then did he straighten up, pushing back his thick black hair. "Sorry," he said, staring malevolently at Crane.

"Bearing is eight-four degrees," said Crane evenly.

Tate slid the door open behind him. "Helmsman?"

"Sir?"

"Steer zero eight four."

"Zero eight four, sir."

Crane left the bridge, giving the startled watchman a slap on the back as he passed.

"Are we doing another station, Captain?" asked the First Mate.

"We are."

"That hurricane's coming up fast and—"

"I'm aware of that, Mr. Johns." The Captain's tone was cold, hard, and threatening. Johns was sorry he'd said that he understood: "Talk about bloody mercurial. He's up one minute, down the next. One second as sane as they come, the next as crazy as a bloody loon. Like a Goddamn yo-yo. I've never met anyone like him."

"Most of 'em are locked up, that's why."

"You think he's on to something this time?"

"No."

It was only then that Tate realized where the new position was. "Son of a bitch!" he said. "We've done this station before. It's Station One. The bastard's gone stark raving mad!"

25

"No way!" Frank was shouting against the wind and the heavy pounding of the two seventeen-hundred-horsepower Fairbanks below.

Crane yelled back through the noise, "Just one cast. One more cast."

"One cast, my ass. I'm an oceanographic technician, not a kamikaze pilot."

Charlie patiently cupped his hands and lit a cigarette as the two of them argued it out. Frank was holding onto the after-lab sink rail, pointing out beyond the poop deck to the thirty- and forty-foot waves, the boiling wake of the ship and the ever-pursuing masses of foam-tipped gray threatening to breach the stern. "That's force ten, Doctor. You want to put over a bottle, fine. You put it over. You go up forward and work the platform—for a change."

"You're frightened," said Crane, looking first at Frank, then at his wife. "You're frightened."

Frank felt the blood rushing to his head. "*I'm* frightened? That takes the cake."

"Yes," repeated Crane.

"You know," bellowed Frank, "you've spent this whole trip telling other people they're frightened. Everyone except yourself."

"I know about myself," Crane said evenly. "Mary wants to know about you."

"Stop it, Joe," Mary said. "Stop it." It was a measure of his obsession with finding sea gold, thought Mary, that a short while ago her husband had been accusing her of adultery with his technician, but now was goading Frank into one more attempt at finding the metalliferous muds.

You bastard, thought Frank, looking straight at Joe Crane. You know where it hurts. His arms flew out in utter exasperation. "What in Christ's name do you want to do a cast here for? We've already done this station. This was the first station."

"We only did one grab," said Crane.

"Right. And there was no anomaly. So why . . . ?" Frank stopped talking as a crewman entered the lab and began collecting used coffee cups. Crane glanced at him suspiciously, then turned back to Frank. "I'd just like to double-check for manganese," he said, for the crewman's benefit. "Even though the map says we're on the same position as before, we're probably miles from the first cast. Even Loran isn't that accurate."

Son of a bitch, thought Frank, seeing Crane's eyes darting furtively toward the crewman. He'd suspect his own mother. But then Frank remembered that he himself had stopped talking when the crewman had come into the lab. The stakes were affecting them all—but what could you do? He caught Mary's eye.

The crewman put the cups and saucers in the lab sink and began to wash them. Frank angrily tore a paper towel from the dispenser.

"Okay," he said to Crane, "what you say about approximate position is true, but it's true of every station we've ever done. What's so special about this one?"

Crane gave no immediate answer, and the four of them stood, looking from one to another, as the crewman continued to scrub vigorously. Sam entered the lab, wiping the spray off his thick blue glasses, wanting to know if he'd be needed for station duty. Then another crewman came in. This time it was the regular winchman.

"Oh, hell," said Charlie. "Come on, Frank. Let's do a cast and get it over with."

"Wait a minute, Charlie." Frank turned to Crane. "I'm not doing a cast until I know why. Why are we working the same Goddamn area again? I'm not risking my neck for the hell of it."

Fuming, Crane flipped down the intercom switch. "Bridge. After lab here. Hold position." Then he motioned Frank to follow him.

Suddenly Frank felt old and tired. Sloop or no sloop, job or no job, it wasn't worth putting up with Crane any longer. Besides, a sloop wasn't any good to a dead man, and in force ten you could end up dead very quickly. He'd wanted to help Joe Crane—but there was a limit.

"Where are they going?" asked Sam.

"I don't know," said Mary quietly, looking sadly at the deck.

Crane ushered Frank into his cabin, then locked the door and turned on his portable Zenith shortwave radio. "In case we're being beamed," he said.

"*What?*" said Frank, incredulous.

"I wasn't just talking about manganese. That was in case anyone overheard us in the lab." He pulled out the pieces of clamshell from the first station. "I've checked the room for bugs," he said, "and they can't beam through bulkheads, so we can talk."

Dumbfounded, Frank rubbed his forehead. "Oh, fuck it," he said under his breath. This was it. His boss had finally gone right over the edge.

Crane didn't hear. Holding a shell fragment, he pointed at an albatross outside the porthole. "It's the heat," he said. "Just as the albatross needs heat currents to glide, so the clams need them to live. For the albatross it's air currents, for the clams, hot-water currents."

"What are you talking about?" snapped Frank irritably.

"That's the trouble with specialization," continued Crane. "We're geologists, so we ignore the biology. The clam should have told us right away. Well, not so much the clam maybe, but the size of it. The first station here was over two thousand meters deep, too. What are clams doing at that depth? It's pitch-black and close to freezing down there. Clams can only survive in waters warmed by the sun, supporting the small microbes that support the larger life systems, including bivalves. But the sun's rays don't go anywhere near two thousand meters deep."

It was then that Frank saw it—like an explosion of light in a submarine canyon. Joe Crane wasn't as crazy as everyone thought. "So it's hot down there or there'd be no clams. And if—Jesus! If it's hot, there must be hot springs. And maybe metal deposits."

"Yes!" said Crane excitedly. "I think the reason we didn't find anything in Big Bess was because the clam jammed the jaws and prevented them from closing. Any mud in the grab at the bottom would have been washed out on the way up. Goddamn it," he said, punching the air. "If we'd only done another grab. We could have found out for sure."

Frank was pacing up and down the cabin. "The old man would've keel-hauled us. We were far enough behind as it was. Anyway, no good worrying about that. We have our chance *now*." He stopped pacing. He was absolutely amazed. "Thanks to you." Frank paused. "They'll have to know."

"Who?" asked Crane, suspicion rushing into his eyes. "Who'll have to know?"

"The crew, the Captain. Charlie and I can't do it alone. They'll all want to know what we're looking for."

"Why? You can do a bottle cast without arousing any suspicion."

"But what if we find a temperature anomaly? Then we'll want to do two or three spot samples with the Petersen grab, perhaps a refractive seismic run, piston coring, and Big Bess—all the stuff you asked the Captain for. No way Charlie and I can do that all by ourselves. Besides, if we dont' have time for more than one piston core, we'll have to use boomerang corers, and we've never used them before—not for manganese. Someone could get wise."

"All right, but cut down. We'll only use one other man. Someone who hasn't worked on research ships before."

"Why can't we play it straight? Just tell them what's happening. That way we can call on some old hands."

"I said I don't want anybody else to know, Goddamn it," shouted Crane. He pulled out a bottle of Scotch and offered it to Frank, who refused. Crane took a swig, holding the bottle with both hands to prevent the neck from rattling against his teeth.

"We've only got four hours," said Frank, watching Joe's paranoia quickly mount again.

"I know, I know. We'll just have to do what we can in the time. We'll have to chance it." Crane looked out at the trawlers. "No one else but us is to know. We're too close. We've come too far to share it now."

"It's not just our ocean, Doctor."

Joe Crane swung around. "Yes it is! After ten years, Frank, this part of the ocean is mine." He took another long swig of the Scotch. "And I'm not about to give it away—to *anyone*. Understand?"

26

The sounder read twenty-three hundred meters—a hundred more than the first time they'd lowered the big grab. The Scottish Mate had done a superb job of keeping the *Petrel* heading into the wind, and they managed to keep the wire angle to a workable thirty degrees.

It took thirty-two minutes for the pinger to signal that it was on bottom, slightly more than fifteen minutes for the messenger to race down the storm-curved wire and trip the bottle, forty-five minutes to roll the hydrographic wire back onto the drum, and another five minutes to do the test.

"The temperature reading," said Crane, as he quickly punched out the conversion factor on the Canon calculator, "is one point eight . . ."

Mary Crane couldn't bear the tension any longer. "Well . . . ?"

When Joe pressed the equals sign on the Canon, Frank saw 15.6 appear. He glanced at the bathymetric chart, checking the calculator's 15.6 Celsius against the normal reading. "Anomaly," he said very quietly. "Jesus Christ, it's an anomaly."

"What order?" asked Crane coolly.

"Six times as high."

"My God!" It was Mary Crane. "What's that in Fahrenheit?"

"That in Fahrenheit, my dear girl, is not less than sixty point bloody zero eight degrees. You can bathe in it."

"You mean we may have discov—"

The bridge intercom crackled. "Dr. Crane?"

"Yes?"

"Weathership reports force ten and rising. Predicting force twelve."

Frank glanced at the clock. They had only fifteen hours in which to travel a hundred and fifty miles before the hurricane struck. He switched off the intercom and looked squarely at Crane. "We'll have to compromise." In that moment something happened. The link of common purpose formed between the two men.

Crane nodded, and spoke quickly to the bridge. "We'll cut out the spot sampling with the smaller grab and go straight to Big Bess. If there's nothing worthwhile we won't repeat, and we'll only do one piston core for a deep sample—six boomerang cores and a seismic run. That will do."

"How long will that take?" It was the Captain's voice.

Crane waited for Frank, who was scribbling on the Formica counter and calculating aloud. "One hour for Big Bess down and up. Same for the long piston corer. Boomerangs we can drop overboard while we're under way. They'll each pop up in about an hour. I'd say about . . . three hours in all."

"We'll do the piston corer last," said Crane. "We'll know better when to drop it after the boomerangs and the seismic run have given us a better idea of the bottom. We'll save you an hour in all."

"You'll save me an hour?" Tate grunted. "Well, thank you very much. Just make it snappy."

Frank and Joe Crane grinned at each other. It was the camaraderie of professionals. Both knew that once the thousand-pound piston corer was over the side, Tate would have no option but to stay on station until it came up. Otherwise, it would be like trying to drag an anchor.

"I'll watch the sounder in the dry lab," said Crane, making off forward with Mary following.

Walking into the dry lab, Mary Crane was still wondering at the sudden change in Frank. "What did you tell him?" she asked her husband.

Joe Crane was watching one of the trawlers. "Nothing."

Suddenly Mary was beginning to view Frank's earlier coldness to her in an entirely different light. It wasn't just that he'd been jealously guarding details from everyone; it was her in particular, she thought. He suspected that she might sell out. But he couldn't know about Nielsen— or could he?

"When the corers come up, who'll be the first to see them?" she pressed Joe. "Who'll do the testing and store them in the cold locker?"

"Frank. Why?"

"You won't see them?"

"No. I'll be watching the sounder, matching our positions on the map with the depth record. Someone has to do it," he said defensively. "Why don't you say what you mean, Mary? You're worried about Frank getting hurt, aren't you?"

"No," she said, quickly sensing another fit of rage building up. "No, I . . ."

Ever since Joe had quietly agreed to Tate's request to turn for home, Mary had noticed that he'd become remarkably composed. After he'd come back from talking to Frank, Joe had seemed almost contented. Otherwise, she wouldn't have dared to bring up Frank's name. Now she could see she'd gone too far. Joe wasn't that composed after all. She'd hit a raw nerve.

"You still think I'm frightened, don't you?" he charged.

"No," she said, "of course not. I just—"

"Yes, you do," he said, throwing down a pencil. "You're on that Goddamn machismo bit again, aren't you?"

"No. I—"

"All right!" he yelled. *"You* watch the sounder! *You* mark the positions—and they better be right. I'll help him. Will that make you happy? Maybe I'll get washed overboard, eh?"

"Oh, God," she said. It was beginning again. Her hand went out in front of her, as if to touch an invisible wall. "Oh God, no, Joe. I never—"

"You never do!" he yelled. "You never mean it, but you *do.*"

Before she could stop him he was gone, out the door and onto the wind-battered deck.

❧ ❧ ❧

Frank was surprised to see Crane crouching next to him beside Big Bess, as he wound open her six-foot spring bite with the crank handle. Charlie quickly slipped in the trip-preventer pin. "If this big bitch slams hard against the side," cautioned Frank, "that safety pin'll come out before we can pull it out. We can't make it a tighter fit, otherwise we'd never get it out."

Tate was using the bow thrusters to ease the *Petrel* into the wind, and the spray on the foredeck became almost continuous, slapping Charlie's face as he sat behind the winch, and drenching Frank, Crane, and a seaman huddled beneath the foc'sle overhang. Although the face was almost hidden, Frank could see the blue lenses of the seaman's glasses. It was the one they called Sam.

The Captain juggled with the rev levers, keeping the ship as steady as possible, marking time against the on-coming seas. "On station," he bellowed into the P.A. mike. "Lower when ready."

Frank lifted his gloved hand and turned it in circles, as if dogging the hatch of a submarine. In response Charlie began cuffling the winch lever. Slowly the cable became taut. Big Bess groaned and began to inch above the deck. The tensionometer needle on the winch jerked to one thousand pounds. Even though they were now headed into the wind with the rolls at a minimum, the *Petrel* was still lurching to angles of twenty-nine and thirty-four de-grees. A long, relatively stable trough passed under them, and Frank cursed. In those roll-free seconds the big grab had not been high enough off the well deck for them to swing the davit over the side.

"Next long trough like that, Charlie, I want you to give 'er the gears. Straight lift up, then I'll swing the davit over and you let her go a little. The next long trough after that, the Doctor can drop the trip weight and Sam can pull the pin. One, two, three, like that, okay? Then let her go down fast before that trip weight hits the side and drops the bloody lot at deck level. Right?"

"Gotcha!"

Waiting in the shelter of the foc'sle for a long trough, they could see the water-smeared shapes of Tate, Johns and Mrs. Crane, watching high up from behind the body-length glass of the bridge.

"I'll pull the pin," said Joe Crane suddenly.

"You sure?" said Frank, surprised.

"Yes—yes, I think so."

"No good thinking. You have to lean out on that plat-form, pull the pin clean but fast, and come back fast. We'll wrap a lifeline around you. Got it?"

Crane appeared to be saying something, but they hit a wave and all other sound was lost in the roar of water.

"Got it, Doctor?"

"Yes."

Frank signaled a long trough approaching. The winch screamed and lifted the grab a foot above the rail height.

The ship pitched high in the first wall of water, and the grab swung back toward Charlie. Snatching at it with a boathook, Sam tried to slow it down before it could crash into the winch and bulkhead immediately below the bridge, but its weight pulled him along like a toy. Frank took hold of the hook too, but the grab dragged them both, taking Sam dangerously close to the winch drum. Charlie slammed on the foot brake and pulled the hand brake with all the strength he could muster.

"For Christ's sake, Doc, give 'em a hand," he yelled. Crane grabbed the boathook as the ship lurched over the wave's crest and slid down into the trough, throwing the grab in the opposite direction, straight toward the bow. All four of them grabbed the boathook and the Mate suddenly appeared, sliding down the forward bridge steps to join them. They slowed the pendulum movement a little, but not enough to stop Bess' thousand pounds from smashing into the foc'sle, demolishing several trunks like so many cardboard boxes and sending a tremor through the entire ship.

Beneath the foc'sle the four men's faces contorted with the strain of trying to hold the grab steady during the next roll. By the time Charlie had swung the davit out, another two troughs had passed. He looked forward for a moment, then signaled to Frank and ran for the winch.

The other four took up the tension on the grab as it was swung to starboard.

"Let go with those hooks," called Frank; then, without taking his eyes off the grab, "Sam, undo the chain."

The seaman quickly removed the safety chain along the cutaway section of the rail. "Trip weight over," shouted Frank.

Sam and the Mate, with Crane looking on awkwardly, lifted the two-hundred-pound weight attached to the five-sixteenths-inch trip wire and half lowered it, half let it slip, through their canvas gloves. It disappeared just beneath the water, pulling down the trip arm with a sharp jerk.

His eyes still on the grab, Frank circled his other hand in the air. "Lower away!"

Crazy, thought Frank, as the grab passed him, its great mouth gaping like a prehistoric carnivore in search of prey. Working with massive equipment in a blow like this was just plain crazy. He signaled and Charlie stopped the winch. The grab was now at eye level, ready for the pin to be pulled. The trip arm, biting down hard on the free-fall wire, stuck out like a one-armed corpse turning slowly in the wind.

Frank swung a boathook out against the main five-eighths-inch cable that held the grab. "Give me a hand, Sam. I'll keep the big bitch away from the side until we get a trough that'll give us enough time to pull the pin. Use your hook to fend off the trip weight cable once the pin is pulled. If that weight hits the side after the pin is pulled, it'll take the tension off that trip arm bite and——"

"I'll pull the pin. I said I'd do it." It was Joe Crane, so eager he was already on the platform, all but jostling his technician aside. Frank looked closely at him. The eagerness, he decided, was really fear. "I'll do it," Crane shouted again. "I'll do it." Frank had difficulty hearing him in the wind.

"Okay. You can pull it, but wait . . ." Frank didn't finish the sentence. Crane was looking at the grab, his face white. Frank knew what was wrong without asking, and bellowed the alarm. "Jesus Christ, the pin's halfway out! Stand back!"

The pin was now resting through only one of its two holes. The impact of the grab smashing against the foc'sle had obviously popped it halfway out of its two-ring sheath.

"Don't back up!" yelled Frank. "Help me push the trip wire off the side!"

The Mate lent his weight to the boathook, followed by Sam, who was watching the pin with terrified fascination. It had to be pulled, but only in a trough where, in the critical few seconds of lowering, the trip weight must not be swept onto the ship's side. A wall of spray enveloped them, and a new gust of wind tore through the rigging. In that split second Crane began to release his grip on the boathook.

"Hold on, for Christ's sake!" Frank urged. "Help us."

But Crane had been the first to see that they were now between waves. "Trough!" he yelled. He thrust his hand forward, pulled out the pin in one clean movement, and cried, "It's out!"

"Down!" screamed Frank. "Down!"

Charlie released the brake and hit the full-power button. In four seconds the grab was beneath the surface, gone in a cauldron of bubbles and creamy foam, the wire tearing sparks from the outer V of the boathook.

Tate had seen the whole thing from the bridge. "Huh," he grunted. "Quick thinking."

The Scotsman nodded, his face white. "Aye. He may not be the full dollar but that took guts. Pretrip then could have taken his bloody head off. Maybe that'll slow him down, you think?"

Tate shook his head, leaving the bridge. "Takes more than that," he said. "He has to know what's down there before he'll slow down."

As the Scottish Mate watched Tate going down to check the late afternoon weather report in the radio room, he lifted his mug of coffee, spilling some in the roll. "I must admit," he said, "I wouldn't mind knowing myself."

Mary Crane had seen nothing of what had happened on the deck. She'd left the bridge several minutes before and was now in the lab, intently watching the thin, gray trace that showed Big Bess racing toward sea bottom over two thousand meters below.

27

The trawler Captain, his Vandyke beard working overtime, had just finished telling Andrea Nolan that no one in his right mind could work in this weather. "Is that so?" she said, pointing. The *Petrel*'s slim bow crested a wave, and they both saw Big Bess being lowered. "We'll stay until they recover it," she said.

"What then?"

"If it's metalliferous muds, our contact will signal."

"But we'll have to wait till dark before we can make the pickup."

Andrea Nolan looked at the sky. It was like a late November day gone mad. She found it all but impossible to imagine the sun's existence, to believe in swimming, warm beaches, hot afternoons, and sunlit elms. For this was another planet, consisting entirely of water and storms. "It'll be dark in two hours. We've waited this long; we can wait two more hours."

Her voice was a little too confident, and the Captain studied her intently. For the first time, Andrea Nolan looked frightened.

"Sure," he said. "What the hell—I'll get overtime."

She smiled tightly. "Of course."

There was a crash from below, followed by the deckhand's cursing. The trawler disappeared into an avalanche of spray.

"Don't worry about him," said the Captain. "He's been through worse."

Andrea Nolan clung desperately to the hold bar. "Do you think we can do it? Pick it up, I mean."

Vandyke shrugged. "Not on the first pass—not in this weather. But we can do it, I guess." He spun the wheel again. "*If* there's anything to pick up."

28

"Never mind the Goddamn *Petrel*," shouted Doyle. "Just watch that *Sea Wasp* son of a bitch. They've got something up their sleeve."

The Captain lowered the revs. Now they were jogging, barely moving ahead, holding position while they tried to figure out what was happening. As another giant swell passed by, a gust of wind blew the Captain's coveralls up like a balloon. "This is crazy," he said. "We should head in."

Tony stabbed a finger into his back. "Hey, Columbus. You ever meet Miel?"

"Who's he?"

"Jay!" said Doyle. "Will you shut him up."

Jay didn't answer. He merely folded his arms and leaned back on the bulkhead.

"Ah, shit," said Tony, waving Doyle's caution aside. "He needs something to keep him going. Don't you, Columbus?"

The Captain didn't answer. Insolently, Tony lit a cigarette from Doyle's Gitanes. "Miel is the guy who hired us in Honolulu," he continued. "His firm hired us to do a job, buddy, and he promised a big bonus if we get the goods. Now, if you head in without getting the job done, you could end up . . . Hey, Mr. Jay," said Tony, "what's the word I want for Captain Canuck here?"

"Eliminated," said Jay, rapping his pipe sharply against the bulkhead.

"Yeah, eliminated," said Tony, stabbing the Captain in the ribs again. "You could find yourself eliminated."

"Leave him alone," said Doyle.

"Why? You chicken, too? I told you we should've fixed that other trawler." Tony turned to the Captain. "You'd be in port by now, Grandma." He rounded on Doyle. "We can hardly see 'em now. What happens when it gets dark, huh? They going to radio us, let us know where they are?"

"Don't be cute," said Doyle.

"Maybe they'll use infra-red scopes," said Tony, stamping his feet. "Hey, can we get some more heat in here?"

Doyle turned up the thermostat. "Infra-red scopes?"

"Yeah," answered Tony. "We used 'em in Houston one time. Right, Mr. Jay?"

"Corpus Christi."

"Wherever." Tony shrugged. "You can see someone a mile away with 'em."

"Not in this weather, you couldn't," said the Captain. "The waves are too high. You'd see one second and be blind the next. They'll have to use a light."

Doyle stomped the remains of his Gitane into the wooden decking and immediately lit another. "You guys ever boarded a ship under way before—in rough weather?"

"We're not fucking pirates," said Tony disgustedly, tossing the empty bottle overboard.

"You might have to," said Doyle.

"What the hell for?"

"If there's a drop, and they try to beat us to it."

"I daresay we'll manage," said Jay, casually.

"Yeah," said Tony. "We'll manage. Whatever comes."

The Captain grunted. "We'll see."

29

To Frank, standing in the bright island of the *Petrel*'s
deck lights, the grab looked brand-new when it broke
surface, its outside washed clean like a frozen carcass.

"Doesn't look promising," said the Mate. No one answered.

Frank ducked his head as the davit was cranked inboard on a roll. The grab swung forward, its lower lip
thudding into the side of the ship, imploding an aluminum
trunk lashed nearby. When it swung back out to sea,
Charlie reversed the winch gear, giving it slack in the hope
of plunging it back into the water until the next trough
came. But the wire wasn't fast enough and Big Bess
swung back in, lower now, smashing into the rail and
sending a shower of wood-and-paint shrapnel high above
the deck. Mary Crane stood nearby, shivering in the
bone-cold wind, as Frank and Joe Crane manned the
davit together. "Inboard!" yelled Frank. "Get it inboard."

When the grab swung wildly again, Frank, leaving the
davit wheel to Crane, tried to steady it with a boathook.
The grab tore the hook from his hands, sending it flying
into the First Mate who dropped, winded, his Day-Glo life
jacket bouncing him several inches off the deck. Ducking
under the incoming cable, Frank ran past the grab and
snatched the Mate's collar, dragging him clear just as the
thousand pounds of steel swept by before crashing into the
deck. "You okay?" said Frank.

The Mate sat up, dazed. "Yeah. Thought that hook had
my balls for a second."

Frank began cranking the jaws open slowly, so as not
to lose whatever sample they might have in a sudden
gush of trapped water. A stench of rotten eggs engulfed
the ship, and when he had the jaws open less than a foot,
a great heap of olive-green mud oozed out like the ex-
crement of a diseased animal. The smell was so powerful

that Crane had to dash to the windward side. An albatross flew into the sulphurous air and immediately veered
away.

Though Frank also felt ill from the smell, he could see
that Crane was jubilant, and he was happy for him. Vile
as the odor might be, this mud was the most promising
sign yet. If nothing else it was evidence of the conversion
of sulphates to hydrogen sulphide in the deep, sunless
waters—a conversion that could only occur at such depths
because of the high pressure and heat present as salt
water traveled through the waterways that honeycombed
the porous rock above the magma. It was in such sul-
phides that the bacteria necessary to feed the clams could
survive.

Rivulets of dark green mud oozed across the deck as
Frank and Crane stooped down together beside the grab's
mouth, anxiously waiting for it to drain completely. The
two men worked quickly, Frank shoveling gobs of the
green ooze onto the sieving screen, and Crane playing
the fine firehose on it. At first there were only a few
small pebbles, isolated and lonely-looking, as the diluted
mud passed through the mesh and ran across the deck
into the scuppers. Then they saw the big clams—a dozen
of them. The pressure change on the way up had killed
most of them, but one or two showed signs of life. Then,
looking back into the throat of the grab, Crane saw it.
A lump, six inches by about four and a half, protruded
from the mound of clam-studded ooze. He got down on
his knees, reached far back into the grab and pulled it
out. It weighed, he guessed, about six pounds. He handed
it to Frank and said, "Wash this, will you?"

But just then a wave broke across the lower part of the
well deck and Crane simply dunked the lump in it. With
most of the mud washed off, they saw that it was a piece
of rock almost completely covered with a black-gold
crust, dotted here and there with tiny pieces of broken
clamshell. It looked like some exotic tidal rock. Except
this was no shoreline tidal rock. This rock had come up
from over a mile below.

Quite casually Joe handed it to Frank, who was staring
at the rock, oblivious to the hose streaming down the
front of his wet gear. "I'll be damned!" he said, noting the
rust-red markings. "It might be manganese!"

Those around him could not hear his voice because of

the wind, but they could see the expression on his face. And, despite the noise of the gale and the almost constant shuddering of the ship, they could sense the excitement.

"Let's make one-hundred percent sure," said Crane. "Set up the test gear. I'll bring in a mud sample from near the rock."

Reaching down with a trowel, Joe Crane filled a plastic bag and walked to the lab, followed by the others. It was difficult to be certain, because his hands were frozen by wind and sea, but to him the mud felt warm.

Charlie turned to Sam, who was heading eagerly towards the workbench. "Put all this stuff into plastic bags and label it 'Station Four' before we get hit by a king-size and lose it overboard."

Sam stopped and pulled up his hood. "Shit," he said, and walked away, peering over the top of the thick glasses.

"Where did the grab hit?" Crane asked Mary, struggling to keep his voice calm in the presence of the First Mate.

Mary studied the trace. "It was on the western slope of the middle ridge leading down toward the middle valley."

"Not actually on the valley bottom?"

"No."

"How deep?"

"Two thousand meters."

Crane stuck a thermometer deep into the mud sample taken from around the rock, then left it and began rummaging through a trunk, pulling out a mortar and pestle. Frank cut off a four-inch piece of platinum wire. Crane broke a small piece of rust-brown encrustation from the rock and handed it to him. Taking it gingerly, Frank braced himself against an oncoming roll. He'd waited a long time, and he wasn't about to fumble. The other three —Mary, Charlie, and the First Mate—watched closely as he put the piece of rock into the mortar and ground it into a fine powder. He lit a Bunsen burner, adjusting the loose yellow flame until it roared like a tiny purple furnace, then took a few milligrams of flux from a bottle, adding it to the powder. The resulting mixture looked like fine brown sugar. Whistling nervously, he put on an asbestos glove. A swell hit and the mortar began to slide. Crane grabbed it, cradling it like an egg. Frank put the tip of the platinum wire in the flame and held it there for about thirty seconds, until it glowed deep red. Then he deftly touched it to the flux-powder mixture. A small bead of the mixture clung to the end of the wire which he then put over the burner, passing it quickly backwards and forwards through the flame like a glassblower till it lost its irregularity and became tear-shaped. They waited for the bead to cool like a group of relatives awaiting a birth.

Slowly but unmistakably the molten redness turned to a robin's-egg blue.

Crane's sigh of relief was audible even over the sound of the storm. An enormous wave of tension ebbed from the lab.

"Manganese," said Frank. "We've found manganese. You were right."

"You rich, Doc?" asked the First Mate, hopefully.

"No," said Frank quickly, glancing at Crane. "No, it's a manganese encrustation, not a nodule. This only means that we know it can form in these parts—that's all. But hell! We've been looking for it all these years. Nothing commercial in it, but, well—it's satisfying."

Joe Crane burst into laughter at the rank understatement. He held the small blue bead in the palm of his hand as if it were the rarest jewel. "It'll give us more money for research. That's for sure."

"Prestige, huh, Doc?" grinned Charlie.

Joe Crane smiled down at the bead. "I guess," he said softly. "And vindication."

Frank looked happily at Mary—and she at him. He turned away and switched off the Bunsen burner.

"Well," said the Mate, anxious to let the bridge know whether the station had ended, "this calls for a celebration, but I'm afraid that right now I'll have to know what you want to do next."

There was no answer. For a moment it looked as if Joe Crane was still mesmerized by the tiny blue bead in his hand, but he was actually watching the thermometer sticking out of the mud sample. Mary touched her husband gently, but he brushed her hand away and began scribbling furiously in the log. Unlike the others, Frank could see that it was a temperature calculation.

Mary touched him again. "Joe, Mr. Johns wants to know what you want to do now."

"What—oh. Uh, I'd like to do a grab of the valley floor. Get down off those ridges and see what the muds are like right at the bottom. Could be geologically interesting, even if we get no more evidence of encrustation."

The Mate's tone was apologetic but firm. "The lull is over, Doctor. The barometer's falling again and we only agreed on one big grab."

Frank saw the danger of pressing the point—of giving a hint of what they might really have found beyond the odd deposition of manganese and iron oxides on the ridge. He knew that now they would not only want to know the depth of the mud in the valley, but the thickness of the rock structure below, where further rich mineral deposits might lie. That meant a refractive profile and cores. In his excitement, Crane obviously wasn't thinking straight.

As nonchalantly as he could, Frank said, "Oh, I don't think we need another grab, Doc. Why not just do a quick seismic refractive run—ten miles—to pick the best core sites? We can do the six boomerang cores first, then go back to the best site on our seismic trace for the long piston core."

The Mate shook his head. "I don't know. That barometer's falling. We'll have that hurricane up our ass pretty soon. Ah, sorry, Mrs. Crane."

Crane looked up sharply, picking up the drift of Frank's suggestion. "All right. How about this. A refraction seismic run to determine the best core sites in the valley, then two boomerang cores instead of six." He looked at the Mate. "Fair compromise?"

Frank, seeing the Mate falter, added quickly, "With the option of a boomerang camera if we find anything worth making a movie of."

"Fine," said Crane.

The Mate scratched his head, the blond stubble moving up and down on the baby-pink face. "You guys! You've proved there's manganese, what more do you want? I don't see how the old man'll go for a refractive in this weather. That means explosives."

Crane smiled. "It'll help us find a good core site. A core would help fill out the geological picture of the area."

"Look great in *Scientific American*," said Frank. "Photographs of the *Petrel*."

"And the First Mate," said Crane.

"And the bosun," added Charlie. They all laughed.

"Son of a bitch," sighed the Mate. "You bloody scientists. All right, I'll try to con the old man. You owe me a beer."

As the Mate walked out of the lab, Crane turned to the bosun. "Charlie, could you help Sam get the rest of those mud samples in? Ten bags will be enough. Then let's rig the first seismic charge. I don't want to move from here till we're ready to start the line."

"Right. Oh, Doc?"

"Yes?"

"The temperature of the muds—was it an anomaly?"

Crane shook his head disappointedly. "No. It was normal. We'll have to settle for the little bit of manganese. Glory, not gold."

Charlie pulled on his gloves. "Well, you can't win 'em all."

As Charlie closed the door Crane's voice exploded. "The mud's fifteen degrees higher than normal. We've got to run metal tests immediately, Frank. My god, if it's as hot on the valley floor . . ."

"Jesus!" shouted Frank, switching on the Beckman absorption spectrometer and scooping up a glob of mud with the spatula. "Jesus! Can you imagine a valley this size? It'd be worth billions. Bloody billions." He patted the spectrometer lovingly. "Tell us, baby," he said. "Tell us what's in those muds. Tell us it's true."

Mary, her heart thumping, watched the two men. The look of defeat was gone from Joe's eyes. But what if the muds on the valley floor, several miles further down from the slope, were not hot? She joined a group of seamen who were coming forward to carry the sample bags of mud from the deck to the cold-storage room. But her anxiety stayed with her, as unshakable as the two black masts she could see riding the waves in the ever darkening sea beyond. Of the two masts only one was topped by a pinpoint of light and carried the red and green sidelights. Even as she watched, the other trawler became invisible as the black sky swallowed the horizon.

30

Five minutes later the Mate came on the intercom to the lab. On seeing the blue bead, Captain Tate had reluctantly agreed to Crane's request for more time on one condition—that he wouldn't ask any member of his crew except the bosun, who had more experience than anyone else, to assist if he didn't want to.

Charlie was surprised to see Sam turn up and volunteer, particularly when behind the blue glasses the seaman still seemed to be sulking about his exclusion from the manganese test. While Frank and Crane were running the metals test on the absorption spectrometer, Charlie and Sam were preparing to launch the eighteen-foot sonobuoy. The buoy was an eight-foot plastic barrel four feet in diameter which would float upright once over the side, supporting a ten-foot whip aerial and dangling a wafer-sized, pressure-sensitive barium-titanium disc a hundred and twenty feet below the surface.

"What's this?" asked Sam, kicking a small box of thumb-nail-sized blasting caps.

"Holy Christ!" yelled Charlie, pulling him roughly away from the box.

"Hey!" Sam swung his arm out.

"You stupid bastard," snarled Charlie. "If they go up, they'll blow your balls off. They're the caps that explode the primary charge. You look after the sonobuoy. Don't let it roll around too much, and mind that hydrophone. Wrap it in rags until we're ready to put it over."

Sam, his long, lean features looking like the Sad Sack of the comic strips, did as he was told. Charlie pulled out a long piece of the quarter-inch black safety fuse. Once overboard, suspended by a meteorological balloon to the depth the scientists wanted, it would fizzle down to the blasting cap and the primary charge, which in turn would trigger the three-foot, twenty-pound ammonia-dynamite

LOSHOK cartridge. On their rebound the shock waves would be picked up by the hydrophones suspended from the sonobuoy lying astern, which would then transmit forward to the ship. The recording apparatus would transform the sound waves into a series of visual lines piled on top of each other like so many undulating stripes, giving a picture of the rock layers beneath the ocean floor.

As the ship jogged into the wind, awaiting Crane's decision, the wind gusted to fifty knots. The gale was nearing force eleven.

The mess boy, standing defiantly at the open door of the dry lab, looked out beyond Charlie at the mountainous wake. Like a boy playing at the seashore, he seemed to be daring the sea to catch him. Holding his coffee mug in both hands, defying the rolls to set him off balance, he asked cockily, "Hey Charlie, why don't they just do the regular seismic profile? You know, send the echoes straight up and down? What do they call it . . . reflective?"

Charlie, helping Sam to lash the sonobuoy to the stern's A-frame, was irritated that George, a mess boy, knew even that much. He scowled as he slipped the tail through the last bowline knot and walked back to the lab, followed by Sam. "A reflective run's like pointing a hose at the ground. Some of the energy bounces back but some just goes straight down and gets lost. This way you're hosing at an angle, so more of it runs along the bottom before it bounces up. The time it takes to go between two points gives a better idea of what it's like under the seabed."

George looked puzzled, and turned down the volume on the cassette.

"It's like a direct hit versus a glancing blow," said Sam unexpectedly. "With a direct hit you lose a lot of energy that just goes down and never comes back. The other way it has time to kind of slide along. Gets better pictures of fault lines."

"Son of a gun," said George, genuinely impressed. "Whaddya know—Doctor Sam."

"And you didn't know what a blasting cap was," grunted Charlie.

"I know what seismic recording is," said Sam, half apologetically. "I read about it in *Reader's Digest*."

George did a little bow of appreciation. "Thank you, Dr. Digest," and fell over in the oncoming roll, spilling his coffee over Charlie's boots.

"You bloody yo-yo."

"Sorry, Bosun, I . . ."

The ship's engines rumbled beneath them and the deck began shaking. "We're off," said George.

"Really?" said Charlie. "You know, George, sometimes I think . . ." He turned and went on deck.

"Charlie, set safety fuse for five minutes. We'll explode a charge at a hundred and fifty feet." It was Frank, suddenly appearing in the shadow of the starboard quarter working light. The bosun nodded, measuring off the fuse. "About a foot every thirty seconds, right?"

"Roughly," said Frank. "Burn rate at surface is forty seconds a foot, but it'll increase with the water pressure. Give it seven feet. That should do it."

Charlie tugged at the compressed air hose and began filling the balloon. "How about putting the sonobuoy out first?" he said dryly. "Might be nice to have something to pick up the echoes."

Frank slapped him on the back. "Good God, I nearly forgot. We'll set the hydrophone at a hundred and twenty feet. That should be far enough below all this turbulence."

Charlie was aware that Frank's voice sounded strange, slightly tremulous, almost to the point of alarm. But it wasn't until he saw the excitement on his face that he suspected what had happened—that Frank and Joe Crane had found more than just manganese on the absorption spectrometer. Kneeling down to cut the safety fuse, he caught another glimpse of the lone mast light dipping madly several kilometers away in the storm. He wondered who else might know by now.

While Frank checked the first charge, Charlie made his way to the starboard aft quarter of the flight deck and switched on the tiny instrument lights that illuminated the Austin-Western control panel. He pulled the levers with the synchronization of long experience, and the telescopic arm whined out as if protesting the worsening weather. He lowered the quick-release hook to the deck, where Sam connected it to the rope sling they had hastily improvised around the waist of the buoy.

Charlie waited for Sam's thumbs-up signal, then slowly lifted the buoy off the deck. The Austin-Western extension would allow them to lower the sonobuoy a good ten feet astern, well clear of the thrashing props.

When the arm reached the black sea beyond the arc of the stern light, Charlie waited for a lull, then dropped the arm so low that it momentarily disappeared into the crest of a thirty-foot wave. The buoy popped drunkenly to the surface, smacking against the quick-release hook at the end of the arm. In the trough Charlie shouted, "Now!" and Sam jerked the rope attached to the quick release hook. Nothing happened.

"What's the matter?" bellowed Charlie. Sam tugged furiously at the line while the trunk of the buoy swung dangerously close to the stern. "Sling must have looped around the arm," said Sam, still tugging. Charlie retracted the arm slowly, simultaneously raising it above the props, trying to shake the loop free. Suddenly Sam felt the taut release line go slack. There was a splash, and the buoy was away.

Its salt corrosive pin began to break up and the hydrophones on the end of their cables streamed out of the buoy through the immediate subsurface turbulence to the quieter and darker regions below. In two hours the bung would disintegrate and the buoy itself would sink, preventing its nonstop beeps from interfering with commercial aircraft signals. This meant that they only had two hours, steaming at five to six knots, a ten- to twelve-kilometer run in which to find good coring sites and metalliferous muds on the valley floor. If there were any.

❧ ❧ ❧

Through Andrea Nolan's binoculars, the afterdeck of the *Petrel* looked like a small, brightly lit stage that had been so constructed as to rise and fall quickly in the darkness, only to emerge seconds later several meters from its previous position. She moved the binoculars up a centimeter or so to look at the flight deck, but a swell came between them and all she could see was darkness. She knew better than to adjust the glasses lower, and simply waited until the trawler rose on a crest. But except for the vertical red-white-red string of special operations lights on the main mast, the flight deck was in darkness.

"Signal!" she said impatiently. "For God's sake, signal! What the hell are you doing?"

❧ ❧ ❧

Two kilometers port aft of Andrea Nolan, and almost three kilometers from the *Petrel*, Doyle watched intently as the four-foot-diameter white meteorological balloon streamed from the *Petrel*, after the sonobuoy, trailing its yellow nylon rope like the tail of a kite—quickly disappearing over the storm-tossed sea. He couldn't see the size of the charge, only the blur of its release from the extended arm of the Austin-Western, and its fizzing safety fuse dropping out of sight like a firefly. From the time elapsed between the balloon's release and the release of the charge, he had an idea of the length of rope attached to the charge, and guessed that the explosion would probably occur more than a hundred feet beneath the surface. "Damn it!" he said. "We won't be able to see a thing if it goes bang that deep."

Tony was half asleep against the starboard door, but every now and then the noise of the winds would awaken him. "How about all those depth charges? You can see them."

"In the movies," said Doyle, "and only when they use four hundred pounds of TNT." He pointed to the *Petrel*. "They're probably using thirty pounds over there."

"Never mind," said the Captain. "Their stern's lit up like a Christmas tree. We won't lose 'em."

Doyle put the glasses down and felt for his Gitanes, but the packet was empty. "I want to know exactly what they're doing," he said. "What happens if they turn ten degrees and we don't see them put over a charge? We won't know whether they've ended the run or not." He crumpled the cigarette packet and tossed it out of the window, but the wind blew it back in his face.

"What difference does it make whether you can see 'em or not, if they don't find anything?" asked Tony.

"What do you use for brains?" snapped Doyle. "Jesus Christ, you think some dumb-ass scientist is going to work on spec in a storm like this?"

"That dumb-ass guy will," said Tony. "He comes back empty and he's out on his ass. He'll work in shit if he has to."

The Captain staggered as the trawler plowed into a high bow wave. "Don't worry," he said. "I've seen 'em do this before. They'll have to increase the charge the further they get away from the sonobuoy. Otherwise it won't register the shock wave. We'll see explosions on the surface as we get near the end of the line."

"We're not worried, Columbus," said Tony, but Doyle saw that he was. The approaching storm was beginning to frighten him, just as it was all of them—except, perhaps Jay, who sat silently waiting in the darkness of the wheelhouse recess. Doyle glanced at the barometer. He'd been frightened for the last hour. A gale was one thing; this weather was something else. But he knew what Jay would do if they went in now. So did Tony—he'd done it for him often enough.

〰 〰 〰

As he retracted the Austin-Western arm, Charlie heard Frank call urgently from below. He flicked off the hydraulic power, leaving the uncradled arm sticking out over the afterdeck like a giant finger pointing into the night, and slithered down the stairway to the afterdeck.

With Sam busy attaching the sling that would hold the waist of the second charge, Frank was having trouble filling the balloon for the next charge. The small compressor astern kept cutting out. While Charlie tended it Frank renewed his efforts. Once the compressed air was flowing again, Charlie took the opportunity to grab a quick cup of coffee from the wardroom galley.

In the wardroom lounge, the Scottish Mate sat half asleep, as he listened to the wild crackle of a shortwave broadcast from Japan. The bosun wondered why he was up so late—it wasn't his shift, but before he could think more of it, he remembered that he hadn't cradled the Austin-Western arm. If the old man saw that he'd have a fit. After only one mouthful he put down the cup and pulled up his parka. As he passed through the dry lab he saw from the recorder that the first explosion had gone off. Crane and his wife were watching the gradually undulating parallel lines closely. Without looking around, Crane said, "Bosun, have you and Frank got those three boomerang corers ready to toss over?"

"Yeah," Charlie lied, knowing they only had one ready, but feeling too exhausted to get into a panicky argument with Crane. Besides, all they had to do was check the electronic flashing units. In each corer these units were set in one of the two glass float balls which would pull the cores to the surface. The flashing units would indicate the core's position for pickup.

∽ ∽ ∽

As Charlie began his climb back up the ladder toward the darkness of the *Petrel*'s flight deck, Doyle, now two kilometers off the *Petrel*'s starboard beam, could see the bobbing light of the other trawler.

Tony saw it, too. "Why've they got their mast light on?"

Anxiously Doyle picked up the glasses. "He wants his contact to see him."

"Christ," said Tony impatiently. "Why don't we just get going with the S.O.S. plan?"

"Better to intercept than tackle," said the Captain.

"Listen," said Tony, "you're the hired hand, Grandma. Just steer the boat. Right?"

"Right," said the Captain. In the dim light of the Decca's scope he could just make out Tony's face. "You look a bit green," he said. "You look a bit sick."

Tony's finger stopped halfway toward the Captain as Doyle put his hand between them. "For crying out loud, you two. Knock it off. We've got a—" He stopped speaking and lifted the glasses. "Smart! Very smart," he said with professional admiration. "Their contact's waited until the work party is busy on the afterdeck—too busy to see anything else."

From the pitch-blackness of the *Petrel*'s flight deck, a light was stabbing the darkness.

On the *Petrel*, Charlie had reached the control panel of the Austin-Western and was about to turn on the hydraulic switch. Then he saw it too. It was yellow, and it blinked two more times. By the time he'd raced, tripped, and raced forward again in the darkness to the rear of the 'copter hangar, where the light had come from, whoever had signaled Andrea Nolan had vanished. The only thing Charlie could hear above the wind was the slamming of a hatch.

"What does yellow mean?" snapped Doyle to the Captain.

The Captain shrugged. "I dunno. Like traffic lights, maybe? Red for stop. Green for go." He shrugged again. "Yellow is standby, I guess."

"You guess? You *guess*?"

"Listen, Mister, I'm only hired to steer the boat, remember? Anyway, it's probably not a standard code, just something they've arranged with the contact. They could hardly risk the time to send out a letter in Morse, could they?"

"Shit!" said Doyle, slapping his palm on the bulkhead. "All right," he said, recovering his composure. "All right, at least we know something's going down."

"Or coming up?" said Tony, giggling.

Doyle ignored him. "So let's all watch that other trawler," he said. "Captain, move in closer."

"But don't you think—"

"Move in closer." Doyle's voice was frigid with anger.

               ~   ~   ~

Andrea Nolan took a bite out of the sandwich, and just from the way she chewed, Vandyke could tell she was pleased. He enjoyed looking at her. He nodded toward the *Petrel.* "Yellow is good, huh?"

"It means they've probably found hot muds." As she turned toward him her face caught the golden glow of the radar screen, and for a split second her eyes were like a cat's. "Now we have to stick to them like butter to bread," she said. "The moment they find something definite, our contact will flash green. Then we'll have our sample in sight."

The Captain belched and apologized. With the wind and sea howling constantly and no time for fishing, he was bored. He knew the coming storm was a potential killer, but he'd decided long ago that if you lived from the sea you had to take chances with her—just as he was taking chances with this woman who'd hired him. But what would the unflappable Andrea Nolan do if the going got rough, he wondered. She was ambitious enough, no doubt about that, but was she tough enough? Would she stick it out, or would she cut and run? "Who's your contact?" he asked.

Andrea Nolan looked down into the galley. "Just someone who can read a thermometer," she said. "Is there any more coffee?"

31

Sitting alone at the recorder, Joe Crane saw the first good coring site in a flaw that looked as if a cross-section of marble cake had been divided into three pieces, the center section sunk lower and wedged between the other two. It was a sign that here in the axial valley floor, between two relatively new ridges formed by the crust's spreading, there was a fissure. Hopefully, convection currents might be percolating through fissures to the rocks below, which had themselves been moved by the massive convection currents in the magma that had caused the spreading in the first place. It was all part of the world-wide motion of the tectonic plates, which in some places caused rocks to pile into ridges and in others had created the deep ocean trenches. Crane tapped the fissure trace as they passed over it. "Drop a boomerang!" he instructed Charlie.

"Where's your wife?"

"What?" asked Crane. He'd heard the bosun clearly enough, but he was far too interested in the possibility of hot springs to let the question register first time round.

"Where's your wife?" repeated Charlie.

"Resting. Why?"

"I like to know where everyone is in a blow like this."

Peering down at the fault line, Crane pushed the inter-com button. "Lab to bridge. Return to half mile from our present position." He turned to Charlie. "I don't know what you're on about, Bosun, but I haven't got time to waste. Tell Frank not to let out any more explosives. We'll turn back in a half-mile circle and then drop a boomerang. Should be bang on target."

∽ ∽ ∽

"Don't let it roll," said Frank.

Sam, cursing the dried salt on his glasses, leaned harder

against one of the boomerang corers. From a distance the corer looked like a four-gallon gasoline drum with a four-foot gun barrel poking out of it. It weighed a hundred and sixty-five pounds, and Frank knew that once loose on the deck it would be a monster to stop. A sheet of spray stung their faces. "Charlie and I'll roll it over to the Austin-Western," Frank bellowed. "That way we can release it clear of the props. You relash the oth—" Without warning the *Petrel* came about in the heavy seas, took a fifty-three-degree roll, and the corer was away. It rumbled across the deck, slammed into the starboard rail, smashing its glass dumbbell float and electronic flash unit.

"C'mon!" yelled Frank, throwing himself toward the corer, pinning its drum-like trunk against the side as the next huge wave came charging into them, pooping the stern with hundreds of gallons of water that poured through the dry-lab door. Frank felt the corer pushing him back, but Charlie arrived in time to throw his weight against the barrel. From the lab they could hear Joe Crane cursing the wave.

Frank could see that the lab was a foot deep in water. The recorder, high on the counter, was safe, but notebooks, pens, and loose rags floated among swamped toolboxes and, worse, the electronics spare-parts box.

Mary Crane peered in the side door. "My God," she said. Putting down her coffee cup she immediately began retrieving whatever she could before the water could rush astern on the next pitch, taking the floating cargo with it.

The wind was now so cold that Frank's hands were numb. In the glow from the lab Charlie could see Sam, balancing one of the float units, coming toward them. The corer started to move again. Both men gave it their full weight and held it steady.

Charlie put his mouth close to Frank's ear, and shouted. "I saw someone signaling from the flight deck."

"What?"

"I saw—"

"Son of a—You tell Crane?"

"No. He's his old self now—well, sane enough. Don't want to start him off again."

"Yeah. Were they signaling to one of the trawlers, or both, I wonder."

"Christ, I hadn't thought of that. You think it's a team out there?"

"Who knows?"

"Someone does."

"Don't tell anyone else," yelled Frank. "We have to play this one close."

Before Charlie could respond, Sam arrived with the new unit. The seaman bent low, nursing it like a baby while Frank pulled out the circuit-breaker pin. The star-white 1.2-watt flash began. It would flash once every two seconds for forty-eight hours, until the Eveready 491 battery exhausted itself. Frank replaced the pin, breaking the circuit until they were ready to drop the corer overboard.

In eight minutes they were above the fissure. Frank pulled the pin out again, and Charlie climbed up to the operating panel of the Austin-Western. As he carefully lifted, extended, and lowered the steel arm, the boomerang corer swinging wildly from the sling harness a few meters beneath the quick-release hook, he kept glancing behind him into the darkness of the flight deck. There was no light.

This time, when Sam pulled the quick-release rope the corer plunged straight to the sea and was gone.

∽ ∽ ∽

Joe Crane saw the second fault exactly 8.3 kilometers from the first. It was two kilometers wider, and the probability of a fissure looked much greater because of the 170-meter-wide, 20-meter-high mounds surrounding the fracture. He decided that this was a site worthy of a boomerang camera, as well as a boomerang corer.

The corer was released first, because of the slight possibility that with its faster rate of descent it could fall on the camera unit. It would take five minutes to descend the two thousand-odd meters, and after it had been driven into the sediment by its speed and weight, the trigger release mechanism would allow the glass dumbbell float to rise free of the drum, extracting the spring-leaf-sealed, plastic core barrel from the metal housing—just as one would pull a refill from a ballpoint pen. The flashing float, with the core suspended beneath, would pop to the surface approximately forty minutes later. By then the Petrel would be about seven kilometers further down the run.

Although, at a hundred and ninety-five pounds, the boomerang camera unit was heavier than the corer, it was smaller and more compact. Its medium-wide-angle, 35-millimeter movie camera, set in a cone-shaped high-pressure housing, was set to run for twenty minutes before a time-release lever jettisoned the last of the twenty holding weights attached to the base of the assembly. As the camera rose from the sea bottom in its nineteen one-minute stages before losing the last weight, the focus adjusted automatically from zero to infinity.

The Austin-Western picked up the camera unit by its nose cone U-bolt, and in a minute it was over the side and released. Although its flashing unit was already working, the phosphorous flares which would provide the high-intensity wide-angle light needed for the twenty-minute movie sequence would not begin burning until the assembly hit bottom and the flares were activated by a trip lever. The camera unit and the corer would be picked up on the *Petrel*'s return run—if she could see their flashing strobe lights in the heavy seas. The weather reports handed to the Captain by a tired radio officer now confirmed what everyone on the ship had already guessed—the storm line was coming in faster than predicted.

∽ ∽ ∽

When Doyle saw the boomerang drop, he was wracked with indecision. Should he go on tracking the *Petrel*, or should he remain and pick up the boomerang corer before the *Petrel* returned? Would he gamble everything on picking up one core, hoping it was hot and metalliferous, so that he could run for home before anyone else? Was that what the yellow signal meant? But what would the other *Sea Wasp* do if he moved on with the *Petrel*? Maybe the signal was a trap to get him to stay and be left behind . . .

"What'll we do?" asked the Captain impatiently.

Doyle picked up the glasses again, as if they would provide the answer. They didn't. He cursed. There would have been no dilemma if the sea had been calm, as the Decca radar could have picked up the other trawler wherever she moved, but now waves thirty and forty feet high hid the other trawler from radar view, and all hope of visual contact was lost in the line of squalls that was periodically obscuring the other's mast light.

"Goddamn it!" said Doyle, sweating, resentful of the buffeting his body was taking in the bucking wheelhouse,

and unsure of what course to follow. If he didn't make a
decision soon, the *Petrel*'s lighted afterdeck would be lost
in the curtain of rain.

When he finally made up his mind, he did so more from
fear of being left alone in a hurricane than from any
cool calculation of what the other ship might be up to.
"Stay with the *Petrel*," he said, as confidently as possible.

It wasn't until ten minutes later, when he caught a
fleeting glimpse of the other trawler's mast, that Doyle
knew he'd made the right decision. The yellow signal, then,
was only a general standby warning.

≈ ≈ ≈

The sixth charge, halfway along the twelve-kilometer
seismic run, was fifty pounds, and now Charlie could faintly
discern the dancing phosphorescence well astern, as thousands of bubbles made a twenty-foot circle in the black
side of a wave. After the next explosion, again of fifty
pounds, he saw nothing.

≈ ≈ ≈

In his cabin Frank rummaged in his seagoing kit until
he found the can of Malachite Green. It took him several
minutes because it had been years since he'd had occasion
to use it. The last time was when they'd suspected a thief
amongst the dock workers. The thief's habit was to casually walk aboard, pretending he was a steward, and riffle
cabins on the pretext of making beds. When the harbor
police caught him, the crew had been amused that instead
of being caught redhanded the thief had been caught
greenhanded—the bluish-green of the unwashable stain
which the Malachite 657 brought out on fingernails after
the hands had come into contact with even a few specks of
its fine powder.

The signal light had worried Frank. He knew that for
anyone to win the race for the muds, they had to have a
sample in hand. That meant getting a sample to one of
the trawlers—or to both. If his plan was to work, it was
essential that he tell no one what he was about to do. He
went down to the dry lab, where Joe Crane was sitting at
the absorption spectrometer while Mary watched the seismic trace. In the raging storm, a quietude had enveloped
Crane, as he felt more and more certain of success. Now
he was rechecking his earlier test and running others from

another part of the grab sample, carefully watching the flickering of the Beckman's gauges.

"How is it?" Frank asked.

Crane smiled at the needle swinging far to the right.

"Rich," said Crane. "We're over a valley almost twenty miles long by five to eight miles wide. If the cores over the wider area are the same as the grab, it'll be worth more than Saudi Arabia."

Frank was tempted to tell Crane about his plan to use the Malachite 657, but then, suddenly, he realized what the Chief Scientist was saying. More than Saudi Arabia . . . As a paid scientist of the Institute, Crane could hardly benefit himself. Unless . . . Jesus, thought Frank, if someone else were allowed to get the jump on us, to get the sample to Vancouver ahead of the *Petrel*, then all they'd have to do would be pay into a Swiss bank account and Crane could "retire" a year later—to all intents and purposes as clean as a whistle. Is that why he had been near mad with expectation? But the informant *couldn't* be Crane. But whether or not it actually could be, Frank told himself to keep his mouth shut, and tell no one.

"You finished with that grab sample now?" he asked Crane.

"Yes. Take it to the cold room, if you like."

"Right."

"And Frank?"

"Yes?"

"Thanks."

Despite the howling of the storm, Frank felt within himself a cone of pure silence: he was unsure whether he was being touched by the warmth of friendship, or by the false comaraderie of subterfuge. His own smile was just as inscrutable as Joe Crane's.

"Don't mention it," he said.

～ ～ ～

Opening up the cold room down below on the crew's deck. Frank pulled on a pair of rubber gloves. He heard a faint ring like a distant dinner gong. It was, he knew, the last charge Sam had dropped overboard. They were getting bigger all the time. This one had been seventy pounds, and either the fuse had burned too quickly or the wind had pushed the balloon forward, bringing the ammonia dynamite too near the ship. Unlike the people on the trawlers, Frank couldn't see the jump of white water from the explosion, but he could still feel the reverberations running through the *Petrel*'s hull.

Looking around to see that none of the off-watch crew were in the laundry nearby, Frank entered the cold room and pulled the door shut. The sixty-watt bulb threw a weak glow over the eight-by-six-foot space. Putting the sample bag down near the other samples from Big Bess' haul, Frank took the can of Malachite from his pocket. Turning the pepper-shaker top to the sprinkle position, he tapped the bottom of the can, watching carefully as the powder dropped like fine dust over the sample bags. Then he carefully returned the can to his pocket and used his shoulder to push open the inside latch of the insulated door. Once outside, he deposited the gloves in a waste bin, pushing them down with oil rags and placing several used pop cans on top.

He wondered who it would be ...

32

The climactic thumping of the drums, the swirl of mauve and orange-gold skirts, had Miel in a sweat as the Tahitian dancers brought the Tavana's special mid-afternoon Polynesian show to its conclusion. The frantic yet controlled pulsation of hips, thighs, and pelvis under the grass skirts held his attention like no other show on Waikiki. His face was flushed and his fingers were drumming the table. The dancers gave one final pelvic thrust in unison and the lights went down. The *Otea* was over.

Freddie slipped in beside him. "Christ!" said Miel, breathing heavily. "You see that? They'd tear your prick off." He sipped at the Mai Tai, tossing the flower into the smoldering ashtray. "How we doing, Freddie?"

"Our guys in Washington are moving ass. We've offered the Canadians a large slice of the George Bank on the east coast, and we're asking for Juan de Fuca Ridge in return.

We drew the Forty-Ninth Parallel out from the west coast and showed them that it put Juan de Fuca inside the U.S. two-hundred-mile zone, and told them we'd press that point at the U.N., and maybe at the fourth Law of the Sea Conference. But we didn't want to push it too hard— you know, or come across heavy. Wanted it to sound more like a trade."

Miel watched one of the short-skirted waitresses. "Hey, beautiful. How about another round?"

"Right away."

"Right away, right away," said Miel happily as he watched her behind move tightly in the green and white plumeria-patterned skirt. "Could you screw that, Freddie?"

"Yeah."

"Yeah, yeah." Miel flipped the young lawyer's tie insolently. "You'd shoot your bolt if she touched you. Yeah, bullshit. Anyway, I don't care about that Washington crap. That'll work out if we get the stuff to lobby with. So tell me the important news—what's Doyle doin'? Pickin' his nose?"

"There's a gale, a hurricane or something. No chance of radio contact with Seattle. They're too far out."

"Terrific. Well, he better not lose 'em."

"He won't," said Freddie confidently.

"How do you know?"

"Not with Jay and Tony there."

"Hey, Freddie, you're getting the idea."

Freddie didn't want to smile but he did. He hated Miel, but a compliment from him always made him feel good. It was sort of like stepping into the major leagues, he thought—an acknowledgment that you knew your way around. "Hey, honey," he said to the waitress when she brought Miel his Mai Tai. "How about a Coconut Willie?"

Miel roared with laughter. "Shit—a Coconut Willie!"

Freddie started to object, but Miel cut him short. Miel's gut was poking out of his red flowered shirt, crushing the white pikake lei against the table. As he leaned forward his blotched purpled face almost touched Freddie's. "You'd better be right about Doyle. You recommended him. This isn't penny poker. Understand?"

Freddie nodded nervously. "I understand."

Miel threw away the purple orchid from his new Mai Tai. "You'd better." He tested the drink. "Too much pineapple," he said. "I tell you one thing, Freddie. I told that guy Jay that I don't want any fucking lawsuits getting in the way of our lobbying."

"So?"

"So I only expect to see one boat coming back with that stuff—if there is any. And that's *our* boat."

"But you can't—"

"I haven't *done* anything," Miel cut in. He was watching the waitress again. "I was just telling him what I'd like. Okay?" Miel leaned over. "But tell me, Freddie—how do you think a sixty-foot trawler can outrun the *Petrel*? Fifteen knots against twenty? No way. Let me tell you something else. I got a boat of my own, and accidents happen all the time at sea. Ever heard of an S-band antenna? A wave guide? No? Well, doesn't matter. The thing is, as this Jay pointed out, in all that salt spray all kinds of things screw up—specially in rough weather." Miel drained his Mai Tai.

"But—but Christ!" said Freddie, alarmed. "Doyle doesn't know that. I mean, I never told him to . . ."

"*Relax.* Jay knows." Miel shook his head derisively and laughed, his stomach jiggling on the table's edge. " 'Hey, honey,' " he mimicked, " 'how about a Coconut Willie?' " He shook his head again. "Shit, Freddie, you kill me."

33

"That's it," said Joe Crane. The ship shook slightly from the last hundred-and-twenty-pound charge. "That's another fissure I want to core. The muds look deep."

"Boomerang?" said Frank.

"No, long-piston corer. Before the boomerangs come up."

Charlie drew heavily on his cigarette. The smoke was making Frank ill. "No way the old man'll go for it," said Charlie, rubbing the tattoo. He looked at the seismic trace and his watch. "We've run ten of our twelve kilometers anyway. We're damn near out of time. By the time we go back and start looking for those two boomerang cores we'll be smack into force eleven."

"Look," said Crane. "If we're fast enough, the Captain won't know. I'll just tell the bridge we're dropping a corer."

"Without telling him what kind?" Charlie held up his hands, palms away from him. "Leave me out of it."

"Charlie, we need this core to know what's down there. It looks good."

"You guys found something in the grab—right? The spectrometer came through with something—right?"

Frank said nothing. Joe Crane grinned sheepishly. "Yes. We did." Sam came into the lab. "So thanks for your confidence in me," said Charlie. "Let's rig the fucking corer."

As Frank followed him out, Crane started to speak but changed his mind.

Sam looked about at the lab's fluorescent tubes, reflecting white bars in his glasses. "Something I should know?"

"No," said Crane, pulling up his parka. "Come on, lend a hand."

Glancing down at the recorder, Sam tried to figure out what all the fuss was about. Nobody ever told him anything.

On deck, Frank tried to apologize. For a second his voice was lost in the sound of the storm. "Charlie, I . . ."

"Hey," said Charlie, spinning around. "It wasn't me who sent that fucking signal, you know. *I* told *you*, buddy, remember?"

"Okay. I'm sorry."

"So am I. How deep is this fucking thing?"

"Twenty-four hundred meters."

As the ship slowed to one and a half knots, Crane, Sam, and Frank unlashed the thousand-pound piston corer. Frank strained to see beyond the circle of bridge and foc'sle lights that rose and fell with the dark green sea, now curtained by spray and foam. But beyond the light there was only an all-engulfing blackness unrelieved by moon or stars.

"Now hit straight on, you big bastard," Frank said, talking to the long-piston corer. The corer was basically the same shape as the smaller boomerang corers, but it operated on the same trip-weight principle as the big grab. When the hundred-pound trip weight hit bottom, the corer would free fall for fifteen feet.

Most of its weight came from the eight hundred pounds of half-moon-shaped steel weights stacked around the central steel column, to which could be fixed any length of pipe from six to thirty feet.

Provided the bottom was soft enough, Frank knew, two things would happen when the corer hit. First, the barrel would thrust into the seabed, its penetration governed by the compactness of the sedimentary layers; second, a loose piston attached to the main wire would move up inside the barrel, creating a vacuum and sucking the mud up. With any luck, the piston wouldn't cause too much distortion in the top few inches of the core.

On the forward Austin-Western, hydraulic fluid had begun to bleed slightly, dripping down in long, thin webs that in the harsh glare of the worklight looked like congealed blood. The Chief Engineer came on deck to have a look.

"Ah, Christ," he said. "That's no trouble. Just keep going and we'll strip it down after." For the Chief, Murphy's law, that everything that can go wrong will go wrong, was an article of faith. Hands in his pockets, he sucked pensively on his cigarette, watching as Charlie lowered the hook toward the inverted U-bolt on top of the corer. "That thing wouldn't pull a prick out of custard," he grunted, with the authority of many a coring station.

Joe Crane looked at Frank. "Thank you," he said to the Chief. "You shouldn't bolster our confidence like that."

"Yeah," said Frank. "It'll go straight to our head." Sam grinned, and the angle of the deck light revealed the true color of his eyes for the first time. Frank was surprised, almost shocked, to see how youthful they were.

The Chief's cigarette bobbed up and down between his lips like a nervous insect. "It'll go straight to the bottom and that's where it'll stay. Twenty-four-foot barrel? Holy Jesus, you'll anchor us."

"Get your fishing rod out, Chief."

"What?" shouted the Chief genially. "And miss all the fun? No way. I'm gonna watch you silly bastards."

Charlie pulled back on the lever. The Austin-Western cried its resistance, and the thousand pounds of steel began to rise. Using rope ends, Frank, Crane and Sam began lowering the trip weight through the unchained opening on the starboard side. When he saw the wave, Charlie yelled, but no one heard him. Sam held position, but Crane and Frank were pushed across the deck by the sheer volume of water. The Chief instinctively stepped forward, grabbing the hundred-pound trip-weight wire until the others regained their balance. But the equalizing roll threw him hard against the rail.

"Drop it!" bellowed Frank, as loudly as he could. The Chief let go the trip weight and the wire sliced across his hand, immediately drawing blood. The weight slid thumping down the ship's side as the starboard side heaved.

Back on their feet, Frank and Crane tried to help Sam steady the main body of the corer. If it began to swing, there would be no stopping it, other than by dropping it into the *Petrel*'s deck. All the time they pushed and tugged at the barrel's nose to get it pointed overboard through the unchained gap, the three men were watching the thousand pounds of steel poised above them. If a strained section of cable gave way and it slid off the block, their heads would crack like peanut shells. Frank also watched the safety pin. If the corer pretripped over water, there was a good chance that the wire would at least whip out over the water rather than the deck. The biggest danger was a pretrip in the few moments when the corer hung high in the semidarkness over the deck. Like now.

Tate's voice crackled into the storm. "Get that thing over before it kills someone."

"Thought he was off watch," mumbled Frank.

"Obviously not," said Crane.

Frank watched anxiously as Charlie lifted the levers and the arm jerked upwards, taking the corer even higher toward the rigging. The thirty-foot wave that lifted them gradually up and over into a comfortable trough was long and smooth, but it swung the core barrel into the Swann winch with a resounding crash, jarring the whole structure. The trip weight smashed against the ship's rubbing strake, and the pin flew out. For perhaps one-tenth of a second the trip arm was lifted up like one side of a beam balance; then the corer fell free. Crane and Charlie swung away at the same time. As he dived beneath the overhanging bridge wing, Frank grabbed at Sam's arm. He missed.

Frank rolled over, looking around. For a moment time was frozen. The silver flash of the free-fall wire across the deck took only a split second, but it seemed suspended in space. He watched helplessly as the wire writhed in the air like a wounded python. Then there was a violent *whack*, a scream, and the loudest crash he'd ever heard as the twenty-five-foot corer struck the deck, pivoted like a grotesque dancer, and fell, wedging itself between the foc's'le and the winch.

As Frank got up, still swaying from the concussion, the general alarm clanged out. He could see only two other figures on deck—Charlie, who had taken less than three seconds to slide down from the Austin-Western control, and Crane.

Dazed, Frank stood shaking his head like a punchdrunk boxer. Charlie was shouting something, but it was difficult to hear anything above the deafening ringing of the alarm bells.

"Get the boathooks! Boathooks!" shouted Charlie.

"What—?"

"For Christ's sake, Frank—the boathook!"

The bridge watchman swung the searchlight out over the water. Fifty yards out, carried swiftly by current and wind but still supported by his bright orange life jacket, Sam's arms were waving frantically.

Frank grabbed a boathook, dimly aware of Crane beside him. Someone was throwing the yellow nylon lifelines, but the wind was blowing them back just as quickly and now they were floating uselessly toward the ship.

The engines' thumping quickened and Frank heard the surge of the bow thrusters as Tate maneuvered to get on Sam's windward side, from where the life preservers might be carried to him by the wind. "Why don't they just go in with the ship?" said Mary Crane to no one in particular.

"In this weather?" said a seaman. "We'd be lucky not to run right over him."

"But he could be lost in the dark."

"I know," said the seaman, his voice taut with anguish.

Already Frank could hear the cranking of the davits lowering the Zodiac—the motorized rubber raft. But he knew that no matter how well they were trained, cold hands would take at least ten minutes to get the raft outboard and two or three men safely on her in these seas.

It was due solely to Tate's expertise that, despite the ever present danger of being swamped beam on, he got the ship on Sam's windward side only four minutes after he had gone overboard. The first in the rain of life preservers that flew out toward Sam was the best-aimed. It landed no more than a foot to his right. He clutched it con-

vulsively, pulling it down over his shoulders. A loud cheer
went up from men ranged all along the starboard side—
but then they lost sight of him in a series of troughs. Then
they saw him again, still locked to the preserver. Another
cheer went up. His glasses had fallen off, and once again
Frank was surprised by how young he looked. Someone
appeared with a pile of navy blue service blankets. Joe
Crane headed the line of seamen who pulled Sam quickly
through the freezing waters. In the heaving green sea
slopping against the ship's leeward side, Sam's face was
white and shocked.

Crane marveled at how light he was, considering that he
must be soaked clean through. Not realizing what had
happened, not seeing the pink blood which was diluted
and almost lost in the foam, he credited the ease of the
pull to there being so many eager hands heaving in unison
on the lifeline. It was not until one man let go of the
rope, stumbled to the rail next to him and threw up,
that Crane saw that in the life preserver there was only
half a man—a head and torso with a few white, spaghetti-
like ligaments trailing where there should have been legs.
It was all very clean, like a filleted fish.

"How—how could he wave?" asked an oiler. "How
could he grab the preserver?"

The Chief Engineer put his arm in front of his mouth.
"Jeez, Jesus . . ."

"How could he move his hands?" the oiler repeated.

The Chief closed his eyes. "Nerves," he said. "I saw it in
the war. Like a chicken with its head cut off. For a few
minutes your brain and limbs keep working. Jesus Christ!"

❧ ❧ ❧

Doyle had watched it all, but even with the glasses his
image of what had happened was fragmentary, as if instead of having watched a movie he'd seen only a series of
slides interspersed with periods of darkness. He wasn't
aware, for example, that Sam had been sliced in half by
the wire. Doyle had seen only the white lump being pulled
up the *Petrel's* side, and thought that he'd been rescued.

❧ ❧ ❧

Andrea Nolan was sick. She too had only seen fragments
of the incident, but her glasses at a different angle had

picked up the full horror of the final moments. Vandyke tried to comfort her, but it was impossible to do that and man the wheel at the same time. The seas were faster now and the danger of a massive wave crashing over the stern and driving them under was increasing.

"My God," he whispered hoarsely, staring out at the dark, rain-spattered sea. "Those sons of bitches."

"Who?" she said.

"Those fat cats back in Vancouver and wherever. They sit and sip their Martinis and dream up plans for higher profits." He pointed to the *Petrel.* "A man—a *man* was just cut in half. They won't talk about that in their soft recliners, but it's men like him who push their Dow Industrials up."

Andrea shrugged. "They're the risks."

"What the hell do you mean? You were just sick to your stomach, lady."

"I know . . . I know how you feel, but we can't give in now. We're too close to—"

Following a loud bang, Andrea saw a pile of debris sweep past, rasping against the wheelhouse as it went. "What was that?"

"The skiff—our lifeboat."

"Don't you have an inflatable raft?"

"Yes, but . . ."

"But what?" she said sharply.

"The inspection—well, we sort of let it slip. We didn't think we'd be—"

"How long ago?"

The Captain, shamefaced, looked at the compass. "About a year."

Andrea was incredulous. "It hasn't been inspected since then?"

"No."

"Terrific," she said. "No wonder so many of you idiots are lost at sea."

"We'll be all right," he said, "if we get *this* fishing over with soon."

"They'll head for the second boomerang they dropped. They won't risk another piston core after that. It won't be long now."

"Then he wasn't our contact—the man who was killed?"

"No," she said. "He wasn't."

"Maybe he was the other's?"

Andrea felt sick again.

❦ ❦ ❦

"As soon as we pick up this boomerang core and camera we go straight on to the first one you dropped, then home. Understood?"

"Thank you, Captain," began Mary Crane. "I think Sam would have——"

"Madam!" Tate exploded, "I don't give a fish's tit for what you think one of my seamen might have wanted. You and your party have only one thing in mind. Fame and bloody fortune. No matter what the cost to anyone else."

Mary looked down at the deck. "I'm sorry for what I said earlier. I had no right to——"

"I'll tell you this, madam." Tate threw down the gleaming steel dividers. "I'll transfer to another vessel before I'll have your lot aboard again. You're bloody mad, all of you! Now, if you'll excuse me, we have to find your bloody boomerangs."

As she left the bridge, Tate's voice followed her. "He was married, you know. Two children. A boy and a girl."

Mary froze for a second on the stairwell, then turned back up the stairs. "I'm sorry," she said again. "I'm very sorry, Captain." She could feel her cheeks burning.

"Goddamn it!" said Tate, his fist smacking the steering console. "Goddamn you people and your bloody toys!"

After Mary Crane had left, there was a cold silence inside the wind-lashed bridge. For the first time in months the helmsman, who'd been watching the pinpoint of light on the trawler's masthead, was aware of the chronometer ticking behind him like a time bomb.

34

It was Johns who first saw the flashing light of the boomerang corer. In the somber mood that lay over the ship,
with Sam's remains now cooling in storage with the geological samples, the commands and responses on the bridge
lost all their usual informality, as if formality could best
express what everyone felt at such a time. Johns had
even felt impelled to spruce up, shaving off his blond stubble out of some vague feeling of respect. He'd never even
liked Sam. He'd been a moody son of a bitch, without
the slightest trace of humor. Still, the Mate had to admit
that the man had done his job well. Trying to put the seaman's death out of his mind, Johns strained his eyes for
the corer flash, glad of something to do. He'd looked for
many a flashing light on many a dark night, so he didn't
look out to sea, but rather moved his gaze slowly along the
glass of the bridge's windows a few feet in front of him.
It was there, in one of the windows, that he saw the reflection. This one was not yellowish orange, like the dots
thrown off by the radar set, but white, like a tiny star. He
lost it in the swells for a minute, but then it came back
and he got a fix on it. "Flashing beacon. Bearing one two
seven degrees."

Tate picked up the glasses to verify. "Steer one two
seven degrees."

"Steer one two seven degrees, sir."

"Bring her around easy, helm."

" 'Round easy, sir."

Frank, sheltering behind the winch on the port well
deck, still felt sick to his stomach. When he saw the second
flashing light—the boomerang camera—it did nothing to
raise his spirits. He recalled Andrea Nolan's efforts to buy
him off. It was people like her—craving for glory and power—it was they, he thought, who should be the ones who

went for the high jump. But things never worked out like that. Instead, it was always some poor bastard like Sam, some deckhand, some working stiff, who got his back busted, his pelvis crushed, or his arm amputated while the fat cats—especially the ones who had never been on a ship—sat around complaining of overtime costs and danger money, whining about the growing power of the unions, while noting that 1970 was a good year for claret.

∾ ∾ ∾

"No, I don't want to go out," said Joe Crane, slumped in the swivel chair that creaked every time the *Petrel* was buffeted by another of the endless onrush of waves. "I caused the man's death."

"Oh, for God's sake!" Mary's voice was sharp and impatient. "Don't be ridiculous."

Joe rubbed his eyes. "We should take that boy's body— we should take him home."

"We're going to," Mary said. "As soon as we pick up this core and the camera and the first core we dropped."

"We should take him home now."

Mary wedged the toilet door onto a folded-up piece of paper to stop it from banging. The sound was getting on her nerves. "What difference does an hour or so make now? He's dead."

Crane looked hard at his wife. "What's come over you?" he asked quietly.

"What's come over *you?*" she snapped. "I nursed you through your . . . your depressions, your paranoia, whatever, so you could get what you always wanted. Now that we're this close to getting it, you're—"

"I'm what? Acting like a human being for the first time in years?"

"Oh, my God, Joe," she moaned. "Spare me your sense of guilt. Please. You're acting just like Tate. Why do you men always do that? Play hard and tough, then use women as sponges for your guilt?" She listened to the howling of the storm. It sounded now like an omen. Perhaps they hadn't come that near to success after all; they still hadn't recovered a sample from the valley floor. And even if they got one, perhaps the valley, unlike the ridge, would turn out to be stone cold. "I'm sorry, too, Joe," she said. "I'm sorry we ever came out, but—"

"But what?"

"We've come this far," she said. "Let's finish it. Get out on deck." She walked over to the porthole.

Crane buried his head in his hands. "Christ, I'm tired."

Mary recoiled as spray splattered the glass. Then the wind swept it clear again and she looked defiantly out into the darkness. "You have to find out what's in that tube of mud," she said. "It could change everything."

Crane folded a wet facecloth and slapped it over his eyes. "Change everything for who? For Sam?"

Mary Crane gripped the porthole latch tightly as the ship bucked hard aport. "No," she said. "For us."

∽ ∽ ∽

Frank clipped his lifeline to the rail and shifted his grip on the ten-foot boathook. The core and the camera unit were a mile apart, and picking them up wasn't going to be easy. But the most difficult task was the Captain's. He would have to bring the ship ten feet from the green netting that enclosed the float and flasher units. Too close in the heavy seas and the units might easily smash against the ship's side. Too far away, and they would be out of reach. The only thing to do was to get to leeward of them and use the wind to push them down on the ship.

On the first pass, the flashing strobe unit of the corer passed just beyond Frank's reach and drifted astern. And on the second. And on the third. Frank was sweating now, and on the bridge the Captain was furious.

"Goddamn it!" he said, and swung the ship hard a'starboard once more. In an hour the winds would be blowing force twelve.

Charlie, looking like an Old Testament prophet in his heavy wet gear, leaned on the winch, surveying the flight deck above. Frank knew what he was doing.

"See anything?" he asked.

"No," said Charlie, shading his eyes. "With all the deck lights on fore and aft, whoever it is won't show up. Too conspicuous. Besides, the signal would be soaked up by our glare."

"Good for us," said Frank.

"Yeah," growled Charlie. "But who is it?"

Now Tate was once again bringing the *Petrel* astride the core unit. This time Frank, using the extended working platform on the starboard side to gain extra reach, hooked the web on his third snatch and began the hard, direct pull up. Charlie ran to help. As the strobelight came aboard, Crane appeared from the wet lab, taking hold of the unit until the plastic core barrel was aboard. Under the deck lights they could already see that it was dark green. Again, there was the overpowering stench of hydrogen sulphide.

"It's warm," said Charlie.

Frank slipped as the next wave thumped the side, but Charlie managed to keep the core upright, so as not to mix the layers, and struggled into the lab with the thirty pounds of sediment. Crane took samples from the top and bottom layers, replacing the stainless-steel spring-leaf catcher on the bottom with a plastic cap before the mud oozed out. Charlie began to leave, but Frank tapped him on the shoulder. "Hey, Charlie?"

"Yeah?"

"Why don't you stay for the tests?"

Charlie smiled, grateful for Frank's attempt to include him this time. "Thanks, Frank, but I'm cold. I need a coffee—or something a bit stronger. You can fill me in later if you want. I'll take your word for it. Truth is, I really couldn't give a shit right now. Not after Sam."

Crane, already busy at the spectrometer, looked up. "It'll soon be over, Charlie."

Charlie's eyes swept the darkness for the trawlers. "You think so?"

∽ ∽ ∽

It had taken the bridge another ten minutes to locate the camera unit, but now they were closing. Charlie tossed the remains of his Bacardi-spiced coffee overboard and grabbed a hook.

The camera frame swept past Frank, tantalizingly out of reach, but the roll pushed it in closer to Charlie and the hook found its mark. The relief winchman lowered the hydrographic line to the water's edge and the special spring-latch block was clipped onto the frame. The combination of sea spray, flashing light, and water streaming from the camera unit blinded the two men, and for a moment it seemed as if the assembly would swing wildly in and demolish itself against the bulkhead, but the pitch

of the ship's port side counteracted the starboard roll and
they managed to fend the frame off with the hooks. Frank
bellowed, "Station finished!"

The *Petrel*'s engines shook heavily and she turned once
more—this time to pick up the first, and now final, core.

Inside the lab, Mary Crane watched as Charlie and
Frank disassembled the camera unit. Frank didn't speak,
not so much because he was tired as because he was almost afraid to ask Crane the results of the tests. When
the Polaroid movie drum was removed, Frank eased himself up from the deck, his back stiff from the cold.

Again Charlie started to leave, but this time Frank
caught him by the sleeve. The bosun shrugged good-naturedly, leaning back against the sink.

Frank turned to Crane. "What's the story?"

Mary Crane reached for the film drum. Frank let it
slip from his hands. Crane switched off the spectrometer.
He was bowed with fatigue, but his eyes were wide awake.
He spoke so quietly they could hardly hear him. Frank
could see he was still shaken by Sam's death. His voice
varied strangely, teetering on the edge of a shout one moment and barely audible the next.

"It's richer than the last," he said.

"Jesus!" said Frank. "Is that true? I mean—how far is
it between this core and the last one?"

"Approximately ten miles," said Crane. "Ten miles
by an average of seven miles wide. The whole valley might
be like this."

Frank sat down on the nearest trunk. "Mother of God.
How many square miles is that?"

"If it extends into the Cascadian Plain—if the final core
turns out the same as this one—it's about . . . thirty miles
by six. Around two hundred square miles."

"How deep?" Frank pressed. "How deep is the sediment?"

"A mile thick. Gets richer toward the bottom of this
core. And there are probably deposits in the rock beneath
that. The video'll give us a better idea."

Charlie was confused. "How much, Doc? What's it
worth?"

Crane took up a felt-tip pen and doodled on a piece of
paper. He could scarcely bring himself to believe it. "Oh,
it's very high grade," he said softly. "If the final core is the
same, then the whole valley is hot. I'd say two hundred

million tons." He handed Frank a metallurgical breakdown he'd made as a result of the spectrometer tests:

Copper: 0.5%
Nickel: 1%
Manganese: 30%
Iron: 30%
Zinc: 5%
Lead: 5%
Silver: .028%
Gold: .001%

"Yeah," said Charlie, caught up in the excitement. "But
what's it worth?"

"Current prices," Crane mumbled, "around two thousand, possibly three."

Frank, his eyes racing over the list, gave out a long,
low whistle. Charlie looked confused. "Two thousand dollars?"

Frank let the spectrometer report fall to the floor and
roared with laughter. Tears came to his eyes. He slapped
Charlie so hard on the back the cigarette nearly dropped
from the bosun's mouth. "Two thousand million!" said
Frank. "Million, Charlie, million."

Mary Crane picked up the report from the deck and
coldly asked her husband for the keys to the chief scientist's safe, adding pointedly, "We're not quite finished in
the valley yet."

Frank's laughter died. "What do you mean?"

"The last core. We need the last core—the first one
we dropped. Even if it's hot all the way along, that
doesn't mean that there are metal deposits all the way
along the valley floor. Could be just hot springs without
muds, couldn't it?"

"But what we've already found is a bloody fortune,"
said Frank.

"Who for? You and Joe are just the scientists. You
can't claim it. You can't claim any fortune," she went on.
"You're employees of the Maritime Institute."

"I hadn't forgotten," said Frank. "But it's the idea,"
he continued. "We've been searching all this time. It's the
idea?"

"That won't make you rich."

"Nor will finding the final core," said Frank, annoyed

by the truth. "So why bother?" he said peevishly. "Why don't we go home now?"

"I didn't mean . . ."

"So what were you trying to say? That you're not an employee of the Marine Institute? That maybe *you* can do something more with the information than we can? That—"

"Let's all cool off!" It was Crane. Rising from the seat, holding onto it as the ship was pummeled by a quick succession of waves, he looked like an invalid.

Charlie, embarrassed, stared hard at his sea boot as it crushed out his cigarette. "Yeah. Let's take a break till the next station."

"Let's see the film," said Frank, looking at the movie drum that Mary was holding. "I love premieres."

"I'll see you later," said Charlie, anxious to get away.

"No, you stay," said Frank. "Come on, Charlie. Stick around. You're among friends." He smiled at Mary. "Isn't he?" Her eyes were cold.

"No," said Charlie. "I'm hungry. Time for a bite before the final core. I'll see you on deck."

As he left, Frank put out his hand to Mary for the film drum. "I know how to run the projector. It's in my cabin. It's a bit tricky."

"I'm sorry . . ." she began. "I . . ." He pressed her fingers gently as he took the cannister.

"I'm going to freshen up, Joe," she said, but all the time she was looking at Frank. "I'll be down in a minute."

Frank watched her as she walked out of the lab. He was just as sorry that he'd snapped at her. It was the edginess of fatigue and uncertainty. Well, soon they would know for sure.

∽ ∾ ∾

Crane and Frank sat back, watching the Polaroid film flicker to life, the bright cherry-red number code showing up on the bottom right hand corner, registering the date, time and station number. The hot, stuffy atmosphere of the cabin, together with the lack of a horizon which he could focus on, made Crane feel slightly sick for the first time on the trip. Mary opened the door and stood silhouetted for a moment, accustoming her eyes to the darkness. Frank stared long and hard at her outline. Something had happened to all of them this trip, he thought, but whatever had happened, he knew he still wanted her. As she sat down, the first frames from the abyss over a mile below them came to life on the screen.

Suddenly the projector ground to a halt.

"Frank—Mary." It was Joe Crane's voice. "I . . . before we see what we've got here I want to . . . I want to apologize to you both. I guess I should apologize to everybody. I'm sorry for the way I've been behaving. I have no excuse really . . ." They could sense the anguish in his voice—the lack of any simple explanation. "I guess I've just let the whole thing get out of proportion."

"Look, forget it," cut in Frank. "You've had to put up—"

"No. I know I've been . . . I've been . . . I don't know. One half of me knew there was nothing to be suspicious of, but the other half just . . . I guess the older you get the quicker your nerves go . . . I—I'm sorry."

There was a long, painful silence, then Mary spoke. "We've all felt the strain, Joe. I know Frank understands. Everyone does," she lied.

"Of course," said Frank quickly, to contain his embarrassment. Self-confessions always made him uneasy.

"Thanks," said Joe Crane quietly. He squeezed Mary's hand affectionately as the film, once again, began.

At first there was nothing but a stream of bubbles and clouds of dark brown-green sediment billowing up about the camera, as the pilot weight struck the bottom, triggering off the camera and its flare. But then, as the brown-green cloud cleared, they saw a clump of small olive-green hillocks, twenty to twenty-five feet high, with what appeared to be dark encrustations protruding through the sediments. The camera drifted on over a small escarpment. For ten seconds or so, the edge of the screen was again blanketed by green-mud clouds; then, sixteen feet down, the wide-angle Edgerton lens revealed a green expanse pockmarked by hundreds of hillocks. Frank depressed the zoom button, then momentarily froze the shot. Despite the whir of the projector and the continuous crashing of the storm outside, he became oblivious to everything but the picture. With a kind of wonder, he and the Cranes watched a passing moonscape of thousands of smaller volcano-shaped hillocks topped with jagged crests of brownish manganese and golden iron oxides. That they were fumaroles, hydrothermal vents, or exhausts, boiling and steaming from the upper levels of the earth's fiery mantle was evident from the hot brines, so voluminous that they were clearly visible, rising in great shimmering curtains like the heat waves above summer fields.

Watching the camera gliding over acres of black, shimmering, pebble-like deposits mottled by blood-red, white, and tangerine stains of ore, Frank realized that he and Crane were the first men in history to see off the west coast of North America young laval flats so new, so polished, that sediments had not yet accumulated to hide them. Here, in front of them, was dramatic evidence that the great rock plates of the lithosphere were being slowly pulled apart by massive semi-molten convective currents.

The water was opal blue, made powdery here and there by the presence of billions of bacteria. Countless clumps of iron oxide and scattered sulphur deposits shone in golden nuggets on the seabed as the camera slowly turned above, like a fish drifting easily with the current. Normally at this depth they could expect no life; but now and then huge clusters of oysters and mussels would come into view, bumping the camera away over yet more heat vents and deep green muds where colonies of white and copper-red, shrimp-sized galacthea crabs swarmed in an attack upon errant orange sponge balls that had drifted into their midst like dandelion seeds. Scores of coral-pink starfish and scarlet sea anemones floated gracefully by. A series of black, finger-length shadows hastily retreated before the lens as a gray octopus shyly withdrew its tentacles, while to the right a dusty brown grenadier fish swam up close to investigate the camera, which was now passing over a field of crimson sea cucumbers lying on the green mud in a pattern suggesting some exotic Asian carpet. Diamond-shaped skates flitted past, bluish white in the camera's eye.

Then, suddenly, the muds gave way to rocky islands. The camera shook violently, bumped into a stony cliff, swiveled and moved on, revealing a crevice-scarred outcrop laden with foot-long Vesicomyidae clams, their years of growth evidenced by the thin contours that girded them like the growth rings of a tree. Soon the living clams gave way to a graveyard of empty mussel shells strewn about the small, rocky plateau in mute testimony to the end of a hot spring—the extinction of an island of warmth in the icy sea. The fleshy debris of creatures long dead hovered above the graveyard, preserved and uneaten because the colder clime was unreachable by the inhabitants of the warmer world nearby.

Zooming the projector in on an area of massive, pillow-shaped basalts shrouded in a turquoise haze, Frank saw an extinct colony of chalk-white clamshells lying still in a cobalt-blue ravine.

"That's what we got in that first grab sample," he said.

There was no answer, and when he turned around he saw that Joe Crane was no longer there. On the screen a shoal of tiny white fish darted by, flashed into a solid wall of silver and were gone.

Above all, it was the fish-infested phalanxes of flour-white tubeworms that intrigued Frank. He was fascinated by their tall stems rising from the ocean's bottom, bending back and forth like windblown grain in the constant shimmering, bubbling gush of a six-foot-wide thermal vent studded with yellow mineral deposits. More than any other sight on the film, this was evidence that there was teeming life where there should be no life at all.

Frank was conscious of how lucky, how privileged he was at this moment, given the time it had taken man to explore the surface of the earth. It was worth all the years of disappointment that he and Joe Crane had experienced. And even now it was well-nigh miraculous; they could have been so close, yet so far. He thought of how the Spanish had for years sailed within fifty miles of the Hawaiian Islands without ever seeing them. He and Joe could have spent a lifetime dredging, coring, and sounding in the vastness of the Pacific and never found the riches of the middle valley.

Had he not been so captivated, Frank might have wondered what Joe Crane was doing. But he sat on in the darkness, increasingly aware that he was one of three people in the world who were privy to one of nature's most awesome creations.

Finally, he could hear Mary's soft breathing, and was about to ask her where Joe had gone when his eye caught an orange-red blur in the corner of the screen. In the phosphorescent cascade of a hot spring whose frosty green jet shot a hundred feet up from the valley floor, two huge lobsters had clashed by a golden spire of iron oxide. Pincers locked, they fought for possession of one of the tangerine sponges that hung suspended in their thousands,

moving slowly toward the sea bottom like an avalanche
of orange cotton balls. The larger lobster jerked backwards, tearing off the other's left claw. The white stump of
the loser's elbow twitched spasmodically, and he fell toward the mud. The victor scrambled away with his prize.

Frank shifted uneasily in his chair. In his excitement
with the film, he realized, he had forgotten the trawlers.

35

Joe Crane was walking aft, thinking. He would be famous. And if he wanted wealth, he knew it was a mere
phone call away. But he could only feel a hollow sense of
victory.

Sam's maimed corpse had shaken him badly. Last time a
man had been killed lowering equipment, the minister had
said it was "for the advancement of science." What would
they say about Sam, he wondered, as he cautiously
made his way toward the stern. He'd never even known
the man's surname. And *was* it for the advancement of
science that he'd died? They'd say so, shying away from
the truth—that he died for other men's greed. But it
wasn't the hypocrisy of others that was depressing Crane;
it was something closer to home than that. The fact was,
he realized, that his disappointment at losing the chance
to use the long corer in the rich muds of the valley floor
outweighed his feelings about Sam's death. True, he had
felt sorrow and sadness; he'd even been physically sick
from shock. But inside he knew he'd do it all over again
if it meant the same chance of winning.

As he neared the stern with the cold, clean wind
streaming into his face, he saw the green light. It was
quick, like a wink in the night. It was repeated. Lost in
his thoughts for a second, he wondered what it meant.
But as it came a third time from the flight deck above, he
knew it was a signal. He froze. Whoever it was obviously
knew that the scientific party was watching the film. This

would be a perfect opportunity—no crew on deck, no
working lights, the ship under way in near total darkness
except for the faint running lights looping the sky high
above. Besides, he realized, whoever it was would have to
act now or lose the race. If they left it until the final core
retrieval, the *Petrel* would beat them home.

As he ran up the ladder to the flight deck, the wind
howled around his ears, snatching at his parka hood. When
he reached the top, he saw the signal winking again.
Green-Green-Green.

～ ～ ～

"It's go!" yelled Andrea Nolan. "Close in. Let's go and
get it, now."

The Captain spun the wheel and the rhythm of the trawler's engine quickened as it ploughed toward the *Petrel*.
"How's the core coming to us?" he said.

"Same way as they got it," answered Andrea, fixing her
binoculars on the heavy black seas about the pinpoints of
light which marked the *Petrel*'s progress in the gale.

"Floats?" asked the Captain.

"Yes," she said. "Watch for the strobe light. He'll dump
it over the side, so it'll be astern of them when we see it.
But we have to see it before the lookout on the *Petrel*'s
bridge. Not that he'll have much of a chance—it'll be
directly behind them. But if he spots it they could turn
and retrieve it."

"So could *they*," said the Captain.

She turned and scanned the darkness for the other
trawler. There were no other lights. "Can't you see them
on your radar?"

"In these seas? Not a chance."

"Where are they?" she said. "Where the hell—"

"Maybe they never saw the signal."

"And maybe water isn't wet. They've been shadowing
us like a hawk. They've seen it. They won't be sure what
it is, that's all. I know what to look for; they don't. That
gives us a slight edge." She swung the glasses back to the
Petrel, so quickly she felt dizzy and had to take hold of
the radar grip. "We'll just have to beat them to it. Get
your man up here with a boathook."

"It'll be ten minutes before we—"

"Now!" she shouted. "He's just stopped signaling. Six
sets of three greens. That means he's going to dump it

overboard any minute. Get your man up here, Captain."
She lifted the glasses again. "And for God's sake, watch
for the flash."

∽ ∽ ∽

"Go!" yelled Doyle. "Go!"

As the trawler's nose reared, spearing a high crest and
diving into another, the increased tempo of the diesel
woke Tony up. Jay took hold of the galley table with one
hand and with the other he reached down into the small
attaché case, clicked it open, and handed Tony four grenades. "Don't let Doyle see them," he said.

"Why?" Tony yawned sleepily. "Christ, that wind's
noisy."

"Because our friend Doyle's too soft. He can read a
chart well enough but he won't pull a pin. If we have to—"

"So okay," said Tony, dragging himself up from the
table. "I don't give a shit. Don't want no sermon. What's
the fuse delay on 'em?"

"Seven seconds."

Tony yawned again, shoving the grenades into his pockets.

∽ ∽ ∽

Joe Crane moved as quickly as the roll would allow.
Just as the last signal ended, he reached the bow of the
long lifeboat on the starboard side of the funnel. Over the
wail of the wind in the rigging, he heard footsteps starting
away from the bow of the boat, where the signaler had
been crouching. As he steadied himself against the next
swell, he was suddenly blinded by a sheet of light, so bright
it was silver. A strobe had begun flashing only feet away.

Joe Crane lifted his arms to protect his eyes, and that
saved him from the first blow, but not the second. He fell
hard against the lifeboat, rocking it in its davits, its movement helping to cushion the shock. In the next flash he
saw an outline and kicked at it. There was a groan and a
muffled curse, then the two seconds of blackness came
down like ink. In the next flash Crane saw a long, mud-
filled boomerang core liner attached to two of the spheri-
cal glass floats, one of which housed the strobe light that
flashed again within the constraining netting, throwing
giant, diamond-shaped shadows on the flight deck, as the
signaler tried to manhandle the core and floats over the

side. Crane reached for the core to pull it back inboard. A boot kicked his fingers away, then smashed into the side of the lifeboat.

On the bridge, Johns heard the thud of the boot, and below in the galley Frank, making himself a sandwich after the film had ended, stood still and listened to the core rolling around on the flight deck directly above. He picked up a flashlight and went to investigate as Johns began to make his way aft from the bridge.

The fifth flash gave the two trawlers another fix as they raced toward their quarry. To Joe Crane it also revealed the face of his assailant. For a moment his eyes stared in shocked recognition. The two were now locked in a close, shoulder-to-shoulder tug-of-war with the floats—a struggle made all the more difficult by the flashing strobe light exploding in their faces every two seconds, as well as the precarious angle of the deck in the rolls. Far below them the sea was boiling along the side, cascading over the propeller guards that were now visible in the crests of the swells. Crane suddenly remembered that there was no rail outboard of the lifeboat. The ship collided with a wave that enveloped the flight deck in a beautiful, phosphorescent spray, set aglow by the strobe light. Struggling away from the ship's side, Crane caught his opponent off balance and managed to get the fingers of his right hand firmly entwined in the strong nylon netting about the two basketball-sized spheres. Over the crest, the ship plunged into a deep trough and rolled hard to starboard. Frank and the Mate raced toward the two from opposite directions, and all four braced themselves for the counterbalancing roll to port. It never came. Instead, the ship slid further into another starboard trough. The flight deck canted even more steeply. Joe Crane felt his boots begin to slide, and then he was moving uncontrollably to the high deck's edge, still locked to his assailant. He knew it would come down to who would let go first, who the core was more important to.

In the next flash Crane saw just how close he was to falling overboard. He groped with one hand for the two-inch-high sill that ran the deck's length, keeping the other locked in the netting. The core and floats bumped over the side. He held on tightly, but the weight of the core dragged him further toward the edge. The ship bucked and his legs disappeared over the side. His right arm felt as if it would

be wrenched out of its socket by the weight of the core
assembly. It dangled uselessly, like a pendulum. Frank
caught a glimpse of Joe clinging desperately to the thin
edge of the flight deck with his left hand, his body and
right hand swinging fore and aft with the ship's pitching,
his blood-streaked face grotesquely illuminated by the
flash of the strobe light. The Mate made a grab for the
signaler, tripped on the lifeboat's guys and fell. The
dark figure swung the signal lamp at Frank, then turned
and drove his boot into Crane's hand. There was a crack
as the fingers splintered.

Frank ducked the lamp and thrust out a hand to Crane.
Joe Crane clutched convulsively and Frank held him, but
then the ship rose hard to starboard, wrenching him loose.
There was no sound from him, only a scraping as his
body, together with the sediment-filled core liner and float,
slid down the side of the ship, and bounced off the rubbing
strake as the *Petrel* rolled sharply to port.

"Man overboard!" yelled Frank, and dived after the
signaler who, having kicked the Mate in the groin as he
lay by the lifeboat, was now making for the narrow gap
between the funnel and mast assembly. Frank caught him
by the throat and brought him to the hard steel deck.
Frank began to hammer at him with his fists. But the man
wriggled away, and was up and running. Frank caught him
by the boot and twisted, and the man flew back against
the lifeboat, the signal lamp swinging wildly. The ship
rolled, and the lamp slammed switch-first into the lifeboat.
Its light came on and it clattered to the deck. As the seaman dived for it, the beam lit up his face, pallid with
fear in the green glow.

"You rotten little bastard!" shouted Frank, lunging at
the other's throat. The mess boy sidestepped, swinging
the lamp again in midroll. It hit Frank on the shoulder,
knocking him off balance. As Frank fell he heard a
scream. For a split second the green light seemed to hang
suspended in midair; then it plummeted into the night
past the lifeboat's bow. The Mate, who had staggered
to the bridge, pressed two buttons—one for the "man
overboard" alarm and the other for "all deck lights."

A moat of light surrounded the *Petrel* as the engines
churned full astern, bringing the ship to a stop even as
she was coming about. Men tumbled on deck, some half
asleep, straining their eyes for the two bodies.

The first one they saw was the mess boy's, wedged head down in the corner of the starboard propeller guard, the thin, brown tape from the cassette recorder streaming around him like seaweed. He gurgled when they brought him aboard, but Frank could tell it wasn't breath. It was simply the sound of the remaining air bubbling out of lungs and nose.

"Is he dead?" asked Charlie.

"As a doornail," said Frank, pulling the parka hood over George's face.

Frank gulped thirstily at the cold air. "What an actor he was. Playing the dummy and all the time figuring the angles."

"Except this one," said Charlie.

"Wonder how much they promised him?" Frank gasped.

"Not enough," said Charlie, easing himself up from the deck. "Stupid little bastard."

"There's the strobe!" shouted a crewman. "The strobe light—that's where Doc Crane must be."

The ship made full speed toward the light. So did the trawlers.

36

Andrea Nolan's eyes were fixed on the deckhand six feet away on the trawler's deck. Each wave's spray covered him as he stood stoically by the wheelhouse. "Is he all right?" she asked.

The Captain nodded. "Yes, he'll be okay. He's just getting a bit damp and cold, that's all."

"I mean, is he capable?"

The Captain frowned, as if the question reflected on him personally. "Henry's been with me ten years."

The palms of Andrea's hands were wet. She caught another glimpse of the core assembly blinking like a distant flashlight half a mile away. "But can he use that boathook? If we miss on the first pass, we might not get a sec-

ond." She peered nervously into the darkness. The only
other ship she could see was the *Petrel*, which was now
turning.

The Captain took a new bearing on the light. It was
drifting faster than he'd anticipated. "If anyone can hook
it in one pass, Henry will."

"He'd better," Andrea began. "Otherwise we'll be in—
my God! The *Petrel*—she's coming toward us, toward the
strobe."

"Don't worry, we've got a head start."

"On who?"

The Captain shifted the wheel, and braced himself as
a wave smacked his bow side on. "We'll beat them to it.
Don't worry."

"Beat who?" she asked. "The *Petrel?*"

"And the others."

"Can you see them?"

"No, but—"

"*But* they could have been between us and the *Petrel*—
closer to the light."

Illuminated by her well deck lights, the sharp cream
wedge of the *Petrel*'s bow was now plainly visible as she
bashed through the crests. She was three quarters of a
mile away. The strobe light was less than a half.

～ ～ ～

By now they'd laid the mess boy out in the after lab,
while someone went to get more of the plastic bags
they'd used to wrap Sam in before placing him in the cold
room.

Mary Crane saw a steward race past the cabin door.
"What's happening?" she called out.

"Man overboard."

"Who?"

The steward kept running.

～ ～ ～

Tony and Gus waited calmly in the wheelhouse. Doyle
was urging the Captain on. "Can't you get any more
revs?"

"We're over-revved for this weather already."

"Jesus Christ, they'll beat us to it by a head. By a
Goddamn head."

Tony began clicking his teeth. "We're gonna have to

use the grenades. Scare 'em off long enough to give us a chance to pick it up."

"I told you I don't want any rough stuff if we can help it," said Doyle.

Jay pulled down the leeward window, spat, and shoved the friction pane hard up against its bracket. "And Mr. Miel doesn't want you to screw it up, *if* we can help it. Look at that trawler's mast light and the strobe light. Ten more minutes and they'll be there. I say swing across and cut them off. Give them a few scares and they'll leave us to it."

"And if they won't?" asked Doyle.

"Then we'll drop a couple real close, won't we?" said Tony.

"And how are you going to judge that, Joe DiMaggio?"

"I've had lots of practice."

"I'll bet."

"Listen," said Jay. "If you don't do something now, Gentleman Jim, you won't have a chance to cut them off. It's now or never. And never means trouble, old man. For you."

A new gust of wind buffeted the wheelhouse, as if bent on breaking through. In the distance they could hear the rumble of thunder. Doyle took his hand out of the deep pile pocket, jabbing it toward the other trawler. "Swing across," he told the Captain. The trawler heeled steeply and began to come around.

"You guys be careful," said Doyle.

"Sure," said Tony. "Right, Mr. Jay?"

Jay nodded slightly, as if at an auction.

∾ ∾ ∾

On the other trawler the deckhand, seeing the light bobbing four points to port, tapped the wheelhouse glass to get his skipper's attention.

"I see it, Henry," said the Captain, pulling hard on the wheel.

The closer the three ships got to the light, the more difficult it was to judge distance. At one moment the strobe seemed a hundred yards off; then, two seconds later and caught on the next swell, the next flash seemed twice as far away. Despite the height of the waves, Andrea Nolan could now see the other trawler on the radar. That meant it must be very close—within a mile. In fact it

was only a quarter of a mile, but the Captain was too busy
watching the strobe light to read off the distance.

"They're closing," she said, watching the tiny, lumines-
cent orange dot breathing brightly each time the white
sweep arm passed over it. "What are they doing?"

"It's not a social call," said the Captain tersely. "Better
warn Henry."

Andrea forced the door open against the wind. Then,
hanging onto the wheelhouse guard rail, she inched her
way forward, bending her head against the gusts that were
now topping fifty-five knots.

〜 〜 〜

On the *Petrel*, four-fifths of a mile from the strobe light,
completing the triangle of ships bearing down on the light,
Tate could see that some of the waves were higher than
forty feet. They were now definitely in force ten.

〜 〜 〜

The orange dot was fast approaching the center of the
radar screen. "They're almost on us," yelled Andrea. The
huge ridge of a wave's crest swept perilously close. In the
east a slash of horizon was visible as bluish-white forks of
lightning darted through the sky and rolls of thunder
moved toward the ships. The Captain glanced at the screen
and simultaneously saw the blunt, black outline of the
other ship's bow. "Christ!" He turned the wheel hard
aport. The other trawler was barely thirty feet away.

Then there was a blinding purple-white flash and a
sound like hail as shrapnel showered the trawler's decks.
The Captain spun the wheel further aport, and Andrea
grabbed his arm. "Go for the light!" she screamed. "Go for
the light!"

There was a muffled thump, immediately followed by a
spume of water streaking skywards not ten feet from their
bow.

"What the hell is that?" shouted Andrea.

"It's a grenade! They's using Goddamn grenades."

"Go for the light!" she yelled again. "We're nearly
there."

There was another flash and they instinctively ducked,
but there was no explosion. It was the strobe light, dead
ahead. Henry was rapping on the glass, pointing. A long,
crooked finger of lightning danced around the dark sea's

edge. Andrea could see the sharp outline of two figures on the foredeck of the other trawler. The thunderclap split the air a second later, and rain began to pour. "Swing to starboard," she ordered. "Cut them off."

"Cut them off? Those are bloody bombs they're throwing."

"Cut them off! If they wanted to hit us we'd have been hit before this. Cut them off from the light. That'll put it on our port quarter and them on our starboard. I hope to hell Henry won't miss the pickup."

The Captain's face was tight with anger, but he steered for the *Sea Wasp's* starboard quarter. "He didn't run away from the grenades, did he?"

"No," said Andrea. "But can he pick up the core?"

"Jesus Christ! You people are unbelievable. What more d'you want—?"

"Cut them off!" she yelled, above the sound of the storm.

The strobe light flashed on their port beam. There was a rending crash that threw Andrea to the deck and flung the coffee mugs high out of their cradles, smashing them against the compass glass.

On the other trawler Doyle fell against the Captain, driving him into the starboard corner as the ship reared and slipped dangerously sideways from the impact.

"The bastards!" shouted Doyle above the noise of the heavy wind and rain. "The bloody bastards! They've rammed us."

Andrea Nolan could now see the black shape of the other trawler sliding off into the darkness, so close that she felt she could touch it.

"Throw the grenades!" screamed Doyle. "Blow them out of the water! The bloody bastards could have killed us."

Groggily raising himself off the deck, Tony pulled out another grenade, but Jay stayed his arm. "No!" he shouted, his voice loud against the gale. "We're too close to the strobe now. Let's have another try at it this way."

Doyle's voice was shrieking from the wheelhouse. "Sink them! Sink them!"

Jay, one hand checking his toupee, wrenched open the door as a river of foam roared past him, spilling over into the wheelhouse. "Doyle!"

"What—?"

"Shut your mouth and get out here with a pike pole."

Doyle began yelling again and Jay grabbed him by the throat. "Thought you didn't want any rough stuff, Mr. Doyle? First kick in the balls and you're screaming revenge. Get hold of yourself. Now help us get this core aboard."

Jay pushed past him, pointing at the rival trawler, shouting. "Drop back and swing around behind them on their left side so we can try to pike that core." For once the fat captain didn't argue. He pulled back the throttle, swung hard aport, then boosted the revs again.

As they bore down on the strobe light, now seventy feet away on their starboard side, they could see Henry bending over. It looked as if he might have hooked the light but was having trouble pulling the assembly inboard. Now, Jay could see a second outline in the rain. It was a woman, hanging on to the pole as the trawler's screws churned the water in reverse, struggling to maintain position. But even with her help it seemed that the seaman was in difficulty. Jay saw that he still had a chance.

～ ～ ～

"What the hell's going on out there?" asked Tate, watching the two dots on the snowy radar. "I can only see one masthead."

"I'm still trying to reach them," reported the radio officer, "but there's no answer. Not even an acknowledgement."

Johns had seen one of the grenade's flashes and thought it was the strobe light. "Maybe they're just curious about the light?"

"And maybe I'm the Virgin Mary," said Tate. "How is Mrs. Crane?"

"She's in her cabin," said Frank. "She doesn't know yet."

"Just as well for the moment," Tate mumbled. "You think *both* of those ships are up to no good?"

"At least one of them," said Frank. "George didn't put that core over for fun."

"I know that, man," said Tate irritably. "But which one?"

Frank shrugged. He was exhausted. Johns shook his head. "That stupid little bugger," he said.

Tate pulled the glasses down and glared at Frank. "Why didn't you tell me what you were after? I could've arranged some kind of deck security."

"That wouldn't have helped. He only needed two or three minutes to signal. Could've done it from the crow's nest."

"But he'd have had to come to me for the key," said Johns.

"What I'm saying is he could've signaled from a hundred different places on the ship. Deck security wouldn't have stopped him. Besides, with deck security the whole ship would have known what we were looking for."

"Obviously you don't trust us," growled Tate.

"I do, but Crane didn't."

"And look what happened to him."

Frank felt a chill pass through the bridge. He remembered what Charlie had said: if *two* trawlers were involved there were two contacts. They now knew that the mess boy had been one of them. Who was the other?

37

Andrea reached out to the full extent of her safety line, jabbing at the float with the boathook. Henry stood by the wheelhouse, calmly conserving his energy. The trawler played cat-and-mouse with the light as it swung in closer, then away, closer and then away with the slopping of the swells on their leeward side. Andrea threw a frantic glance at the other trawler. It was only fifty feet away now. She lunged again, cursing as the end of the ten-foot pike plopped uselessly into the water two feet from the light. Though the strobe was glistening in the rain, and bright enough to be seen over miles of sea, it was only a small, sharp light and didn't illuminate the water around it to any extent.

The other trawler was now only forty feet away.

Andrea gripped the spotlight handle directly above the radar console.

"What the hell are you doing?" bellowed the Captain.

"I—I thought the spotlight would help us pick up the strobe. We can hardly see—"

"Don't be an idiot! You'll light it up for the opposition as well."

She gripped the railing as the boat lifted, and saw Henry brace himself against the bulkhead, thrusting with the pike as if he were harpooning a whale. "Got it!" he said. "Lend a hand!" His voice was swallowed by a thunderclap overhead.

Andrea saw that Doyle's trawler was now only thirty feet away, threatening to slip sideways on a swell and crush them. Then she saw three other aluminum pike poles darting frantically at the net from the other boat, and heard shouts and obscenities directly across from her. She pulled hard with Henry, but the core seemed enormously heavy. She wondered how they would ever get it inboard. But now at least they had a secure grip on it. If only they could hold out against the others. One of the other poles caught the net, but the next swell shucked it loose. There was violent swearing as the other trawler drifted away from the light.

It was the next flash from the strobe that saved her. She saw a glint of aluminum aloft in the air, coming straight at her through the spray. She ducked. The incoming pike struck the wheelhouse three inches above Henry's head, then clattered lifelessly to the deck, whacking him hard on the knees.

"Are you okay?" she called.

"Yeah," said Henry. "We have to get this inboard right now. They'll come back for another pass at it."

Now the lightning had swung around behind them, dancing spastically westwards in great crackling leaps of frost-blue light. The two of them heaved until the float and core assembly was smacking the rubbing strake. The next few flashes from the strobe, reflecting off the hull as the glass floats moved back and forth with the pole, showed them why the assembly was so heavy. At first Andrea thought it was some kind of white shark fin sticking into the net, but then the strobe flashed again and she saw the body of Joe Crane stretching out behind, obscuring the core that dangled from the nylon cord beneath the floats. She gasped, automatically relaxing her grip on the pole. "Hold it steady," said Henry. Lowering himself as far over the side as the safety line would allow, he pulled his splicing knife. Halfway over he could see that the other trawler had completed its turn. "They're coming back," he called. "When I say 'now,' turn the spotlight right at them. That'll stop 'em for a few seconds. I'll work the pole now that we have it in close."

There was no answer from Andrea Nolan.

"You hear me?" he shouted.

"Y—yes," she stammered, and in the next flash of the strobe Henry saw that her face had turned to chalk.

〰 〰 〰

For ten minutes, the *Petrel* had lost sight of the boats in the rain. Only now did the radar pick them up again.

"Give me the bullhorn," Tate commanded.

"Why not let them pick it up for us? Then we can ask for it. Save us the trouble," said Johns. "If we get in too close we could have a collision."

"Get me the bullhorn," growled Tate. "Apparently nobody can hear us on radio. Maybe they'll understand this."

"Not likely in this wind," murmured Frank.

"How far away are they?" demanded Tate. Johns checked the radar sweep. "They've drifted. Two miles to the southwest."

"Damn! Any acknowledgement yet, Sparks?"

"Nothing, sir."

"Damn!" Tate turned angrily, his beard jutting at Frank. "I'll tell you one thing, Mister. There'll be no more coring. Just as soon as we sight that first boomerang core we dropped, we pick it up and head in." Frank didn't bother to remind the Captain that he'd already made that abundantly clear some hours ago. When he looked up he saw that Tate had taken over the wheel, as they continued to head for the beckoning light.

〰 〰 〰

Without switching it on, Andrea brought the spotlight around to face the oncoming trawler. She could barely see the three dark figures readying their pike poles again. Henry was still struggling with the knife. He saw the other trawler disappearing in a trough, and knew that the next

time it was in sight it would be almost upon him and
Andrea. He slashed furiously with the knife and when he
spotted the trawler's nose poking over the next crest, he
shouted, "Now!"

Andrea flicked the spotlight on. Its beam penciled out
through the spray, sweeping the length of the gray trawler, settling like a full moon on the three figures barely
twenty feet away.

Temporarily blinded in the rain-streaked light, the three
figures turned away from the glare. Henry heaved up
with all his remaining strength. Realizing that after their
initial surprise the others could easily smash the spotlight
with a well-aimed U-bolt, or anything else handy, Henry
gave another heave and yelled, "Go!"—praying that he
could hold on to the load once the boat was under way.
The Captain pushed the throttle forward and turned the
trawler to starboard, sending his wash rolling in to smash
against Doyle's boat. Henry felt the sudden drag on the
pole. He didn't know if he could haul in—even if he
could hold the weight.

∽ ∽ ∽

The spotlight went out and the other trawler steered
off. Doyle could see the strobe still flashing. "They've
missed it!" he shouted. "They've given up! The sons of
bitches have missed it!"

When Tony felt the weight of the glass floats, he called
Jay to help him. It wasn't until they had it halfway up
the side that they realized that all they had was a flashing
strobe light and the body of a man, the gashed face gazing
at them stupidly each time the bulb flashed on the frozen
eyes.

"Goddamn!" said Tony, letting the pole drop. "Those
bastards have got the core." Doyle watched as the floats
splashed into the water and floated away.

"Get the jelly ready," said Jay, without emotion.

"What are you going to do?" asked Doyle.

"We're going to slow them down, old man."

"Just delay them, you mean?" said Doyle. He was
calmer now.

Jay snipped off a piece of fuse from the coil. "Yes,
that's right," he said, passing the rest back to Tony.
"We're going to delay them."

∽ ∽ ∽

The strobe unit was now drifting dead ahead of the *Petrel*. No one had any stomach for pulling it aboard—least of all Frank, who'd seen Crane hit the rubbing strake. As Captain Tate watched, the trawlers moved away. "Damn it all! What are they up to? What were those explosions?"

Johns had half expected an S.O.S. from one of the boats. "Maybe an engine blew up."

"Engines don't blow up any more, Number One."

Johns remembered reading in *Shipping News* about one blowing up off the Queen Charlottes only a month before, but he didn't press the point. He knew the old man was just being testy because, like the rest of them aboard the *Petrel*, he didn't know what the hell was going on.

Tate scowled at the chart. "Damn that drift. We'd be on them in another ten minutes."

"Strobe light in sight," came the call from the lookout. "Two points to starboard."

Frank snared the unit on the first pass. Johns, who had made his way down from the bridge, helped him. Suddenly his arms froze. "Jesus, Jesus!"

A young seaman beside him began throwing up. "Oh, my—" began Frank, and then, the smell of vomit still in his nostrils, he looked down at what had been Joe Crane's head.

After his fall, he figured, Crane must have been sucked in by the propellers. They'd ripped and mangled him almost beyond recognition. From the red, bone-splintered pulp that used to be a face, two eyes stared up in utter surprise. The clean, pink skull had burst like an overripe melon, the gray brain spilling loosely into the sea. The right hand, or rather the few ligaments and three finger-stumps that remained, was still grimly clutching the shredded green netting.

"Where's the core?" a seaman asked cold-bloodedly.

"Probably sliced off by the props," said another.

"Poor bastard. Why didn't those trawlers pick him up?"

"In this weather?" proffered another. "We were lucky to gaff him."

"Maybe the core just worked loose on the way up. Hope that first one we dropped didn't come loose. We—"

"Christ!" exploded Charlie, his voice furious and impatient with fatigue. "Never mind the fucking theories.

Worry about the first core later. Clear the way. Let's get
the poor son of a bitch aboard."

"Where's Mrs. Crane?" someone asked. "Shit, don't let
her see this."

"Someone'll have to tell her," said Johns. "I'll get the
old man."

"I'll tell her," said Frank, reaching out with a pole and
grabbing the lacerated leather strip that had been Crane's
belt.

"What do we do now?" came a voice from the rail.

Frank hauled up on the pole. "Get even," he said.

"Even? Even for what?" asked Johns.

"For Christ's sake!" Frank exploded. "That could have
been me," he said, pointing to the corpse. "Or *you*. It could
have been any of us!"

∽ ∽ ∽

"Joe's dead." Frank hadn't planned to say it that way,
but that's the way it came out. He had to stop her before
she pushed past him to the commotion on deck.

"No, no, no," she cried hysterically. Frank held her
closely but she was inconsolable. "Oh, my God," she
sobbed. "My God, my God . . ." She cried it over and
over again, sinking in his arms, until he didn't think she
could cry any more. He tried to speak but words were of
no use, so he simply held her tightly, letting the rib-
wracking sobs tear out of her, trying to absorb some of
the trauma from her body, to take away some of the pain.
Then, without warning, she passed into a deep silence. He
couldn't hear her breathing, the shock seemingly stifling
her very heartbeat.

"Mary." He shook her. "Mary!" Lifting her into his
arms, and fighting the roll of the ship, he took her to her
cabin. He stayed with her until she asked to be left alone.
He feared leaving her but finally relented. "Mary," he said.
"Don't you think . . . ?"

"Please," she said. She spoke so quietly it was almost a
whisper.

"I'll come back," he promised, gently closing the door.
But after he'd left and headed down towards the deck, he
asked the Captain to send someone to check on her soon
and, above all, to keep her away from the deck.

38

In the foc'sle Doyle was watching Jay and Tony preparing the charge. He was frightened now. He didn't believe they would merely "delay" Andrea Nolan, and Jay knew it. The Englishman clasped his hands about the galley heater, warming them before handling the explosives. The mole on his face was dark with blood. "Look, Doyle, you're up to your eyeballs already. So what's the difference? That woman got a damn good look at us. That wasn't just a flashlight she hit us with."

"She wouldn't remember," said Doyle, too quickly to sound convinced.

"You want to bet on that, old man?" asked Jay, slowly pushing in the detonator. "You really want to bet on that?"

There was a long pause. "No," said Doyle quietly.

"All right, then. Keep Captain Canuck here on their tail and tell him to swing this tub away when I throw. We can't use a long fuse."

"Why can't we?" asked Doyle ingenuously, his authority crumbling by the second. Tony clicked his teeth and looked disgusted. "You want to catch it back, eh? Want to play handball with it?" He snipped the fuse to five-second length. Doyle looked frightened. "So what do we do now? Our contact won't be able to get a thing off the *Petrel* now that they're on the alert. Besides, it's lit up like a Christmas tree."

"Use your S.O.S. plan," said Jay.

"Should've used it first off," grumbled Tony.

"I was only trying to save us work," whined Doyle, "letting them do it for us."

"Yes, I know," said Jay, "and 'intercept.' Wasn't that the big word, Tony—intercept? Isn't that this week's big word?"

"Yeah."

"We almost had it," Doyle said angrily.

"Tell that to Miel, sweetheart."

"I'll send the S.O.S. to the *Petrel* after we, uh, delay that bitch," said Doyle. "Your explosion'll make it sound more convincing."

Jay nodded approvingly, wrapping a tape round a bundle of Forcite sticks. "Now you're thinking. How far away is the trawler? I can't see its mast light."

Doyle stuck his head into the wheelhouse. A few seconds later he returned. "Skipper wants to go home."

"How far is the trawler?" repeated Jay.

"Three hundred yards."

"You ready, Tony?"

"Ready."

"Okay, tell Canuck to pour on the coals. And remember—swing hard the moment we throw."

"But he might head in," said Doyle, nodding up toward the Captain. "In this weather he could do it without us knowing for an hour."

Jay shoved past Doyle. He paused, turning his back on the incoming wave that threatened to fling him into the small, warm wheelhouse. He pulled out the .357 magnum and shoved it hard into the Captain's ribcage. "You steer for that trawler—now! And you swing hard when we throw, and you do just what I tell you to do or I'll blow your kidneys out. Understand?"

"Yeah, bigshot," the Captain wheezed. "And then who'll navigate this boat? You?"

Jay pushed the gun in until the barrel was almost lost in the fat man's coveralls. "I can wait till port if you like. You'll die just as easily there. Now let's have some more speed."

The Captain eased the throttle forward. Immediately they could feel the powerful thrust of the diesel.

≈ ≈ ≈

Andrea Nolan was tracking the other trawler on the radar. It was gaining. "Can we get any more speed?"

"Not unless you want to drive her under," said the Captain. "They're a bit bigger than us. They can afford the extra knot or two." He glanced at the radar. A hundred and seventy yards away and closing. "Keep an old Lee Enfield down below for sharks," he said.

"What's that?" asked Andrea without taking her eyes off the radar.

"A rifle. Three-oh-three calibre."

Andrea was bent over the Decca console, her auburn hair turning golden in its glow. "They're holding at one hundred and seventy yards," she said hopefully.

The Captain shook his head. "Doubt it. They're wallowing in the same swell that hit us a few minutes ago." As he finished speaking Andrea saw the blip moving in closer. "A hundred and fifty yards," she said. "Henry! Get that three-oh-three."

As the distance between the two trawlers narrowed, Henry, using the wheelhouse as cover from the wind, tied himself to a stanchion on the port side and set the rifle's sights for fifty yards.

It was so dark that as he pulled back the bolt he could barely see the steel-tipped bullet pop from the magazine and click into the receiver. He had ten shots. He hoped he wouldn't have to use any. He was a fisherman, he told himself, not a guerrilla, but he'd nearly been speared with a pike a short while before, and if they wanted to play that game he'd have to play it too. If he didn't, he might end up like that guy floating in with the core.

◇ ◇ ◇

Doyle, too, was watching the radar. The ever-growing blip showed that the other trawler was only a hundred yards away. He tore open a fresh carton of Gitanes and looked out of the windscreen, through the wipers that were now screeching from overtime and lack of oil. But he still couldn't see the other trawler's running lights. "We'll be on top of them before you can throw it," he said.

"We'll see them soon enough," said Jay.

"What about their spotlight? What if they throw that at us?"

"Relax," said Jay. "Tony'll take care of it."

"How?" demanded Doyle, his hand shaking slightly as he lit a cigarette. The blip was now ninety yards away.

"Relax, Doyle. You're coming apart."

"How are you going to do it? I'm in charge here."

Jay took a sip of whiskey and screwed the cap on, looking at Doyle all the while. "You're in charge," he said. "Really?"

∾ ∾ ∾

When she got no response from the trawlers, the
Petrel had moved on to pick up the final core. It was
Tate who'd first seen its strobe light twinkling on a high
crest three miles further west. Although it signaled every
two seconds like the one before it, it was only visible
every thirty seconds or so. Most of the time it was hidden
by spray.

It took Charlie, Frank, and four seamen five passes
to hook the core, and when they finally got it Frank
gashed his right index finger on the pike as they were
hauling it over the rail. Frank taped the finger quickly
and put his canvas work glove back on. Then he scooped
out samples from the top and bottom layers and immediately tested them on the spectrometer.

"Is it as good as the other core?" Charlie asked.

"No," said Frank, "it's better. Joe was right. It's a valley. A whole valley—full of metalliferous muds."

Charlie shook his head. "Not that it'll do him much
good now."

Frank taped the caps on the plastic cylinder and made
his way below to the storage room. Charlie was trying as
best he could to pack away the floats, but halfway through
a roll he lost his balance and one of the bottle-green
globes smashed on the wet lab floor. Cursing, he made
his way to the machine shop to get the dustpan and
brush.

In the cold-storage room Frank took out the small vial
of Malachite Green. He hesitated for a second, then
dusted the new core barrel with the chemical powder and
threw away the canvas gloves he'd used.

On the bridge Tate rang for another knot, and put the
ship on a direct heading for Vancouver Island.

39

"They can't be more than thirty yards away," said Andrea. Henry nodded and tumbled back the safety catch of the .303.

"Don't do anything unless they do," she said.

"Don't worry. I'm no hero."

〰 〰 〰

Tony watched the faint glow that was the *Petrel*. She was on her way home. He would have to work fast if the S.O.S. plan was to succeed. He sucked hard on the Gitane he'd mooched from Doyle and touched it to the fuse, which immediately started spitting a yellow light into the darkness.

"Just delay them," yelled Doyle. "Throw it behind them."

But as the bundle of explosives left Tony's hand the trawler rose so sharply to starboard that the Forcite sailed almost straight for the other ship's wheelhouse. Then a gust caught it and it was blown astern of Andrea Nolan's trawler, nearer to Doyle's. Even in the howling of the storm the explosion was deafening. A hundred-foot circle of water erupted into phosphorescent white-green columns, then boiled white, spreading like some giant, undulating bedsheet over the swells.

"Jesus Christ!" cried Doyle, swinging around toward Tony. "What the fuck are you trying to do?" Tony didn't answer. His dentures were giving him trouble.

Inside the wheelhouse, Jay spoke quietly to the Captain—almost with respect. "Can you bring her into the wind, old man? Hold her steady?"

The Captain's face was gray, and shiny with sweat.

"Can you?" Jay repeated calmly.

"I'll try."

"Don't try. Do it. Now."

233

The trawler steadied and Tony picked up the next charge. Suddenly he found himself bathed in a white glare. He brought his arm up to shield his eyes. Then he realized it was the other trawler's spotlight. There was a sharp crack and a hiss of steam as the .303 bullet struck an engine pipe.

Jay ran out of the wheelhouse, reaching toward his left armpit. He braced the magnum against the funnel and fired three times. The spotlight went out amid a tinkle of glass.

∽ ∽ ∽

After Jay's third shot, Henry clutched convulsively at his arm and sank to his knees. "I'm hit!" he cried.

Helping him into the wheelhouse, Andrea could already feel the warm blood. When they were inside she helped him off with his coat and sighed with relief. His arm had only been sliced by the flying glass. There was a lot of blood, but the wound wasn't deep.

∽ ∽ ∽

"Stick with them," encouraged Jay. The Captain, his legs trembling visibly, tried to maintain an even course while Tony held the second charge ready. "They won't scare," he shouted angrily. "That bitch wants to fight. I coulda been killed."

"Go for broke," said Jay.

The next charge was smaller because the other trawler was only forty feet away, and Tony had no intention of getting mixed up in the explosion. The bundle of forcite hit Andrea Nolan's boat just forward of the foc'sle in a saffron burst of flame. It ripped the bow apart like a pine box. The boat gulped water and began to sink. The Captain and Henry never got out of the wheelhouse, and Andrea's exit through the door was purely accidental, due solely to the suction created by a huge wave as the boat listed rapidly to port.

By the light of the burning vessel's stern, Jay could see the woman struggling and splashing wildly toward some splintered remnants of the boat. He could see the *Petrel's* glow becoming brighter. She was obviously steaming full ahead to investigate. They mightn't have heard the explosion too clearly, but must have seen its flash.

Andrea's body was already numb with cold. She clung

desperately to the remains of a bunk mattress as it rose skywards, but suddenly it was torn from her grasp when a high crest smacked her face-on, driving her down into a wide, deep trough. A menacing swell slid under her, and for a moment she was treading water in a calm created by the opposing forces of the frenzied sea. In the calm she caught a glimpse of Jay, at the top of a shining slope twenty feet away. He was smiling. Fear clamped Andrea's stomach. She looked for the *Petrel*'s lights, but all she could see were the black hills of freezing water. For some reason she found herself trying to remember in detail the last good thing that had happened to her. It was the picture-postcard ride from Grindelwald to Kleine Scheidegg—the sun warm on her back as she rode the small red train up the flower-strewn hillsides. She must go there again—she was determined to go there again, and this trip there would be no Klaus, only hours and hours to take pictures, to lie in the sun, the deep, warm sun, and time to watch the great mountain filling the peaceful blue sky.

On the next crest Jay was visible again. Looking down at her imperiously, he was still smiling. The explosion of the trawler would fit in beautifully with Doyle's S.O.S. plan, he figured—beautifully. But not if the lady was free to talk. She'd probably drown anyway. It was a million to one chance that she'd manage to hang onto a piece of wreckage and be picked up by the approaching *Petrel*. But the chance was still there—many a lone survivor had beaten the odds before. He had to think fast. On the next swell Andrea wondered why he was pointing at her with what looked like a finger. Perhaps the *Petrel* was closer than she thought and had seen him, and now he was forced to show them where she was. Eagerly she listened for the sound of the Zodiac rescue craft. It never came. In a second all of Andrea Nolan's self-discipline was gone. Now she was screaming hysterically. In less than a second a series of minutely detailed color slides flickered through her brain with incredible speed —a favorite doll, a small girl crying, struggling, growing up; a beautiful woman, self-assured, insecure, self-assured —tough. And now this.

"No!" yelled Doyle, rushing at Jay.

Jay stepped back, smacking him aside. There was no time for argument. The trough would disappear from view any second and so would Andrea Nolan. Jay lifted the .357 Magnum and blew her head off.

The Captain swung at him and missed, but Doyle's aim was better. He hit Jay in the stomach, throwing him back on the radar. Recovering quickly, the Englishman whipped the Magnum against Doyle's head and slapped the Captain into the port aft corner. "She knew the rules," he said. "Now, Doyle, we're finally rid of your competition. Send for your contact."

Doyle, wedged into the corner of the confined space of the wheelhouse, was wide-eyed with shock.

"Use the explosion as a plus," said Jay. "Put it into that message you've got all prepared." There was no answer. Jay pulled down the radio mike, shoving it forward. "Over to you, Mr. Doyle!"

Doyle's hands were quivering uncontrollably. He turned the red band selector to the 2182 kilohertz international distress channel. "Hurry it up," snapped Jay. "They've one blip less on their radar screen by now. Report it before they become too suspicious."

Doyle's voice was hoarse. "*Sea Wasp* to *Petrel*—come in!"

There was no response, only the fierce static of the storm. "*Sea Wasp* to *Petrel*," he said again. "Do you read me? Come in, *Petrel*."

The acknowledgment was broken and barely understandable. "*Petrel* to . . . *Wasp* . . . over."

Doyle turned down the volume to filter out some of the atmospherics. "*Sea Wasp* to *Petrel*. We've had an explosion on sister ship. No survivors. Shock wave from explosion, ah . . ." Jay jabbed him with the Magnum. "Ah, shock wave hit us hard and shook off the bulkhead fittings on the oil cooler. Fittings must have been worn already. They need brazing back on but, ah, we—we don't carry any welding gear. Can you assist? Over."

The rupturing of an oil cooler had happened to many a fish boat. Doyle knew that the *Petrel*'s machine shop would have the high-temperature torches necessary for the silver brazing. It would only take ten, perhaps fifteen minutes to solder the brass fittings back onto the copper casing. And he knew they would help. No matter how suspicious the *Petrel*'s Captain might be—and having lost the first core from the strobe he would be very suspicious—Doyle knew, with a sudden stab of conscience, that under the unwritten law of the sea, the men aboard the *Petrel* wouldn't deny aid to any vessel in distress.

There was only a fifteen-second delay before the *Petrel* replied. "*Sea Wasp.* This is *Petrel.* Repeat number of survivors off other trawler. Over."

Doyle stared at Jay. "None," Doyle said. "Repeat, no survivors."

After a few moments of silence, the *Petrel* came on again. "*Petrel* to *Sea Wasp.* Have you reported to Victoria Rescue Command? Over."

Doyle looked at Jay, who nodded.

"Ah, *Sea Wasp* to *Petrel.* Have reported." This time there was a long silence. "All right, *Sea Wasp.* Can help. Show all lights. Weather conditions permit only transfer one of you with broken oil cooler. Will transfer via Zodiac raft. Approximate ETA seventeen minutes. Prepare to assist raft. We will notify Victor Alfa Echo."

"*Sea Wasp* to *Petrel.* Understood. Am standing by. Thanks. Over and out."

As regulations dictated, Doyle got off the 2182 kilohertz channel as soon as he'd finished.

"Good," said Jay. "Hook, line and sinker." He reached behind, grabbed a half bottle of bourbon and handed it to Doyle. "Okay. I'll go and fetch the cooler." In the jaundiced light the black stitches where Moody had hit him were starkly visible on Jay's forehead. He looked up, first at the Captain and Doyle, then at Tony. "Watch them, Tony."

"Okay."

Jay disappeared toward the small, cramped engine room. Tony grabbed the bottle from Doyle. "Don't get pissed, eh? Don't want nobody blowing it, do we? Just stay cool."

"After that?" Doyle jerked his head back in the direction of the wreckage which was scattered in a crimson glow of burning oil.

"All right, then, act concerned," said Tony. "Tell everyone how it upset your Jello gut, how terrible it was. But stay cool. We don't want anybody gettin' suspicious. Just stick to the story like you told it, Doyle. Right?"

Doyle turned away. Tony jabbed his finger into Doyle's ribs. "All right?"

Doyle grunted. "I can handle it."

"You can't handle shit." He turned to the Captain. "Victor Alfa Echo—where's that?"

"Tofino listening station. They probably heard it all anyway."

"You think they'll send out a search plane?"

The Captain shrugged. "Maybe an Argus with flares. Depends on the duty controller at Victoria Rescue Center."

"Big deal," said Tony. "What can they find in this pea soup?"

Doyle began apologizing to the Captain. "I'm sorry. I—I didn't expect all—all this," he said, lifting his hand ineffectually toward the burning debris. The Captain was silent.

"I didn't expect . . ." Doyle began again.

Tony looked at him contemptuously. "It ain't over yet, sweetheart."

Tate wrote in his log: "0100 hours. As per instructions from V.R.C. am responding to distress call from Canadian trawler *Sea Wasp*. Will seek further information for V.R.C. regarding earlier explosion and disappearance of radar echo at that time."

Bending low in the crawl space around the *Sea Wasp*'s ninety horsepower G.M. diesel, Jay was searching in the mess that was supposed to be the toolbox. Like most fish-boat equipment, the equipment was out of date and incomplete, particularly for an emergency that might mean the difference between life and death. Eventually he came up with a monkey wrench.

He crouched down beside the old oil cooler that Doyle had brought along for his S.O.S. plan. The honeycombed interior of the copper casing had once been flushed with a constant stream of water that cooled the boat's oil and so kept the oil pressure up. Jay unscrewed the old rubber oil-feed line from the brass nut brazed onto the cooler's casing, and hammered at the nut until it fell off, bringing out a piece of the casing with it. Then, nauseated by the heavy diesel fumes, he wrapped the cooler up quickly in an old rag and made his way back to the wheelhouse.

40

Johns watched the great swells roll past in the darkness. Although he'd chosen the two most experienced men he had—himself and Charlie—Johns knew that this launching of the rubber Zodiac raft would be the trickiest he'd ever supervised. The French-built, Coast-Guard modified craft with twin outboards was seaworthy in winds up to sixty kilometers per hour, but he wasn't looking forward to the launching, particularly when he saw a thirty-foot wave followed by a trough just as deep. The great advantage of the raft, its light weight, was also its biggest drawback; for while it made for superb maneuvrability and was relatively easy to lower even in heavy seas, it was just as liable to flip if the wind got under it on a sharp crest.

Half a mile away the *Sea Wasp* sat riding the swells, lit up like a harbor ferry.

∽ ∽ ∽

While Johns supervised the lowering of the raft, the Scottish Second Mate sent by Tate was doing all he could to comfort Mary Crane. Not content to simply watch by her door, he wanted to help but it wasn't working. Redfern's idea of dealing with bereaved women was derived from his mother; you took them a nice cup of tea and told them everything would be all right. He spoke quietly, offered to get a little brandy, asked if he could send someone up to fix the loose bolt on the door. "It must be annoying, banging away like that," he said. But there was no answer.

Mary Crane heard every word as clearly as a bell tolling, but she understood nothing. Still numb from shock, her consciousness floated about her like a particle around an atom, enabling her to say "yes" and "no," but nothing else.

Now the Second Mate stood awkwardly halfway to the door, not knowing what to do. Finally he decided to give her the pills he'd brought. They mightn't be the best thing for her, medically speaking, but obviously tea and sympathy weren't doing any good. He held out two chloral hydrate capsules to her. She accepted them without a word, and he left.

It took Mary Crane a while to realize what they were. She stared at them a little longer, then rose and flushed them down the toilet. Without Joe she was totally alone. She would have to look after herself. Unhurriedly she turned to her handbag, upended it, and began sifting through its contents. She stopped. Her mind was clearing by the second. Nielsen's message was in the secret pocket.

~ ~ ~

For several moments the raft was lost in the night, further obscured by a light rain that peppered the long, froth-strewn swells like tiny hailstones. A streak of white light reached out toward the *Petrel*, blinding Frank and the others on deck. The beam receded, becoming shorter, zeroing in on the Zodiac. Frank glimpsed Johns shielding his eyes with his left hand while the right gripped the wheel, adjusting the throttle of the Mercury outboards, whose sound was now no more than a faint gurgle lost in the craters of water. For a few fleeting seconds that drew murmurs of admiration, even from the hardened salts at the *Petrel*'s rail, the tiny raft in the outer reach of light from both vessels hung suspended, high on the crest of a forty-foot wall of water. The two men were plainly visible in their bright orange life vests, standing atop the mountainous gray sea in clear defiance of the storm. Then they were gone.

~ ~ ~

Doyle zipped up the beige goose-down jacket and nervously lit up another Gitane. As Jay watched the Zodiac's black triangular bow approaching, jutting out of the spotlight beam, he murmured to Doyle, "Make sure you do it right, old man."

Doyle said nothing. All they could hear through the wind was the sporadic choking of the Zodiac's outboards. "If you don't do it properly, Doyle, we're all in a jam.

Remember that," said Jay, shuffling his feet for warmth
and blowing smoke through the pipe bowl.

"Christ!" Doyle exploded. "In a jam! What do you
think we're in now? That woman you killed . . ."

"Not me, Doyle. *Us.* We're playing for keeps—or
hadn't you heard? So stay cool. You get a piece of that
core they just picked up. It doesn't matter what they
suspect later. They won't be able to prove a thing."

Jay saw the gray-blue of the raft, now twenty yards
off. He leaned so close that Doyle could see the toupee
was slightly askew from the wind. "And don't think of
staying on board the *Petrel*. One, you're in too deep already, and two, even if there was a chance you'd be given
immunity it would do you no good—if you don't make it
ashore."

Tony made a sucking noise with his upper denture.
"Yeah. Our contact on the *Petrel* can pull a trigger as
easy as I can. Get me?"

"Give me the cooler," snapped Doyle.

Tony thrust it at him like a sausage. "You get the hammer?"

"Yes."

"You know where to look?"

"I arranged it."

"Just make sure you don't louse it up. Do it good."

"You're full of advice, all of a sudden. *You're* not the
one going over."

"I'd change places, old man, but my orders are to stay
on the boat. Right, Mr. Jay? Besides," he grinned, "I'm no
fucking mullet-head."

Doyle's voice got higher. "Why don't you just shoot
them full of holes? That's your style, isn't it?"

Jay spoke without taking the pipe from his mouth.
"Get a grip on yourself, Doyle. If our man did what he
was told, we're away."

"I can handle it."

"Of course, like that little business back there. You
cracked up, Doyle."

"Yeah," Tony cut in. "You can't handle shit, Doyle."

∼ ∼ ∼

For the last ten yards, the Zodiac surfed on the trawler's leeward side. Johns put the outboard into reverse,
and as the swell slid under it he shifted into neutral. When

they rose high on the next swell, Charlie grabbed a painter from the *Sea Wasp*'s side to steady them, and Doyle stepped easily into the raft, as though he was getting off a streetcar. Johns gave the Zodiac full throttle, sending it swiftly back toward the *Petrel*.

After a nod to Johns and Charlie, Doyle put the oil cooler between his knees like an expensive gift and began worrying. The problem wasn't making contact—after all, no one on the *Petrel* knew who the contact was. The problem was making the *Sea Wasp*'s request for help stick. The suspicions of *Petrel*'s captain must have been aroused by the missing core beneath the strobe light. No matter how much you tried to anticipate, Doyle thought, there were always unexpected questions. He tried to think of them all, but he knew it was hopeless. He'd just have to fend each one off with the best act he could muster.

⌐⌐ ⌐⌐ ⌐⌐

Tate didn't try to be subtle. He didn't like unexplained entries in his log—particularly explosions, and the minute Doyle stepped aboard, gingerly handing the oil cooler to the Chief Engineer in the machine shop, Tate started the questions. "Why the hell didn't you pick our man up?" he demanded, his face turning purple with anger.

Doyle, shaken by Tate's sudden barrage, tried to tap out a cigarette from his pack, dropping three of them on the deck. It was only Tate's first question and Doyle hadn't a clue what he was talking about. "What—what man? I don't—"

"Our Chief Scientist," barked Tate. "He was hooked up in that damn strobe. Didn't you see him?"

"No." Doyle was recovering fast, the blood returning to his pale cheeks. "I'm sorry, Captain. Jesus, I didn't realize—we made for the strobe—wondering what the heck it was. We saw the strobe, all right, but nothing else. Even if we had seen him, what can you do in these seas? We were only at half revs anyway."

Tate charged on. "Why are you out this far?"

Doyle didn't hesitate. "We came out for tuna. Water temperature seemed perfect when we left—sixty-one Fahrenheit."

Tate grunted. "Should've headed in, away from this lot."

"Wanted to, Captain. Trouble was, we had problems with the fuel-injection line. Then this," said Doyle, indicating the oil cooler in the vise grip and the Chief Engineer, who was striking up the oxyacetylene torch ready for the brazing.

"What caused the explosion on the other trawler?"

"No idea. Probably a leaking gas tank," said Doyle. "Damn fool probably kept his stove on."

Tate frowned. It was hardly the way to refer to the skipper of a sister ship, thirty minutes after he was dead. "Didn't you know him?"

Doyle realized his mistake, but countered quickly. "No, ah, not really. New guy. Too bad."

"Yes," said Tate pointedly. "It was."

Watching the welding, Doyle was in a cold sweat. In ten minutes or so the job would be finished. He didn't have much time.

∾   ∾   ∾

Frank tapped gently again on the cabin door, but there was still no answer. He opened it softly. Mary Crane was sitting primly on the bunk, looking straight ahead.

"We're on our way home," he said. He had no idea what to say, so he said the first thing that came into his head. "Is there anything I can do?"

To his surprise she answered without hesitation. "Yes," she said. "Finish the second run. Finish what—what Joe . . ."

"Of course," said Frank, feeling guilty because he'd intended to do it anyway. It was normal procedure on the run home, and wouldn't cost them any time in this weather. They could only travel at six to ten knots maximum anyway. Might as well use the resources. Not doing it wouldn't help Crane, or Sam—or anyone else. "Of course we'll finish the line," he said softly.

"Frank."

"Yes?"

"When—when you've finished, come back."

∾   ∾   ∾

Tate wasn't letting up. "Didn't you hear us calling you earlier?"

Doyle shook his head. "That bum radio set of mine.

It's acting up all the time. Sometimes it's as clear as a bell, and the next moment you can't hear a Goddamn thing. Thanks for sending in the distress call."

"No trouble," said Johns, standing nearby. "They'll send out an Argus from Comox with search flares, just to confirm no survivors."

"Yeah," said Doyle, clutching the lathe as the ship dropped. Suddenly he doubled up.

"You all right?"

"Where's your toilet?" mumbled Doyle, his hand over his mouth.

"Take him below," said Tate to the Scottish Mate, who'd been relieving his boredom by watching the welding. The Mate opened the door of the machine shop and led Doyle below to the lavatory.

Once he was alone in the toilet-shower room, Doyle acted quickly. He flushed the toilet and made his way to the shower cubicle. Then he drew the curtain, felt underneath the polished wood changing seat, and pulled out the four-by-three-and-a-half-inch length of plastic core liner that had been carefully taped to the wood. Inside the liner he could see the dark green mud, and outside, scratched onto the plastic, the latitude and longitude where the core had been found. For a moment he looked at it, almost disbelievingly.

Diamonds sparkled, gold gleamed, but this green ooze —this sea gold that would make some men barons of incredible power and wealth—was no more than a cold, repulsive slime. He checked that the plastic caps were securely taped at both ends, then dropped the core piece inside one of his large wet gear pockets. He taped a message for the contact underneath the seat where the core had been, then, making certain that no one was coming, he pushed back the shower curtain, made his way along the aisle, nodding pleasantly to a passing seaman, and walked up the stairs to upper deck number two. He looked around him. No one was watching.

He took the nine stairs to the flight deck three at a time, turned right just before the radio room, and stepped quickly out through the starboard exit door. In the icy air, it took several seconds for his eyes to get accustomed to the darkness, as he felt his way forward along the side of the funnel to the crow's nest mast assembly just aft of the bridge. High above, just below the covered crow's nest, he could see the aircraft-wing shape of the fifteen-inch-wide, twelve-inch-long S-band antenna which transmitted and received the signals for the Marconi radar on the bridge. His fingers slid inside each edge of the four triangular steel pylons that stretched upward in a twenty-four-foot pyramid to support the crow's nest and antennae. He found the wave guide on the inside of the third pylon. A hollow rectangular pipe, one inch by a quarter, it ran from the bridge radar set to the S-band antenna carrying the electronic waves. Wherever it had to bend, it did so at right angles. Small mirrors, attached as in a periscope at different angles inside the tube, reflected the waves in perpendicular lines between the bridge and antenna. Anywhere along the wave guide would have done for Doyle's purpose, but he wanted to be sure. His fingers moved quickly and silently down the guide from head height until he felt a right-angle bend just above the deck where the tube bypassed a cross strut.

∽ ∽ ∽

The Scottish Mate stepped into the machine shop, grimacing as his teeth sank into a particularly fatty piece of corned beef. Tate stared at him. "Living Jesus, Scotty! Where's that guy from the trawler?"

The Mate, his mouth full, stared back at Tate.

"Good God, man. Use your head," said Tate. "Don't leave him running around the ship. There's something funny about that guy. Says he's got no idea what caused the explosion."

The Scots' accent was almost shrill, the face florid in self-defense. "But he's only having a crap doon there, or being sick."

"*Is he?*" answered Tate. "Johns, go find him." As the First Mate left the shop, he passed Frank on his way in. Tate shot him an angry glance. "I see you're not on your toes either."

"What?"

"Why aren't you watching that Doyle fella? Christ! We're more concerned than you people." Before Frank could answer Tate turned to Charlie. "Bosun, give Johns a hand to round him up."

"Aye, aye, sir."

∾ ∾ ∾

Holding the right angle with one hand, Doyle took the hammer out of his pocket. He waited for the covering noise of crashing water below, then smashed the wave guide hard. He felt the right angle to make sure it was now caved in. It was a good spot—near the deck so the rupture would most likely be blamed on strain caused by the storm. Pocketing the hammer, he quickly retraced his steps. As he walked down from the flight deck to upper deck number one, he saw Johns descending the steps to the toilet-shower room. He hurried along the passageway, calling out, "Any coffee round here, Mate?"

Johns stopped and turned around. Before he could say anything Doyle grinned ingratiatingly. "Christ, I dunno what that was all about. Musta been something I ate. I'm feeling a bit better now, but I'm sure as hell thirsty." Johns led him wordlessly to the galley.

When they returned to the machine shop, the welding was finished and they were testing for leaks in the water bath. Every time the ship rolled, water slopped onto the deck. So far, thought Doyle, so good. He had the sample, and *Petrel*'s radar was out.

The Chief gave him the oil cooler. "A-one," he said.

"Thanks, Chief. Might've been a wee bit of overheating without this."

"Just a bit," said the Chief, appreciating the understatement.

Johns and Charlie were waiting by the Zodiac, and the trip to the *Sea Wasp* was even quicker this time. When Jay and Tony grabbed the painter Charlie caught a glimpse of their faces. If they were fishermen he'd eat his Bosun's spike.

41

In the dim beam of the stern winch light, Frank cut the black fuse cord for the next charge. It was lonely here on deck, carrying out a dead man's orders. It had only been five minutes since Johns and Charlie had returned from the trawler, but the ship's company had disappeared below out of the cold.

He pulled the trigger on the air gun and watched the balloon puff up until it was five feet in diameter. Tying the balloon's tongue with his canvas work gloves was impossible, so he took them off and straddled its neck, the sphere sticking out behind him.

"My, what a big ass you have!" It was Charlie, putting on his gloves and coming out to see if he could help. Frank stood up and attached the balloon to the rope. He looped the rope's mid-section on the winch brake to keep it moored until they got far enough along the seismic line for the bridge to tell them to drop another charge. He pulled his gloves back on, enjoying the feeling of well-being they always gave him. "Knotting these balloons is a real pain in the neck. I lost one once—just farted off like a rocket into the night."

Charlie laughed, then fell silent. Finally, he said, "Well, Frank, old son. It'll soon be over. What a shambles, eh?"

Frank nodded slowly, as the gruesome memories of the last twenty-four hours washed over him. He was sick of the mad race. But deep inside he knew he wasn't that different from Joe Crane—none of them were. He wouldn't settle for second place. Not now.

"What do you think of that lot?" he asked Charlie, pointing into the night.

"The trawler?"

"Yeah."

"If they're fishing for tuna, I'm my mother's uncle."

"Rough customers?"

"Like fucking rocks. Strictly King Kong."

"You think they had a contact aboard?"

"No idea." Charlie squatted, drew out his spike, and from habit rasped off a flake of rust from the deck. "I thought you would've been watching that Doyle guy?"

"Not me," said Frank. "Why should I? I mean, if they'd had a contact they were hardly going to announce it over the P.A., were they?"

"No, guess not. But they could've tried to smuggle off a sample or something. Like that silly bastard George.

You know, one of those floating flash units. Would have been easy enough."

Frank waved his arm seawards. "You see any flashing lights?"

"No."

"Prepare to drop charge—ten minutes!" came the warning from the bridge.

Frank yawned. "Christ, I'm tired."

Nine minutes later the bridge intercom crackled again. "Drop charge!"

Frank went inside the lab and looked at the records to make sure the styluses were still burning the paper. He pressed the timer and marked "Charge Away," while on deck Charlie began letting the arm out. Frank lit the fuse, then, once the arm was well astern, he pulled the quick-release cord. The white balloon streamed away into the night like an errant moon until the LOSHOK pack hit the water, sank, and stopped it dead. The white rubber sphere settled down on the sea as tame as a gull, supporting the explosive charge a hundred and fifty feet below.

Once inside the lab Charlie closed the door leading to the stern.

"God, it's cold!"

Frank would have preferred the door left open. The diesel was blowing down the vents again and he was feeling queasy, but he didn't say anything. Suddenly he was preoccupied with the remarkably detailed picture that they were getting of the bottom rock layers. Joe Crane would have admired them.

❧ ❧ ❧

Mary read Nielsen's message again. She could even hear his voice, reassuring her: "All you have to do is give it to the radio officer . . . They're very strict about the privacy of personal messages." She got up from the bunk and made for the door. But as she put her hand on the cold brass knob she hesitated. Her old self was un-equivocal—she shouldn't do it. But she was alone now, and that changed everything. She stood there, paralyzed by indecision.

❧ ❧ ❧

Jay was through arguing. While Tony prepared the cluster of seventy-five-percent Forcite with the five-second fuse, the Englishman stuck the .357 Magnum into the skipper's back. "Cut your lights."

First the green starboard, then the red port light went off, and finally the masthead. The only light in the wheelhouse now was the dull orange glow of the Decca radar screen. The skipper began winding his self-winding watch and turned slightly, looking down apprehensively at the barrel that was pushing into his coveralls.

"No, it isn't my finger. Do what I tell you."

The Captain saw the stitches and the long, purplish scab on Jay's forehead. He wished that whoever had hit him had finished the job. He'd agreed to take Doyle out because he'd never been offered so much money before in his life for a few days' work. He hadn't asked any questions. Now he wished to God he had. Running parallel with them, two hundred yards to starboard, he could see the mast light of the *Petrel*.

"Listen carefully," said Jay, as Doyle stood morosely in the port aft corner of the cabin. "We know that now they're getting further away from that sonobuoy, they're dropping the charges closer together—to give them a better picture of the bottom. So after this one explodes," he said, roughly indicating the area where the balloon had stopped, "we cut in at ten knots . . ."

"That's—awful fast in this weather," interrupted the skipper.

"We cut in at ten knots behind them and drop our charge at their stern. It ruptures their props," he patted the skipper's head, "no one gets hurt, so no one'll get upset, and they're slowed up. They don't see us, and blame it on their own fuse fouling up. We offer help. But unfortunately—" Jay smiled, "there is no way that a sixty-foot fishboat can tow in over two hundred feet of research ship. We wish them well. Adios—sayonara. Over and out!" Jay paused. "All right, everyone?"

"Isn't there any other way?" the skipper proffered weakly.

"No. It's simple arithmetic, old man. The *Petrel* can do twenty knots—we bust a gut doing fourteen. It's fifty-fifty in this chuck—neither of us can go any faster than ten knots, as you said. But once we hit calmer water, they'd be in Vancouver making that mineral claim while we were still messing around in the Strait. Correct?"

The skipper knew Jay was right but, still desperate for

an alternative, he asked nervously, "What makes you so sure they'll blame the fuse?"

Jay gently smacked his ear. "You know as well as I do that anyone can have a near miss. Nothing's perfect, old man—from weevils in your cereal to safes."

"Including your plan," said Doyle sourly.

"What's wrong with it, Einstein?" growled Tony.

"It's risky," said Doyle.

"So's living," said Tony, winding tape round the dynamite, grinning at his repartee.

Jay poked the gun at Doyle. "You saw to their radar, didn't you?"

"Yes."

"So they won't see us on the screen? Will they?"

Doyle was peeling off a fingernail. "No. They won't see us."

"And we're running without lights."

"What if someone is on their stern?"

"Who'll be on the stern in this weather—at this time of night? They throw the charge and go inside. That's how they've been doing it."

"Maybe."

"Maybe shit!" said Tony. "I thought your contact was supposed to make sure no one was on deck. Didn't you leave that message?"

"Yes, but no one can guarantee the stern'll be clear. Someone might decide to take a leak, get a breath of fresh air, whatever."

"If your contact doesn't keep that stern clear, Doyle, there's gonna be no fat envelope back in Vancouver."

Doyle fell silent.

"All right," said Jay. "You ready, Tony?"

Tony nodded, clicking his teeth in anticipation. "This'll mangle those fucking props."

"Good. So the second we see that next balloon, we go in and deliver our package. Right?"

"I need a drink." It was the skipper. "Could I have a drink, please?" Jay handed him the bottle, patting him again on the head.

"Good, get a shot in you, old man," he said, winking at Tony. But Tony was busy checking the fuse.

∾ ∾ ∾

Frank felt a mounting irritation with Charlie. The bosun had been harping on about the man with the oil cooler, and Frank was getting damned tired of it. Now he was at it again.

"Captain Tate sure as hell watched that guy, didn't he?"

Frank sensed an implied accusation. Before he could stop himself, his temper erupted. "Will you shut up, Charlie? If you're still wondering why I haven't been snooping around, the answer's simple. I can hardly keep my bloody eyes open—"

"I wasn't saying that you—"

"Yes, you were. You're as bad as Tate. Jesus, man, just work it out. What can a trawler do?"

"Do?"

"Yeah. How fast can she go? Ten knots—maybe fifteen, tops?"

"Uh, no more than fifteen."

"So what can we do?"

"Twenty."

"Twenty-two, when you want to," snapped Frank. "When you're headed home. You only do twenty when you bring us out."

Suddenly it dawned on Charlie. "Oh, I get you. Yeah, 'course. No way they can outrun us."

"Right," said Frank grumpily. "Even if that oil-cooler business wasn't on the level—which I think it was—it's a common enough accident on those boats. But even if it wasn't, they can't outrun us. So why worry about them? Why spy on their skipper? Besides, as I said before, I didn't see any flashing units dumped over the side. Did you?"

"No. Yeah, I guess you're right." He punched Frank on the arm good-naturedly. "We're all getting paranoid."

Frank grunted, his good humor returning. "Better believe it."

"Sorry, Frank. I—Christ, with George and Crane and . . ."

"Yeah, I know. Forget it. Let's rig that other charge. We'll be due for the next drop soon. Son of a bitch, I'll be glad when we're in port."

"You and me both," said Charlie, pulling the door shut hard as they went on deck. "Christ, I'm cold and it's supposed to be heated in there."

"Ah well, those who go down to the sea in ships, Charlie." They both laughed and crouched under the winch light, using the Swann as protection against the wind. Frank pulled out a safety fuse. "Sea seems to be dying a bit. Maybe the weather boys are wrong and that hurricane's changed its mind."

"I hope so—Chrriiist, I'm cold!"

∽ ∽ ∽

Johns turned on the Marconi. The screen instantly came to life and the arm began its sweep. He bent down over the glare shield like a man peering through a spy-hole. There was no blip on the screen. Without looking up, his voice sounding like an echo from a tunnel, he asked the lookout, "Can you see that trawler any-where?"

"No."

"Can't see it on the screen either. We only left her ten minutes ago. She should be aft of our starboard beam. If they've got any sense they'll stick with us. She was pretty well lit when we pulled up alongside her."

"Maybe she crossed over to the port side?"

"She should still be showing up on the screen, doesn't matter where the hell she is."

"Maybe the waves are too high, Mate, blocking the signal."

"Not this close. Ought to be getting the occasional bounce."

Johns slid open the port door and stepped out on the wing. The wind grabbed at his hair and turned his baby face taut with its chill. Hunching his shoulders, he looked high above the bridge toward the crow's nest. The S-band antenna was faithfully rotating. He closed the door again.

"Want me to call Sparks?" offered the lookout.

Johns thought hard. He didn't like waking the radio officer, but better safe than sorry. Last thing he wanted on his record was that he'd bashed into a trawler. "Yes, all right. Tell him I'm not getting an echo. Something's definitely wrong."

Johns then rang the after lab. Charlie answered. "Yeah?"

"Bosun, the radar is on the blink. Can't - see that trawler anywhere. And no chance of hearing her engine in this wind. If you see any lights from the stern, let us know, eh, so we can get a fix on her."

"Will do."

"What's up?" asked Frank.

"Radar's screwed up."

∾ ∾ ∾

The radio officer cursed the roll as he lumbered up to the bridge. If only the ship's officers were taught more about how the whole electronic system works, he thought, it would save a lot of trouble. Half the time they called you up for some piddling thing they could easily have fixed themselves with a minor adjustment to the controls.

But after he'd checked the bridge radar, he had to admit that this wasn't a matter of knob-twiddling. It looked like the wave guide was acting up, and that meant going topside in the wind and wet. Reluctantly he made his way back to the radio room, pulled out a flashlight, donned his fur-lined parka, and headed toward the top.

∾ ∾ ∾

When Mary Crane heard the voices, she thought the radio officer was in. But when she entered the dim, pantry-sized room, she saw that it was empty. The voices were the incoming radio chatter coming all the way from Vancouver to Norway. She sat down to wait for the officer's return in the chair by the door, shifting it a little to make sure she couldn't be seen from the passageway. She unfolded the strip of paper containing Nielsen's message, and looked again at the coordinates that she'd filled in for the fake address. The incoming chatter ceased, and in its place was the crackle of static. She tried to relax by watching the rows of lights winking on the control panels, but there was no apparent pattern to them and in the semi-darkness they seemed like feverish, accusing eyes.

∾ ∾ ∾

It was just a glimpse. No more. But it was the key. Frank had just cut the fuse to explode the hundred and thirty pounds at a hundred and fifty feet. Simultaneously Charlie took the air hose, inserted it in the neck of the balloon and with one long squeeze inflated it to a six-foot

diameter to better support the extra charge weight. He
waited for a long trough, straddled the balloon beneath
the winch light and took off his gloves to tie the knot in
the balloon's neck. Frank had started to say, "What a big
ass you . . ." when, just for a second, he saw Charlie's
fingernails. They were green. Not dark green—Charlie
probably didn't even notice himself, it was so faint. But
they were green, bluish-green. Having tied the knot in
the neck of the balloon, Charlie pulled his gloves back on,
took hold of the heavy hook at the end of the Austin-
Western arm and looped the balloon rope through, ready
for the quick release. The afterdeck intercom crackled.
"Prepare to drop charge. Ten minutes."

"You okay, Frank? Christ, you look sick!"

"What? Yeah, yeah," said Frank. "I think I'll go take
a Gravol."

"You'd better. You look bloody awful."

"Back—in a minute." Frank half stumbled through the
lab into the alleyway and down toward the storage room.
He pulled the heavy insulating door open. The first thing
he saw was the black plastic sack that contained the
corpses. The draught from opening the door inflated it
slightly, making him start. He glanced around quickly at
the samples. None of them looked as if they had been
touched—until he examined them more closely. The bottom six inches of the final core had been siphoned off
and replaced with what was obviously bulk from one of
the grab sample bags. Which bag it had been taken from
was difficult to tell. There were plenty of unused sections
of empty core barrels into which the stolen sample could
have been transferred. The bag samples were rich too,
but the piece of core had no doubt been taken because it
would give a more optimistic sample of the subsurface
layers. It would be the best "in hand" sample of all. But
whoever it was had been careful not to take the whole
core, in hopes of avoiding detection.

No, Frank told himself, it couldn't be him. It . . .
He looked at his watch. Five minutes till they dropped
the next charge. Suddenly he yelled at himself, his voice
bouncing eerily off the locker walls. "You silly bastard.
He probably just came down to check it out. Christ,
man, he *is* the bloody bosun. It's his job to keep his eye
on everything, including the storage lockers." He leaned
against the door and exhaled slowly. "All you have to do,

Frank, is ask him when you calm down. Just say, 'Charlie, have you been down to the storage room? I know you didn't take any of the samples down from the deck *before*, because you were helping me topside all the time. But did you go down *after?*' 'Yes, Frank, I went down to check stores.'" Case closed. Paranoia over. Frank laughed at himself again as he walked tiredly up toward the lab, thinking how good it would be to get home, to get some rest. To live like a normal human being again.

In the lab it was just over four minutes to drop time.

"Feeling better?" asked Charlie.

"Yep. Miraculous recovery."

"Atta boy!"

∽ ∽ ∽

A hundred yards astern of the *Petrel* and blacked out, the *Sea Wasp* was invisible. Tony stood behind the wheelhouse, so that when he flicked his lighter to start the fuse no one would see the glow—not that anyone would be looking. Jay wound down the starboard window. "All set?"

"Those props—they're gonna have one heck of a hernia. I'm tellin' ya."

"Good, but remember you only get one shot—when you see them leave the stern after dropping their charge."

"So get Grandma to take us in close."

"I will, but it'll still be fifty feet away."

"Hey, I'm not gonna slip this time."

"You'd better not."

Tony waved him away. "Stop worryin'. It's in the bag."

Jay turned to the Decca set, looking at his watch in the halo of the sweep arm. "They'll be dropping the charge in three minutes. Take her in, Grandma. Three minutes, Tony!"

"Gotcha!"

The skipper pushed the rev lever forward, glancing nervously across at Doyle. "If it lands on that deck, you'll sink the whole ship."

"So a big accident instead of a little one," said Jay. "Main thing is to stop it, slow them down." He was smiling.

"Jesus," said Doyle. "You crazy bastard. There's over thirty people on that boat."

Jay waved the Magnum at Doyle. "You want to play a numbers game, Doyle? I'll give you numbers. We've done in three already on that other trawler. That alone would get you put away—same as three thousand. So shut your face."

The lurching stern of the *Petrel* was four hundred feet dead ahead.

∽   ∽   ∽

"Drop charge!" commanded the voice from the bridge.

As Charlie opened the door to the afterdeck, Frank asked for his lighter to ignite the fuse. Charlie tossed it to him and moved quickly up to the Austin-Western control panel. Frank pulled down the main afterdeck light switch, and instantly the stern was bathed in bright yellow.

∽   ∽   ∽

"Beautiful," said Tony. "Like a fucking birthday cake, fellas. *Merci* blow through."

Doyle watched as Frank released the balloon and saw it streaking astern far beyond the LOSHOK pack, bouncing over the high crests like a playful beach ball until the Austin-Western arm had extended far enough beyond the troughs for Frank to pull the quick-release rope. The white pack dropped into the sea and the balloon settled on the swells.

∽   ∽   ∽

Shutting off the Austin-Western, but not bothering to retract the arm, Charlie slid down the stairs to the lab entrance. "Let's get inside. It's like the bloody North Pole out here."

"I'll be in in a sec. Got to fix this next charge."

"Fix it inside. How about a coffee?" asked Charlie, closing the stern door, taking off his wet gloves and slapping his arms on his ribcage against the chill.

"Thanks," said Frank. "I could do with four cups. Nearly dead on my feet. And all I can taste is dieseline."

"I'll buy you five." As Charlie went for the coffee, Frank reopened the stern door. Charlie might be cold, but Frank's head was starting to throb from the diesel fumes. All he wanted to do was rest, but now that the charge was away, it was time to settle the matter of the green stain on Charlie's hand. Then he could rest.

When Charlie returned from the galley with the steaming mugs, Frank asked as easily as he could, "By the way, were you down in the storage locker—after the crew took the samples down?"

"Yeah. I took Sam down, or what was left of the poor bastard." Charlie walked down the length of the lab and firmly closed the stern door—again. "Bloody freezing," he said.

Frank watched him closing the door—again.

"Why?" asked Charlie, spinning the lock wheel. "Something wrong down there?"

"No, just thought things'd been moved around a bit."

"Probably the swells."

Frank's eyes were on the clock. Four and a half minutes until the explosion of the last charge. He didn't know why he was so preoccupied with the time, but something impelled him to watch the clock. Something wasn't right. He couldn't define it clearly, but things didn't fit: Charlie walking all the way back to the stern door again to make sure it was closed, even though he knew Frank hated the stuffy, fume-soaked atmosphere; his leaving the Austin-Western arm extended, as if he was in a hurry. And the Malachite Green stain on his hand. So all right, maybe Charlie was just tired and crotchety. The stain wasn't proof positive of any tampering with the samples; taking Sam's body down would explain that. Just brushing against one of the bags would stain the skin. Even so, the pieces still didn't fit. Frank rubbed his eyes. All he wanted was sleep—twenty-four hours straight. But the pieces didn't fit. He hadn't seen green stain on the hands of any of the other seamen.

"Who else helped you?"

"Helped me what?" Charlie said irritably.

"Carry Sam down?"

"Shit, I dunno. Johns, two or three of the guys, I think. Listen, Frank, if something's buggin' you, you'd better—"

"No, no. It's okay. It's okay, really." Scowling, Charlie walked brusquely from the lab. Frank slumped in his chair. Charlie was right. If he had anything to say he should say it. If he wasn't sure he should shut up. He felt ashamed of what he'd done—snooping around like some half-baked private eye—and now the dieseline fumes were making him feel sick. He looked at the clock again. There were three minutes and twenty seconds to go before the explosion. It would be the biggest bang so far. Maybe he'd try to catch a glimpse of it blowing right up into the sea's surface, and get some fresh air as well. He got up, unwound the stern door lock and stepped out on the afterdeck. He couldn't see anything except the long finger of the Austin-Western poking aft. As always, the chilling wind whipping the diesel fumes away from his face felt good, like a bracing shower the morning after. It was strange, he thought, that he couldn't see the trawler anywhere. It hadn't been long since it had steered off from the *Petrel*. Even in the giant swells an occasional running light should show.

Revelation came slowly at first, but then it gained speed. It was as if the wind was blowing the cobwebs out of some dusty corner of his brain. Christ! he thought. That American comes aboard, part of the core disappears, the radar screws up . . . Jesus. If they have the core, they mean to beat us home. But how can they do that if we're faster—unless—Jesus Christ!

He hit the switch panel for every light on the stern. In the half shadow beyond the flood of light that now covered the sea, the bow of the *Sea Wasp* loomed out of the darkness only thirty yards away. He ran into the lab, grabbed a three-pound LOSHOK pack, cut a fuse for five seconds' delay, crimped it into the end of the blasting cap and wound it around the pack. The door flew open and Charlie dived at him, knocking the charge to the deck and yelling, "Get out of here!"

Frank lashed out and fell, dropping the charge.

Wrenching a pike pole from its clips on the bulkhead, Charlie swung the hook toward his face. "Stay out of it, Frank."

Frank's mouth twisted in anger. "Why? So your pals can blow our ass off? So you can collect your payoff? How much they pay you, you bastard?"

"Get off the deck. What's the percentage in this for you, eh?"

Frank ducked as the pike swung overhead. "And you called George a dumb bastard. You're the dumb bastard. You think they'll just try to outrun us? What do you think they did to the other trawler?"

Charlie swung the hook again.

∾ ∾ ∾

"What are those assholes doing over there?" moaned Tony.

"Throw it!" yelled Jay. "Throw it!"

Tony lit the fuse, grasped the port rail, and waited until he was high on the wave's crest. Then he tossed it. It was a long, slow lob. It bounced off the Austin-Western arm and dropped overboard on the starboard side, exploding four feet below the starboard prop. Like an animal kicked from behind, the whole stern suddenly jumped, spumes of water rising and falling on Frank, knocking him to the deck and sweeping the pike from Charlie's grasp.

Immediately, the *Petrel* was slowed. The props, lifted clear of the water, jerked and thrashed spasmodically, screeching against the buckled plates.

There were only two punches—Charlie's jab at Frank's head, which missed, and Frank's uppercut to Charlie's groin, which connected. Charlie crumpled, writhing in agony on the deck like a freshly landed fish. Frank grabbed the LOSHOK pack, lighting the fuse as the *Petrel* yawed out of control and the general alarm sounded from the bridge. He ran to the ship's rail, and when the next swell lifted the *Petrel*'s crippled stern high into the air, he threw the charge well forward of the trawler's bow, allowing for the wind. As the charge left his hand he saw that the *Sea Wasp*, in mid-turn, was now beam on. The explosion was too soon. Hitting the water ten feet in front of the trawler, it did little more than cover her in a blanket of foam and rupture her bulkhead fixtures. But at least it had stopped her momentarily, and Frank turned to get another charge. He knew that the next charge the trawler threw at the *Petrel*'s stern would be the last—for the *Petrel*. Turning back toward the explosives box, all he saw was the glint of the pike coming at him from somewhere near the winch as Charlie stumbled toward him. Frank stepped aside. His right hand darted out, grabbed the pole and jerked. As the two men collided, falling hard on the deck, Frank still held the hook. The first sailor on deck, seeing his fellow crewman in trouble, instinctively swung at Frank. Frank twisted and caught the blow on his shoulder but managed to smack the sailor with the pole. He brought the handle back and thrust. He felt it stop abruptly and heard a soft gurgling sound as the bosun

slumped to the deck, grasping the pike, trying to pull it
from his stomach.

Frank ran to the trunk and pulled out another LOSHOK
charge. There was no time to cut the fuse. He rammed it
into the blasting cap and quickly wrapped it around the
pack. He lit the fuse midway, two inches from the blasting cap, so that it began burning in both directions.
Then he took careful aim and threw it at a point ten feet
in front of the *Sea Wasp*'s bow. A gust of wind caught it.
The charge arced over the trawler's wheelhouse, struck its
Beaufort life-raft drum astern, and fell over the side. It
exploded level with the gunwale—tearing the boat open
like a carcass and spilling its innards into the sea. In seconds she was on fire and going down fast.

Doyle and the Captain dove overboard. Tony was de-
capitated by a flying splinter from the prop blade. Jay,
bald, bloodied and still in the shell of the wheelhouse, began firing the Magnum. In the heavy swells, Frank could
see that Jay had little or no chance of hitting him or anyone else on the *Petrel*. If that was what he was trying to
do. But the Englishman kept firing until the remaining
dynamite on the *Sea Wasp* blew up under him. The explosion showered the *Petrel* with debris, driving shock
waves against her side and sending Jay's blood-sodden
toupee flying high above the sinking trawler like the pelt
of some tiny animal.

∽ ∽ ∽

The unnerving sound of the static was finally getting to
Mary Crane. Ten minutes sitting alone had seemed like
half an hour, and the radio officer still hadn't returned.
She couldn't stand waiting any longer. She had got up and
reached the alleyway just as the *Sea Wasp*'s dynamite
erupted. The blast picked her up, throwing her head first
into the bulkhead. There she lay still. One of her shoes
fell off, tumbling noisily down the steps to the lower deck.

∽ ∽ ∽

By now, Tate and most of the crew were on deck,
moving through the floodlit and spray-filled confusion like
shadows through an incandescent fog. Tate bellowed for
lifelines to be thrown to Doyle and the trawler's Captain.
But with her props badly damaged, the *Petrel* was virtually
unmaneuvrable in such seas. Under Tate's direction from

the aft intercom, Johns tried as best he could to use
the bow thrusters to turn, but the high waves made it
hopeless. They never did find the skipper, nor did the
Argus, which arrived forty-five minutes later from the
Canadian Forces base at Comox. The plane's flares picked
up some wreckage but no bodies were sighted. Doyle
had been found by the *Petrel* but when they dragged him
aboard, the back of his neck was a bloody hole where the
Hi-Vel Magnum bullet had hit him at a range of not more
than twenty feet, and in any case the concussion of the
final explosion had snapped his neck.

∿　∿　∿

Seeking respite from the deafening noise of the engine
room, the Chief Engineer came onto the bridge, but even
there he found it necessary to shout above the ear-split-
ting shaking of the ship's plates below. "Four knots and
that's the limit," he said.

"Will the plates hold?" asked Tate.

"Oh, we're taking some water aft. Looks like a swamp
down there. But we'll get home all right."

Tate grunted his appreciation, adding, "I'm in no hurry."

"I am," said the Chief. "This damn vibration'll shake
the crown and bridge right out of my mouth. Is the Coast
Guard sending out tugs?"

"Yes. They'll give us a tow once we're in the Straits."

"How's the forecast?"

"The same."

"Terrific," growled the Chief.

"Well, they'll be shepherding us in. We'll make it."

"I bloody hope so."

∿　∿　∿

Alone on the stern, Frank looked back in the direction
of the sunken trawler. He was the angriest he'd ever been,
but the only visible sign was the graceful arc made by a
green signal lantern which, for lack of anything else nearby, he'd grabbed and flung savagely astern. For a moment
after it struck the stormy water, the green light bubbled
like an effervescent fish—full of life—then it was gone,
sucked down by the ship's wake into the vastness of the
middle valley over a mile below.

∿　∿　∿

"I . . . the radio . . . the message. I have to send . . ."

Frank eased Mary's head back gently onto the fresh white pillow. "It's all right," he said. "You fell. Just stay still. You have to rest."

"The message. I have to—"

"It's all right." He pushed her down gently again. "Everything'll be all right."

She lay back and groaned, shielding her eyes from the cabin light. Frank turned it off and switched on the dimmer bunk light. Along with the shoe the stewards had found, there was her handbag and the message to Nielsen. Frank tore it up. He didn't know what the rest of the message meant—the part about a Mr. Browner and a Mrs. Lindert—but he'd guessed it was a cover sign. In any case, he knew damned well that the address was the lat and long of the hot-mud find. If after the concussion had passed she asked him about the message, he'd just profess ignorance. It could have gone anywhere when she fell, he'd tell her. But he hoped she wouldn't ask. Once she calmed down a little she wouldn't want to go through with it—or at least, he hoped she wouldn't. Not when he told her that he knew how, through both of them, Joe Crane's long ordeal could pay off in a way that no one else could possibly have imagined two days before.

But it wasn't until five minutes later, as he sat quietly beside her and started putting the remaining pieces together, that he realized the danger that he and Mary Crane were still in, and what he would have to do. Alarmed, he got up quickly from the bunk. He'd tell her after he did it. But no one else must know.

42

Fifteen hours after the news reports of the explosions and missing trawlers, while the crippled *Petrel* was not yet halfway home, Miel and Klaus, known to each other only by reputation until this moment, sat facing each other

across the café table. By five p.m. the waters of the Limmat, rippling out of Lake Zurich, were golden in the late
summer sun. Although it wasn't cold, it was cool enough
for Klaus to order hot chocolate instead of beer. Miel ordered coffee with Kirsch. The Swiss banker smiled at the
American. It was a forced smile. Both of them knew it and
neither of them cared. This was strictly business.

"You enjoyed your trip?" asked Klaus.

"Yeah. Bit crowded inside."

"So I understand. But marvelous food, yes?"

"Chow's pretty good."

"Perhaps you would have preferred the big plane—
the . . ."

"Jumbo."

"Yes, exactly. Jumbo. But it was important that we
meet as soon as possible. For that, the *Concorde* is the
best."

"Guess so."

"Sugar?"

"No, thanks."

"Crowded or not, the *Concorde* is a tribute, don't you
think, to international cooperation?"

"You think so?"

"Oh, absolutely. It was so sensible for the French and
English to—how do you say it?—throw in their lot with
each other?"

"To join forces," said Miel bluntly.

"Exactly, Mr. Miel. To join forces."

Miel drank the Kirsch in one gulp, grimacing with
pleasure as it burned into his stomach. Klaus patiently
stirred his chocolate until it was uniformly smooth and
creamy. "Joining forces is the key to success," he said.
"There is too much time wasted by useless fighting. These
muds, for example. Unfortunately there was no time for
us to talk. Being men of initiative, we had to act quickly,
and act we did—but independently. And what have we
now?"

"Zip," said Miel.

"Zip?" Klaus looked perplexed.

"Nothing. Zero."

"Precisely. We have nothing. But now, Mr. Miel, it is
time to talk. These muds, they are rich?"

"Very," said Miel, looking out on the river, watching
some of the pedal boats starting out toward the lake.

"You are sure?"

"What else do you think those two explosions the Coast Guard reported were about? And the report about the scientist—Crane—dying from working in damn near hurricane conditions?"

Klaus nodded his agreement, then asked suddenly, "Who else is interested?"

Miel called the waitress and ordered another Kirsch. "Who else is interested?" he said. "A Canadian company —Canadian Oceanic Resources—which you control. The outfit that must have told you you had some seagoing opposition. Guess you got a message from that broad, Nolan, eh?"

"Ah!" Klaus smiled. "You have—how do you say it? —you have done your homework, Mr. Miel."

"Yeah. And there's a guy, Nielsen, that wanted part of the action from an outfit called Vancouver Oceanics. But he's not interested any more."

"Why is that?"

"He had an accident," said Miel, gulping at his coffee. "With his legs. Both of them were broken."

Klaus meticulously removed a crumb from his lapel. "That is the trouble with competitive sports."

"Yeah."

Klaus toyed for a moment with his spoon. "So, until others find out—which will not be long, once the *Petrel* has moored—there is you and me, Mr. Miel. Correct?"

"Correct."

The waitress delivered Miel's second Kirsch and brought the long stick of fresh, saucer-sized pretzels and a plate of small cakes. Klaus took a pretzel, breaking it neatly in half. "The area. Juan de Fuca?"

"Yes?"

"It is in dispute between the Canadian and the U.S. governments, is it not?"

"There's negotiations going on," said Miel cautiously.

"But the outcome is not yet known?"

"You know what bureaucrats are like."

"Exactly. And the International Law of the Sea Conferences?"

"More bureaucrats."

"As I thought. More time. In fact it is possible, is it not, that there will be no resolution of exact national boundaries?"

"It's possible."

Klaus smiled. It was genuine this time. "Precisely. It will be grab as grab can. Am I correct, Mr. Miel?"

"That's right. Whoever has the muscle."

Klaus broke off another piece of the pretzel. "Of course, the companies interested in mining the minerals could approach their own governments for jurisdictional decisions of the Juan de Fuca area, but . . ." He waved his hand imperiously. "There would be no need, if two companies could come together—to agree to share the profits, to—"

"To join forces."

Klaus was delighted. He pulled out his silver cigar case. "Exactly! Then no matter what the official outcome of the border disputes. You agree?"

"Yeah," grunted Miel. "Guess you're right."

Klaus' face lost all trace of easy humor, and he looked hard at Miel. "Better for both to fish than none, Mr. Miel. If the bureaucrats decide it is in Canadian territory, then we use CANORE as—"

"The front," cut in Miel. "And if it's in U.S. waters we use my company as the front."

"Precisely!"

Miel nodded thoughtfully. "What do you propose? Fifty-fifty?"

Klaus beamed. "Mr. Miel, how happy it is for me to meet a man who does not beat around bushes. Some you would not believe. They haggle like—like street vendors." His hand rose in a grand gesture. "Fifty-fifty? Yes, of course."

Miel grabbed another cake as if they might suddenly be taken away. "What should we call the company?"

"Yours is North American Oceanics?"

"Yeah."

"Ah, N.A.O. Mine is Canadian Ore—CANORE. Let us find some common ground. Let me see. How does Oceanics West suit you? O.W.?"

"No," said Miel. "It sounds funny. That's an American word for—you know, 'ouch'—'ow!' "

"Oh, I see. Have you a suggestion?"

"United Oceanic Industries. U.O.I."

"Yes. Very good, ja. United!"

"Divided we fall," said Miel.

"I don't understand."

"It doesn't matter. It's a joke."

Klaus thought for a second. "Ah, yes. If not, we fall. I see. Very good," he laughed. "Very good." Klaus took out his notebook and turned to the "C" section of his diary to the CANORE entry. Next to it, he wrote, "CANORE + N.A.O. = U.O.I." He saw Andrea Nolan's name written next to CANORE and erased it briskly, leisurely blowing the erasure dust away. Snapping the diary shut, he pushed his silver cigar case forward.

As he accepted, Miel was busy watching the waitress bending over the next table. Klaus lit the pencil-thin cigar for him. "Do you like Switzerland?"

Miel blew out a long stream of smoke, still watching the waitress' bottom, which was wiggling as she cleaned the table. "Yeah," he said. "I like your country very much."

"You have arranged for someone to meet the ship?" asked Klaus.

Miel didn't take his eyes off the waitress. "Yeah. We have a man on the dock. A longshoreman. He checked the *Petrel* out for me before she left."

"If your plan does not work?"

"It will."

"Your last one didn't."

Miel shot an angry glance at Klaus. "Neither did yours."

Klaus tapped the ash off his cigar. "Touché, Mr. Miel. But there is no point to our agreement if we do not get a sample before others have a chance to interfere."

"I know that," said Miel, chomping down on the cigar. "My man will get a sample before they even finish unloading." Miel looked at his watch. "Soon as she docks, he'll be aboard her. I fixed up some people to help him. He'll find it."

"Let us hope so, Mr. Miel," said Klaus coldly. He pushed the lighted end of the cigar into the ashtray until, starved of oxygen, it went out, leaving a black smudge. He waved the stub toward the pedal boats that Miel was watching as they crawled about on the Limmat. "Ridiculous machines."

Miel glanced again at his watch. "I'd better be going."

"The *Concorde?*"

"Yes."

"Now there *is* a useful machine. You'll be in Vancouver before the ship docks."

"Yes. About three hours before."

"You will let me know immediately?"

As Miel rose from his chair, he watched the long string of smoke from Klaus' dead cigar wafting high into the air, like a poison gas, amongst the green vines that surrounded the table and trailed off toward the river. "Don't worry, I won't double-cross you, Klaus. I know a good deal when I see one."

"Forgive me. I do not mean to imply——"

"Sure. It's okay. I'll let you know."

Klaus rose and extended his hand. "Bon voyage."

"Sure," said Miel.

"Oh," said Klaus, "I nearly forgot." Reaching into his thick overcoat pocket, he took out a small box of Sprungli chocolates and gave them to Miel. "I think you might like to try some of our Swiss chocolates. They're very good for the nerves."

Miel started to grin, then stopped. He could see that Klaus wasn't joking.

43

The moment the ship came alongside Centennial Pier, Larn was ready. Two other longshoremen stood behind him, wearing Customs uniforms and rather enjoying the masquerade.

When the gangways came down, Larn gripped his clipboard and walked aboard with such authority in his sparkling Customs uniform that no one even thought to ask for credentials. At the bottom of the gangplank, Johns was supervising.

"Customs clearance," Larn said tersely.

Johns waved carelessly toward the bridge. "Second Mate has the forms. Flight deck cabin number one."

"Right! Thanks. Have you had some rough weather?" said Larn in passing.

Johns nodded.

Once inside the wet lab, Larn approached the first seaman he saw.

"Customs. Where are the geological samples stored?"

The seaman didn't know why Customs would be interested in mud, but they'd tax each bag, for sure. He jerked his thumb below. "Lower deck for'ard."

Larn wrote briskly on the clipboard. "Have they been unloaded yet?"

"No, they leave 'em cold right until the last minute before they put 'em in the trunks. They'll still be in storage."

"Good, thanks. Heard you had a rough trip?"

"Roughest I've been on."

Larn patted the sailor's arm. "Well, good to see you back."

While he left his two cohorts to check the assembled trunks in the wet lab just in case, Larn quickly descended the stairs to the lower deck.

On the upper deck Frank, walking off with his bags, saw the two men looking through the gear he'd helped stack ready for the crew to load on the trucks. "What're you doing?" he asked, an edge to his voice.

"Customs," one of them mumbled.

"There aren't any cigarettes on the sea bottom," said Frank. "They get rather soggy." One of the men glared at him. "Don't break anything," added Frank, and left.

The two men waited for a few seconds, then one of them followed him off.

Down below, excitedly wrenching the door open, Larn surveyed the interior of the storage locker—and nearly dropped the clipboard. He checked with the man topside, and in four minutes he was on a dockyard phone to Miel.

∽ ∽ ∽

The girl, dressed only in her underwear, brought the phone over to the end of the bed where Miel sat trying to unwind from the quick trip back from Zurich. Naked, his belly looked like a great pile of veal in trauma, as the girl continued to work on him, kneeling beneath his knees at the edge of the bed. Miel looked out the window at the big red and black time-weather sign flashing on and off at the corner of Georgia and Burrard: 3 p.m.; 21°

Celsius; gray skies. He listened to Larn for a few moments, then jumped up, knocking the girl to the ground with his ham-sized thigh.

"*What?* It's not there? Well where the fuck is it? What? Whaddya mean, they're all gone?" His face turned purple, in stark contrast to the lily-white mound of his stomach. He listened a little longer, then yelled, "Well, check the ambulances when they take the stiffs off. Check every Goddamn thing that comes off the ship. Everything!"

The girl sat at the window, sipping a gin and tonic and blankly watching the crowds crossing from Christ Church Cathedral.

"Who's in charge?" shouted Miel. "No, not you, you dummy—the geology guy. Frank—Frank who? So if he left, follow him. All right, so you did. All *right*, I said. Keep your shirt on. When you know where he's gone, call me back. And have that other guy of yours follow that scientist's wife."

Larn's voice sounded frightened. "Mr. Miel—"

"Yeah?"

"Ah, I got a chance to snoop on the bridge, like you told me."

"So?"

"The logbook. It's gone. The old man must have locked it away in his safe."

"Great! Fucking great!" bellowed Miel. "Now we don't even have the Goddamn coordinates. Well, move, Goddamn it! Ring me back!" Miel hung up and paced around the room for a few seconds while the girl watched him as if he were a monkey in a zoo. Finally, he grabbed a handful of twenties and flung them at her. "Get outta here."

After she'd gone, he rang Zurich direct.

"Klaus?"

"Yes? My God, what time is it?" asked the banker, squinting at the clock-radio at his bedside.

"Never mind what the fucking time is. There's no samples."

"Who is this?"

Miel remembered Klaus' dread fear of the telephone, but he couldn't give a damn right now. "Cut the crap, Klaus. I haven't got time to catch a friggin' plane."

"What did you say?"

"You heard me. No samples." There was a brief silence.

"What happened?"

"Don't ask me. There were dozens on board. The crew says so."

"Then what . . . ?"

Miel's brain was racing. Suddenly he smacked the wall. "Son of a bitch! It's that scientist's sidekick—he must have it. Son of a bitch—he must have dumped 'em overboard and hung on to one or two. The fucker!"

Klaus was gradually waking up. "Can he be reached?"

"Reached? What the hell do you mean, can be he *reached?*"

"I mean can he—?"

"You mean can he be bought?"

"Yes."

"Who can't be bought? Why the hell do you think he's playing it so close to the chest?"

"Then contact him immediately, Mr. Miel." The moment he put the phone down, Klaus turned on his reading light and opened up a box of Sprungli chocolates which he always kept by his bed—for those rare occasions when he was so agitated he found it impossible to sleep.

∾   ∾   ∾

As soon as he put it down, Miel's telephone rang again. It was Larn, telling him that the technician, Frank Hall, had driven directly to a post office and then out to the Maritime Institute. Miel immediately rang the University. He knew he had to work with extraordinary speed. Vancouver would be crawling with mining scouts, who by now would have had time to learn of Shae's paper and would be looking for a chance to buy a sample, hoping to hawk it to the biggest bidder, pending the settlement of boundaries.

∾   ∾   ∾

Frank was still hanging up his jacket in his small, crowded lab when he heard the telephone ring. He didn't know exactly who it might be, but he guessed the type. "Yes?" he said.

Miel was smooth. He gave the name of Parks. He was very sorry to bother Frank—he'd heard it had been a very bad trip. The average Joe didn't have any idea of how dangerous it could be out there, but anyway, why he was ringing was that he was interested in collecting "geological samples," and speed was of the essence. He would pay very well for such samples.

"How much?" asked Frank.

"Twenty thousand. Cash. In an hour."

"No, thanks."

"Name your price."

"I don't have one."

"Thirty thousand."

"Sorry, I'm not interested."

There was a long silence. "Bullshit! Okay, okay. Fifty grand—last offer."

"I said *no.*"

Miel exploded. "You stupid bastard! Who are you trying to be? Honest John? A man of the people? You jerk. You could be on Easy Street. You . . ." There was a knock on Frank's door.

"Excuse me a moment," said Frank. He was enjoying it. When he opened the door, Mary was standing there crying. "I—I came as quickly as I could. They had to take Joe off the ship but I couldn't . . ."

Frank put his arm around her, led her to his chair and said softly, "I'll be right back."

Frank lifted the receiver again. "You were saying?"

"You stupid jerk!" continued Miel, unabated. "You could've been on Easy Street." His voice dropped. "You dummy. You coulda had it all."

Frank looked over at Mary. As she breathed quickly, trying to regain her composure, her breasts rose tightly against her dress.

"You smart-ass!" continued Miel. "I could have your legs broken."

"You could," said Frank coolly, still watching Mary, "and what would that get you?"

Miel was about to hang up, but the temptation was too great. "So what did you do with it, bright boy? You didn't throw all of it over the side."

"You should know. You had me followed from the ship."

Miel thought about what Larn had told him. Frank had gone to the post office, and . . . "You posted it! You stupid son of a . . ."

Frank glanced over at the can-sized bulge in his

khaki down jacket, grinned to himself and hung up. He walked over to Mary. She was frightened. "Oh my God," she said. "Is someone trying to get it already?"

"Yes," he said. "But don't worry. I told you I'd look after it. It'll be all right. They're not getting what Joe Crane found. I promise."

"What did you tell them?"

"Nothing. But I stopped off at the post office when I saw one of those thugs following me off the ship. So they think I've put it in the mail drop. They'll probably hire fifty more thugs to rip the post office apart. Anyway, it'll make them think we haven't got it. That'll keep them away from us long enough to finish the business."

Trying to rid her mind of all that had happened by concentrating on something she'd never seen before, Mary surveyed the lab. On the far wall there was a print of Cezanne's last painting of Mont Sainte Victoire. She studied it intently. From six feet away, the painting was clearly that of a village hugging a green mountain. But the more closely she examined it the more the village became a series of clay-orange dabs interspersed with shadows, so that the sense of order and security it had imparted at a distance was now gone. In its place was a tension borne of unrecognizable patters of color and darkness. She was terrified. She swung around at Frank. "But I don't understand? Why can't we take the sample to the Claims Office right now? It's still open."

"We can't take it there. It's too dangerous. Someone else has to take that sample in hand, and register it in Joe's name. I'll get a graduate student to do it. That'll be safe."

"But why? Why can't we . . . ?"

"Because whoever rang me on the phone won't take long to cotton on to my post-office red-herring bit, and once they do they'll be waiting for me—or you."

Mary shivered as Frank went on. "We wouldn't get within a hundred yards of that Claims Office."

Mary was crying again. "All right, but why—why do we have to go to Joe's office? I don't ever want to see that place again. I—"

"We have to. I told you. Not just for Joe but for you. For us."

He could hear her sobbing silently, deeply. "I—" she began, "I feel so guilty. For Joe. For . . ."

His voice dropped and he spoke as comfortingly as he could, pulling her gently toward him. "Don't," he said. "Don't feel guilty. Joe couldn't help what happened—nor could you. It just happened. But now we can even the score. Trust me."

"Hold me," she said. "Hold me, Frank."

"I'm not leaving you," he said. "I'm never going to leave you. That's why I want you to come with me to Joe's office. Right now. I'm not going to let anyone hurt you. I . . ." He kissed her hair. "I love you."

∽ ∽ ∽

Mary didn't even see the graduate student leave the Maritime Institute in the cab—heading for the Claims Office with the sample in hand. She was far too engrossed with the TV-sized microfilm screen in what had been Joe's office. She and Frank were alone in the southeast corner of the building, now made unexpectedly warm and bright by a sudden rush of sun as the storm's wind blew a gap in the stratus cloud that continued to hang over the rest of Vancouver in a vast, gray, brooding blanket. What had transformed her mood, what had dried the tears and brought back the smile and beauty to her face, was the long list of station records of Joe Crane's past cruises. Every now and then Frank would stop turning the machine's handle and back up to read the sample description more fully. Wherever he saw that a geoduck clam had been found in a sample, he wrote down the latitude and longitude of the station. By the time he'd finished, there were eight such sightings recorded—all of them over two thousand meters deep, all of them within the two-hundred-mile limit. All of them just waiting to be mined.

"How—?" began Mary, so excited that she couldn't find the words.

Frank finished the question for her. "How come no one got on to it—that an ugly geoduck clam could mean sea gold? Joe was right, that's why. 'We're too specialized,' he said. 'The whole world's too specialized.' Geologists studying muds in the area didn't take any notice of the clams. And biologists studying clams weren't thinking of sea gold. It's as simple as that. Joe was the first to make the connection."

Frank walked over to the wide window and watched

the clouds parting even more, as the storm's wind kept pushing the nimbo stratus eastward toward the Rockies. "We'll let Vancouver Oceanics and the government split the core we've just sent in. They paid for the trip—it belongs to them. But now," he said, turning to Mary and smiling, "now we form *our* company, and we go out and get *our* samples in hand. All eight of them. We're the only ones who know. Joe told no one but me."

"And you told me," she said.

"And I told you," he answered, drawing her to him.

"And I love you," she said.

"And I love you."

44

In the Zurich darkness, the Hugentoblers were shocked! After a good meal of the city's famed veal dish at the Kronenhalle, washed down by a half liter of beer, they had been in good spirits. But walking home past Ernst Klaus' house on the Tobystrasse they were distressed to hear shouting. Never, they told each other, had they heard such language, not in such a respectable neighborhood. Herr Klaus had always been such a quiet, dignified man. One of them stopped to listen, the others nervously beckoning him on. "It's none of your business, Karl, Come!"

But Karl stayed, watching the large square of orange light through the tall, dark thicket of linden trees. Soon the whole group stood watching and listening. They looked at each other in amazement, as the dressing-gowned figure of Herr Klaus hurled the telephone across the room, then strode back and forth past the huge picture window, yelling like a madman that all his chocolates were gone.

A Special Preview
of the opening pages of
the #1 Canadian bestseller

ACT OF GOD

The super-thriller novel by

Charles Templeton

"Superb. I was spellbound. I do not recall when
I last read a book so totally satisfying in every
way."

—Arthur Hailey

Prologue

The box had been three days in the belly of the Pan Am 707 cargo aircraft, having been shipped from Amman, Jordan to John F. Kennedy airport but being delayed in Amsterdam by reason of the need to replace an engine in the aircraft. In the freight warehouse, a cargo-handler picked it up and dumped it onto a long steel-sheathed table.

"Goddammit!" the supervisor snarled, "It's marked fragile. Can't you read?"

"I can read."

"Then read, for Christ's sake."

The box, three feet long and a foot wide, was made of unpainted half-inch pine. It had been securely nailed and was bound with metal strapping. A bill of lading, glued to the rough surface of the wood, yielded the information that the box had cleared customs at Amman and weighed 11.4 kilograms. A rectangular piece of paper, also glued to the wood, read:

SHIP TO: Dr Herman Unger
Curator, Department of Anthropology
HOLD FOR: Dr Harris G. Gordon
Museum of Natural History
Central Park West at 79th St
New York City, 10024, USA

Carefully hand-lettered in red ink on the wood itself were the words: FRAGILE! HANDLE WITH CARE, and beneath them the neatly printed injunction: *Contents archaeological artifacts. Not to be opened except in presence of addressee. Avoid extreme cold, heat or humidity.*

The cargo-handler pivoted the box on the table, picked it up and placed it on a wooden pallet. A forklift truck thrust its tines beneath, wheeled and trundled away. On a long aisle of open-shelved racks the driver spied a space. He stopped, raised the lift, dismounted and slid the box onto a shelf alongside a carton containing a computer keyboard, a box of pharmaceutical supplies, a crate of Jensen automatic rifles and a metal container for motion picture film bearing the label, *Sex Practices in Sodom.*

The cargo-handler made a note of the coded digits on the shelf, mounted his machine and drove off.

Chapter One

That late afternoon in Rome the setting sun was gilding towers, cupolas and crosses, and impatient traffic contended in the streets as a small black Fiat bearing the distinctive SCV license plates of the Vatican State separated from the flow at the lower end of the Via Venetto and turned in at the entrance to the United States embassy. An enormous flag over three wrought-iron gates waved an indolent welcome and two marines in dress-blues drew themselves taut to snap and sustain a salute as the car moved the length of the building, made a 180-degree turn and drew up before the bulletproof glass doors within the security of the inner courtyard. The driver leaped from the car to open the door, and the Most Reverend Michael Cardinal Maloney, Bishop of the Archdiocese of New York, his fame less suited to Fiats than to limousines, emerged. As he approached the doorway, the ambassador strode swiftly down the broad sweep of the marble staircase, hand outstretched.

"Good afternoon, Your Eminence," he said, his voice sepulchral in the vaulted vestibule. "Right on time, but then you always are. Good to see you."

"And you, Mr. Ambassador."

The ambassador was a very tall man, taller by inches than Cardinal Maloney's six feet two, and lean to the point of gauntness. He had a narrow, bald head and lank hair hanging in spikes down the back of a long neck. Not wanting to intimidate by his height, he compensated by thrusting his head forward.

Michael never saw him without recalling the great blue herons that stilted solemnly about in the stony shallows near The Cottage in summer.

"You had a good flight from New York?" the ambassador asked, pumping Michael's arm as though trying to draw water.

"Couldn't have been better."

"The Holy Father, he's well?"

"I'll tell him you were asking."

The ambassador flicked a glance at his wristwatch. "I think perhaps I'd better get you to the telephone. It's going on five and Mr. Lieberman . . ." He left the sentence dangling, and cupping Michael's elbow lightly, disdained the tiny elevator and turned him toward the staircase. "I've put you in the conference room," he said, "There's a scrambler on one of the phones there. . ."

What would be on Josh Lieberman's mind to cause him to take the most extraordinary measure of having him come to the embassy? There was only one likely explanation: Lieberman had heard about the Holy Father's illness. But why the embassy; could he not talk more easily and as safely—and certainly, more appropriately—at the Vatican? Perhaps, for all the recently intensified security measures, the telephone system there was not invulnerable.

On the telephone a light flashed. He picked up the receiver and said, "Hello."

"The Secretary of State calling from Washington, Your Eminence. Will you hold please?" There was a sustained buzz, a series of automated beeps and the line cleared.

"Are you there, Eminence?"

"Yes, I am," Michael said, his voice cordial. He held a particular affection for Joshua Lieberman. They had met often and had spoken on the telephone daily during the period just before and after the Communist party took power in Italy.

"Good to hear your voice," Lieberman said, the hint of a chuckle in his tone. "I won't ask how you are because virtue must reward its possessor with a serene mind and a—"

Michael feigned a groan: "Beginning like that you must want an enormous favor . . ."

"Sorry to have brought you to the embassy," he said.

"Am I to take it that our switchboard leaks?"

"The way things are I wouldn't be surprised. But if you have bugs they're not ours." He laughed. "At least not that I know of. It's just that I feel more confident on this line."

"I understand."

The Secretary's manner changed. "Three things on my mind: Number one, I hear the Holy Father is ill."

Michael's hesitation was so brief as to be undetectable. In that microsecond he balanced the wisdom of admitting the truth against the risk involved and knew that the secret would be secure. "You have good sources," he said.

"How serious is it?"

"He's had a stroke."

"I'm sorry to hear that. A bad one?"

"He's been in a coma off and on for days."

"I *am* sorry." He paused a moment. "My second question is a somewhat indelicate one but I think you'll understand. If the Holy Father should pass away . . ."

"Who will succeed him?"

"Yes."

"It's not a matter about which there can be any certainty. We like to believe that God takes a hand in the choosing."

"Let me put it another way: there must be certain men who are more likely to be selected than others."

"There will be perhaps five candidates."

"Would you be among that five?"

"It would mean a radical break with tradition, but to answer your question, yes."

"Good."

"Why?"

"Because it'll make things a hell of a lot simpler at this end." He was silent for a moment and Michael could hear his wheezing over extraneous sounds in the background. "Sorry to leave you hanging but I wanted to put my hands on a report here. The reason for my chasing you down—beyond my concern for the Holy Father, of course—is that I've just learned that the Italian government is about to take steps that may seriously affect your church and I thought I'd better get the information to you while you're in Rome. Our people over there tell me that, after a bit of kite-flying to test the wind, Premier Gordini has plans to . . ."

When, ten minutes later, Michael put down the telephone, his face was grave.

The summons to Rome had come in an early morning telephone call from Paolo Cardinal Rinsonelli, Dean of the Sacred College of Cardinals and one-time visiting Professor of New Testament at the North American College in Rome with whom Michael had done graduate work after his conversion to Roman Catholicism. At eighty, straight as a pillar and with the vitality of a man half his years, Rinsonelli was the terror of the Vatican bureaucracy. He suffered fools not at all, was intemperate with temporizers, impatient with mediocrity and disdainful of subtlety. He was a man of patrician tastes and often earthy language, whose seamed and craggy face, beneath a mane of purest white hair, suggested a relief map. A Sicilian, he delighted in intrigue, and when he had occasion to telephone Michael long distance—seeking his counsel or relaying messages from the Holy Father—often used the name Giovanni, employing an elaborate code and speaking exquisite Italian in what he fondly believed was a perfect simulation of underworld argot. He was indifferent to the six-hour difference in time between Rome and New York City and as a consequence often broke Michael's rest. On this morning, when the private telephone beside the bed jangled him from his deep sleep, Michael had glanced at the illuminated face of the clock beside his bed, noted that it was just past four, and on hearing Rinsonelli's organ tones identifying himself as Giovanni (double fortissimo because it was long distance), muttered a sleepy, "Damn."

He was soon fully alert. Rinsonelli spoke of "your pal Tony in Genoa"—his code name for the Holy Father—and despite the convoluted ambiguity of his sentences, it quickly became clear that the pope was seriously ill and that Michael was to come immediately. . . .

There was no reason to discuss the arrangements to be made should he die: they had been established by long tradition and specifically in the Apostolic Constitution of 1945. Those cardinals resident in Rome—the Curia Romana—would meet in "preparatory congregation" on the day of his death to choose a *cardinal camerlengo,* a chamberlain. He would immediately decree that the papal apartment be sealed, take charge of the properties of the Holy See, require that the Fisherman's Ring and all other papal seals be brought before the Curia and the seals defaced in its presence, set in motion the complex preparations for the burial and name a date for the beginning of the conclave to elect a new pope.

Gregory, his body having been prepared for public viewing by the embalmers, dressed in full pontificals, a mitre on his head, would be borne to the Sistine Chapel to lie between gigantic white candles beneath Michelangelo's fresco of *The Last Judgment.* With the Holy City draped in black and Rome itself solemnized by the tolling of bells from every tower, they

would mourn him with nine funeral Masses, give him nine ab-
solutions and, his face covered with a purple veil and his body
with an ermine blanket dyed blood-red, bury him on the third
day in the sacred grotto beneath the Basilica close to the tomb
of Peter: bury him in three coffins, one of cypress within one
of lead and both within one of elm, to make him in death kin
to the humblest of men borne to their graves in a plain wooden
box.

Chapter Two

Despite a difference of nearly twenty years in their ages and centuries in the worlds from which they'd sprung, the two men had become each other's best friend. They were walking idly now across the spongy turf, shoes gleaming with dew and with the musk of night in their nostrils. Michael had just finished recounting the burden of his conversation with the Secretary of State: specifically that the Italian government was about to withdraw all tax exemptions and privileges granted the Vatican State, not only in Rome but from all Catholic churches, schools and monasteries throughout the country, and after testing the wind, would so announce.

"In effect, tear up the Lateran Treaty," Rinsonelli rumbled.

"Lieberman says the economy is in worse shape than outsiders dream. Their balance of payments is way out of line and the probability is they'll have to devalue the lira again. Probably raise taxes."

"So much for election promises."

"So much for the workers' paradise."

They need a scapegoat, and who better than the church?" Michael imitated the intonations of a public speaker: "No longer should a wealthy church get a free ride on the backs of the workers. *Their* rhetoric."

"The rhetoric of all our enemies," Rinsonelli gloomed. "Little do they know."

"Let's face it, Paolo, it's an argument they can sell."

"Our wealth!" Rinsonelli snorted. "In real property we are as Croesus; in cash-flow we approach beggary." . . .

Rinsonelli was fuming: "I wonder what those tongue clacking critics of our wealth would have had us do? Would they have had Michelangelo and Leonardo use their gifts only for emperors and princes? Would they have had Bernini render unto Caesar that which is God's?"

"That's hardly the point, Paolo——"

But Rinsonelli wasn't listening. He pressed on, tugging at the dewlap beneath his chin with brown spatulate fingers. "Where would they have placed the *Pieta,* these critics? In the parliament which now has an atheist majority? Should Michelangelo have painted the *Creation* on the ceiling of an army barracks?"

"I agree, I agree," Michael said. "But will you not in turn agree that that same conspicuous wealth in a world in which millions have hunger as their daily companion is to many a reproach? I almost said a scandal."

Rinsonelli shrugged and turned up his palms. "The trouble with you, Michael, is that you're an American. Not enough centuries flow in your veins. The poor you have with you always; are they advantaged if the church also is in rags?"

They walked on in silence for a moment. "I keep remembering that summer in Ethiopia," Michael said softly. "Thousands of people literally starving to death; old and young, mothers with babies like bundles of sticks at their dry breasts, children without the energy to cry." His voice thickened in the memory. "I saw a skeleton draw his last breath before an altar plated with gold."

Rinsonelli stepped in front of him, tilted his massive head and peered at him over his half-spectacles. "But suppose," he said pianissimo, "suppose, as some would have it, that that altar had been taken to the smelters and sold to buy bread. There would only be more poor tomorrow, and in the meantime something of infinite value lost. That supplicant of yours came to die at the altar because it was the one place he encountered God. Swords into plowshares, perhaps, but altars into bread . . . ? Your man would have been fed but empty." . . .

Michael had not seen the doctor when he entered; he had been seated in the shadow beside the door. Now he approached and stood with Michael by the bed: a swarthy man of fifty with a hound's face, stooped and cadaverous but with an inappropriate paunch. "I'm Dr. Sabatinni," he said in a whisper. "You're Cardinal Maloney?"

Michael had to clear his throat. "Yes."

"I'm glad you're here. The Holy Father was asking for you again this morning, but I don't know . . ." He sounded dispirited. "He hasn't moved now for three hours."

Michael looked down at the waxen face, blotched with liver spots. "Perhaps it would be better if I didn't stay," he said.

He had seen death often, but a primeval fear was on him, a dread that the man on the bed would convulse and die before his eyes, that he would be there when the wrench from earth to heaven happened. He thrust the thought away with a flash of anger at himself, but it remained.

"No," Dr. Sabatinni said, "he wants to see you. I told him it was unwise, that he must save his strength, but he looked at me in that way he has . . ." Sabatinni spread his hands in a gesture of impotence. "Who am I to instruct the Holy Father?"

"Is he sleeping?" Michael asked.

"Sleeping . . . ? In a coma . . . ? Who can tell much of the time?"

"Will he recover?"

Again the noncommittal shrug. "The first forty-eight hours we were sure he would never come back to us. Some of us stayed with him right through, expecting the end. But now he seems stable."

"I'll stay awhile and pray," Michael said.

As he put a hand on the bed to lower himself to his knees, the frail figure stirred. As they watched, it seemed he summoned his spirit from far off and brought it to the room. There was a quiver, a sudden shuddering intake of breath, a slight flushing of the skin and the eyes opened slowly. It was a moment before they were drawn into focus. They rested first on the doctor and then moved to Michael's face. The voice when it came was not much more than a breathy whisper. "Michael . . ."

Michael forbade the tears that blurred his eyes. "Holy Father," he said.

This was the man, this fragile figure in the great bed, who had loved him, had seen the possibilities in him, had encouraged him. This was the man who, when he was himself a cardinal, had singled him out and set his feet on the ecclesiastical ladder, who had intervened with Paul VI to have him made a prince of the church and who had helped him with his vestments before the Consistory in which he had received his cardinal's biretta. This was the man who, when he became pope, had taken him into his counsel, with whom he used to meet privately and correspond and speak to at length on the transatlantic telephone, explaining the attitudes of presidents, the vagaries of Congress, the mood of the American people. This was the man who had set his faith in the papacy to soaring after the difficult years of Paul VI. Antonio Giulio d'Annunzio, son of a Genoese pharmacist, trained as a lawyer, member of the Society of Jesus, specialist in foreign affairs, papal nuncio to France, named a cardinal by John XXIII and elected Pope Gregory XVII on the first ballot. And this man was his friend.

The fingers of a hand fluttered like a broken butterfly. "Come closer," the voice whispered. Michael knelt by the bed. Gregory's eyes turned toward Sabatinni. "Leave us alone," he said.

Dr. Sabatinni hesitated. "Your Holiness . . ."

"Enrico," the pope said. "I shall leave this world when *I* decide to."

The doctor went off quietly, drawing the door closed behind him. The slightest smile touched Gregory's lips. "Doctors," he said. "They understand the body; they know little of the spirit."

Though some of his words were blurred, he seemed to be gaining strength and Michael's hopes began to rise only to plummet with the next words: "Michael, come closer. This may be the last time we'll speak . . ." Michael began to remonstrate but Gregory shook his head slowly. "We must all die," he said. "My time is not far off. Don't fret, it doesn't trouble me." The breath suddenly caught in his throat and he was racked by coughing. It was a minute before he could continue.

Michael asked, "Are you all right?"

It was as though Gregory hadn't heard. He ran the tip of a dry tongue over his lips and swallowed hard. "Michael," he said, "Our Lord may call you to succeed me . . ."

"Holy Father . . . please."

"No, no. Hear me out." Again he paused to gather his resources. "It will be you or Benedetti or Della Chiesa, and I want a last word with you. There are difficult times. They'll be worse. You must be strong." There was a pause, a frown, and a wandering of the eyes as though the thought was a bird that would not alight. "Yes. . . . Be strong, but be wise. Try to avoid confrontation. . . . God can use you with your countrymen. Perhaps he has raised you up for such a time as this." His breathing grew shallow and pain drew the corners of his mouth into a grimace. "No time . . ." he said, "No time."

Now the tears would not be forbidden. They inundated Michael's eyes and fell unnoticed to the floor. He lowered his head. "Bless me, Holy Father," he said.

Gregory began to raise a hand but it faltered and fell back. He opened his mouth; the lips worked, trying to form words, but the only sound was a dry exhalation. The concentration that earlier had enabled him to summon his strength ran out as sand in an hourglass and he slipped again into a coma. Michael remained on his knees, his mind numb. He thought he should pray but couldn't; he was empty. There were no words in him. He struggled erect but didn't look again at the motionless figure on the bed.

When he opened the door, Dr. Sabatinni looked past him. "Good morning, Eminence," he said, and went into the room. Michael closed the door.

At Rinsonelli's quarters there was a note. Michael tore open the envelope. In a script as precise as hieroglyphic were the words:

Madame Ovary has lost her Bee—or does the memory-bank of a cardinal retain such trivia? Spotted you at the airport but you were gone when I got through customs. I'm at the Hotel Lombardia. Can we have dinner? It was signed, *Harris Gordon.*

Harris!—the name exploded in his head and each fragment was a memory. Harris! The irrepressible, the zany! Best friend of his undergraduate years at Princeton, roommate in his senior year, fellow member of the track team, fellow graduate *magna cum laude,* he in philosophy and Harris in archaeology. After the ceremony in the chapel there had been pledges, soon forgotten, to keep in touch. Later, as Michael had gleaned from newspapers and periodicals, there was celebrity: Harris Gordon, discoverer of the lost city of Horan, Dr. Gordon with the Leakeys at Olduvai Gorge, Dr. Gordon with Yigdal Allon in Israel. . . . A half dozen times Michael had made a mental note to be in touch and each time had procrastinated. And now here was Harris in Rome.

He rang the hotel and gave the operator his name. There was nothing familiar about the voice that came on except the note of banter.

"Mike Maloney, I presume," the voice said, "or do I call you father, Father?"

"Harris! How marvelous to hear from you."

"So you *do* remember Madame Ovary."

The film, *Madame Bovary,* had played the Princeton Playhouse and the ribald comments of the undergraduates at each line of dialogue had kept the theater in an uproar. Afterward, Michael had boosted Harris onto his shoulders and he had removed the letter *B* from the title. For the remainder of the run the marquee read, MADAME OVARY. They had mounted the battered metal trophy in a place of honor on the wall of their rooms in the dorm beside a STOP sign in French and English smuggled from Canada.

"I remember *all* the crazy things we did," Michael said.

"Even that blind date at Mingles?"

A slow smile moved on Michael's face. "I refuse to answer on the usual grounds," he said.

"You're one hell of a correspondent," Harris grouched. "You were going to send me your address. We were going to get together at least once a year."

"I presumed you were too busy digging up somebody's mummy."

"Or you, kissing somebody's ring."

"Believe it or not, I've followed most of your adventures through the newspapers, even the honorary doctorate at Oxford. Then you dropped out of sight."

"Been in Israel the past four years," Harris said. "On digs with Freeling and Allon. Spent about six months at Hazor Tell. I was getting ready to head home at the end of my sabbatical when I got . . ." a slight tension entered his voice even as it continued lighthearted, ". . . how shall I put it?—waylaid by history."

Michael wasn't sure how to respond so he said, "Uh, huh."

"I was planning to come see you about it back home, and here you are. What are the chances of our getting together?"

Michael was apologetic. "I'd love to," he said, "but it's impossible. But why not in New York? I stop off in London on the way back but—"

"Could we have dinner in London?" Harris asked. "I'll be there from tomorrow."

"Perfect."

They refined the arrangements and chatted on tangentially for another five minutes, each relishing the resurrection of the past, both discovering that nothing of their old camaraderie had altered.

"Question," Harris said.

"Ask away."

"I thought your old man was a Presbyterian."

"He was."

"A preacher."

"Right."

"So how come you're a mick? Nobody was about to nominate you altar boy of the year when I knew you."

Michael laughed. Harris's irreverence pleased him. He was so accustomed to sycophancy and formality that his old friend's impudence gave delight. "Happened during the war," he said lightly.

"I even hear talk you may make pope. Mike Maloney, pope! Boggles the mind."

"I wouldn't hold my breath."

"No, I'm impressed. I really am. In my line of work you don't get to meet many of the Almighty's Mafia. When I finally buy it, can I use you as a reference?"

There was more of the same, and when Michael put down the phone he was warmed, smiling. It was a few minutes before the memory flooded back of that frail pale figure on the great bed upstairs . . .

Dr. Harris G. Gordon, Chairman of the Department of Oriental Studies (Emeritus) in the Faculty of Archaeology at Albright University, Philadelphia, Pennsylvania, was taking inventory. Shouldn't take but a few seconds, he thought with a wry grin. There on the glass stains on a grubby hotel room table were most of his worldly possessions: in cash, $442.78, two American Express travelers' checks for $100 each, and a one-way plane ticket Rome-JFK. In the closet, two suits, a pair of slacks and two sweaters. On the luggage rack, two scruffy suitcases stuffed with a mix of mismatched and threadbare haberdashery and assorted toilet articles. Aboard a ship en route to New York City, a steamer trunk filled with those oddments commonly described as "personal effects." As well, in the care of Manhattan Storage, perhaps two dozen cartons of books and papers, concerning which a professional bill-collecting agency had been hurling intemperate *Last Warning!* thunderbolts at him for months now. There were also—if one might list them in an inventory—three wives: one lost somehow, one divorced and one deserted. And seven children by wives Two and Three, although the children, he thought, had always been more of an expense than an asset. Granted a few inadvertent omissions, that was about everything he owned in the world . . .

It was not that Harris Gordon was feeling sorry for himself. He had never been an accumulator of things and never thought of himself as rich or poor—they were categories into which it would never occur to him to place himself. What was important at the moment was the fact that his scarcity of tangible assets was damned inconvenient. The airline had charged him $46.75 to insure and ship home his precious box, and that, as the saying has it, had made a small dent in his bankroll. The box would by this time be safely ensconced in the atmosphere-controlled storage room at the museum in New York and probably better housed than he would be. Which, he decided, was not inappropriate.

The immediate problem was: where was he to live when he'd finished his research and was back stateside? He grimaced; last thing in the world he'd do would be to go crawling to the university. "Bastards," he said aloud. How did the letter go? *I regret exceedingly, my dear Harris, having to inform you that it has become necessary to terminate your employment here at Albright. Your sabbatical has already been extended twice, and the Board of Trustees etc. etc. etc. . . . Permit me to say, Harris, that your obduracy in refusing to disclose the nature of your discovery or the location of the dig has left us with no option but to etc. etc. etc. You upbraid us, it seems to me, unfairly.*

So be it, but they would dance to another tune shortly. By God, wouldn't they though!

His thoughts returned to the telephone call. It had been good to talk to Mike. He'd sounded a bit stuffy, but only a bit, and that was to be expected. Perhaps he was the man to talk to about his find. He'd had the secret bottled up within him so long that it was becoming unhealthy. What he needed more than anything else at the moment, more even than money, was someone he could take into his confidence and from whom he could get counsel. Mike would, of course, be shocked when he broke his news—it would be fascinating to watch his reaction—but he was a sophisticated and worldly man and would soon adjust. And who better to tell? *Cardinal* Maloney, no less! He grinned: after all, if you can't trust a priest, who can you trust?

THE LATEST BOOKS
IN THE BANTAM
BESTSELLING TRADITION

Bantam Book Catalog

Here's your up-to-the-minute listing of over 1,400 titles by your favorite authors.

This illustrated, large format catalog gives a description of each title. For your convenience, it is divided into categories in fiction and non-fiction—gothics, science fiction, westerns, mysteries, cookbooks, mysticism and occult, biographies, history, family living, health, psychology, art.

So don't delay—take advantage of this special opportunity to increase your reading pleasure.

Just send us your name and address and 50¢ (to help defray postage and handling costs).